Jefferson's Chef

JAMES HEMINGS—FROM SLAVERY TO FREEDOM

A NOVEL BY

SHARON O. LIGHTHOLDER

Albedo Press

Also by the Author

Fiction

The English Rendition

The Baldwin Portolano

The Paris Draft – The Road Back from Dementia

Nonfiction

Vietnam: The War Zone Dictionary In Their Own Words

*The cause of freedom is not the cause of a race or a sect or a class –
it is the cause of humankind, the birthright of humanity.*

Anna Julia Cooper

Contents

AUTHOR'S NOTE

This imagined biography of James Hemings is based, when possible, on what documents exist about his remarkable life. As Jefferson's personal servant, confidant, industrial spy, and America's first French chef, he changed the way we eat and cook today.

Although this is a work of fiction, it includes many well-known characters who were associated with the founding of the United States of America and with the American and French Revolutions. Hercules Posey and Oney (Ona) Judge were the enslaved cook and house servant in the household of President Washington where James visited with Jefferson. It is likely that they came to know one another.

Lesser known, but key to understanding the complex relationship Jefferson had with the enslaved Hemings family is that Thomas Jefferson's father-in law, John Wayles, fathered six children by Elizabeth Hemings, who was enslaved to him. Those six children—Robert (who was also called Bob), James, Thenia, Critta, Peter, and Sarah (who was called Sally)—were therefore half-siblings to Jefferson's wife, Martha. Robert came as a gift to Jefferson as his personal servant upon his marriage to Martha. The other enslaved half-siblings were inherited by Jefferson.

James Hemings was the only one of the hundreds of enslaved men, women, and children who were owned by Jefferson who was unconditionally freed. In so doing, it is my opinion that this act and his respect for James influenced his decision to abolish the importation of the enslaved when he became President.

BOOK I

THE NEWLY UNITED STATES OF AMERICA

1782–1784

Wherein Thomas Jefferson is invited to France
on behalf of the new Government,
and
James connives to accompany him to gain his liberty.

CHAPTER 1

MONTICELLO PLANTATION, VIRGINIA
NOVEMBER 1782

"**B**oy!"

James ignored the knee prodding his backside and tried not to rustle his straw- stuffed pallet. When he felt his brother's foot nudge his rump, he threw off his blanket. "What'd you do that for? You got no call kickin' at me!"

"Hush now, Jamie."

"Don't call me that baby name no more."

Bob chuckled. "Well, *Mister* James Hemings, best you get up and don't back sass me." Bob stripped off his nightshirt and took his morning piss in the slop bucket by the door. He ran a wet rag over his body, splashed on rosewater, and dressed. After buttoning his vest, he put the half-busted pocket watch that Jefferson made him carry into its pocket and grabbed his coat from the peg beside the fireplace. "Don't tarry. The man's as jumpy as a water bug these days. So, be quick. Empty the slops, stoke the fire, come to the kitchen."

James tangled in his long shirt when he rolled off the pallet. "I got sweepin' to do in the big house."

"Kitchen! And be quiet about it." James glanced at their mother. The worn blanket was pulled tight to her face. The early light through the small window fell on her salted hair. She moaned and turned. The bed ropes under her creaked like timbers on a ship.

He whispered, "When ya gonna teach me to tend to Massa in the mornings, like you do?"

Bob pulled on his coat. "Best learn to shave yo' own face proper first. And remember your place."

After the door shut, James turned toward the piss pot. As he relieved himself, he huffed, irritated by his big brother telling him not to tarry. Everyone knew that Jefferson lived by the hands of his clock and said his house servants had better too. House servants! *Like we didn't know we was slaves.*

Although crisp air found its way through cracks in the thin-timbered walls, he knew that theirs was the best cabin on the row. Still, he liked it better when they all slept together like a pack of pups. Now that Peter was in the trade cabin learning to make beer and Sally had joined Thenia and Critta in the big house, it was just Bob and him by the fire. Mam's youngest, little John and Lucy who were fathered by another slave, were snugged into blankets under her bed. He liked it before Mam's hips and fingers stiffened so's she could only do patching needlework and tend the youngsters and the sick. He wanted it like it was but knew things were changing. He felt it in the air, in Bob's voice, and in the hurry that was starting in the house.

He dressed, put twigs on the embers, and left them to catch while he emptied the bucket into the slops barrel by the road. Chilled from his time outside that morning, he lingered longer in the cabin than he knew he should. He stoked the low fire, closed the cabin door quietly, and started up the hill.

From his hilltop study, Thomas Jefferson saw Bob hurrying toward the kitchen, looked past him to the barren trees, and realized how much he hated this November. The dull idleness of the bleached landscape weighed on him in normal years. Now, two months a widower, he barely tolerated living in his unfinished home.

Temporary bookcases huddled against three walls of raw brick. The heavy scent of wet plaster from the one finished wall taunted him. He turned from the window and swept the last of the probate papers from his desktop into a drawer, shut it with more force than he had intended, and blew out the candle. Martha was still with him, from the lavender scent of their bed linens to the way their daughters echoed her delicate features and fine auburn hair. Always frail, bearing Lucy had been too much for his wife's constitution.

Dressed for the escape of his morning ride, he had pulled on rough linen breeches and a scuffed leather coat over a wool shirt. His copper hair was still sleep-tangled. He edged around the scaffold, selected books from the shelves, and made teetering stacks on his desk. He glanced up at the thud of boots in the hallway. Mathew Miller lumbered into the study carrying a small trunk, which he placed beside the desk.

"Harden James up while I'm gone."

Miller looked up from filling the trunk with books from the desktop. "James?"

"Working in the house has kept him soft and given him airs."

"You want him in the field? He's sixteen and able bodied…"

"No. The kitchen, and not just carrying trays to the house for you. By the time I return, I want him skilled in basic cookery. Lizzie can teach him, but he'll need to think it is his idea or he'll buck like the spirited colt that he is."

"But that's women's work."

"Not in France, the great cooks, *chefs*, they call them, are all men. When we return from Paris, I'll have Bob train him as my under-chef."

"How long you figure you'll be gone?"

"Sailing to France alone is a month, so two or three in travel, a few more in Paris to negotiate the peace treaty. I'd venture you'll have a year to turn his mind right."

"If you say. I had planned to hire him out as there is little need for the house staff when you leave."

"No. Hire out Thenia and Critta if you find a suitable home, but not James. Keep him to the kitchen and to what little housecleaning there may be. Elizabeth's others are too young to hire out."

Miller straightened his vest. "About the production report, do you want to do that this afternoon?"

"Best I hear it now. I'm having guests later."

"Yes, sir. Like you asked, I went to look at that girl that Mister Mason offered up."

Jefferson shrugged. "I still can't understand why he had me do that boundary survey if he couldn't pay for it."

"She's scrawny but should be good in the kitchen. A good worker, he says."

"You trust him?"

"I trust my eyes. She's healthy and got a lot more cooking years in her."

Jefferson frowned. "Why the kitchen?"

"Two of Lizzie's helpers gonna foal any day now and leave her short-handed. Suzanna and that other one. I know you don't cotton to selling or buying them."

"I need not sermonize to you on the matter. You know my feelings. However, I see the exception in the current circumstance and will draft the bill of transfer discharging his debt. Do you have her name and particulars?"

Miller handed Jefferson a torn paper. "He wrote it for me."

Jefferson leaned over his desk and penned the conveyance while Miller reported on the plantation's production and resources. Once the document was written, Jefferson paced and glanced out the window. Jefferson's height and accomplishments as a horseman rendered him fit and looking younger than his forty-one years. When he saw his roan stallion being brought up by his stableman, he turned back to Miller hoping to speed his overseer's report.

Just younger than Jefferson, an inch shy of his height but a foot wider, this bear of a man was all Jefferson could want in an overseer. He knew how every part of the plantation ought to operate and could do any chore himself, from making nails to clearing land, logging, and farming. He could shoe a horse, hitch and drive any team, sharpen a plow, fire the charcoal kiln, instruct the smith, get prime crops to market, and oversee the slaves to accomplish any of those tasks all within the time and funds Jefferson allocated.

Although he objected to Jefferson's tolerance for the occasional lapse in work or the shenanigans of his slaves, Miller still managed to meet both the constraints on discipline and his production goals. Often, he urged the purchase of more slaves, but Jefferson consistently refused him. Slaves were traded only to hold a family together or remove an unruly or thieving slave instead of resorting to the lash. The occasional birth in the slave quarters along Mulberry Row only served to enrich the plantation, to which neither objected.

Jefferson's pacing hinted at his impatience. Miller hurried. "Wheat's coming up strong. Should be a good summer harvest."

Miller was not a man who was comfortable indoors. His black hair had the sheen of grease and a dent from the rim from his broad-brimmed hat. His ivory shirt was clean, a tribute to his pale wife, yet his homespun trousers had the trace of saddle and his leather vest was stained on the belly and under the armpits from long days in summer fields. The smell of the stable followed him.

The man puzzled Jefferson. His manner was coarse and brutal, yet his mind for matching skills to tasks and his management of the fields and trades was the best in all of Albemarle County. "Sheep's all good. Looks like fine wool come shearing time. The older bay mare has gone lame in the left front. Not a breeder anymore, so I'd like to sell her off."

Jefferson recalled the bay as Martha's favorite. She had boasted that when that horse trotted, it was like being in a rocking chair. "Might just need a new shoe. Have the blacksmith look at her and let me know."

Then Jefferson asked, "Are my daughters liking their new maid?"

"Seem to. I thought Sally too young to tend the girls, but you were right. Her brother helps her. Brings in extra wood for overnight."

"Bob?"

"No. The younger one, James. Miss Elizabeth knows how to rear 'em."

Miller took note of Jefferson's opinion before continuing. "Now that harvest and planting are done, if you want, I could cull some of the older ones."

Jefferson raised his hand to Miller. "Put them to trades over the winter or to repairing fences. No sales." Jefferson glanced at the conveyance, ascertained that the ink had dried, and handed the paper to Miller. As Jefferson started for the door he said, "Have him sign it before taking her. Leave it on my desk if I am otherwise occupied. Is that all?"

"Yes. I'll get her this morning."

"Have this trunk removed to my bedroom by noon. And not a word of my travel plans. I'll tell the girls when I deem it prudent."

The morning was crisp. Jefferson's breath fogged as he took the horse from the stableman. After mounting the roan, Jefferson held the stallion to an easy walk. James stopped on the path up the hill, stepped aside for the horse, and bowed his head until his master had turned down Mulberry Row.

Once past the big house, James sprinted toward the kitchen when he did not see smoke curling from its chimney. He rushed through the doorway expecting Bob to be giving Lizzie what for and why. She was alone at the far end of the kitchen in front of the stone fireplace, which was tall enough for a man to walk into and wide enough to hold a whole deer on a spit. The metal cranes that extended into the firebox from hinged iron gudgeons could hold several potbelly iron pots over the blazing fire at the same time.

Lizzie looked around. The best of the Darby pots, spider skillets, and kettles that lined the shelves against the wall weren't a bit of good without her helpers to get the work done or start a fire in the hearth.

Everything else was as it should be. Windows along the opposite wall were open to get the draw of air when the fire started. The lidded wooden cool box held chunks of ice from the icehouse in wet sawdust to keep a chill on the milk and cheese. A large worktable commanded the center of the room with an equally large rack hanging above it. The wall opposite the windows had a long sideboard holding crockery jugs, trays, and serving pieces. Plates and glasses were stacked on the lower shelves. A grandfather clock stood in the corner by the door. James glanced at it.

Less than an hour before the trays had to be in the big house. All thoughts of an easy morning vanished when Bob brushed past him, carrying small sticks of wet wood. Bob glared at James. "Go bring in kindling. Pull dry wood from deep in the pile."

Lizzie twisted her apron into a knot as tears ran down her cheeks, but Bob ignored her. "Where's your lard tub?"

She shoved a small covered pail from under the big worktable with her toe. Bob took the lid off, scooped out three fingers' worth, and spread it on several sticks. He held a small twig over the oil lamp's flame until it flared. Kneeling at the hearth, Bob fired the tinder and stacked the lard-coated sticks above it. They sizzled, snapped, and then flamed.

"James! Get some wood in here!" James sprinted outside and brought in several split logs, leaving a trail of chips behind him and getting his homespun shirt full of splinters. The logs clattered into the woodbox. Bob selected several small kindling sticks and set a wobbly stack over the fire. It hissed and steamed.

Lizzie sighed as she watched the fire catch. "Got one girl laying in, and I don't know where Suzanna is. Gotta talk to Massa. Gonna tell him straight. I needs more help in here if he's gonna keep having menfolk over."

Bob looked up from fanning the fire. "Tell old man Miller. Make it his burden, not yours."

She planted her fists on her ample hips. "He be the overseer of the field and trades, but not of me."

Bob held his hand in front of him as if shielding off blows. "You think one way, but maybe he thinks another. Go slow there, girl."

Bob had taught her to tell time to meet Jefferson's needs. Breakfast was usually at eight. Supper was at three. Tea later if needed. On Sundays he had added a noon meal for all the slave children. Some of the tradesmen from town got a sit down at his table after some special thing happened on one of his building projects. Then there was Christmas for the house servants, as he called them.

Today, the schedule was upside down for everyone but baby Lucy. Supper at twelve; light for him, heavy for his daughters, Patsy and Polly. Then a groaning board for his guests at six and feeding their servants. Lizzie shook her head as if to make these new demands go away. Ham on the table, eggs in the basket. Just needed to make the hoecake batter and get lard in the pan up to heat, then she could start the day over again in her head and make sense of all that she had to do.

Pausing at the grandfather clock by the door, Bob set his pocket watch. Seven fifteen. He looked back at the fire. The flames were dying, and the embers were almost ready to cook over. He wound his watch with the key attached to the end of his watch chain.

A ten-year-old girl rushed into the kitchen and ran to Bob. "Suzanna say she can't come. She's having them baby cramps."

Bob returned his watch to its pocket. "Is Miss Elizabeth there?"

"No."

"Go get her. Suzanna might need a potion."

Shortly before noon, Lizzie sent James to deliver Jefferson's lunch tray to his study. Pausing in the doorway, he saw Jefferson seated at his desk and a stocky tradesman standing behind him looking at a drawing on the desk. "You see, Mister Maybridge, my plan is to enlarge the main house and add matching pavilions extending to the north and south."

Jefferson had changed from his riding attire to fine breeches, white stockings, silver-buckled shoes, and an embroidered vest in deep blue over a white shirt with flowing sleeves. His reddish hair was perfectly combed and captured in a ribbon at the nape of his neck. In contrast, Maybridge was a decade older than Jefferson, well rounded and worn at his edges. His brown, homespun trousers were clean, faded, and stuffed into ill-polished boots. In spite of the chill, he wore only a leather vest over a band-collared, white shirt.

Jefferson tapped the drawing on his desk. "To extend hospitality as befits my duty and station, I will need to enlarge the main house from eight to twenty-one rooms."

Maybridge squinted at the drawing. "Planning to brick these dependencies as well?"

"Yes. The North Pavilion will incorporate the privy, washhouse, stables, carriage stalls, and perhaps an icehouse. I calculated that the Rivanna River is close enough to harvest sufficient ice to last a season, even with increased guests. The South Pavilion will extend to include the current bricked kitchen, a smokehouse, and dairy."

"Smart to keep the kitchen as far from the main house as possible but still convenient. I see it is a bit downhill from..."

Jefferson nodded. "I'll add fill and elevate the new kitchen at that location so a connecting wing will be at the same level as the house. I have witnessed far too many house fires to have it any closer, yet a covered passage would speed the delivery of hot foods." He handed a paper dense with figures to the man. "Here are the exact dimensions. I estimate some ninety thousand bricks will be needed. Would you agree?"

Maybridge studied the paper for almost a minute in silence. "Yes. I agree with each of your calculations. Perhaps another five or six thousand to account for breakage in transit."

"Could you move your kiln and brick-making operation here to the end of Mulberry Row?"

He looked puzzled for a moment. "By the slave cabins?"

Jefferson shifted in his chair. "Yes. By the charcoal kiln. Could you give me an estimate by the end of this week for the cost of your labor and materials, both at your location and here?"

"Certainly."

Jefferson noticed James and motioned for him to enter. After placing the meal tray on the table near the desk, James turned to leave. Jefferson stood and shook Maybridge's hand. "I'll be interested to see your estimate." He towered above him.

"James? Would you escort Mister Maybridge to the door and then ask Bob to fetch both of the jackets I left on my bed."

"Uhh. Sir, he's in the barn tending to a broken wheel on the carriage."

Suddenly, Jefferson turned. "Then you fetch the jackets after you show this gentleman out!"

He bowed and left with Maybridge trailing behind him.

Jefferson was standing statue-still reading a paper when James returned carrying two silk jackets. There was an adolescent awkwardness in his manner and, although almost as tall as Jefferson, he adopted the subservient stoop that Bob had taught him to appear shorter. He held two cutaway jackets with short tails fashioned in the latest French style. One jacket was garnet and the other a pale blue.

"Well, James? What do you think of the newest fashion in French jackets? Be honest."

"Sure 'nuf fine cloth."

"Silk. Doctor Franklin sent them from Paris."

"Maybe not warm enough for a winter day. But…you just gonna put the ladies to shame with your fine jacket."

Jefferson cleared his throat, somewhat embarrassed. "No," he stammered. "No ladies at tonight's supper. Just four of President Washington's envoys. Which jacket?"

James paused, glancing between the choices. "The blue is as bright as the sky. Fits the season."

"Blue it is. Drape it over the back of that chair. I hope to get these accounts in order before they arrive. Are you clear on how to send up the wines from the cellar?"

"Yes, sir. You got 'em lined up in the order I'll send them up in that thing."

"I'm calling my vertical trolley a dumbwaiter."

"The white one goes first."

"That's the hock wine from Germany. I've just opened them. Has Bob showed you how it transports wine directly to the dining room?"

"Yes. Rope's on a spring thing to draw the bottles up easy."

"Right. For simplicity, we'll only use the two compartments on the right side of the fireplace, not all four. When I take out a bottle, send the next one up so it is waiting for me. I'll put the empty bottle in the other compartment. Listen for the door to open."

"Yes, sir."

"And it will be chilly down there, so take a blanket or coat."

"I gonna do that right now."

Jefferson looked up from his papers and took care to speak with precision. "It is 'going to' not 'gonna.' You read very well, James. But I want your spoken language to be refined. Strive to be precise. Remember, precision in all things leads to grand results. You have applied it to your violin lessons, and so you shall to other endeavors. That is the scientific method, which we can apply to ourselves as well as our tasks."

He nodded. "Yes, sir."

"I think that more diplomacy has been conducted over a fine meal than has ever transpired in all the courts of Europe." He returned to his desk. "Tell Lizzie to bring your dinner down to the cellar. A plate of venison, not the chicken."

"Thank you, sir."

"And James, set one of the boys as a lookout to come running when he sees their carriages pass by the orchard."

"Yes, sir."

"Tell Bob that I want him to escort my guests into the house, whether or not that wheel is repaired. You will attend to their servants, then play your violin in the parlor, and then go to the cellar. Remember, we may be known for our wit or craft, but we are remembered for our hospitality."

After he notified Lizzie and Bob of Jefferson's requirements, James went to his cabin to retrieve his violin and a blanket. Dropping the blanket in the cellar, he took a moment to sniff each of the open bottles to see if they were as different as Jefferson had said. One smelled like vinegar and old, wet paper. James crinkled his nose and thought that couldn't be what Jefferson would serve guests. He hurried upstairs, left his violin in the sitting room, and rushed to alert Jefferson.

He saw William Short entering the study as he turned the corner. Lean and handsome, he had light hair and a chiseled profile. He also wore a half-smile when he knew ladies were appraising his charms at dances. Although only in his early twenties, Short had made a name for himself in Virginia as an astute lawyer, having graduated from the College of William and Mary, being president of Phi Beta Kappa, and having demonstrated a solid understanding of the law to Jefferson and the other examiners. Short had become a valued family friend and pro-tégé of Jefferson, who had called Short his "adopted son" over dinners with Jefferson's wife and daughters. The combination of his talent and trust, as a distant relative, led Jefferson to hire him to handle matters of Martha's estate upon her death.

Hearing Short laughing, James paused before entering. In that mo-ment, James overheard Short saying that he accepted. Wondering what he accepted, James lingered.

Jefferson said, "Good. I know of no one I could trust more with the finances of the plantation while I am away in France. Miller is a good overseer, but there needs to be financial oversight and monitoring of his efforts to have the plantation prosper in my absence."

"Are the girls going with you?"

"I'll take Patsy and Bob. Their aunt can manage the younger girls. I'll send Sally with them so as not to burden her further."

"Do the guests know you are planning to go?"

"Washington's men? No. They are coming to convince me. I'll play coy."

"Shall I greet them with you?"

"No need. That would just delay their business with long introduc-tions and hint that I have already accepted the posting. They are here but one night and then I will be gone as well."

James backed down the hallway, came forward as loudly as he could, and shouted, "Come quick, sir! One bottle's gone bad. Spoiled. Smells like vinegar and mold."

"Set it aside. I'll be down in a moment." James lingered outside the door, waiting for Jefferson.

Short spun and looked at Jefferson in astonishment. He pushed the door shut. Leaning his palms on the desk and facing Jefferson, he strained to keep his voice low. "You let him talk to you that way? Interrupt our conversation? I'd as easily have him lashed. His lack of respect for your authority, for you! How dare he?"

"Listen to yourself. Have I taught you nothing?"

Short sat in the side chair as if slapped. "Sir?"

"Think back to the lessons I gave you as a young lawyer. What is the first rule of developing a strategy for the courtroom or the larger political stage?"

"Know your enemy? Listen?"

He nodded. "And how would either strategy be enhanced if I let that boy be sullen and quiet?"

"You let him back talk like that."

"For a reason that he would not understand. But I would have expected you to have seen my strategy."

"It was so guileless. I am embarrassed to confess that I mistook your intention."

"My point precisely. Applied with skill, forbearance may appear either as weakness or as patience to achieve a common goal."

"Does it work?"

He cast a sideways glance at Short and smiled. "It always has with you."

Blushing, Short continued. "But you would not permit that haughty attitude from others of your slaves."

"No. For most, fieldwork is the best you can hope for. For a few, the trades. I am well aware that there is no point in expending energy teaching most slaves the tricks of grammar or tools for reading either music or books. But that boy has a gift. He has shown a keen intelligence and wit ever since I inherited him."

"Is that why you have him as a house servant now?"

"That and his mother raised him well. James is the brightest of the lot."

"Was it true she was mistress to old man Wayles?"

Jefferson snapped at him. "Some things are not talked about here, even after Martha's passing. Remarks on her father's behavior do her a disservice."

"My humblest apology, sir."

"When Bob gets long in the tooth, James will replace him, just as I had Bob replace Jupiter as my personal servant. Best he starts to know my wants and needs as early as possible by observation and commerce with his brother."

"I see. You want to train him early."

Jefferson stood, adjusted his vest, and started for the cellar. "More than that. He is of the mind to either be my best ally or fiercest foe. He does not know that about himself, but I do. I know him as the boy he is, but as he grows, I shall discover if he responds better to the carrot or stick." He paused before opening the door. "Then I shall determine how to hold the reins on him."

Having heard Jefferson's chair scrape as he stood, James rushed to the cellar, wondering what Jefferson had in his mind to do next, yet finding a sense of pride in his words.

After showing the suspect bottle of wine to Jefferson, James hurried back to the kitchen as Lizzie had instructed. She looked up when a cloud of dust rolled past the window, then turned to James and asked, "Now, what dang fool would pull up near my kitchen blowing dust all over? Them delivery boys know better."

When Mathew Miller filled the doorway, Lizzie stopped working to meet any demand he might make. A slim girl followed him. Looking toward the sunlight, Lizzie saw just an outline that gave the impression of an adolescent. Once in the kitchen, Lizzie searched her polished ebony face. There was no hint of any lines at the corners of her eyes. No gray in her short, bushy hair. Maybe twenty. Hard to tell age on the scrawny ones. Her floor-length dress was simple in cut and made from white flour sacking that had small blue flowers. It was clean and hemmed just above the ankle so as not to sweep dust about the kitchen. A stained white apron was over her thin dress. She shivered.

Lizzie pointed to James. "Get them dishes from the big house, then you set to washing them here." He slipped past Miller with his head down. As he passed the girl, he noticed that she fingered a seashell on a cord at her neck.

Walking to the water barrel near the hearth, Miller drank from the dipping ladle. "Got you a kitchen girl, Lizzie. Some farmer sent her to cover a debt. Picked her up just as she was starting his breakfast, smelled just right. Says her name's Marie."

He turned and left. Just as Lizzie was about to ask the young woman something, Miller returned and dropped a bedroll and a plain cotton sack. "Best she sleeps in your cabin to start. I'll be by later to see if she can work as good as he said."

Lizzie looked at the slim woman and wondered how in the world she was ever going to get her cooking done with such a tiny thing. She cleared her throat to settle her thoughts. "Marie? You et today?"

"No, *madam*." She shivered again and crossed her arms.

"Go stand by the fire." Lizzie brought a slice of ham to her. "What you cook for that farmer?"

"About everything, I suppose." Her voice had a singsong to it that Lizzie had not heard before.

"Name one thing he like best over all others."

"Ashcake. I make better things, but that what he like. He's a simple farmer. Not like when I was in New Orleans." She said the city's name as if it were one word.

Lizzie folded her arms over her full bosom and fixed a hard eye on the thin woman. "How you make it?"

"I knows how to make them lotsa ways, but how he like 'em was like this: I'd take a quart a cornmeal, some salt and soda, with just enough sour milk to wet it and then a little sorghum molasses to make it sweet. Stir that into a stiff pone."

Lizzie tipped her head. "Then what ya do?"

"Brush back the ash from a hot firebox and lay down the pone just until it's crusty. Then I's cover it with hot ash and red coals just until it smokes. Brush away the ash with a damp cloth. Some nights, that be all he et. Just my ashcake with some sorghum syrup on it. He not know finer foods. Not like I make in New Orleans. There, I made some fine vittles. Shrimps and all manner of creatures from the sea. Some little creek critters called crawdads, boil 'em up in their shells and then put 'em all into a stew."

"We ain't got them critters here, so tell me two other things you make."

"Dumplings. You blend up like making a pie dough then put berries inside and put them in a bag and boil until firm. Then cut up for a plate. Did that in New Orleans too. Squirrel pie be the other. That cheap farmer brings in squirrels for me to fix up. So's I steamed the dressed-out squirrel until tender, pull off the meat, put on it some salt and pepper, and make a thickening of flour and sweet milk. Then I put in a deep pie dish, cover with crust, and bake it off 'till done."

Lizzie nodded seeing that her new helper did indeed have some knowledge. She handed her an apron. "Cover up your dress with a fresh apron. I keeps a clean kitchen. We got a big day. Gotta get three different suppers ready. Chicken and rice and carrots and turnips for his two older girls. Baby's got a wet nurse, a young gal what just lost her own. After that, 'bout eight slaves gonna get ham and beans with greens and cornbread. They's traveling with Massa's guests. Then a lotta covers for Massa and his company—four men plus Massa—all gotta be ready at six."

Marie nodded, waiting for instruction.

"Girl? You think you can get that bean pot off the fire and on the table?"

"Yes, *madam*." Although slim, she easily swung the pot off the fire and hoisted it over to the worktable.

Lizzie laughed. "Got some strength after all. Let me see how fast you can get them chickens broke down for a boil."

"I need a small, sharp knife."

Lizzie opened a drawer of the cabinet and showed her the knives. "Take what you want, but these gotta be washed and back in the drawer every night. Any slave caught with a knife gonna get in a world a trouble. Hear me?"

"Yes. I do."

"Good. 'Cause I gotta count them up every night and tell if any go missing."

Marie nodded as she picked a small knife from the drawer and tested its edge with her thumb.

Lizzie worked beside Marie, dressing a leg of venison and several rabbits for the spits. She nodded approval at her new helper's skills. "Where be that New New?"

"New Orleans. Go south 'till you hit water."

"Was you in a big house like this?"

"Family with six chillens, youngest was eight years of age, so not too much tending to them. The house be in town, Massa was a banker, so we buy food every day from the market of farmers who carted goods into the square. Go to the docks and buy shrimps and fishes off a boat."

"Gonna be different here. We grow all we eats. There be a market we go to maybe once a month for some spices and the like. Good to go if you can. About the only way to get news, pass the word along, and meet others like us. And some free men too."

"Down in New Orleans, house slaves got Sunday off. My massa even let us make *calas* and sell them."

Ca-lay. Lizzie tested the new word slowly. "*Calas?* What's that?"

Marie shut her eyes, a memory seducing her. "It's like a fritter, almost. Leftover cold rice is mixed with an egg batter with some sugar in it. Then made into small balls and fried in deep fat. Dusted with fine sugar and eaten hot. Makes my mouth water just telling you of it."

"Your massa let you sell these?"

She nodded. "I'd make up a tray and walk along the street calling, '*Belle calas! Tout chauds!*' and people would buy them to eat on the street or take to their homes. Some of the older ladies would have a huge basket of them they would balance on their head. But they had their own money to buy the fixings. Some even made enough to buy their freedom under a law called *coartacion*. That's a Spanish word. But we mostly talked French. You get to sell things you make and keep the money here?"

"Depends. Some have coops for chickens or rabbits. Eat most of 'em themselves or trade with others. But some sell to Massa and he pay them. A copper here and there. Some do handwork at night and sell it."

"In New...."

Lizzie lowered her voice. "You here now. So listen. Every Sunday, Massa Jefferson bring the chillen in for a noon meal. On a long table outside if the weather good or we sets a table in the weaving cabin if it be too cold. Looks 'em over tight. Any one of 'em sickly, he tells ol' woman Hemings to fix them a potion. That be Miss Elizabeth, that boy's mama. Them powders she makes cleans out their stuck bowels or cools a fever. Salves for a blister. Poultices for a boil. But it ain't all good wishes on his part. I see his eye going over them. I see him reckoning which of 'em gonna be working in the trade shops pounding out nails, joining wood for furnishings, brewing beer, working the forge, learning to drive a wagon or be a carpenter for the plantation. I sees him look at the lighter ones for the house."

"So, who be fair here?"

"That Hemings family. Miss Elizabeth's fair and her chillen fairer yet. Now you seen James, that boy that left when you got here. He's 'bout the color of ginger cake just done. His little sister Sally been taken for a white child more than once."

Marie stopped slicing and looked up when James came back. Lizzie checked the clock and pointed to the boiling water in a large pot. "James, get them carrots and turnips from the table and toss 'em all in the big pot."

In the next hours, multiple dishes for Jefferson's dinner were made and put aside to stay warm. Lizzie pulled out a pan for the cornbread, let Marie grease it, and slid it onto the hearth's edge. "What other things you know to make?"

"That banker's wife was from the North. She teach me how to make jams and Boston steamed brown bread. Got the fixings in a bread poem for my memory."

"Tell me."

She thought a moment then recited in a singsong manner. "One cup of sweet milk. One cup of sour. One cup of cornmeal. One cup of flour. Teaspoon of soda. Molasses one cup. Steam three hours. Then eat it all up."

"How you cook it? Like a pudding?"

Marie nodded. "Use a tall tin mold, like a tankard with straight sides, or a pudding mold. Put the mold on a wet cloth in a covered pot so's the bottom don't burn, put the pot over coals, and put boiling water half way up the mold. Fix the lid tight, hold to a low boil, and then it be done in three hours. Keep them bubbles low so it don't tip over or get wet. Tap outta the mold and slice across. Sometimes she have me add raisins or nuts."

"Three hours? Ain't got that kinda time today, but you make some tomorrow when the visitors are gone, and we see how it taste."

When Lizzie turned to James, he opened a paper and pointed to it. "Massa gave me the list of what he want on the table for tonight. Want me to leave it?"

Lizzie shrugged. "I'm busy just now, so read it to me."

As James read the listing of platters Jefferson expected, Lizzie nodded at each one, then sighed. "We got 'em all. Thank the Lord he ain't added any new things like he do sometimes."

James left the written list on the table and went to wash the dishes.

Marie shook her head and whispered, "He got hisself some airs. Pretending he reads."

"He can."

Marie fingered the shell on the string around her neck. "Lawdy. Don't tell."

"Mas' Jefferson taught him hisself. Same as he's teaching Sally."

"Don't he know the law don't allow that? He gonna get into a mess a trouble."

Lizzie scowled at her. "He knows. He's a lawyer. Check on that pan. Turn it if need be."

"Where I from, they cut off a finger if they catch you trying to read. Even tarrying too long above stairs when they's doing lessons can get you stripes." Marie rotated the pan of cornbread.

Lizzie shook her head and grimaced. "Massa comes and goes. Things change when he goes. The overseer got a hard hand. Not shy with the lash on the field hands if they don't hop-to. I don't think Mas Jefferson likes that so much but if he gone, he gone. And without Miss Martha here to hold him back. Well, you just watch yourself and step lively. Keep yo eyes down and your feet moving."

CHAPTER 2

J ames had just finished pulling on his brother's old coat when he heard two boys shouting as they ran past his cabin. "Carriages! They's here!"

As he buttoned his jacket, he looked at Bob. "You gonna get yourself out there?"

"In a minute. You run and tell him."

He sprinted from the cabin and hurried to the library to alert Jefferson. At the doorway, he stopped and tapped.

Jefferson sat at his desk writing on a large paper with a quill pen that he had dipped into the inkwell just as James arrived. Jefferson did not look up. "Yes?"

James sucked in air and caught his breath. He calmed himself and spoke as clearly as he could. "You asked to be told when your guests arrived."

Jefferson finished a line, put down the quill, and added the page to a stack. "Um hum. It will be interesting to see how they try to lure me to France. I've already decided to go, but let's see if I can improve the terms of the engagement over a fine dinner and an abundance of even finer wine."

"You going away, Mister Jefferson?"

"If I get my terms. I have a mind to take Bob as my personal servant and put him into training as a chef, that's a French cook."

"In France? I'd go. Tend to you when he's busy."

Jefferson laughed as he slipped into his blue jacket. "Best you tend after your mother and my Monticello when we're all gone."

"All?"

"My oldest daughter will accompany me. The two younger ones will remain in Virginia with their aunt, Missus Eppes. They need a woman's hand, now that their mother..." He walked into the hall, shaking his head.

By the time Bob arrived on the porch, the four enclosed carriages, each drawn by an elegant matched brace of horses, were almost to the house. Each carriage had a liveried driver seated on an elevated platform. Travel cases were strapped on a shelf at the rear of the carriage where a second slave rode, facing backward.

Jefferson buttoned his coat as he marched onto the porch. He planted his feet apart and put his hands on his hips, looking like the captain of a ship. He stood motionless with the open door behind him.

The drivers halted their teams. The slaves on the rear platforms sprinted to grab the bridles of the prancing horses. The doors opened. A man stepped out of each carriage. Only one wore a fancy jacket similar to Jefferson's. The others wore plain colonial brown homespun suits. Jefferson knew them all, almost better than they knew themselves, he thought as he ran inventory on them. Samuel Browning of Boston, Francis Stanton from South Carolina, Edward Cooke from Pennsylvania, and William Litton, a fellow Virginian. The carriages and servants were from Litton's plantation, only hours away from Monticello. Jefferson smiled as he thought how they must have convened and plotted to entice him.

The man in the silk coat was the first to approach with an outstretched hand. Jefferson took it. "Welcome to Monticello, William."

"I see Doctor Franklin's gift arrived." William was half a head shorter than Jefferson but smartly dressed, athletic, and slim. He shared Jefferson's slow Virginia drawl, but his voice was deeper than Jefferson's and somewhat hoarse.

"It has been far too long since we had the pleasure of your company." William stepped up onto the porch to allow the next guest to be greeted.

A gaunt older man in plain attire said, "Your orchard is planted now, I see." Slower in speech than William but with a clear voice.

"I hope you will come again some spring to see it in full bloom. I know you admired the 'fruitery,' Francis. I have a crate of apple and peach seedlings for you to take back to Charleston."

"Thank you, Thomas. It certainly looks like you are well on your way to self-sufficiency here." Jefferson shook his hand and took him by the elbow to move him onto the porch. Then he greeted the third man.

A portly fellow with a wide grin shook his hand like he was pumping water. "Edward! How are things in Philadelphia? You will need to give us all a full report as soon as we get settled."

"It will be my pleasure, Thomas."

The last man walked with some difficulty. "Thank you for having us on such short notice." His voice was thin and reedy, but his words were well formed and forceful. "Very gracious of you to have us spend the night as well."

"My pleasure, Samuel. No need for a long carriage ride or musty tavern room after a good meal. I have a Madeira wine for dessert that I don't think you have had before. Even better than the bottle we shared the last time I was in Boston."

"Wonderful. Just the thing to toast to your success in France negotiating our peace treaty with the British." The oldest of the lot, he was more direct and his speech more clipped than the others, more like the English, although no one would ever say so.

Jefferson chuckled and held up his hand in protest. "Now. Now. I have not accepted the commission offered by the Congress to be the country's negotiator."

Samuel laughed. "Offer? Spoken just like a lawyer. Offer. Acceptance. I suppose you want to negotiate something betwixt the two."

Jefferson laughed and turned. "James! Show the footmen where to put the luggage and then take them to the servants' quarters. Tell Cook to have the soup ready by six. I'll have Bob tell her when to serve. Then come to the parlor with your fiddle." He turned to his guests and smiled. "Gentlemen, I have a splendid sherry set out to wash away some of that travel dust and warm you. After you make yourselves comfortable, we can relax and then enjoy a leisurely supper. The jakes are at the end of this hallway. Bob will guide you. See you all in the parlor at your convenience."

James led the eight men in livery to the room in the far end of the stable set aside for the slaves accompanying their masters who visited Jefferson. While this was referred to as slave quarters for visitors, it was nothing more than the big end stall that had been boarded in to offer some protection from the weather. A small kettle for coals on a bricked base offered to take some of the chill from the air. The pile of straw-stuffed mattresses by the door would be spread on the floor later. The room smelled of horses.

"Cook's got dinner ready for you all. I need two of you to bring it down."

The tallest one asked, "Got any cider? Been a dry road coming up from Charleston."

"I'll ask the cook."

"What'd she make for us?"

"Pot a ham and beans, one of greens, and cornbread."

"Sounds fine."

James smiled. "Will be. She is good. That one thing we got over city folks is good food."

The man shook his head. "True, but they don't need to look to winter with the notion that they's gonna be sold off 'cause crops are in and there be no need to feed another mouth until spring."

Both nodded. They walked in silence to the kitchen. Lizzie had mugs, plates, and spoons set on a wooden tray. She had the men carry away the cooking pots to keep the food hot. She sent James to get a couple of crockery bottles of cider as well as a bucket of rainwater for them.

Jefferson's guests found their seats in the parlor near the fireplace. Bob returned holding a silver tray with a decanter and five small glasses. Jefferson motioned for Bob to pour. James followed him with his fiddle in hand. Francis chuckled. "I cannot express how I have longed for your fine taste in spirits after Washington's sundowners."

Jefferson scowled. "I thought you liked the colonial whiskey he made."

"It takes a poor second to your taste, even with his new copper still."

When Bob had poured full glasses and placed the decanter on the sideboard, he presented the tray to each of the men. Jefferson lifted his glass. "Gentlemen! It is a pleasure to have you all here. Please refresh your glasses at will. Thank you, Bob, that is all."

James cleared his throat, reminding Jefferson of his presence in the doorway.

"James? Please favor us with some music as we chat. Begin with Pachelbel's *Canon in D*. Then play whatever suits you to continue in that mood."

James went to the far corner of the room where he would be out of sight but still able to hear some of the conversation. After Bob closed the door behind him, Jefferson turned to Samuel. "How are things in Boston?"

"Still rebuilding after the war. Idle shippers are turning their hands to carpentry. Building homes and stores along the waterfront. A few keels have been laid. Barely work for half of the labor available."

"Good. A recovery is starting. What news of John Adams from France? Has he become Frenchified yet?"

Samuel laughed. "Hardly. He writes me that he is put off by the elegance of the French, their manners confuse him, and their morals shock him."

"So like him. But there is work to be done to craft a treaty of peace with the British and work to be done here to prepare us for future trade agreements."

William drained his glass before asking, "And what might that be, Thomas?"

"Money. Currency. We need a simple and reliable monetary system if we are to draft trade treaties with other nations. It is still nearly impossible to draft a contract of sale between parties in different states. Let me give you but a simple example. Just yesterday, one of my late-paying clients finally paid me for some survey work I had done for him, but he had no money. Wealth of land but no currency."

William got up to refill his glass and poked Jefferson on the shoulder as he went by. "Try to pass off Continentals?"

"Hardly! Not worth the paper they were printed on by now, as you well know. I contend that without a backing fund, our money system is bound to be a continual hindrance in trade between states, let alone with other nations. Each state has its own rate of exchange and…well, just consider how I was paid. The survey was paid by giving me a commodity."

"Bushels of turnips?"

"Almost. Last week another man paid me for legal services. He came here with a bag of this motley mixture of silver and gold. Portuguese half *joes* and *moidores*, Spanish dollars, doubloons and *pistoles*, and a few English half crowns. It would take a mathematical savant to calculate the actual value of such a collection. Yet that is how we operate today. That and barter and payment in kind."

James observed the men and tried to memorize which voice belonged to which man for when he would be in the cellar. He shifted to a series of Bach exercises that seemed to him to be in keeping with the soothing manner of the canon he had played twice without interruption. He strained to overhear their conversation above his own playing.

Francis asked, "Can't the states regulate their currency better? Set a national standard but let each state print their own?"

Edward shook his head. "Unlikely. Have you forgotten so quickly how the British flooded our market with counterfeit Continentals and sped the devaluation of the currency? We still have old British pounds being used for trade as well as state-issued script. It's a hash." Turning to Jefferson, he asked, "You still favor a national currency?"

He nodded quickly. "Yes. For security and control at the minimum. In fact, I think there is a good basis for it in the Spanish dollar."

William plopped into his chair without spilling a drop. "What? You are mad. That is a decent silver crown, but then merchants slice it up in half, quarters, and then again into eighths, call these slices 'pieces of eight.' Now while those slivers of the coin are supposed to stand for a lesser value, they are not consistent. They are deucedly odd. And sharp. And hard to calculate, being in bits."

Jefferson cleared his throat. "Exactly the problem with the British system as well. Odd fractional subordinate monies, hangers-on from Roman times. I propose that we create a national system based on the decimal system. A dollar would be worth a hundred pennies. We should also have a five- and ten-cent piece as well. A decimal system would be splendid."

Edward raised his glass to interrupt. "But Thomas, I know of no country that has a decimal system, although I do see your argument for its simplicity."

Jefferson grinned. "Then we shall be the first."

Edward said, "It will take some serious explanation to Congress to adopt such a radical notion."

"Then explain it I shall. I have already started some notes, which I shall refine and send forward as you suggest. So? What is the latest of Franklin? Candidly."

Samuel chuckled. "He and Adams are at constant odds. John, the prude, is very uncomfortable with Mister Franklin's more liberal attitudes toward the ladies of court. And I understand that Ben is equally irritated by John's plain attire and homespun morality lessons that he imparts at almost any gathering of more than two."

Jefferson sipped then said, "He has been away from his Abigail for too long. She tempers him."

"Yes, I do think that if Abigail were to join him, his sourness toward the world would diminish."

Jefferson sighed. "She is indeed his better half by twice."

William paused and seemed relieved that Jefferson could now jest. Any spark of wit seemed to have died with Martha. He had fallen into darkness and shut others away, leaving the house just to ride alone or with Patsy during those mourning months. Perhaps he had recovered enough of himself for this post after all. He laughed. "Both better company and better to gaze upon than stumpy John."

Samuel nodded. "Quite so. I myself could do but half what she accomplishes. I marvel at how she raises their children and manages their farm in Braintree when he is so often gone, and all without an overseer."

Jefferson frowned. "Hard to imagine, even on their small farm, but a plantation such as this is quite another matter. I am fortunate that my overseer is a man of sound business practice. He knows how to manage the livestock, implements of farming, and the field hands to promote the highest yield of their labor in planting, tending, and harvesting the crops I designate, while, at the same time, he manages to find the minimum subsistence of food, lodging, and attire required for their labor to reduce the costs of their maintenance."

Samuel matched his frown, but Jefferson continued. "But by allowing them to raise a crop or have a few chickens on the plot adjoining their cabin, I allow the industrious to prosper. I encourage their crafts for my purchase or their sale in the town's Sunday market. I also encourage family bonds and find that calms many an issue."

Francis interrupted. "Of course. They are less prone to wander off. And a child anchors a mother to the land."

Jefferson added, "Precisely. Rare is it that I need to sell a slave. Just for theft or fighting, really. They know their cabin is warm and their place here is secure as long as they attend to the proper activities and attitude."

Francis was interested. "As to your overseer, do you form an annual contract, as we do?"

Jefferson chuckled. "No. You change overseers as often as some change their stockings. But I prefer an ongoing employment agreement. I doubt that I could know the full capacity of an overseer in just one season, particularly as I continually try new crops and farming methods.

But having the same overseer year to year is a benefit to me that you may not find as you grow your same Carolina rice year to year and face the horrid health risks of the flooded rice fields."

As James played, he looked at the sunset and lost track of who was talking about what. A light breeze was fluttering yellowed leaves from the row of mulberry trees.

William cleared his throat to interrupt. "I find the young men wanting to do the work have little attachment to the land."

Francis chuckled. "Best you attach them. Look for one with a wife and lodge them both on your land. A young buck of an overseer and a henhouse of servants can lead to mischief in the evenings and consternation some months later when a strangely pale infant yowls."

All laughed. Jefferson turned his attention back to their conversation as William continued his analysis. "Better yet, if his wife has some domestic skills to spin, weave, or sew as to manage the domestic industry of the girls, particularly if you have no slave driver acquainted with those arts."

Francis said, "True, and in the most perfect of worlds, their domestic union would be bliss, and neither would have any draw from their attention to your tasks, such as family in a nearby village."

Jefferson laughed. "So, the perfect bonding of orphans who are skilled in all the domestic and farming arts, and newly married. Is that the ideal we should seek, Francis?"

"In a dream! But I agree with you, Thomas. I found that an annual agreement or using a first-year production measure tends to put the emphasis on the crop to the expense of the slaves and implements, so the second year falls short as implements need to be repaired or replaced and slave labor has been diminished by illness, injury, disability, or death. No, I want an overseer who can manage a balance of these competing interests to find an ongoing betterment in all of the areas under his purview."

Francis sighed. "But you don't have the challenges we have growing rice. A goodly number of my workers are lost to disease in those flooded rice fields every year. I need continual replacements as well as added slaves for my expansion into new rice fields. You know those boys from Africa, not the ones born here, but the ones who worked rice in Africa have brought some new means of clearing and flooding fields that have increased my production almost twenty percent in just two years."

Samuel sighed. Jefferson looked at his discomfort. "Edward? Are you sufficiently ready to enlighten us with the latest doings in Philadelphia? How is the shipping trade?"

Bob opened the door slowly, stood in the doorframe, and looked at his pocket watch. Jefferson nodded to him. "We will have our soup at six, please."

Jefferson turned to James and dismissed him with a tip of his head toward the door. The young man left the violin on a side table and hurried out of the parlor. Bob returned the watch to his vest pocket with a flourish and closed the door.

William huffed, "Don't want my boy getting ideas on him needing a pocket clock."

Jefferson shook his head. "In actual fact, it has saved me a great deal of oversight. I run by the clock and so must my plantation if there is to be order. Bob keeps all servants and events on time at the house. My overseer does so for the trades and fields. I plan to install a chime clock on the front of the house that can be heard across the plantation. Besides, all he has is one of my old watches with the *verge fusee* mechanism that never held to more than five minutes late a day, no matter how many times I sent it to the watchmaker in Philadelphia. And I cracked the glass out riding one day, so it is not really an object of envy."

"So, you say." William looked at his empty glass theatrically before he motioned toward the sideboard. "Time for another before we proceed to your supper?"

Jefferson nodded and grinned. He had inspected the dining room just before the carriages had arrived. Lizzie had James set the table with Jefferson's finest wares. At each place was a sterling setting from England.

There were three stemmed glasses at each place, two for wine and one for water.

The chinaware was French. Flat soup bowls rested on large dinner plates. Above the forks were bread plates. Between the bread plates and glasses rested dessert spoons. A large white napkin was folded on the back of each chair, as was the latest style in Virginia. At the head of the table, a small silver coaster sat empty, awaiting whatever wine Jefferson had selected to accompany each of his dinner offerings.

The room sparkled as Jefferson opened the door for his guests. Dusk had fallen and the candles had been lit. A small fire danced in the fireplace, spiking rainbows off the crystal. In the cellar, James put his blanket aside when he heard laughter above him through the shaft of the dumbwaiter.

CHAPTER 3

Edward was the loudest of the men upon entering the dining room. "You have come a far distance from our colonial days, Thomas. I can recall our eating boiled beef in taverns from wood trenchers that we had to share and hoisting our beer in carved wooden cups."

Jefferson laughed. "We worked through some of the most complex puzzles over such humble fare. I trust supper today will be less humble but the conversation as stimulating."

Rather than going to the table, Jefferson walked across the dining room to the center of the fireplace, which protruded into the room by several feet. To its left was a square-wheeled walnut trolley with four shelves. He pushed it aside and turned to his guests. "Now, you shall see my latest convenience for the dining room." Jefferson opened the door to the dumbwaiter. "Gentlemen, in a moment, you will see a bottle of fine German wine appear, perfectly chilled from my cellar." James pulled the rope smoothly until he heard applause and the door click shut. He loaded the next bottle and let it ascend carefully against the counterweight. Now that the good German wine was being poured, he knew that he had a few minutes while they ate their soup before he would again send up a new bottle of wine. He strained to listen.

Jefferson proceeded to lecture his guests on his latest invention. "The dumbwaiter, as I call it, drops down a shaft directly into the wine cellar. I have a shaft on either side of the fireplace. Each has two counterweighted platforms that bring us a new bottle as its weight drops. All I need do is pull it out and pour it without the intrusion of servants."

Someone clapped Jefferson on the shoulder as they returned to the dining table. William's southern drawl rose above the rest. "That's some magic trick, Thomas. Doctor Franklin would be impressed."

Jefferson poured the wine evenly between the five glasses on the table. "Will he remain?" The men took their chairs.

William answered, "For a time. But his role is diminishing. Now he lives outside the city, at Passy, and entertains there. The carriage ride into Paris is getting to be too much for him. He's almost eighty and not well, but he tries to mask it. I understand Abigail Adams will go to Paris if she is not already there."

Jefferson paused before saying, "I find her quite a sharp wit, but as to John I am at a loss for words."

William mocked concentration before putting his finger to his temple. "A duller wit and a prude?"

The men all laughed.

When Jefferson heard a tap on the small dining room door beside the fireplace, he stood, motioned for his guests to watch him, and quickly crossed the room. Once at the mahogany door beside the fireplace, he pushed the edge of the door, which then rotated on a center rod. Soon, shelves on a flat panel replaced the faceted face of the door. On the largest of the shelves, which was at waist height, sat the covered tureen of soup.

Jefferson put the soup on the rolling trolley cart and pushed it to the table. He glanced around the room and smiled. "No servant is in sight. We have all the privacy that a king should want yet will never have. So now we may speak candidly as we eat and drink well. To your health."

Samuel raised his glass toward Jefferson. "And to our union of states." All took hearty draughts from their glasses.

Jefferson filled their soup bowls from the steaming tureen at his side. As they lifted their spoons, Jefferson said, "Gentlemen! I would have you know that the peas in this soup were grown and harvested last year on this property. The intent of this experiment was to see if they could be reconstituted as close to fresh as possible. Have we met that challenge?"

Shortly after they finished the soup, Jefferson retrieved a new bottle from the dumbwaiter, leaving the door ajar allowing James to hear their conversation clearly.

Holding a new bottle aloft, Jefferson said, "I think you will like the Gevrey-Chambertin. Splendid Burgundy. Shows the Pinot Noir grape to great advantage." After Jefferson had emptied the bottle, he sauntered to the mahogany door by the fireplace. Rotating the tall door again, the empty soup tureen had been replaced by an abundance of tinned covers over Lizzie's platters. Jefferson carried the largest platter to the sideboard, at which time Edward and Francis both jumped up to assist in transporting the other platters.

Once the dishes were lined up on the sideboard, Jefferson uncovered them and announced the bounty. "Tonight, we dine on spit-roasted venison and rabbit. Boiled chicken and vegetables in the colonial manner." He pointed to the steaming bowls of rice, and boiled vegetables. "Accompanied by Carolina rice, Monticello vegetables, and sliced pickled beets from our garden and kitchen." A basket of bread rolls sat beside a platter of thinly sliced cold ham. "The ham, I should point out, was born here, fed a controlled diet, and smoked here. Finest dry smoked ham in the state, if I say so myself."

Francis was the first to lift his plate from the table and partake of the variety of the buffet, laying down a bed of rice on which he placed the roasted meats. To the side, he set a small portion of the vegetables. The others followed quickly and took very different approaches to the buffet. The northerners, Samuel and Edward, took the roasted meats and vegetables and only modest portions of rice. Jefferson took small portions of the meats and had mainly rice and vegetables. His guests knew that Jefferson reserved his ham for the second trip to the buffet table and followed his approach.

William had several bites of venison before he looked at Jefferson. "Splendid dinner, Thomas. If you can do half as well negotiating the treaty."

"So how is Congress on the strategy?"

"You know, Congress has been clear that we need to fix our treaty of peace with England before we have a legitimate position to negotiate on matters of trade with others."

Jefferson nodded. "These trade treaties are essential to our economic survival. We cannot trade with England and are not yet self-sufficient."

"After the peace treaty is agreed upon, your access to the French leaders of industry and commerce is unique and will be of great value to us through your friendship with Lafayette."

Jefferson turned to the others. "A friend he is indeed, to our nation as well. When I think of his arrival here from France, I marvel at it. Did you know he was a mere nineteen-year-old lad but talked his way into a commission as a Major General. He commanded our troops with distinction and was wounded in our service. His assistance here during our Revolution was invaluable, as will be his role in our future plans. What trade do you see as key to each of your regions?"

Samuel was the first to reply. "Our Boston whalers want to increase whale oil sales in France and Germany. Coopers, lumbermen, and shipbuilders each have a place in your talks, as well as do our fur trappers. And don't forget about our rum."

William chuckled, holding his fork at the ready, loaded with chicken. "No need to emphasize tobacco for our Commonwealth."

Francis added, "For the Carolinas, rice and indigo in addition to tobacco. And a continuation of the importation of labor."

Jefferson scowled. "That won't sit well with our Quaker friends in the north."

Francis snapped back, "Would they prefer breeding farms? We must have replacement labor."

Jefferson turned to Edward. "How about Pennsylvania?"

"Grains and cattle. Dried meat for ship stores. Our Quaker and Methodist brethren do oppose slavery, whether imported or traded or owned."

Jefferson nodded back to him. "We all know that slavery is a hideous blot. You know during the drafting I offered a clause that abolished it, which was not unlike the one adopted by the Congress in '74 that banned importation."

Francis pointed his fork at Jefferson. "You know damn well that the Continental Association was merely a ban on trading with Great Britain as a pressure point. A pressure point! Adopting such a measure universally is utterly impractical and you know it."

Samuel put down his glass. "But not for Adams. His Declaration of Rights in the Massachusetts Constitution has caused no end of discord in that state by interrupting the legal relation: master to servant and state to state."

Jefferson cleared his throat. "His is a state with little reliance on labor, and Adams is, you know, Adams." Taking a deep breath, he continued. "But at Monticello, we have met our increasing labor needs by natural procreation, not importation. That is the model on which I drafted my proposed ban on the importation of enslaved Africans in 1778 for the Virginia Legislature. I hope that this model will be adopted in other states. But Adams went beyond this sensible point."

Samuel asked, "Why not send your wording to be introduced as federal legislation in the next Congress?"

Hoisting his glass but pausing before responding, Jefferson said, "Oh, no. The time is not right. I would view that as anti-democratic and quite opposed to the principles of the Revolution to impose such a broad law. The states each must come to their own conclusions on their own needs and merits. Without continual importation, South Carolina would suffer. Charleston would find its demise within a year. But I agree that ultimately abolition should be the goal, or it will put a fissure in our union."

Samuel looked puzzled. "Yet you continue to have slaves."

"Yes, which are the economic engine of this plantation. I feed and clothe them well. And, their work feeds and clothes my family. Look at the model I have adopted from the Utopian writers. Plato's *The Republic*.

Sir Thomas More in his *Utopia*. Have you read it, Plato?"

"No."

"Do you read Greek? I have a copy in my library I could loan you."

"No, afraid not."

Jefferson's voice was strong. "Pity, I should translate it for you. Interesting view of what constitutes a just city-state and indeed a just man. More wrote of an ideal community on an island in the Atlantic." Jefferson smirked. "As he was English, perhaps he intended us as his ideal community!"

Edward put down his glass. "Ideal? I doubt you could have an ideal community in which one would not gladly trade places with another. Would any of you exchange places with any slave—even your own, Thomas?"

Jefferson slid his chair back and picked ham and a roll from the buffet. Returning to the table he said, "We know that among the Romans, the condition of their white slaves was much more deplorable than that of the black slaves here. The two sexes were confined in separate apartments, because to raise a child cost the master more than buying a new slave. But in this country the slaves multiply as fast as the free inhabitants. Their situation and manners place the commerce between the two sexes almost without restraint. Cato, on a principle of economy, always sold his sick and superannuated slaves. He gives it as a standing precept to a master visiting his farm, to sell his old oxen, old wagons, old tools, old and diseased servants, and everything else as it becomes useless. As much as my overseer protests, my slaves cannot enumerate this among the injuries and insults they receive."

Samuel said, "But look to Homer."

"But weren't his slaves generally white men capable of learning and tending to their affairs? They weren't Africans."

Samuel continued, "Ah, have you read the abolitionists' tracts about Phillis Wheatley?"

"Who?"

"That Negress poet."

Francis scoffed. "A Negress?"

"Truly. Wrote something called *Poems on Various Subjects, Religious and Moral*. That is how she titled her book. Had to have it published in England. Poems? Perhaps, but so laced in religion that I hesitate to call it poetry."

Francis continued his disbelief. "Nevertheless! A woman. A Negro! But, point taken, they taught that dog to stand up on its hind legs and bark. But not all dogs can be taught."

"Today, Monticello has more than a hundred black slaves, over half working the land. But in my trades, I have hired two free black men and five indentured whites who are no less free from my control than my slaves."

Samuel raised his voice. "But their term of servitude is fixed by contract. They bargained for the duration and a specific remuneration."

Edward took up the argument. "And in so doing, bound themselves for a term of service, three or five years. You bought their contract for labor, but not the person or their offspring in perpetuity."

"Correct, but you miss my point. By having a free black man at my forge, I show others that you can become a blacksmith. If there is a goal, people will work for it. If there is no hope and horrid conditions, people may revolt. I simply am finding the balance that leads to a harmony. A balance, like wheels of a watch mechanism. I want to improve their condition in a way that improves mine as well. I am reducing my tobacco plantings and introducing wheat, short-grained rice, and other crops that require less labor."

Samuel countered. "That has little to do with slavery and more to do with profitability. Besides, to free a slave is to abandon your own responsibility for their well-being."

"The enslaved and indentured complement each other. But on this matter, slavery is like holding a wolf by its ears. We can neither hold it forever nor can we safely let it go."

Samuel held up both hands. "Gentlemen. Can we agree that slavery is a conundrum for another day? Now let's talk about Paris."

Jefferson nodded. "Sound recommendation. But as to Paris, what is a widower to do in that social swirl? I have no hostess."

Edward suggested, "Your daughter."

"Patsy? She is but twelve years of age! Quite the innocent. Not ready for that role."

He persisted. "Don't cosset her."

Jefferson scowled. "Of course, I am being overprotective. She is my daughter."

Edward winked at Jefferson. "Think of the opportunities Patsy could have. Presented at court. Polishing her French. It may open new *liaisons* for you both. Fancy a wealthy French count for a son-in-law? One with a vineyard, perhaps."

Jefferson laughed a bit too loud. "I am just now planting the winter crops and starting an expansion of the main house. Do not tempt me with new projects."

William said, "With all due respect, Thomas, we need you to build a nation, not just your precious Monticello."

"But how can I maintain Monticello, have a suitable residence in Paris, and travel throughout Europe on the scant budget that George has suggested? It is barely sufficient to live like a monk in some provincial hovel. I'll need a local cook, housemaids, and servants at the least. I'll bring my own valet and driver to defray costs. Bob is invaluable. And a trusted personal secretary is essential."

"Understood."

"That settled, we need to find ways to import their ideas and export our products if we are to become a great nation."

Without waiting for a reply, Jefferson stood and took the empty bottle to the dumbwaiter. James then pulled the rope down with the empty bottle, sent the next one up to the dining room, and continued to listen easily through the open door.

While Jefferson sauntered back to the table, his guests all returned to the sideboard and refreshed their plates by taking slices of ham. Jefferson held a bottle above his head. "Bordeaux. Château Haut-Brion. History goes back to the sixteenth century."

Samuel said, "Your cellar is quite remarkable."

"My wine merchant sent this shipment in bottles. Rather than casking the wine for export, they bottled it at the winery, used a cork stopper, sealed it with wax, and shipped the bottles in wood crates padded with straw. It's the latest innovation, proving the source and halting pilfering. They seemed to travel well. Wouldn't you agree?"

William worked the notion out loud. "Bottled there. I often bottle from my casks to take my wine with me on travels or use a decanter at home. But bottled there? Interesting."

Francis tapped the table. "Much better than trusting casks to those river pirates. On my last shipment, they drained off a goodly amount and replaced it with water. I did not discover the theft until I tapped it a month ago."

"I see merit to the sturdy glass bottle, even if you must use a screw or thin-bladed knife to remove the cork."

Samuel added, "You see, bringing ideas like that back to us with the peace treaty will..."

Jefferson raised his voice. "Will what?"

Samuel leaned forward in his sincerity. "If our financial situation were improved by peace and trade, there might be increased support for you as the next president."

"Kind of you to say."

Francis was stern. "The boycott of English goods is starting to vex some. I know you don't want to rekindle those relations. But we must put the matter of a peace treaty ahead of all else."

Jefferson was stern. "I won't support any resumption of trade with our former masters. Peace first. Trade later, much later."

All muttered approval.

Francis said, "All the more reason for you to join in the negotiation. You see the issues so clearly."

"And without using Franklin's little eyeglasses."

Francis chuckled. "He once adopted the French attire, but now has become a rustic curiosity wearing his plain brown suit of clothes and that odd fur cap. They even sell gimcracks with his face on them, from snuff boxes to chamber pots with the slogan, 'He wrested lightning from the gods and their scepters from tyrants.' But you! You are revered by the French as a philosopher and the author of the Declaration of Independence."

Jefferson smirked and tested his support. "Who still owns slaves."

William shouted, "Irrelevant!"

"Not to everyone. Remember, when I introduced a bill in the Virginia legislature—and a similar clause in the first draft of the Declaration—to abolish slavery, for total emancipation, I made enemies."

Samuel argued with him. "But those of us in the north who oppose slavery feel that you made progress by opening that discussion, even if the measures failed."

Jefferson snapped, "And what came of it?" He emptied his glass in one tip.

"Eventually, your Commonwealth adopted a law granting any owner the ability to free a slave either by an indenture or deed of manumission while alive or by a testamentary bequest in their will."

Jefferson took on a professorial tone and spoke with emphasis. "Manumission is as rare as hen's teeth. But it does offer a theoretical pathway to freedom. But at least in a testamentary bequest, the owner need not suffer the scorn of other owners for his act."

Jefferson left the door open and failed to announce this new red wine. He walked around the table pouring freely and raised his voice. "Attacks on character and ability? This appointment is political. One must expect it."

William said, "But your philosophy is consistent. Adams is from a free state. The French have abolished slavery, except in their colonies, in large part based on your dissertations."

Jefferson sighed. "It creates a quandary between head and heart. I do believe that all men are created equal, which means free. But that is not the state of the law today or the economic necessity for plantations. In the north, you don't have these issues."

Samuel argued, "We still have labor needs, but I admit they are not as intense."

"If I elect to accept this commission and go to Paris, I must take my valet, Bob. I find him indispensable. But I can see Franklin poking at me for doing so."

Francis smirked. "Wrong! He wants to forget the poverty he knew as a lad. You do know that his father indentured him out as a bond servant?"

"Really?"

Francis adopted a conspiratorial tone. "Ran away from his master. My father knew his bondsman, so I know this to be true. No, he does not want his past brought to light."

Jefferson cocked his head. "Interesting, his rise in station."

"Indeed. I hear there is even a wax likeness of his head in a little shop in Paris. People pay a coin or two to gawk at him, alongside other notables and a few infamous for the murders they committed. No, he will not meddle with you. He is too busy being celebrated as the inventor of the lightning rod."

"I shall not take away from the practical value of his inventions. Spectacles have no doubt helped some see more clearly and his lightning rod has saved a goodly number of homes from burning after a strike, but it is not as though he invented lightning itself."

CHAPTER 4

Less than a week later, Jefferson's sister-in-law, Elizabeth Wayles Eppes, arrived and assumed charge of his girls while the household servants packed for him. Soon, he was ready to travel. After attending to Jefferson's last-minute needs and instructions, Bob returned to the cabin he shared with his family. He closed his travel bag and pulled on his heaviest overcoat. He nodded to James. "Go out and watch for the carriage to pass while I say my goodbyes to Mam." The scent of rosewater lingered in the cabin.

James stepped into the chill of the day wondering if Bob would claim his freedom in France and this goodbye was forever. He heard his mother weeping and paused before he called, "It passed. It's up at the big house now."

The light carriage would make better time to the coast than the wagon with their trunks. Dispatching the wagon two days prior to Jefferson's departure should allow its arrival to coincide with Jefferson's at Baltimore. The ship cabins were booked, and passage paid. Their warmest attire had been sent ahead for the winter voyage.

The farewells between the sisters were tearful.

Lucy, just nine months old, refused to release her sister when Patsy tried to climb into the carriage. Sally, who was only nine, held the squalling Lucy as the carriage jerked forward. Bob quickly settled the team into a comfortable trot. In spite of the November crispness in the air, the sun was bright. Jefferson elected to leave the cover of the carriage down. Bob could easily put it up if the day became colder or rain emerged from the few clouds over the mountains.

Jefferson sat tall in the open carriage, facing forward, bundled in a heavy coat. He pulled a lap robe across Patsy's knees. As the carriage passed the wintered orchard, he took off his tricorn hat and held it high in a farewell salute, knowing all were watching from the lawn of the big house until the carriage rounded the turn and sped down from the mountaintop.

In the quiet of the house that night, Missus Eppes walked through the home her sister had made and felt her loss as if fresh again. She decided to stay a few days longer to let Polly and her baby sister get over their father's departure in familiar surroundings.

November seemed colder the week after Jefferson left with Bob and Patsy. James and Sally tended their duties with added attention to detail and precision, heeding their mother's words so they didn't get a cross look from anyone during this time of change. Sally continued to tend after Lucy and Polly and frequently looked in on Missus Eppes, asking if she would like another log on the fire or a cup of tea or a biscuit or another shawl. By measuring her responses, Sally quickly adapted to the wants of her new mistress. Jefferson's daughters were calmed by Sally's presence and their aunt's soothing ways.

Just after lunch, several days after Jefferson's departure, James was at the dining room table polishing the glass globes from the oil lamps on the walls. Sally rushed into the room. He looked up. "No call to have this much soot on the glass if you'd trim the wicks like Bob say to. But no. Now I gotta polish it harder."

Sally put her hand up to stop him. "Miller's lookin' fo' you."

He put down the cloth. "Me? Don't see me working from can't see to can't see for him. I'm no field hand."

"Didn't say you was. He sent me to fetch you. So, you gotta hop to. He's in the library, leaning on Massa's desk like he own it."

James threw the sooty cloth on the table and stood quickly. He tugged down the hem of his vest and scrunched up his face in displeasure.

"Best you put on your face, like Mam say. With Massa away, you know."

He marched toward the door.

Sally grabbed his sleeve. "Don't go takin' airs with him; he can make a passel a trouble. For all of us."

James pushed past her and marched toward the library. Halfway there, he tried to consider what business Miller might have with him. He was a man who was feared, but not respected. His lash was random, and his methods grew in harshness as the harvest approached if Jefferson wasn't there to cool him down. James drew a deep breath.

Last corn harvest, he was put to helping in the kitchen when Cook made batch after batch of cornpone. When the pans cooled, he cut the bread into hand-sized squares and stacked them in apple crates so that pickers could eat and work at the same time. Cook told him that Miller was working the field hands over night, night after night, to bring in the corn harvest before the big rains. Men were sleeping an hour or two in the mud and taking a square of cornpone from the crate and drinking rainwater from the ruts in the road. Someone said he told Jefferson it was easier to let the barrel go dry than driving the water wagon through the mud, not wanting to risk a mule breaking a leg.

James knew that it wasn't just during the push of harvest that Miller was a hard man. Planting tobacco was sunup to sundown, then he'd call on ol' Moses to come and play his fiddle outside the overseer's house while he ate his supper with his wife. Gave him a copper for it. But the old man's hands were already cramping and his fingers bleeding from the day of work. Maybe Miller had some heart after all giving him a copper for it, or maybe his wife made him.

James thought that women could make men do things they alone wouldn't think to do. Although he had no real recollection of his father, James had heard his brother, Bob, tell of how Mam had wrapped ol' Massa Wayles around her little finger until the day he died. He'd tag after her like he was tied to her apron strings. James nodded to himself as he thought of how Bob talked crazy about being with Dolly and running. *Now he's gone to France.*

A few steps before the library door, James stopped, then took a slow, deep breath and squared his shoulders. "Calm your mind and hurry your body." That's what Mam would say. Put on the face. Now go into the room. Look like you hurried.

As he started toward the door, he heard Miller talking to someone. James stopped and listened. Miller's voice was low and unhappy. "Now? You want me to start this now?"

"We need to increase our income. Jefferson's expansion of the house is far more costly than he planned, and with his new expenses abroad…"

"What do you want me to do, Mister Short? Go back to planting tobacco? Makes him more money."

"I think there is an opportunity for income in our nail production."

"We barely make enough here now to avoid buying kegs of nails in town. That's a saving, I suspect."

"Exactly. But, if you can increase nail production beyond our needs here, we'd have a new income source."

Miller's voice went to a low growl. "And you think that a slave, even a house servant, has the wherewithal to monitor production? What's he gonna do, make chicken scratches of tally marks, four up and one crossing it, for me to recount later?"

"James can read and write. Jefferson taught him himself, if you can imagine that. He'll be able to manage a ledger. Just show him once. Jefferson says the more you tease him with knowledge, the more he wants."

Miller lowered his voice. "If you say so."

"Better he count the kegs of nails made daily than you or I. Besides, he need only check in the morning to be sure the boys are at their tasks and count kegs at night. Other than that, you can task him to kitchen work."

"You are tying one hand behind my back."

"No. What I am doing is creating the opportunity for James to develop basic cooking skills without complaint. He thinks cooking is not for house servants. It's women's work."

Miller chuckled. "See, when he coddles them, that's the attitude I get."

"Nevertheless, Jefferson asked that I create an environment in which James is exposed to cooking skills in a way that he won't run off or be insolent. That boy does not do well with orders, so making the other jobs less attractive might make the kitchen more so."

After a moment, Miller responded. "I understand. Couple weeks in the new brickworks with them tender hands might get his attention."

"Not yet. Let him see that working in the kitchen is in his interest. If not, we can reform his view by some added labor that is not to his liking."

James backed down the hallway silently then ran to the doorway, boots clattering on the wood floor. Miller had his back to the doorway and stopped talking when Short looked up at James.

Miller turned and then glanced back at Short. "*I'll* talk to James now."

Short frowned at Miller's dismissive tone but said nothing. He stalked out of the room, barely missing James, who jumped aside.

Miller sat at Jefferson's desk and watched the young man walk to the front of the desk like he watched a horse before a race or slave at auction for muscle and attention. He looked at James with a sternness that James had heard was usually a prelude to beating a field hand with a short truncheon, now that Jefferson had taken away his favored whip. Eyes fixed on his target. Mouth pressed to a slit. They said his voice would go low into a whisper so you had to really try to hear him, maybe even need to lean close, and then he would order someone to strip off his shirt and two others to hold his arms during the beating right there in the field. He knew that since Jefferson tore down the whipping pole at the end of Mulberry Row, all of Miller's beatings were done in secret in the field with his short horsewhip or truncheon so Jefferson wouldn't know or complain about the reduced price a scarred slave would bring if a sale became necessary. But James saw his handiwork when Mam tended to the slaves' wounds in secret.

And he heard their stories.

They talked about him when Mam was tending their lash cuts or broken bones. James overheard them. "Miss Elizabeth, do what you gotta." Once she'd looked over the harm, she would hand them the leather-covered stick to hold between their teeth to quiet the screams while she did what was needed. Patting a tar salve on the rawness left when the whip snapped just right and bit off a chunk of flesh. But when the whip just ran across someone's back, it left a long stripe, a shallow but longer cut.

The stripes mended easier by themselves. She'd make up her salt-water brine and pour it over the still-bleeding stripes. "Clean it out so it can start the healing," she said, knowing the pain from the brine was almost as bad as the salt and pepper that the previous overseer used to rub into the lash lines. "Season 'um up," he'd say. Jefferson put a stop to that by firing him. But Miller had his own mind and did not always follow directions. He also knew how to wield his truncheon to inflict pain without breaking a bone.

James stood silently at the edge of the desk, his hands at his sides. His thumbs pressed into the seams of his trousers to stop his hands from trembling.

Miller slowly cocked his head, and closed one eye, like he was sighting down a musket. He hovered above the center of the polished walnut desk that separated them. "Mister Jefferson has commented to me on occasion how you are improving in your skills as a house boy and were starting to assist Bob in attending to Mister Jefferson's personal care."

Miller had just said more to James during the last minute than he had in his five years as the overseer at Monticello. James blinked and leaned forward to focus on Miller's words as he learned that he was assigned to duties in both the nailery and kitchen.

Mister Orr, a free man who worked for wages, would run the nail-making effort, but James was to verify and record the names of the enslaved workers at the start of the day and the number of kegs of nails they had produced by day's end, whether Orr was in the nailery or off drinking, as was his habit. In the hours between, his labor was under the direction of Lizzie. Once a week, James was tasked to dust the library. As James left the meeting, he felt the weight of Miller's capacity to alter his life—and not for the better.

A week later, the morning was crisp with frost on the ground when Sally packed her case and the trunks for Lucy and Polly for the long ride to the Eppington Plantation. Missus Eppes decided that nine-year-old Sally was sufficiently personable and trained to help with her two nieces both during the long journey to traverse the ninety miles between the two plantations and continue her service at Eppington.

By ten that morning, the frost had melted off and the sun was bright. Lizzie packed a large food basket and sent James to the carriage with it and extra lap robes for the girls. The driver, an oak of a man, held the bridle of the near horse in the team while Missus Eppes, Sally, and the two Jefferson girls settled into the closed carriage.

James and Mam watched the carriage leave from their cabin door. He started to say something to his mother, then stopped when he saw her face. She let her tears fall without regard, making no effort to brush them away. James hugged her. She gave his back a couple of taps and pulled away but held his shoulders to look at him. "James. You gotta know that I'll always want the best for all my chillen. I want their days to be better day-by-day, wherever that takes them, even if it is far from me. Now Missus Eppes is a good lady. I seen her when she was just coming up from a little thing. So don't fret on Sally, hear. Tend to your new duties with care. Make your own way."

James took this to heart. He hurried back to the kitchen as soon as the carriage departed, arriving just before lunch preparation began. He watched how Lizzie sliced the ham and then carried the light meal to the dining room for Short and Miller. In the days that followed, James soon became friendly with Marie, who was also new to the kitchen. One afternoon, he glanced up from peeling turnips and said something that made her laugh and nod.

Regaining her composure, Marie said, "*C'est vrai.*"

James frowned. "What?"

"Said, 'It be true.' That the way we say it where I come from. It's French."

"You talk French?"

Marie winked at him. "If you live in New Orleans, you gotta talk some French and some English there if you want to get on."

"Can you teach me?"

"You really want to learn?"

He grinned. "*C'est vrai.*"

Once a week, James continued to do the dusting and polishing of the furnishings in the big house to keep them in perfect condition, ready for Jefferson to walk through the door. James would never let the brass handles tarnish or the glass fog or the hinges squeak in his master's absence, both to honor the home and never to chance going to fieldwork.

Dusting the books in the library was the one job that Jefferson had instructed Mister Short to put solely on James; his care in handling the books met Jefferson's high standards for that task.

Along with this special duty came the opportunity to surreptitiously borrow from the extensive library. After he had brushed the feather duster over all the books, James slipped a new title under his vest and arranged its neighbors to hide the gap on the shelf. Holding it tight to his side with his elbow, he hurried to his cabin and read by firelight in those few hours after Mam and the youngsters had gone to sleep but before the fire dwindled. He sped through each book and returned it in perfect condition to the exact location in the library from which it had been plucked.

After James read every book in English in the library, he fanned through Jefferson's schoolbooks in French, Greek, and Latin. Putting aside the Greek and Latin textbooks, he slipped the beginning French primer under his shirt and consumed it in three sleepless nights. Soon, he and Marie conversed in French freely in the kitchen, more to the amusement than annoyance of Lizzie.

When he found a slim volume of French poetry in Jefferson's library, he committed one verse to memory and recited it to Marie when they were picking vegetables in the garden. She chuckled at his pronunciation and corrected him occasionally. Once he had listened to her, he recited it with perfection. Her grin matched his.

So bold he became that he took the advanced French grammar book from the library and kept it in his cabin for months to study at night. Sitting by the fire, his back against the wall to cast light on the pages, he mouthed the words to practice the pronunciation.

Squinting up from her bed, his mother frowned at him. "What you say, James?"

"Nothing. Just practicing."

"Practicing what?"

"French. I talk it with Marie in the kitchen, but I want to know more than just the names of foods and garden matters. I want to know what the words look like and how to spell them. I want…"

"Anyone say you can take that book?"

"No, Mam."

"Best you get it back before anyone misses it. And don't you get it all sooty, sittin' so close to the fire. And don't let the youngsters see you with it."

"I'll try."

"Trying ain't the same as doing. Overseer catch you with that, it means lashes. Maybe for me too. Tomorrow, first thing, it goes back. You getting too comfortable for your own good, boy."

"Yes, Mam."

"And another thing."

"What is it, Mam?"

"That Samson boy, he gone on the run late today."

"Oh no. The one in the nailery?"

"Same. But his brother found him. Sent word and is bringing him back. But he won't be there at the start. Maybe by noon."

"You knew this all night and just now tell me?"

"Ain't about you or me. It about keeping him from harm's way. You gotta say he got the flux and hope his bowels calm by noon."

"I ain't gonna lie for that fool. Think I want to bring Miller's wrath down on me instead? Or on you?"

"Then don't say nothing. But don't give him up or Miller'll know someone told me 'bout it, then we both in a mess."

James banked the fire and tried to sleep.

The following morning, well before dawn, James did return the book to its place on the lower shelf. But he took another look at the Latin and Greek textbooks from Jefferson's school days. The Greek letters still mystified him. He shrugged and returned that book to its shelf without added thought. Scribbles in the margins of the Latin text offered a guide, however faint, to the words. James fanned through the Latin book and found a table in the back of the book that translated words in Latin to English and another from English to Latin. *Agricola* - Farmer. Jefferson loved agriculture. The link between the languages now teased James, who slipped the Latin book into his cabin that night and waited until he heard the deep sleep sounds from his mother before he dared open it. Over the next few weeks, he made connections between words in French to Latin to English and found a web of relations and mental stimulation that he had never known.

In the spring, Miller and Short went to Richmond to buy new farm equipment. In their absence, James ventured into the cabinets under the bookcases. Opening the boxes that were stored there, he found a jumble of loose pages. These were more souvenirs of a time past than any orderly dissertation. He extracted a handful and laid the loose pages on Jefferson's desk.

He fanned through the wrinkled and stained pages. Drafts, copies of speeches, fragments, a few letters from others. A few copies of letters he had dispatched to others. A list of clothing purchased for school. Folded letters of commendation on school achievements. A crumpled envelope with a smudged address on it. He fingered through the pages. A speech, or perhaps a paper for school, was more tattered than others. He picked it up and read it. When he realized that it was a plan for the reduction of slavery, he became lightheaded and had to force himself to start breathing again. He read it again, slowly. It was choppy and consisted of listings and disconnected phrases. James wondered if it were notes for a debate, notes for a speech, or legislation. It had many marginal notes beside what passed as paragraphs. Some in pen, others in pencil, some more faded than others. He skimmed the body of the text then struggled to decipher the scribbled notes.

On slavery. How to reverse its onerous pathway. Freedom by deed of manumission—a paper to legally release from bondage, without the consideration necessary for a sale. To will away at death, by testamentary bequest. To place into trust but release from duties, enslavement continuing but duties none.

Suddenly the fragmented notes formed a whole and James discovered Jefferson's private thoughts. Stunned, James leaned against the desk and read it again to be certain of his understanding. This was the pathway to freedom.

He leafed through drafts titled as briefs for court cases. A neatly folded page dated 1770 had a court name on it. He pulled it from the stack. The caption at the top indicated that Jefferson was the lawyer representing two mulatto boys in their challenge for their freedom. Attached to the page, by thread, pierced and knotted in the upper-left corner, were notes on the case, pages of random phrases, incomplete lines, scratch outs.

Then on the last page, there was a clearly written block in a firm hand:

Use in closing argument: "Under the law of nature, all men are born free, everyone comes into the world with a right to his own person, which includes the liberty of moving and using it at his own will. This is what is called personal liberty, and is given him by the author of nature..."

Although his hand trembled, James hurried to return the pages to their box and restore the order of the shelf. He calculated that Jefferson posed the premise of liberty as a universal right six years before the Declaration of Independence. He had exposed his heart and set a dream to ink. James thought he had discovered Jefferson's mind and possibly his soul.

In late March, James overheard Short reading a letter to Miller in which Jefferson advised that he had been unable to sail to France because ice had blocked the harbor. He had rejoined the Congress, Bob would remain with him, Patsy was boarded with a woman near him, and his younger daughters were to stay at the Eppington Plantation.

James felt that the plantation's core was still missing. Missus Jefferson's death had been like a fog that changed everything. No copper for a treat or kind word. No Bible stories. No gentleness. His family had scattered, Bob with Jefferson, brothers to the plantation trades. Sisters hired out. They too might as well be in another world for all that he saw of them on a daily basis. And now Sally was away at Eppington. James felt adrift. Mam was there, but only for the few moments between his return and when she fell asleep after tending the youngsters.

He leaned against the raw brick wall. Tears came unbidden. He felt as though he were orphaned on an unfamiliar island.

CHAPTER 5

Like clockwork, James dutifully checked that the boys in the nailery were present and operating under Mister Orr's guidance before going to the kitchen, helping as Lizzie instructed him, and then recording the number of kegs in the little book at the end of his workday. He mastered and simplified his kitchen duties and found idle time during which he and Marie were often missing from their tasks or taking longer than necessary in the barn or orchard. For months, one day had blended into the next without challenge, but he measured as success that Miller and Short ignored him as he went about his chores.

The sameness soon weighed on James who began to ask for more difficult tasks. Within months, he was as accomplished as Lizzie in all facets of the kitchen and assumed more and more of her duties. Marie became more attentive as his skills developed and she saw him as the certain successor to Lizzie once Jefferson returned and the kitchen became challenged to increase its production and variety of dishes.

James dressed in the faint light and slid out the door, shoes in hand. Hopping on one foot then the other in the cold, he put them on. Halfway to the nailery, he pissed against the trunk of a mulberry tree. Chinese trees in Virginia? Just another one of Massa's strange ideas. Who else would plant a row of trees just for their leaves? Then he got some special worms all the way from China that only ate those leaves. Built the worms their very own house with two fireplaces, where they ate all the leaves they wanted. Let them spin cocoons. He held some cocoons back for breeders and let them go to moths. But all the other cocoons, no bigger than the end of a thumb, he'd boil, kill the worm inside, and soak until the threads came free. Had girls with a light touch pull off the threads that formed the cocoon. Some of the threads, he swore, were a mile long and fine as a spider's web.

He remembered Jefferson's instructions, as it seemed an impossible task even for the girls with nimble fingers. Take eight of the nearly invisible strands from cocoons and twist them together to form a thread. Put the threads on a spindle. Put the spindles on the special loom he got from China. Weave the threads together. All that effort made only a few yards of lumpy silk. James shivered. Maybe Virginia was too cold for the worms and all China was like a warm kitchen.

As he walked past cabins and workhouses toward the forge, he saw three young blacksmiths hammering on nail blanks in the swirl of charcoal smoke. Two boys worked the bellows. With the warming of spring, Mister Orr let the new smiths set up out of doors to point and head the blanks. He heard the snapping of cutters against the iron wire as he approached the nailery. Looking into the dim room, he saw seven youngsters cutting blanks from reels of wire. Production was high and there was a profit in the industry. James opened the ledger book and entered the personnel for that day: three smiths and seven cutters, followed by the note that the eighth cutter was absent with a stomach illness but expected to return the following day.

James closed the ledger and walked across the sloping lawn toward the kitchen. Following him was the sound of nail making, as regular as the ticking of a clock. He knew each sound: the clatter of blanks being tossed into a bed of hot coals, the squeak of tongs grabbing the red-hot blank and holding it against the anvil, and then hammer taps, three to form the point on smaller nails or four for the largest of the nails. A moment of silence followed while the smith held the raw end of the nail in the fire until it glowed again. Then he'd slip the blank, point down into the funny pliers they called a header. Two crashing blows to the red-hot iron formed the nail's head over the rounded header. Once made, it was tapped out into the quenching barrel where it sizzled. He had been hearing it for so long, he even knew when a blow was hit badly.

As James jogged up the hill to the kitchen, smoke from the chimney put him in a good mood. All was as it should be. He smelled ham as he entered the kitchen and smiled. "Morning, Lizzie."

"Might be morning, but not a good one. That Emmaline done got sick."

"The one who cooks for the field hands?"

She nodded. "Gonna fall on us today. Make a couple a pots of cornmeal mush. You gotta drive it out too. Go get the food wagon."

"Her wagon?"

"You got a wagon I don't know about? She's got the heaves and ain't in no way to cook or drive the food out to the men."

"I gotta serve breakfast to Mister Short."

She turned to him and planted both fists into her ample hips. "You think you too good to carry vittles to hungry men?"

"No."

Turning to her stove, she said, "Thought not. Have Marie help carry to the wagon. But she stays here! Not gonna have him looking her over out there."

Ten minutes later, he hitched an older chestnut gelding to the small food wagon. The wagon's flat back made for easy loading of crates of food or pots of mush. A fifty-gallon water barrel was lashed to the back of the driver's bench.

Tying off the reins, James came into the kitchen. Lizzie was stirring the largest pot over the open fire. Sweat darkened the collar of her blue dress. "This one's almost ready to load."

Marie was adding water to a second, smaller pot before stirring it. She looked up. "Be another few minutes before the mush sets up."

"No hurry on my account."

Lizzie snapped at him. "Maybe not, but you ain't been cutting lumber out there since before sunup. That barrel full?"

James went outside and jumped up on the wagon bed. He tapped the barrel's side and heard a hollow echo. Then he pulled off the flat wood cover and looked inside. "No."

"Fill it at the stream on your way out, hear?"

"Yes. They got plates and spoons?"

She nodded. "Keep 'em out there."

James followed Lizzie inside and leaned on the worktable while she stirred the mush. When she was finished, James loaded it on the wagon. As soon as the cornmeal had boiled in the second pot, Marie hauled it to the back of the wagon and handed it up to James. After he tied the pots down, he climbed into the driver's seat and called to Marie, "Got a bucket for the stream water? I don't want to go back to the shed and waste time."

Lizzie handed him a bucket and motioned for him to lean down to her. "You ever drive out there?"

"No. But I know where they're clearing."

"Good. Don't tarry. Deliver the pots, trade out the water barrel, and get straight back."

"You know I will."

James clicked to get the horse moving and eased the wagon down to Mulberry Row. His mother sat in a patch of sunshine on the cabin's step sewing a dress hem. "James?"

He pulled the team to a halt. She dropped her sewing on the step and hobbled out to the wagon. "James, where you off to?"

"Taking food to the cutting crew."

"Be careful. Miller's got a new driver out there. White fella. I hear he lay back on the edge of the clearing and don't much get off his horse, but when he get a notion he just rides his horse into the man or he ride past and knock some heads with this little club he got on a string on the saddle."

"Who said?"

"I patched up a boy yesterday that got sideways with him. Calvin, and you know he don't start nothing. Don't give him no reason to take offense, hear me?"

"Yes. Gotta go."

"Watch yourself."

Driving down from the mountaintop, he heard the dull thudding of axes biting into the pines echo across the valley. The Monticello Plantation was being carved out of the raw, wooded wilderness. Before he forded the stream, James took the bucket and dipped into the water, climbed on the wagon, and poured it in. At this rate he would be making a dozen trips.

He drove the wagon halfway across the ford and stopped with the wheels in the deepest part of the stream. He lashed the end of the reins to the bucket, dropped it into the water, hauled it up, and emptied it into the barrel. In this manner, he quickly filled the barrel that he thought should have been filled the night before. Putting the top on the barrel, he continued uphill.

Thirty men were clearing trees. Most were bare chested and shoeless. The older men by the road who were trimming off branches of the cut trees had homespun shirts hanging free over tattered trousers or knee-high pants. Axes striking the tall white pines at the far edge of the clearing set the pace for those cutting branches from the downed trees just like Jefferson's metronome when he taught James to play the violin.

In the northern part of that tract, there was a stand of oak and beech that were harder to harvest due to their irregular shapes, but valuable for furniture making. Once a tree crashed to ground, ten men got on a rope and pulled it to the edge of the clearing. After branches were trimmed off by hand hatchets, two men on a saw sectioned the trunk to the length of a wagon bed. Crews of six were needed to hoist or roll the sections onto the long-bedded wagon.

In the time it took James to unload the pots of mush, three men had taken the heavy water barrel off the wagon and lashed an empty barrel in its place. Before he could get back on the wagon, two older men had taken the mush pots to the side of the trail and motioned for him to leave. A white man on horseback came riding fast from the far edge of the clearing. Seeing the pots of food, he slowed as he approached the stacked bowls. With a riding quirt, he leaned down and hit the bowls, sending them flying to the muddy edge of the trail.

The driver shouted to one of the men by the pot to start serving the mush. He knocked the mud off a bowl, dipped it into the still-warm pot, and handed it to a slave. He took a few paces away from the wagon before being joined by four others. They ate their mush by the handful, shoving the food into their mouths as fast as possible. James kept his head down and got into the wagon's bench as fast as he could. He turned the wagon around and clicked twice so the gelding started back at a fast walk.

Usually the rolling hills of green pine accented by brilliant white patches of dogwood trees in early bloom brought joy to him. But today, the stench of piss and mud and sweat and the ragged hands of the men eating from muddy bowls crowded his thoughts.

He stopped at the stream and filled the water barrel so it would be ready for the next meal. He looked back, but the turn in the trail blocked the cutting crew from view. He knew that one wrong word and he could be there hauling timber. He knew it as sure as he knew his name.

At the crest of the hill, he stopped and looked back on the timber crew at the edge of the tall pine stand. To the east, across a small valley, other men drove horse-drawn plows and turned over the rich loam for planting in a field cut two years ago and cleared of rock and roots only last fall.

James felt his neck muscles relaxing as he drove the wagon past the manicured orchard containing several hundred fruit trees. Jefferson had arranged them in small groves of apple, peach, apricot, and almond. Buds were turning into blooms and the flowering trees sparkled in the spring light. A spiced scent wafted from the early blossoms.

He chuckled as he remembered Jefferson planting rows of pears nearest the big house. That first spring, the orchard smelled of dead fish. Only after some serious sniffing did he discover that pear blossoms of the variety that he had selected had a putrid stench. He removed the pears to the farthest part of the orchard and planted sweet-smelling apple nearest the house. He inquired prior to buying crabapples and learned that they too lacked the sweet aroma he intended to waft into his home on temperate days. So, as lovely as the crabapple bloom was, those trees were relegated to the far lot with the pears.

As James unhitched the gelding, a long timber wagon with a team of four rattled past him on its way to the sawpit. James watched it stop. Men used long metal rods to roll the timber from the wagon bed to the far end of a pile of freshly cut pine in the timber yard. Young boys worked the other end of the pile with hatchets removing bark and putting it in baskets for the slaves to burn in their cabins.

Closer to the road, two sawyers were at work in the sawpit planking a pine that had been harvested a month before. The bark had been stripped and the amber timber leaned against a wood rack over a four-foot dugout in the soil. The saw-master had chalked the saw line on the timber as the guide both men should follow. One sawyer stood above the log while the other was on his back in the pit. Both labored on the two-man saw, following the chalked line with care. Two older men carried the cut planks away to cure.

Past the lumberyard, joinery, and carpentry shop, was the weaving hut. James always stopped to wave at Suzanna and her boy, now a toddler. In a way, he measured his time in the kitchen by the boy. When he saw him, James thought of that hurried morning when Bob pressed him into service in the kitchen when Suzanna and another girl had their babies. He smiled. It was like replacing her and meeting Marie was supposed to be.

That evening, James finished with his kitchen duties and left Marie and Lizzie to go to the nailery. As he finished counting the newly filled kegs, he heard Lizzie shouting his name as she ran toward the open door of the nailery. Fearing some disaster, he ran to the door, still holding his logbook. "Here! I'm here. What?"

Lizzie pointed at the big house while she gulped for breath. "Massa

Short. Wants you. Real quick."

James dashed off his notation, tossed the book on the desk, and hurried up the hill. Stopping only to knock the mud off his boots, he went to the doorway of the study and waited for Short's nod before entering. Short was glaring at a ledger. Miller was at the window. When Miller turned, he crossed his arms over his chest. His face was pinched as he stared at James.

James pressed his hands against his side seams of his trousers and tried to ignore the sweat that bloomed under his arms and the cold, metallic taste in his mouth.

Short looked up and motioned James to the front of the desk. "James, your skills in the kitchen and nailery, as fine as they are, don't bring in any extra funds to the plantation." James barely heard him for the pounding in his ears. "Yesterday's messenger brought a letter from one of Mister Jefferson's associates, a Mister Henry Martin of Richmond. Have you ever been to Richmond?"

"Yes. Yes, sir. Once when Mas Jefferson had both Bob and me accompany him on a trip."

"Good, then you know how to get there." James tried to slow his breathing as Short continued. "Seems that Mister Martin's boy has taken ill so he is in need of a new riding valet. Do you know what they do?"

"Clean the tack, polish the leathers, accompany the rider carrying his guns, game bags, or picnic bags as they desire. Some do stable duties as well."

Short flicked his hand as if shooing flies. "He has a stableman for all that. But I think it would be a better use of your time to take on this job of work for pay."

James took a deep breath. *He said, 'for pay.' I'm not being sold!* James forced himself to listen as Short continued, "He has offered a decent sum, of which I will be pleased to remit to you one-quarter thereof upon the completion of your services there."

"Massa wants me to hire out?"

"In fact, this is my decision. This contract will benefit Mister Jefferson's accounts quite nicely."

James relaxed. Richmond, he recalled, was quite an interesting place. No wonder Miller looked like he had bit into a sour apple. Splitting pay was something Jefferson might do on occasion when he hired out a slave, but Miller wouldn't consider it. James forced himself not to look at Miller. "When do I go?"

"Tomorrow. Get your things in order. You'll travel light on one of our older horses. See me for your travel papers and directions by nine."

James nodded and turned to leave. Miller called after him. "Take the bay gelding."

Looking over his shoulder, James said, "As you wish." He was able to hide his smile until he left the big house and started running.

By the time he reached the kitchen, he was grinning. Marie had finished her chores and he motioned to her to come outside without Lizzie seeing him. In the twilight, they hurried from the kitchen to the barn. She listened to him, dropped her head, and pushed straw with her toe. When she looked up at him, she held her hands to his cheeks and studied his face.

James held her and kissed her.

She kissed him and pulled his shirt free from his breeches. "When you leave in the morning for Richmond, what if I was to walk off before daybreak? We could meet and go north."

James pulled back. "Go? We couldn't get far together at all. What are you thinking?"

"If you got you a horse, we could make some distance before they'd know I was gone too."

He stepped back and looked at her as if he had never known her, never rolled in the orchard with her, never trusted her. "You'd put my family at that risk?"

"For us."

"For you! No. I will get my freedom. You'll see. But not that way."

Throughout the spring of 1784, James served Henry Martin well and faithfully. On days that Martin rode, the groom brought Martin's chestnut stallion and the plantation's older bay gelding for James from the stable to the townhouse and held their reins until Martin and James were in the saddle. Together they rode to Martin's meetings with bankers and visitations with others, with James serving as the custodian of his riding cloak, portfolio, and ledger books for meetings as well as being his personal courier on occasion. When Martin took to the field, James was an able gun handler and game spotter. On those days when Martin wanted a ride for distance or sport, he provided a swift black stallion for James to test their speed and agility overland. On those days, James packed lunches he made in the kitchen to the cook's dismay and Martin's delight.

Those days when Martin was consumed with his correspondence, James put his master's riding attire into shape again, cleaning and polishing the boots, wet-rubbing his jacket or great coat before drying by the fire and then brushing it to restore the nap to perfection. Brushing hats and wiping interiors, stretching wet gloves into shape, and anticipating what outer attire or comestibles Martin might desire became James's delightful challenge. He became more of a personable companion than a riding valet as he was able to give name to the plants and animals of the region for Martin, who had only recently come to Richmond.

All this changed in mid-May when Martin's valet called James from the stable, where he and the groom had determined that the chestnut's sudden limp was from a stone under the shoe and was easily cured.

In the library, Martin held a sheet of paper and glanced at it and then at James. He hemmed and hawed before clearing his throat and frowning. James asked, "Is there something I have done to displease you, sir?"

"Not in the least, James. To the contrary, I have found your service to be careful and assiduous and your company a pleasure. But now, I am in receipt of correspondence from Mister Short directing your services to Mister Jefferson in Philadelphia. It seems he has been called to France and wishes you to accompany him. He says he wants you for the 'particular purpose' of learning the art of cookery. From Philadelphia you will go to Boston wherefrom you will sail."

James felt the silence press on him. Too many thoughts collided, but he said, "Of course. But to leave America without seeing my family once again or leaving with just the meager possessions I brought here..."

"I could suggest to Thomas that you return to Monticello to bid your farewells and meet up in Boston. I understand he has a wagon of his own goods being gathered there as well. Do you know how to drive a wagon?"

"Yes, sir."

And so it was that James returned to Monticello on his way to Boston. Upon arrival at Monticello, James collected his part of the wages from Mister Short and was given a list of goods Jefferson wanted crated and driven to Boston. He went to the kitchen with several pages in hand and waited until Lizzie turned to him.

"James! You back?"

He gave her a hug and grinned at her. "Just for a bit. He's finally going to Paris. Here's the list of provisions he wants to take with him. Strawberry preserve, peach preserve, and apple butter. Hams from the smokehouse. Cornmeal. Fine and coarse ground, both."

Lizzie frowned. "Ain't they got food in Paris?"

He shrugged. "You know how he gets."

"Bring the list. We'll need to look in the basement stores."

His first night home, James was exhausted from the travel and packing during the day. He washed the dishes in a bucket outside the cabin and returned them to the mantel to dry of their own accord. Mam and the two youngsters were asleep. James knocked down the last of the cooking fire and blew out the candle. He stretched on his pallet. He knew that he had grown. He ran the nailery. He once had a gal. Or at least they spent time together, in the kitchen and rolling in the barn or fooling in the orchard. She had taught him to speak French. He taught her to read. She had tempted him to run off. She thought she had nothing to lose, and maybe she didn't.

But risking his family? No, he and Marie were not a family and would never be. He knew that the itch he still got seeing her was less than love. But Bob's Dolly? She was solid as brass. Sturdy and reliable. Tender with Bob. He had seen the way they looked at each other and wanted someone to look at him like that someday. How could Jefferson not have seen it? How could he have sold her off to that doctor?

James locked his fingers together under his head and stretched his back. Time seemed to stand still when he thought of all he wanted to see and know of the world that he had discovered in Jefferson's library. He sighed and shook his head. He turned on his side and thought of the letters that Bob had sent to him. He told James that the planned voyage to France from Baltimore Harbor on the *Romulus* in December of 1782 had been delayed when the ship was icebound until February. Days turned to weeks and then months. Jefferson's frustration often flared into anger. That man was not one to be idle. Before Jefferson was able to sail, word came back from Paris that the preliminary peace treaty had been signed.

With frustration, Jefferson returned to Congress. His daughter, Patsy, was boarded with a woman to be schooled in both lessons and manners. Bob remained with him and travelled as the locations of Congress moved. Through his various travels, Bob became well acquainted with the cities of Baltimore and Annapolis in Maryland. Philadelphia and York in Pennsylvania. Trenton in New Jersey. All of these Bob made vivid in his letters to James. His comments on life and foods he encountered in these cities only served to expand the interest James had in the world beyond the confines of the plantation. But it was by overhearing Jefferson's conversations long ago at Monticello that James learned that in France, he could learn a trade as a cook and be free. Free to do and say and go or stay. It was barely imaginable. It was there that the dream began. Bob's letters continued to bemoan Jefferson's plan to take Bob, even after Jefferson's letter requesting James. What was Jefferson's intent? James fell into a light and restless sleep after midnight.

The next morning, he finished with the kitchen inventory and went to the cabin to see his mother. He packed his violin and winter clothes into a trunk. She looked at him and smiled. "This is what you want, isn't it? Going away?"

"To learn and be free? Yes. To leave my family? No. I'm still not sure he won't take Bob and send me back here. He says one thing about me to Short and another thing to Bob. You know how he is. And how much Bob wants to be with Dolly at the doctor's house where he sold her." James latched the trunk and smiled. "Then maybe we can help him make his mind who to take."

"What're you thinking, son?"

"Jefferson will go to France. He is drawn to it like a bee to honey. He'll take one of us. So, perhaps we should reduce the choice to no choice at all."

"You lost me. James?"

"I think you might have a potion to make Massa see the way of reason."

"He ain't gonna take no potion, you know how he gets the skitters about cures."

"Who said the potion was for him?"

CHAPTER 6

Within three days, the crates were made. Jars of pickled goods were brought up from the cellar and padded with straw in one. Hams were pulled from the smokehouse for another. Books from Jefferson's list were retrieved from the library. His second-best violin was cased, wrapped in blankets, and packed with the books.

While others were consumed in the chaos of gathering and packing, Miss Elizabeth calmly went to her herb box and selected roots and dried flowers from her collection. The blood red of both roots and flowers stained the board on which she had pounded the dry materials into a powder. Once fine enough, she took the edge of a metal spoon and split the powder into two doses. Finding a scrap of brown paper, she tore it in half, placed one dose on the center of each, folded the papers into tight packets, and put them under the candlestick on the mantel.

Once the list was completed and all manner of foods and other items packed, Miller hammered the crates shut. James noted with some pride that the nails were ones made under his supervision.

Miller had the crates loaded and lashed tight to the wagon that was still in the stable. No need to have it out in the summer sun before the team was ready and in harness. James brought his trunk to the stable and saw the horses being hitched. He ran back to the cabin.

"They're almost ready, Mam." He hugged her.

She took the two folded papers from under the candlestick and handed them to James. "I made two doses, but have Bob take just one. Hear me? Only one. I made two in case the first don't take."

"How long should it take?"

"Be about an hour to get to its fullness. But if it don't take, then have him use the second one. But wait first."

James put the folded papers into a slit he had made in the top of his boot.

She nodded, sniffed, and wiped her eyes with her sleeve. "Got something to eat?"

"Lizzie packed a good basket."

"Take care, son. Love you."

James hugged his mother, mumbled that he loved her too, and left the cabin.

The journey to Boston began with confusion. James climbed up to the driver's bench of the heavily loaded wagon. At first, the team balked at the load, then moved forward slowly. The load shifted and needed to be tied again. Finally, he was on his way.

An hour out, James stopped to let the horses drink at a stream. He opened the basket Lizzie had packed and smiled when he saw cornbread and thick slices of ham.

On the third day when the basket was empty, James boiled cornmeal for his dinner while the hobbled horses grazed. Then he fitted their feed sacks and the horses chewed their grain and nickered. James had allotted himself ten days to get to Boston and kept a calendar so he would arrive on Saturday, July 3, as Short had directed. The night of the second, James slept on the wagon at the edge of town. In the morning, the way markers were clear as James approached Boston. When he saw the harbor, he stopped the wagon and wondered at the anthill of activity. He had never seen a port as large or industrious as this. *First things first*, he counseled himself as he pulled Short's directions from his pocket.

When James saw the sign with the two black cannons belching fire, he knew he was looking at the inn that Short had specified. He felt his shoulders relax. As James pulled the team to a halt, his brother Bob jumped up from a bench in the shade of the inn's porch, grabbed his sack of belongings from the porch, and tossed the sack behind James. James jumped down from the wagon and landed on both feet in front of Bob, who hugged him. Bob lifted him off the ground, grunted, and laughed, "You not so little anymore, brother. Got taller, put some meat on your bones."

"And you got wider."

Bob patted his stomach. "Good ocean food in Annapolis and Baltimore, fish and crab." He lowered his voice. "You still got that idea of going free once you are there?"

"After I learn enough to be able to make my way."

"Brother, you are a godsend. He sees it in my eye that I am not happy being away from Dolly. He let me visit before we went away almost two years ago now. He sees my longing, most like he still misses his Martha."

James smirked. "Been over two years since..."

"Time ain't a healer in such matters. You still a boy, ain't ya?"

"Not so much. I can whip your ass any day, old man."

"You still my little brother. Always will be. I just hope he doesn't change his mind like he is so easy to do."

"Mam thought of a way to hold him fast to his..."

"Not now. Tell me later. We gotta get the goods on board before noon. Massa and Patsy are staying at the Cabots', so let's get the wagon unloaded and the horses stabled before Jefferson shows up about one."

"Where? I didn't see it."

"A few streets back. That's where the phaeton is being crated. He's already paid them to hold the wagon and board the horses." He pointed to the *Ceres*. "That's your ship. The cream-colored one."

When James thought that Jefferson was going to France years ago, he had searched Jefferson's library for books on sailing ships to gather knowledge of how such a voyage might be undertaken. Nights when he should have been in bed, James read page after page and memorized the line drawings at the back of the book of sailboats and the great ships. Now, he had a notion of what he was seeing on the ship that would carry them to France. The freshly painted brig was tied at the long dock. In the harbor, there were boats of all forms. Sloops and schooners, shad boats, flat-bottom transport boats like barges carrying iron, and the smaller dinghies and tenders moving men and materials to and from the anchored ships. He scanned the harbor and was pleased at his knowledge of the ships. He knew a clipper from a ketch and a tender boat from the similar fishers; he also knew that the *Ceres* was a top-of-the-line brig.

She had square-rigged sails on her two masts and a small gaff-rigged sail at her stern. Tender boats were in cradles on both the port and starboard rails. Two small signaling cannons showed on her quarterdeck facing astern. He wondered if the ship had defensive cannons on deck behind the wooden doors, painted to match the hull.

Having never seen a ship like this in real life, James took a moment to study its frame and apply the diagrams in the books to the sight before him. The names of sails that he had memorized seemed to match, but the ropes and lines seemed more of a jumble than in the book. He reckoned the ship to be at least 100 feet in length. Each of the two tall masts had a plentiful abundance of lines, some falling to the deck and others looping out on the crossbars, called yards, that were high on the masts. Bright white canvas sails were pulled up and tied atop the crossbars, gleaming like the first of a snowfall piling up on a wooden fence rail.

The intricacy of the lines going fore and aft, up-and-down, and at all angles suggested a spiderweb. The sails at the front and rear of the boat were called the fore and aft sails, not only because they were fore and aft in their position on the ship but also because they were able to take the air on either side of their canvas, unlike the sails of the square riggers that only took wind from the stern.

Bob tugged the bridle to turn the horses and called to James, "Come on, boy, you can gawk at it later. We got work to do."

James snapped the reins to advance the horses onto the dock. At the clatter of their hooves on the dock's timber, both horses startled. Bob's firm hand on the bay mare and James calling calmed the team as it navigated the crowded space.

A sailor on the raised rear deck saw James approaching, jumped down from the quarterdeck, and ran to the wagon. He had a three-cornered hat, a blue jacket, and carried a ledger book of the same type that Jefferson used for his accounts.

"You have business at this place?"

James dismounted and faced the man. "I do, sir, if you are authorized to speak for the *Ceres*." Bob jiggled the bridle of the nervous horse and patted her shoulder.

"That we be. I'm its first mate, Mister Fox. What be your business here?"

"These are the crates and cases for Mister Thomas Jefferson and his daughter Miss Patsy Jefferson."

James looked past him to the deck of the ship. The sailors on board were wrapping lines into neat coils and lashing them to wooden pegs in a row along the interior of the waist-high wall of the deck.

All smiles now, Fox relaxed his clenched fists and yelled orders for three sailors to unload the wagon and move the crates to the hold below. "And cases for the cabin?"

Bob called down. "They's got their overnight cases with them. They'll bring them when they come to the ship."

"How much for the cabins?"

"Just a small trunk each. Smallish." Bob motioned about three by two feet and the man seemed relieved. "But they's gonna want things from the larger trunks marked such." James pointed to two trunks marked "Attire."

"Certainly. We will have those put in the salon's cabinet."

"That all?"

"Just his valise and a sack and small trunk for his manservant."

Fox frowned and opened his book as a sailor pushed past him and grabbed a wooden crate marked "Hock" and started to push it roughly down the bed of the wagon.

James shouted, "Stop! That is his wine. It needs to go to his cabin."

The sailor laughed. "Cabin? Ain't no room for such in there. How much is there?"

"Four dozen bottles."

Fox came to the wagon to manage the dispute. He directed the crates of wine to go to the galley and told the sailor to charge the cook with their safekeeping. He then turned to the sailors, pointed them in directions, and spoke in such a clipped manner that James could not discern all that was said. Once the men were dispatched, Fox turned back to James.

"Is this all the crated goods?"

Bob answered, "There is a carriage. A phaeton. It is being disassembled now and crated. The carriage maker should have it to you in an hour or so."

He turned the pages of book and ran his finger down the page. "Yes. I have that on the manifest. Their small cases to their cabins, two trunks to the salon storage, and the remainder to the hold with a case of wine to the kitchen. Is that it?"

"Yes. Except for his servant."

Fox read the passenger manifest again and looked at James. "He booked no cabin for a manservant. Here, look. Copied right from his letter of booking, two cabins for Mister Thomas Jefferson, *et svt*, and Miss Patsy Jefferson."

"That's how it is. Jefferson *et svt*. Means 'Jefferson and servant.' Latin, I think it may be. That's how he would reply to invitations or booking a room in an inn to let people know he's bringing along a servant so they can arrange space."

"This is painfully unclear. Mister Jefferson should have been clear. He should have included a name. Well, I suppose he intended his manservant to sleep in his cabin on a pallet on his floor, but that is just not possible. Space and provisions, you see."

Fox laughed, turned, and called over his shoulder, "Well, too late now, all the other cabins are booked. Have your Mister Jefferson see me as soon as possible to correct this matter."

James turned the horses to leave the dock and glanced at the men on the ship. The sailors looked smart enough. Dressed neatly, not with the ragged hem of rough canvas trousers like most of the men on the dock. The captain, in a dark frock coat, was on the higher quarterdeck and watched the exchange between James and Fox with his hands behind his back. Fox reported the conversation to the captain.

They passed a wagon stacked with baskets of vegetables and several crates of live hens. Once at the foot of the dock, James pulled the team to a halt and motioned for Bob to join him in the wagon. "Come on. We can drive to the stable."

"No. There's not enough time. It has to be close to one and that's when he said to be at the inn. We can stable them after he gets our rooms." The two brothers sat on the rear of the wagon and watched the loading activities. Bob pointed at the ship. "What do you think he intends to do about the missing cabin?"

"No idea, but Massa is going to be in a fit about it. Just wait."

"That's all we can do."

After the produce and poultry were unloaded, another wagon clattered down the dock. On it were three crates of small hogs. Each crate was heavier than four sailors could manage on their own, so they ran a thick line off one of the yardarms from the mast and tied the end to the crossbars at the top of the crate. With men on the deck holding down the line, the crate soon became airborne and was guided from the wagon across the deck toward the open hatch. Just as it reached the edge of the hatch, the upper boards of the crate snapped. The pig crate crashed only a few feet onto the deck. When the end of the crate fell open, the pig made his break for freedom. After circling the deck twice and evading sailors scurrying to capture it, the animal started for the boarding plank.

James jumped from the back of the wagon and sprinted toward the ship. Although he and Bob were house slaves, they had helped others raise pigs in a small patch behind their slave cabin. Hollering and waving his arms, James blocked the pig's path. The escapee turned halfway down the plank. In short order, a net was brought from below and the panting pig captured. Both he and his companions were lowered below in the net and put in a straw-covered pen in a forward hold.

At the end of this chaos, the sailor who had met the wagon slapped James on the back. He was browned by the sun and dressed in new attire: a square-cut, short-sleeved shirt and canvas trousers, each of a bright cream color. "Thanks for your help." He looked skeptically at James. "You shipping out with us as a last-minute sign-on to France?"

"No. I'm a manservant to Mister Jefferson."

"That explains it. I would never take you for a sailor."

Initially, James was indignant that someone had so easily dismissed his ability to learn a trade beyond that of house servant. "How so?" Suddenly he regretted his insolence, yet the sailor seemed to take no offense. He looked back at the men on deck who seemed to have matters in hand, so he took a minute and looked James up and down.

"First, you walk like a landlubber. Feet just under you. Sailors have a wider stance and a different sense of balance. We tend to roll once on land, but you walk like you are balancing a book on your head."

For some reason James stood taller. Now he was a good two inches above the sailor, yet the other man continued. "Second, your attire. You're dressed well, not in farming attire made of that coarse cloth—what's it called? Ozenbrig?"

"Osnaburg linen. Called by the town in Germany that started making it."

"If you say so. I mean, you have not the look of a runaway slave trying to pass himself off as a sailor, not knowing a topsail from a forecastle."

James pointed up the mast to the location of the topsail and pronounced as he heard on the docks, not as he had read it in Jefferson's books. "Tops'l." Then he pointed to the hull just under the forward deck and stumbled over the truncated pronunciation sailors seem to use. "Fox-ill."

He laughed. "Not a bad try. But still you are no sailor, just look at your hands. Show me a rope callus or a knife scar and I'll buy you a glass of cider."

James laughed and threw his hands up in surrender, but still asked, "What do you mean 'last-minute sign-on'?"

"One of the lads got into it last night and broke his arm. Can't go aloft or scramble a rigging with a busted wing, so's we might be going out a man shy. Captain had took on a...darkie once before, a free man from New York, so's I didn't know if you were trying to sign on."

"No. I won't pretend to be a sailor."

"Too bad. This is going to be a good sail. Young lad like yourself could do worse. This passenger service is a new thing for the captain. I've shipped with him fishing out a month or two, and once before on a whaler out three years. Never find a better skipper. A Bible-reading Quaker man who don't go shy on grog for the crew. Rare a harsh word unless a man is going to do harm to himself, others, or the ship. Fair as sunlight."

"Sounds like a good man to work for."

"He is that. But this trip is gonna be special. I can see it. Passengers of this esteem will eat well, and we'll get the tailings. When a hog goes under the knife, we'll get a goodly share too. Not just fish we pull from the sea." He looked at the deck, then up into the rigging and savored it as a man looks at a fine woman. "She's a good ship. What we call yar, easy at the helm, fast on the abouts, agile, well rigged and provisioned. Hope for a fast voyage."

"How fast?"

"Never know, but hope for thirty days; she's provisioned for forty-five. Fitted with a good crew. Captain, first and second mate, steward, cabin boy, and us sailors, ordinary and able. But he also has a carpenter, sailmaker and cook so's we be well cared for. And the cap'n, he be a good soul. Kept a sailor on to cook after his sailing days was rightfully over. No, you couldn't do better. Nevertheless, I thank you for your help and wish you well." He extended his hand. His grip was firm and his palm as hard as horn.

Soon, the *Ceres* was loaded and little of interest was happening on the dock. But as directed, the brothers sat on the bed of the wagon in the shade of a chestnut tree and waited for Jefferson. They watched the quick pace and constant flow of men and goods in the harbor. Like a disciplined anthill, it was. Then from behind him James heard a voice. "Hey. You can't be just staying here."

He turned to find a man, dark as coal, stocky, and about thirty years of age, staring at him with his hands on his hips. James jumped off the wagon to face him. The man scowled. "What're you doing just sitting here?"

"Excuse me, sir, but I am new to Boston and mean no offense. I am awaiting my master."

"Trying to be fancy?"

James frowned. "What?"

"Your manner of speech."

"That is how my master wishes me to converse with others. Formal like."

"You still a slave?"

"Yes. Aren't you bound?"

He laughed. "You *are* new. I see you and think, *Those boys are gonna get into a heap of trouble if they don't keep their eyes sharp.*"

"Trouble?"

"You'll want to steer clear of the waterfront, 'specially at night. Some captains send a sailor out to find an able-bodied person to fill their crew if they are short a hand and have no means to pay. You both be dark enough that you might just be taken and sold down south as a slave."

"Kidnapped, you mean?"

"Just so. Some slave catchers don't go south empty handed, even if it ain't who they started looking for."

"Thank you."

"Ned."

James extended his hand. Ned took it without hesitation. "James. James Hemings. From Virginia. My brother Bob."

"How long you gonna be in Boston?"

"Just until our master sails on Monday." Jefferson emerged from a small side street and walked toward the inn. James pointed at him. "That's him now." Bob hopped off the wagon and went to greet Jefferson.

Ned spoke quickly. "Where you staying?"

James nodded toward the inn. "There."

"You at liberty tomorrow?"

"Think so. Why?"

"I'll be glad to show you my city, you and your brother both. If you want, be here at nine. Be safe 'nuf with two of you."

"Thanks. Hope to see you then."

Bob took a large valise from Jefferson, who also held a few new books bound in a leather strap.

Jefferson motioned to the wagon. "James. I thought you would be stabled by now."

"Just finished loading, sir. Didn't want you to wait in the sun if we were delayed there."

Bob glanced at Jefferson and saw his color rising, then he noticed the inn's sign, two crossed black cannons belching red flames under simple block letters that declared it to be the Two Cannons Tavern and Inn. Bob diverted his attention by asking, "Why the two cannons, sir?"

Jefferson relaxed and smiled. "From the British cannons captured at Fort Ticonderoga and brought over the frozen Hudson River to our aid. That and recovering the cannonballs shot at us from the British gunships and firing them back well turned the tide in our favor." Jefferson motioned to James. "Get your things. Bob, get it stabled and then come back for your brother." Jefferson took back his valise. James easily lifted his travel trunk. Bob balanced their sacks on it.

The tavern was a rustic, open-beamed room with a large brick fireplace. There was one communal dining table, a side bar with casks on it, and a stairway to an upper level. The innkeeper looked up from drawing a beer from a large barrel and grinned. "Welcome you be, sir. I'm Harlan Sturgis, proprietor. How may I be of service?"

"I, sir, am Thomas Jefferson of Virginia. I wrote to you months ago seeking accommodations this day and you kindly answered and confirmed our two rooms, which I appreciated."

"Certainly, sir. I haven't separate accommodations in back reserved for servants as your letter requested. But I did assign them to a lesser-appointed room, but not so far from yours as would be an inconvenience should you require them." He took two keys from a drawer and walked up a stairway without another word. The innkeeper opened the door to an airy room at the front of the inn. "Yours, sir."

Jefferson pushed past him and went in to examine the room. Nodding, he dropped his valise and books on a dresser and took the offered key. The innkeeper crossed the hallway to the rear of the inn and opened the door to a much smaller room. James put down the trunk at the foot of the one bed. Again nodding, Jefferson said, "Yes, these will suit our needs." The innkeeper handed James the key. "Is there anything I can get for you, sir?"

"No. The rooms are fine. I am dining with friends and may or may not return tonight."

"As you wish, sir. If the front door be locked, just give it a sharp rap. My room is close so's I'll hear you and open the door right quick."

"Very good."

After the innkeeper left, Jefferson said, "Your suppers are paid for tonight, and breakfast and dinner Sunday. I also arranged for you to have a breakfast on Monday after we sail, but don't tarry past mid-morning." Jefferson took a drawstring bag from his pocket. "Here is money for a midday meal Sunday and for your food, board, and stabling on the travel home. It also has passage letters for you both, I didn't know who would be going until this afternoon. The papers show that you are mine; if anyone stops you and questions your being alone, these should put the matter to rest. Understand?"

James nodded. "Yes. I've had to show your letters to patrollers before."

"Fine. And James. It was good of you to bring a trunk for your brother's journey."

"Just a few things from home, sir." Jefferson locked the door. James followed him out to where Bob was waiting on the porch.

Speaking to Bob, Jefferson was quick in his directions. "You and James are at liberty to explore the town today and are free to participate in the Independence Day celebrations tomorrow. I expect you back at the inn, packed and ready to board the ship, by eight. That's just before sunset, so mind the time well as I will be collecting Patsy and then you, so we will board together. We sail at dawn on Monday the fifth. Is that clear?"

Bob trembled as he answered. "Yes, sir."

"I do expect you both to comport yourselves properly tomorrow, even with the celebration." Jefferson handed Bob a few silver coins. "I just had the thought that you both might enjoy a tankard of Boston's renowned ale."

As Jefferson left the porch, James steeled himself to report the problem on the ship's manifest. "Sir?"

He frowned as he turned. "What is it?"

"The man, Mister Fox."

"Who?"

"The man at the ship who had our manifest for the crates and cabins. He tells me that there is no cabin or fare paid for Bob."

"Wha...what? I explicitly wrote that the cabin was for myself *et servant*, perhaps I abbreviated it. Bu...but can't the man re...read?"

James tried to be as calm as possible and not react to Jefferson's stutter, which only seemed to increase it. "He seemed perplexed when I told him that you were bringing Bob on the voyage."

Angered, Jefferson snapped, "Ta... take me to him now. We'll get this set right."

"Yes, sir."

"Tell me everything that transpired while I was gone." As angry as Jefferson was, he interviewed James as they stormed across the square to the dock. He garnered all the facts he could in those hundred-some steps. James informed him of the following: Mister Fox was the first mate, which he took to be just under the captain in authority. That he ran from a written ledger, not memory, that was correct to the dot on the cargo and he made a decision on the wine storage to benefit Jefferson's convenience and its protection. Also, that they were a sailor short due to some accident and a broken arm but that the crew was looking fit and were eager for the voyage. He then recounted the numbers and duties of the crew for him and mentioned the captain's charity toward the cook, but without knowing the related details.

At the side of the gangplank, Jefferson stopped and took in the longest breath and fixed a smile to his countenance. At the top of the gangplank, he waited for the captain to come to greet him. Even after stepping down onto the main deck, he towered above the rotund captain.

"Ambassador Jefferson."

He motioned dismissively and said, "Just Mister Jefferson for the voyage."

"Captain Nathaniel Tracey at your service. Is there something?"

"In fact, there is a minor issue." As the captain leaned his left ear toward Jefferson, he immediately discerned that the man had some deficit in his hearing and elevated his volume and spoke even more distinctly, making their exchange plain to observe. "Your man seemed not to have understood that I am traveling with my servant."

As James had noted in some of the elderly slaves who had worked in the blacksmith's shop, those who heard poorly often responded in a loud manner. So it was with the captain. "Mister Fox did inform me of some confusion. It seems we in the north are ignorant of what the abbreviation *et serv* means or your intent to have a servant accompany you."

Jefferson smiled slowly and shrugged. "Communication! Isn't that the plague we all face? Even in our own country and language, let alone when I land in France and need to speak to them in that confounded tongue where modifiers are the reverse of normal."

"Indeed."

Jefferson smiled again, what Mam would have called his sugar tit smile, all warm and welcome to get you comfortable and loving him. "But what do we need to do to clarify my intent?"

"Oh. Your intent is clear. I think the question is how to manage an added person on a voyage that could last two months. Added victuals…"

"I understand you are a hand short, so Bob could easily assume his portion of the foodstuffs already on board."

"But there is no cabin for him to be near you."

"That sailor's bunk will do. He can still attend me."

The captain pressed Jefferson. "But the fare of passage…"

"Could well be reduced as you have both a steward and a cabin boy to perform many of his duties. Bob is a splendid server for dinners at your captain's table. A fine man overall to whom you may attach whatever duties you wish during our voyage. I will need him to attend to me only briefly every morning. Perhaps he could assist your cook as he has no experience as a sailor on deck."

The captain looked at Jefferson with some suspicion about how he might know of the cook's needs. "Yes, that may do very well to offset some of the fare."

"Well then, that settles the matter of passage for my man."

"But there is another matter, sir."

Jefferson tilted his head. "That is?"

"Do I understand that he is enslaved to you?"

"He is mine indeed. Is that a problem?"

"As a Quaker, I cannot countenance demeaning treatment."

Jefferson raised his hand. "Rest assured, he will be treated as any other servant would be while on your ship. As an indentured man, not a slave, if that is what you require."

The captain puckered his lips as if tasting an unripe lemon. Jefferson persisted. "Would that meet your standards?"

Nodding slowly, the captain mentioned a figure. Jefferson had it reduced by half by contracting out Bob's labor to the ship's benefit. Then he extended his hand, and they came to terms. Then Jefferson asked, "How long do you estimate we shall be at sea?"

"Fair winds and calm seas, I've made a crossing in as little as twenty-two or twenty-three days. But I provisioned for more than twice that time. A practice I adopted after I sailed on a short-provisioned whaler as a lad. We ran low and fished for our suppers or went hungry on more than one night, so I am doubly cautious in planning."

"I see. So, the provisions were never the issue." He smiled at the captain.

"I think we have come to a positive resolution." Jefferson was about to say something when the captain grinned. "I understand that you are something of an inventor, so once underway, I am sure you will want to see the new Brodie stove below. Have you heard of it?"

James smiled when he saw Jefferson puff up to the praise as the captain continued. "It is a superior cooking improvement. In the past, my other ships had a bricked area and an open hearth for cooking, just as in a home. So, in a heavy sea, you were doomed either to cold food or the threat of fire below."

"Interesting. Not unlike Mister Franklin's stove that he calls his Pennsylvania Fireplace. Made of iron as well."

"But significantly more complex. It is a solid iron box, coal fed, and with the principal elements of the fire behind iron doors. In the front is a hearth that we can bake on, a spit to rotate large items in front of a bank of racked coals, all on a metal plate to catch any embers. Built into the body are two great cauldrons, so no pitch of the ship can tip them over. And best of all, is a chamber in which I can distill sea water into the purist of all water so there is never any fear of not having drinking water even if our water barrels run dry."

"Interesting. I look forward to seeing it in operation."

"Oh. Mister Jefferson?"

"Yes?"

"Looking at the weather and my tide charts, it would be most auspicious to set sail just before daybreak on the fifth. So, I would remind you and your party to be aboard the night before sailing, after your evening meal."

"Mister Fox suggested eight o'clock."

"Until then."

Once Jefferson left, Bob and James strolled along the waterfront promenade. They saw tables and stalls that food vendors were assembling for the Independence Day festivities and celebration on Sunday. When Bob stopped to examine some leather goods, James noticed a stack of books spread across the back of a wagon. Coming closer he discovered a small book in French of stories, not verse. He paid a copper for it and slid it into his pocket.

Some of the smaller vendors were cooking. James sniffed the air. Turning, he saw a stout redheaded woman in a loose blue dress frying something in a big, cast iron skillet. Her fire was wood gone to coals in an iron box on tall metal legs, so she cooked standing by it, not kneeling over a ground fire. He walked closer. In the sizzling pan were small cakes, not hoecakes, but something the size of a goodly biscuit, but with a rich aroma he had never smelled before. He started to ask what she was frying, but hesitated, that being an impropriety that could bring stripes on the plantation, as she was a white woman.

She smiled. "Best crabcakes on the harbor!"

James glanced behind him to confirm she was speaking to them and looked at Bob for approval before he ventured a reply. He took a step closer and asked the cost. It being within their midday meal allocation from Jefferson, they both nodded.

She put two sizzling cakes on two chipped dishes, handed them forks, and bid the brothers to sit at the small table beside her. "My crabcakes. Best you'll ever have. You can ask anyone here." They prodded the browned and still-sizzling cakes and watched steam escape. A bite later, James was transported by a new taste. He had no words for such a sweet, rich, morsel. He closed his eyes and tried to lock the taste into his memory.

He had heard Lizzie talk about crabcakes and how Jefferson loved them. But when she made them, there was never a bite for anyone in the kitchen, only Jefferson and his guests. This light, crisp, salty taste was beyond anything James had experienced. When they finished and handed her their plates, she asked if she didn't make the best crabcakes they had ever had. Both eagerly agreed. James said it was like a bite of heaven and the sea all at once. She laughed and smiled. "Be here all day tomorrow, so come back." James grinned.

Bob took James by the elbow and half shoved him toward the water. "What is in your head, talking to a white lady like that?" Before he had an answer, they were walking fast along the water's edge and not looking back.

Once clear of the town, they slowed their pace and found a downed log dry enough to sit on. Near the shore, seals chased after each other like sleek racehorses. Others lounged on an outcropping of rocks sunning themselves and barked like dogs.

Bob dropped his head in his hands and sobbed. "I can't go. I just can't! I'll run if need be."

James held his brother's shoulder. "Stop. There's a way. Mam and I considered that he might change his mind."

"So what? What he says is the law."

James laughed so hard that he choked on his words. "Not nature's law."

"Are you sick in the head? This is not a matter for humor."

Turning to face Bob, James lowered his voice and became somber. "No. It is a deadly serious matter. Mam and I had an idea. She made a powder for you to take."

"Why? Why would I take something? I'm not sick."

James whispered, "That's the whole idea: to make you appear ill."

"How?"

"Mam's potion gonna give you the chills and heaves. Scare Jefferson into leaving you and taking me to France in your place."

Finally, Bob said, "It might work."

"He'll not have a say in the matter if we plan it right. The dose is big. Should come on in a half hour to an hour and last five or six."

"Should I take it this afternoon? Interrupt him today?"

James shook his head. "It gives him too much time on Sunday to make other plans. I say let him get on with his celebrations, speeches, and whatnot."

Bob nodded. "He sounded like he's gonna be running all over Boston until midafternoon. We might not be able to find him and let him know."

"I overheard him say he's due to collect his daughter at three after some speech in a square and then have dinner at the Cabots' home. I suspect he'll arrive at the ship just before eight, not a minute sooner."

Bob nodded. "I know where the Cabot house is. We went by there on the way back. That's who gave him them books."

James grinned. "Can you draw me a map to find it?"

"Why?"

"So's I can interrupt his dinner with an emergency, maybe about seven."

"Maybe later? Closer to when they have to go aboard."

James shrugged. "We'll need him to go into a tizzy and don't give him time to do anything other than take me in your stead."

"Better than a map, we can walk by there after breakfast tomorrow to be sure you know where it be."

"Best we go there now. I told Ned we'd meet him in the morning so's he could show us around Boston. Man's got things to tell us about how it is up here."

Standing and brushing sand from his trousers, Bob looked over the ocean. "Then let's walk by it now." He draped his arm around his brother's shoulder.

Each seemed lost in thought and said little during their walk. Bob found the house and navigated directly back to the inn. James memorized the route with ease. Once at the inn, they ate an early supper. When the innkeeper asked if they wanted ale with dinner, Bob agreed. "Best I enjoy it now, seeing as Massa was kind enough to offer. I reckon I'm not going to waste any coins on a drink tomorrow."

A few minutes later, the innkeeper went to the barrel and drew two pewter tankards of a lightly foamed ale. Holding both in one hand, he dropped them on the scarred table. Later when he served oily crabcakes and carrots, boiled into a pale reflection of what a carrot once was, James started laughing. "She was right."

"Who?"

"That red-hair lady. Her cakes were better than these."

Then James lowered his voice. "Brother, you need to tell me how to tend to Jefferson's specific schedule and needs."

"Things you gotta know? Let him be when he wakes so's he can have a piss and move his bowels in the commode, or he'll get bound up and be a miserable person. Gets plain ornery. Soaks his feet in cold water every morning while I shave him. Stone-sharpen the blade once a week and strop it hard before every shave. Use your boot top, not a strop. Gives a better edge. Hang and brush off his jacket and fold the breeches each night. Launder his long shirts as he leaves them for you on the floor, but not if he leaves them on the bed or a chair. But wrench them out twice. In hot water both times. Clothing rubs him raw easily. And he got fine linen underdrawers he wears, made with the seam on the outside not to rub on him. Wrench these twice as well."

"Underdrawers? What's that?"

"What's it sound like, fool? Like short breeches, under his breeches."

James puzzled on this. "You mean he don't just pull the tail of his long shirt 'tween his legs to keep the breeches clean like we do?"

"Nope. Skin like a baby's. That's what Miss Martha always said. Remember how Mam made him that skin salve in winter?"

Bob described Jefferson's disappointment at the turn of events holding him from his assignment in France and how he threw himself into the work of the new Congress, introducing some thirty matters to the body and having them adopt his proposition that the expansion northwest of the Ohio River would be by new states, not extensions of the current states. Bob said that Jefferson added the proposition that slavery would not be allowed in these new states. It failed adoption but suggested that his thoughts of freedom for slaves were not extinguished.

James looked at Bob in disbelief. "He talk to you on this?"

"Yes. Openly. Often while I'm shaving him. Some days I think he likes the sound of his voice, even though he don't do much talking to others."

"Maybe he's just trying an idea on to see how it fits."

"Maybe. He's an odd duck."

James nodded and fell into silence as he finished his meal and thought of how Jefferson was a pile of contradictions. As steadfast as he was in his view of the government and its position in the universe, he was as flawed and inconsistent in his personal life. He spoke for freedom for slaves yet held his in bondage. He abhorred the purchase of slaves, preferring to let natural growth account for replacement, yet James had overheard Jefferson bowing to South Carolina's need to import new slaves to the rice plantations where death outpaced birth in the rice swamps.

He was a man who yearned. Sometimes James thought Jefferson himself didn't know what itch he was trying to scratch, but it had to be new, more, different, and challenging. James knew a part of that itch himself. The only thing Jefferson was firm as rock about was his desire to go to France.

CHAPTER 7

Independence Day began with a cannon shot booming across the harbor. After dressing, James and Bob went downstairs for breakfast. The table holding the beer barrel now also held several plates of various dried fish and a covered tureen of a hearty porridge with a pitcher of cream beside it. On a smaller table sat a large pitcher of cider, small mugs, a tankard holding large spoons, and a stack of wooden trenchers, deep enough to serve both as a plate and bowl. Bob loaded his trencher with porridge, splashed some cream on it, and put it on the table. As his brother poured two mugs of cider, James took a large scoop of porridge and balanced a sample of every dried fish on the elevated rim of his trencher. Once the two were seated across from each other, Bob screwed up his face. "Smells like low tide."

"Thought you liked fish."

"Fresh fish."

James sniffed the various fish. He took his spoon and tasted each one carefully with a small bite. Bob shook his head, hurried to finish, and waited on the porch for James. They walked around the harbor, being certain to return to the chestnut tree at three minutes before nine. The square was crowded by the time Ned found them. The trio hurried from the square and walked up the strand where Bob and James had been on Saturday.

Ned continued at a good pace and made for a rocky outcropping as he told them about Boston. Several men with broad-brimmed hats were fishing from the crest of the rocks. As they came closer, James saw they were all much darker than he and Bob. Beyond the rocks, the shoreline gave way to a sandy cove where women and small children played at the edge of the water.

Ned shouted up at the men fishing from the rim of the rock. "Hey, Tom!"

The slim man handed his fishing pole to another man and scrambled down. "How you doin'?"

"Fine. Showing couple boys from Virginia how it is up here before they sail out."

Tom nodded and the brothers did the same. Tom said, "Fish are running good today. Want a couple? Gotta mess of 'em."

"Thanks. Got three for me?"

The fisherman called to a boy to bring the string of fish to him. Soon a barefoot lad scrambled across the rocks holding a line with four fish tied to it. The line had been passed through a gill slit and out the mouth. Each fish was tied off, so it was separated from its neighbor. Ned said, "Good size to smoke dry."

Tom nodded. "Take 'em all. I'll start another line."

Ned took the line from the boy and touched his shoulder. "When you gonna come by and get measured for your boots, Sammy?"

The boy became shy and stood behind his father, who answered for him. "Let summer end, then he's gonna be fishing on the boat."

Ned shook his head in a teasing manner. "I gotta have some time to make them."

Tom smiled. "Gonna let him run barefoot and happy this summer. But when he starts going out with me, he gotta have boots on. His mama has spoken on that matter."

"Just so's you know, I got the leather now and time to make 'em in the long summer light."

"That so? I see you soon."

Ned took the string of fish, turned, and walked from the beach quickly with his guests trailing after him. Once he got to the road, he paused and waited for the brothers to catch up to him.

Moving inland, crossing one street then another, Ned pointed out various shops and homes and spoke of families he knew. They soon came to a row of shops, the likes of which James had never seen. The brick buildings went up three levels of windows and butted into each other forming a solid wall along the street. Signs signified a dry goods store, milliner, tailor, barber, and a newspaper office. A fishmonger had empty wooden bins in the front of the closed store. Today, the shops were locked drum tight. Red, white, and blue bunting was draped above several of the shop doorways.

Turning into the next street, Ned pointed to a sign with smart black riding boots painted on a gold background. "That's my shop. Front's where I work. I live back here." Opening a padlock on the rear door, he led them into his one room and hung the line of fish on the hook of his cold hearth.

A large window lit the room well, showing a small cot against the far wall, a sailor's flattop trunk in front of it, and a spindle-back chair by the fireplace. On the rough timber mantel was an oil lamp, wooden bowls, earthen mugs, and several books.

The small fireplace had a grid over the andirons that held a pot and a large fry pan, each of old cast iron. Ned set to making a small fire. He moved the pot and pan off the rack. His steel met flint and the shavings sparked to life easily. In a minute, there was a decent flame and he returned the pan to the grate.

"Have a sit down. On the cot or chair. Don't matter. Won't be but a minute." He stepped outside to clean the fish.

James looked around the spare room and thought how quickly he would exchange all his fancy clothing and fine foods at Monticello for a room this small, but a life a hundred times larger than his. James wondered if Bob was thinking the same thing as they sat in silence.

Ned returned with the gutted and scaled fish, put a dab of lard in the pan, and slid it over the center of the fire. "Hope you like my cooking. It's simple. I don't hold with no pepper the way some up here do. That way, you can taste how sweet the meat is this time of year." Once the pan was sizzling, he fried the four fish and divided them between the three wooden bowls. He took the lid off the pot and pulled out a half wheel of hearth bread. He placed it on the trunk and put a long knife beside it with a nod toward the brothers to cut their own slices. From a crock on the floor, he ladled cider into three earthen mugs without handles.

They ate their fish with hand-carved spoons, mopping up the fat with the bread and downing the cloudy cider. James noticed that without salt or pepper, the firm flesh did have a freshness that he had not noticed when Lizzie pan-fried fish. Satisfied as kings, they studied each other. The brothers nodded appreciation.

Bob was the first to break the quiet. "So, you work for a cobbler?"

"Did. This be my shop now. I finished my indenture contract a year past. There be a number of us freemen in trades here. Most Sundays we get together, share some news, and have a lively time. Make a boiled dinner on the shore in fair weather or at someone's house in the winter. It get god-awful cold in the winter here."

"Some even got houses?"

"Small, but yes. Even got a Negro lady what wrote a book of poems."

James said, "Real? When I heard one of Massa's guests talk of a Negro poet lady, I thought he made it up like a story to amuse folks."

"On my word. Phillis Wheatley be her name. Lives here in Boston in a boarding house with her daughter, just over there." He pointed inland.

"Like I said, I heard talk of her once. And that there was free Negroes here, but I did not believe it. How could there be such numbers since you don't have big plantations like we do in Virginia? You really free up here?"

He laughed. "Let me lay it out simple for you. In the past, an owner could free a slave just by writing a manumission statement on the bill of sale that says he be free. That be the end of it. But some owners did this just when a fellow got too old or sick to be of worth, or care for himself. Then the city say if you free a slave, you have to register it and pay a sum for his care if he goes into the city poorhouse. Gets looked after by a City Overseer. Then 'bout four years past, the state made a constitution saying all men is free. Last year, July 8, a judge of the state supreme court says all slaves is free. See, this slave named Quock Walker sued for his freedom. Say the part of the constitution saying all men are free means us too. Judge says yeah. Then the state then went after his master, a Mister Jennison, on charges for holding him prisoner."

"Did that really free all the slaves?"

"Here, it did. Took some lawyering after that to make it so, but really that be the case." He patted the deep front pocket of his trousers. "I got my paper to prove I am free since age twenty-nine. Been a free man for almost a year now. Some don't carry their paper, but I do. Ain't the same in other states, so I carry it. That, and a knife in my boot."

James spoke softly. "Can I see your paper?"

"Ain't you never seen a released bill of sale?"

"Not that I know."

"Ought to be one if you was bought by your master?"

"No. We come through his wife's family."

"If you ain't never seen a free document, I guess I can show you." He wiped his hands on his trousers before he pulled out a small, folded leather wallet. He opened it with care and held up a yellowed paper that he reverently unfolded and flattened on the table. James looked at the sheet and read it, mouthing the words to slow himself down. "*Know all men by these presents that I Mathew Rogers of Worcester in the County of Worcester yeoman in consideration of forty pounds lawful money paid me by John Cooper of Petersham in said County which I hereby acknowledge I have this day received of him have bargained sold conveyed & delivered and do hereby bargain sell convey and deliver to the said John Cooper his executors administrators or assigns, a certain negro boy named & called Ned about fifteen years old, to have and hold in servitude as his slave & servant during his natural life and hereby warrant that he may so lawfully hold him and that I have good right to sell him in manner aforesaid. Witness my hand and seal this 13th day of February A.D. 1770. Mathew Rogers. Signed Sealed & Delivered in presence of us.*"

James stopped trying to read the two signatures of the witnesses that followed when Ned nudged his elbow and said, "Turn it over. That's the important part."

James wiped his hands, as Ned had before he touched it. "*This shall certify to all persons that I John Cooper do hereby give to the within named Ned his freedom...*" He had to stop and catch his breath. "*...his freedom and discharge him from my service and the service of my heirs forever. John Cooper. Witness Kenneth McCray.*" James glanced at the date and sighed.

"That's what they call a manumission. Means I'm not a slave no more."

Bob looked over his brother's shoulder at the paper and whistled softly. "Why would he just give you your liberty?"

"Because a judge up here was telling masters to free their slaves who petitioned the court. Just give 'em up. Let them walk away. If I took him to court, and there be lawyers who do that for you for free, then I get freed and the lawyer gets his fees paid by the owner. See now?"

Bob nodded. "He did not want the burden or cost of going to court."

"Exactly, so he made me a bargain. I agreed to be indentured to a cobbler in town. Cobbler paid him off. I got room and board and some pocket money. I did my year indenture. Now I am rid of any duty to the man."

James was confused. "Why did you trade one master for another, if you coulda just walked away?"

"Now...truth be told, I had no place to go or way to eat, so I agreed to the indenture. It was good to work for a man too old to carry on his shop on his own. I learned a trade I could take with me after my time was up. Let me sleep here in the back of the shop and gave me a little spending money when I did extra work for him. Saved my money. Now, he crippled up and lives with his daughter. I rent his shop so he has money and I have a place. Worked out good for all of us."

"Make it sound easy."

"Wasn't. Only thing that was easy was figuring my name. Ned was what I was called, and all I was called my life long. I was Mister Cooper's Ned. But when I got free, I decided that his name was a part of me so's kin could find me. I became Ned Cooper. Lotsa others done the same, take their master's name as their free name to be found."

James held the paper and looked at it as though it were enchanted. "With this paper, you became free."

Ned grinned. "Right so."

The arrival of two of the men who had been at the shore fishing ended that inquiry. Each brought a fish on a string. The taller one asked, "Still got enough fire for us to fry these up?"

"Sure. Clean 'um out there." Ned threw a few more small sticks on the coals and used bellows to freshen the fire. He pointed to the tall man. "That be Charles, and the fat one is George."

George shouted back, "No I ain't!"

Soon both came inside with their cleaned fish and tossed a bit of lard into the frying pan and let it sizzle before they laid in the fish. Ned pointed at the men. "You might a seen 'em on the rock fishing with the others. George works in the shipyard. Charles goes out a week at a time fishing, then back here he mends nets and drives fish inland to markets, then out he go again."

Charles flipped the fish in the pan with his bare fingers. "True. Trade time in a boat with another man. We both like some land time with our women."

George laughed. "You talk like you got a string of women."

"Hell, no. My Sarah'd beat me like a rug if she even think that." He took two empty wooden bowls off the hearth and slid the fish from the pan in an easy motion. "But I makes a good way for us by fishing and her doing crafts to sell at market. She weaves rag rugs and puts up preserves."

James looked at George. "What do you do in the shipyard?"

"Most anything. Been there a few years. Right now, we's caulking the seams on the hull of a merchant ship. Gonna rig it like a schooner to sail to the Indies. Hammering in the oakum between timbers in the hull.

Then gonna tar it over. Boat's gonna be as dry as a preacher's throat by the time I get done."

They laughed. Charles nudged George in the ribs with his elbow. "Ain't nothing dry 'bout your yard."

"True that. Got a good foreman who call out clear as a bell at eleven, 'Grog-o!' and at four too. We gets us a tankard."

James looked puzzled. Charles laughed. "Grog? Ain't you heard of rum and water?"

James was astounded. "They let you drink?"

"Yeah. That the way they do it here. Work is daybreak to dark."

Ned pointed at Charles. "Tell him what you make so's he can see you can get a job up here."

"Makes a dollar a day."

Bob whistled. "I never."

Charles said, "Fishing, I make what the sea lets me take. But if I was to sign on as an ordinary sailor, I could make fourteen to seventeen dollars a month. Now that don't sound like much, but when you figure that the captain is buying me food and my bunk is free, I could make out, but Sarah wants me home some nights."

"And you know how that is. You got a good woman. You better keep her happy."

Bob looked away and tried to hide the spasm in his throat and the start of tears with a cough.

James slapped him on the back. "You all right, brother?" Bob coughed again and waved him away. James took a long, slow breath. "Your paper. Can anyone just write them up?"

Ned shook his head. "Not a wise idea. They got to be in the courthouse record. And it be a crime to run away and another to write out false papers."

George added, "Besides, most everyone here knows who's free. Now sailors coming and going don't get much heed if they stick close to the harbor, but if one was to be marching hisself past town, then I suspect there would be notice of it."

James said, "The war split up slave families in Virginia. Those what run to fight for the English got promised a freedom that never came. British left them behind after they lost. Least those I know. Those fighting for the Revolution stayed slaves in their own country."

George nodded and said, "Some up here did get their freedom after wearing a red coat. Friend of mine did, made his coat into red shoes for his baby that was born in seventy-eight. Maybe it be different up here, but in the south ain't nobody gonna give up their slaves no more than they'd give you their horse if you walked up and asked for it. We just property there, not people."

James said, "But there is a movement to free slaves. I hear Massa's dinner guests telling him about abolition societies. Mister Franklin has joined one. The Methodist Episcopal Church say nobody owning slaves can come into that church soon. The Quakers in Virginia setting to free all the slaves."

Bob smirked as he said, "All that's true, but it ain't happening fast enough."

James pointed to Ned. "No. But he's free."

Ned smiled. "Remember, I worked off the indenture."

"But that day came. I hear folks at Massa's dinner table talking about setting us at liberty like it be the end of the world."

Full of fish, bread, and cider, James started to feel groggy. Knowing what had to be done in just a few hours, he asked Ned about their life in Boston. He told them how Negroes bartered goods or services among themselves because cash money was scarce. Fish for boots. Garden crops or an old hen for a belt or a wallet. Working on a fishing boat all Sunday for a tenth of the catch. As the afternoon grew late, both brothers seemed reluctant for their time with the men to end.

Bob stood. "I thank you for your hospitality to travelers. I fear we could not return it should you be in Virginia."

"It be my pleasure to meet you both. I hope you come back."

James stood. "That might be. Thank you."

Bob reached into his pocket and pulled out the coins Jefferson had given them for their midday meal and jingled them. "Here's what we planned to spend for a meal not half so fine as you provided."

Ned brushed his hand away. "We all help each other out, or we'd not make it to the next week."

Bob took two silver coins and pressed them into his open hand and closed it. "Not payment. A gift. Thank you."

They made their way back to the inn through a crowd watching a parade of children wearing sashes of red or blue. Seeing a table of rounded crusty breads and other baked goods, Bob wove through the crowd to it. He asked for prices, bought a small round of hearth bread, and put it under his arm. He turned to James. "Think I'm gonna need something to help calm my innards."

At the inn, James hid the bread in his traveling sack and stowed it in the corner of the room. About six, cannons were fired across the bay. The window of their room rattled. Bob walked over to it and looked across the harbor. "Getting on to time for an evening meal downstairs."

"That time, already?"

The brothers ate a light supper. After which, James bought a tankard of cider, telling the innkeeper that Bob felt ill. Shortly before seven, Bob opened the paper packet his mother had prepared for him. "Wish me well, brother." He then tipped the envelope of red powder into his mouth, shuddered, and washed it down with the full tankard. He handed James the paper to hide and asked if his mouth was stained. James shook his head.

In less than half an hour, sweat was coming off Bob's forehead. Soon after, he was on the floor doubled with cramps. Then he motioned for James to pull the chamber pot from under the bed. He vomited into it. He laughed before a chill rattled him almost like a fit. "Best you get Massa now."

James started for the door, but Bob called him back. "Go to France.

Stay there. Become a free man." He doubled over and sucked in his breath. "Mam'll understand. She see how your eyes shine talking about freedom. Now go."

James ran all the way to the Cabot house and banged on their door in a most improper manner. When the butler answered, James barely caught his breath enough to say that he needed to see Mister Jefferson right away. His agitation startled the butler, who told him to stay on the front stoop. Jefferson came to the door holding his dinner napkin.

"Come quick. Bob took ill."

A look of revulsion fell across Jefferson's face, which he failed to hide. The brothers had counted on his fear of disease and hoped that it would impair his usual careful evaluation of matters. Jefferson told James to wait and excused himself. Moments later, he came back to the door and they hurried to the inn. Jefferson was sweat covered when they arrived and took the stairs two at a time. James pushed open the unlocked door to their small room. Bob hunched over the piss pot, groaning.

Jefferson squinted from the rancid stink of vomit and sweat and stepped back into the hall. "Good Christ, what is going on in here?"

"Bob's got the pukes."

"I did not give you money to go out and get drunk."

"He's not drunk. He's awful sick. He started getting the chills this morning. We went out for a look-see anyway, thinking some air might do him good. I took some food about midday, but he don't. We had a light supper here. He starts with the shakes, so's we come back to the room straight away."

Jefferson looked at Bob from the doorway then turned back to James, who continued. "He took to bed. I got a wet rag for his head and water, but he got worse and worse. Burning up, then got the sweats and chills. Just started puking real bad so's I come for you."

Jefferson glanced at Bob vomiting above the chamber pot. "Did he eat anything red today? Beets? Cherries?"

James put on a scared face. "No, sir. I think he's gut bleeding."

"Go get the innkeeper. Now."

Bob rolled to his side and accentuated a case of the chills resembling a fit and added a painful groan for emphasis. Jefferson backed out to the center of the hallway. Moments later James returned with the innkeeper, who was huffing to keep up with him.

"What's the trouble here?"

Bob's groans told the tale when the innkeeper peered into the room.

Jefferson looked stricken. "We're set to sail before dawn. Can't you get a doctor or something for him?"

"I can send for a doctor, if you'll stand the charge. Or I can bring up some ginger beer and soda crackers and see if that calms his gut."

"Try the ginger beer."

For the next hour, Jefferson waited downstairs. When James told him that the crackers and ginger beer came right back up, he had the innkeeper send for a doctor.

By the time the doctor arrived, in a top hat and swallowtail coat, fresh from some celebration, it had become almost eight in the evening. Although he smelled of brandy, he comported a good examination of Bob and went to advise Jefferson of his findings.

Jefferson stood when the doctor came down the stairs. "Well? Is he fit to travel or not? We sail tomorrow."

"I doubt that any captain worthy of the name would allow him on board in his condition. We will not be able to determine for another few days if his affliction is from tainted food or some contagion."

"But we are already tardy in boarding."

"Then board and sail you shall. Time and tide, you know. I can care for him at my residence and send him on to you when he is well enough to travel."

Jefferson held up his hands in frustration. "But his passage is paid on this ship for this voyage alone."

James stepped forward to face Jefferson. "Massa Jefferson. Take me in his stead. You already wrote a passage letter. He can take the wagon back when he gets his health."

"It seems that I have no better choice. Go clean him up and pack all your things while I come to terms with the doctor."

James sprinted upstairs and leaned over Bob. "You gonna live?"

Bob groaned as he whispered, "Barely. Maybe I took too much of Mama's root powder."

"Should wear off in a couple hours, Mam said. Got the bread?"

Bob nodded and clutched his belly. "Dried beets sure did the trick. Looked like I was bleeding out like a stuck pig. Think she overdid by putting in bloodroot and boneset. Felt like I was gonna purge and sweat forever."

James helped him into bed. "Think you be strong enough to drive the wagon back in a day or so?"

"Not going back."

James whispered. "You planning to run?"

"No. Gonna hire out to the doctor where Dolly is. I'll send word back to Miller where I am so I'm not a runaway and he can send someone for the team and wagon. I figure if I split wages between him and Massa, he be fine with me being gone. Be safe, brother."

James laid his hand on Bob's shoulder. "You too."

Bob flinched at the sound of several musket shots and then a trumpet blast outside the inn. "What?"

"It's still Independence Day."

Bob chuckled, then winced. "Yes, it is."

CHAPTER 8

It was dusk when James balanced his canvas sack on his trunk and walked down the dock to the *Ceres*. As he boarded, a bell on the quarterdeck sounded. He looked at the sailor ringing the small bell and wondered if all the passengers got the same welcome. He relinquished his belongings to a sailor who said he would stow them on his bunk below deck. He stood alone by the main mast and waited for Jefferson. Although the day was dimming, the celebrations seemed to be continuing unabated. Laughter and music carried easily across the calm of the harbor.

The captain stood at the bow of the ship with a man and his daughter. The men had wineglasses in hand. The girl, slightly older than Patsy, laughed at some remark made by the captain. James had overheard Jefferson give Patsy a summary of the passengers she would meet on the voyage and tried to attach names to those on deck. The girl, Rose Richards, should provide companionship for her. Her father, a widower like Jefferson, was in the business of importing fabric from France to his stores in New York.

Two older men at the rail opposite the dock were no doubt Mister Whitehead and Mister Turner. They too had wine. Both were bankers and lean. One was bald and the other had dark hair and a beard. James had no idea which one was which, but his deduction was simple as there were only six passengers on the voyage and the two tardy ones were his owners.

The bell on the quarterdeck rang once as the Cabots' carriage rattled down the dock and delivered Jefferson and Patsy. James hurried to the dockside and took their small valises from the carriage. When he arrived on deck again, he handed them to a sailor who was tasked to transport them to their cabins. Jefferson took Patsy by the arm and introduced her to their fellow passengers. James was shocked to see the resemblance Patsy had to her mother as she tipped her head and nodded upon meeting the others with a new formality.

Although Patsy was nearly fifteen, both her height and presence made her appear several years older. She moved across the deck as if it were a ballroom floor, meeting the others, offering a short curtsy to each of the men. They stood at the rail and the captain joined them, presenting a glass of wine to Jefferson, who smiled and started to convince Richards to expand his enterprise to include the export of American goods to Europe.

They talked into the dusk. When the lights of the taverns and homes along the harbor's edge showed lamps or candles in their windows, the passengers were escorted from the deck into the salon that was their parlor, dining room, and also held the map-reading table for the captain and first mate. Their cabins were on the starboard side of the parlor while the captain and his crew were on the port side. Although there was a privy off the parlor, each cabin had a chamber pot for any needs that might arise at night or when the passengers were otherwise indisposed.

As Jefferson passed James, he said, "That's all for tonight, James."

"What time should I assist you in the morning?"

"I'll manage tomorrow and take my shaves from the steward, who the captain says has a steady hand at sea. I want you to be of use immediately in the kitchen and assist elsewhere as you can."

"But..."

"James, I will summon you if I need any assistance. Until then, you reply to the cook's direction."

"Yes. As you wish."

A sailor came to James and offered to show him to his bunk. James made his way down the steep stairs with care, thinking the pitch was more like a ladder than stairway. After struggling to hold his balance in the dim light, he saw the wisdom of having the passenger cabins on the same level as the upper deck. There was a dim lantern lighting the bunks built into the bow of the ship. No sooner had James arrived and found his sack of belongings on a bunk when a burly sailor turn to him. "Piss pot is that bucket if you need it. Privy is down the hall toward the kitchen, but you'll never find it in the dark, so hold your bowels 'till morning if you can." With that, he reached for the lantern and blew out the flame.

James shoved his sack to the foot of the bed, stretched out in his clothes, and wondered how his brother was recovering. In minutes he was asleep, only to be awakened at midnight by sailors rustling about in the dark.

Sometime before four that first morning, there was a thunderous drumbeat of wood belaying pins on the deck above his head. All the sailors but two rolled out of their bunks, pulled on their trousers and shirts, made for the passageway in a single line, and snaked up the stairs. No ablutions were performed. All were gone from their wooden cave in the bow of the ship before James got his bearings. He lurched after them and scrambled up the steep stairs to emerge on the forward deck. Some were still taking a piss off the railing, watering Boston Harbor with the residue of significant quantities of beer. James joined them, wondering how this was to be arranged at sea with passengers on deck. The bell rang again.

As he was buttoning his trousers, a whiff of coal smoke blew past him. James was surprised to see that its source was a metal chimney on their own deck. The still-dark harbor was now without the gaiety of the Independence Day celebrants, their music or laughter. In the distance, he thought he heard the slow clop of a horse on the cobbled street, perhaps going to market. Lines on small sailboats in the harbor tapped and rubbed against masts. The soft lapping of the tide against the dock's pilings and the cries of seagulls replaced all human sounds.

As soon as any one of the sailors had buttoned his trousers, he moved to some preordained location on deck or scrambled up the rope footholds on the shrouds. Soon the yardarms of the mast were populated with silent sailors awaiting the order to release sails. But then all activity stopped. The order was not forthcoming.

At the rear of the ship, the captain was arguing with a man. Although James could only hear random words, the drift was clear that the captain was displeased that the harbormaster had let another ship dock so close that it was blocking what little wind there was to propel the ship from the dock. After some shouting and arm waving, the man stomped off the ship. Fox called the men down from the yardarms.

After he shouted out new orders, sailors pivoted the large tender boat on its davits and lowered it into the water. Eight sailors jumped onto the lines holding the boat and, hand over hand, lowered themselves into it. They released the lowering lines so those on deck could retrieve the ropes from the pulleys. Once the tender was at the bow, a line was dropped to it. Just a moment later, two of the harbormaster's tenders arrived and took lines as well.

After sailors on the dock cast off the mooring lines and scrambled aboard, the men in the three tenders pulled hard on their oars and the bow of the *Ceres* pulled away from the dock. Silent as fog, they moved past two anchored ships into an open area of the glassy bay. Although James could not feel the wind, he saw the banner at the top of the tallest mast flutter and extend.

Fox called in his men, who were then pulled aboard, and their craft secured in its cradle on deck. Although the two harbor boats continued to pull hard, Fox eyed the banner and consulted the captain, who nodded. Fox pointed to James and said something to the captain that James did not hear.

James ventured toward the quarterdeck, where Fox and the captain stood. Having seen him the night before, they both nodded their approval. Fox motioned for him to come closer. "Ever been aboard ship?"

"No, sir. Can I watch?"

"Stand clear of me, a step behind but clear of the tiller." James guessed that the tiller was the long timber that moved the rudder on this ship in the place of the wheel in the illustration he had seen in Jefferson's book.

Fox cupped his hands around his mouth and shouted, "Stand by to set sail!"

When the captain nodded, Fox shouted, "Lay aloft and prepare to let loose all sails!" As the sailors scrambled to the side railing and up the tarred rope web of the shroud, they seemed to move in a splendid harmony. Then without added orders, each man balanced on a footrope under the bright spars and walked along it untying the sail. The men held it against the yardarm until the command "Loose all sails" was issued.

It seemed to James that at that moment the sun broke between the horizon and a thin bank of clouds, offering the lightest of a peach hue to the air, a honeyed glow that made him hold his breath to lock it into his mind. The sails fluttered down and brightened into a reflected gold while the crewmen descended.

Once they were on the deck, Fox yelled out a barrage of commands that were unknown to James. The crew scrambled, set the triangular fore and aft sails, and the ship now began to move of its own accord. The tender boats cast off the lines and pulled back into the harbor. A sailor returned the wet lines to the deck, made two neat coils, and then tied the coils off over a belaying pin on the interior of the deck's railing.

The crew on deck then pulled on the many lines that turned the yardarms, tensioned the square sails, and raised the triangular sails named jibs. What Fox called to the sailors was only vaguely familiar to James. His calls were fast and abbreviated like an auctioneer at a tobacco warehouse. Whilst Jefferson's books clearly labeled the sails from the top to the deck as royal, gallant, and main, Fox's commands seemed to be in an accent from another age. Calling the topsail the "tops'l" was the only term he knew. The topgallant sail was the "ta'gallant." The main sail was called the "m'ns'l" and the largest of these he called the "course." The large rear jib, he called a "spanker." The canvas sails filled slowly in the light breeze. The sails, set and trimmed, gave a crisp snap before holding steady as full as a cushion filled with goose down.

The dawn was now a bright gold on the horizon as they passed the lighthouse on a small island at the outer edge of the bay. Mister Fox pointed to the tall white shaft. "That there is the Boston Light on Little Brewster Island. Brought me home on many a dark night." He offered a salute to it, as if the keeper were watching the *Ceres* heading into open water.

The captain held his hat high toward the lighthouse as well and turned to Fox. "Hold her steady until our passengers are awake and fed. We want to gentle them into the motion of the ship."

"Aye, sir."

James stood at the rail and watched the shore grow more distant and a second lighthouse come into view. He pointed to it and before he could ask, Fox said it was the Highland Light at Cape Cod. The low sand hills of the cape were glowing amber. The wind increased, or at least James thought so as he felt the breeze on his face and the ship's speed accelerate. Lines tied up, half the crew quietly vanished below deck.

Captain Tracey turned to James. "Hungry?"

"Yes, sir."

"Then go get your meal. You know where the galley is?"

"No, sir."

"See that smokestack? That's the chimney to the stove."

"Sure. I can find it downstairs."

The captain corrected him. "Below." He whistled and pointed to a sailor who immediately came to the foot of the steps. "Show him the galley and be quick to return. I want to set a top watch."

James rushed after him down the steep stairs and into the bay in the middle of the ship. A blast of heat met him. A layer of acrid coal smoke clung to the ceiling and assaulted his eyes. James choked at the stink, which was somewhere between that of a wet goat and a cheap cigar. He barely noticed a beam that ran across the width of the ship, just at his eye level. Ducking under it, he entered an area some fifteen feet square. Bins and barrels were affixed to an inner rail along the length of the starboard hull. Along the port side was a long worktable butted into the hull and fixed to the floor, with cabinets above and drawers below. In the stern, there were two tables suspended from ropes. Each could seat four to a side.

In the center of the space squatted a huge black iron box that glowed red from chunks of coal in an elevated hearth with a grate in front. A chimney rose from the roof of the open hearth and up through the deck. On the opposite side were two lids flat on the top of the box.

Taking another step to the side to look at the contraption, James found himself face-to-face with a barrel-chested man with copper hair and a beard to match. His eyes were so pale that they had only a hint of blue. Unlike the other sailors, his complexion was fair.

He put his hands into his pockets and looked James over. Just then, the ship pitched. James took a step back and knocked his head into the beam. The cook laughed as James rubbed the back of his head. "So, you are the uninvited guest?"

"Pardon me?" James said, not understanding his meaning and barely understanding the man's words; he had an unfamiliar accent.

"Mister Jefferson's servant, ain't you?"

"I am, sir."

"Good, then you will be my helper for the voyage as well." He shoved out his hand. "Donald McArthur. Call me Donald. Good you have arrived unbidden to start…" He looked at James, saw his confusion, and stopped. "What's the matter, son?"

"The captain sent me to eat my breakfast, sir." He blinked away the tears from the smoke.

"Then so it shall be. After that you can start your chores for me down here. Where's your kit?"

"My what?"

"Your knife and spoon and bowl."

Seeing he was ill prepared, McArthur said, "Grab a large bowl from that rack and follow me."

Without waiting, McArthur went to the back of the contraption in giant strides, used the huge towel at his waist to pad the handle of the smaller lid, and lifted it off, took the ladle, and dug deep into the pot. James held out his bowl for a huge serving of porridge.

McArthur motioned to the farthest of the hanging tables. James sat where his gesture with the ladle suggested. At each side, a bench was fixed to the deck, and having four sides no doubt counted as storage for something; the ship so far had impressed him as having great economy of design and forethought on the placement of items. James saw that each of the eight spots, four to a side, had its area framed on all sides with an inch-high rail, no doubt to hold the plates in place during high seas. James stared at the porridge recalling how the tree-cutting crew had eaten with their hands at Monticello. McArthur came back with a wooden spoon and gave it to him. "Sailors keep their own spoon and knife with them."

James looked down. "I do not have either."

The cook sat on the bench across from James and smiled, an odd, crooked smile. "Then keep that spoon. There'll be knives here for you." He crossed his arms across his ample belly and sighed. "Now what are we to do with you? Ever worked a galley before? A kitchen?"

"Just to help."

"Well that's a start."

James was shoveling the porridge into his mouth as fast as he could, given how hot it was, yet he found in it a nutty flavor and complex texture more satisfying than the uniform cornmeal he was served at Monticello. When he was almost finished, the cook uncrossed his arms. That was when James saw a vivid scar that started at his left elbow and shot like lightning to his wrist. His hand had a waxen quality to it. The fingers were fused into a unit not unlike a seal's flipper. James tried not to react but shivered when he thought of how the man must have burned himself to get such an injury.

"Noticed it, did you?"

"Sorry, sir. I mean no disrespect."

"Was a long time ago. No matter now. As you can see, I could use another *hand* in the mess." He laughed at his own joke. "So, I'll teach you what you need to do to help. Right?"

"Right, sir."

"Start now. Eat your bowl clean. There be a slop pail just there for garbage, a large bucket to rinse off your bowl. Dry it on a towel and put it back in the rack. Ask me if you are not sure of something; you can get killed down here if the sea pitches just right or if you get too close to the Brodie." He nodded toward the glowing coals in the massive stove.

Above them, a bell rang in short bursts. McArthur motioned for him to listen. "How many bells?"

"Five or six? I'm not certain."

"You need to know! Listen sharp. That way you know where you need to be and what you need to do. All is run by the clock on a ship."

James was afraid that he had made a very serious error in going aboard with so little understanding of the expectations.

"You going to be sick? You looked…"

"No, sir. Just thinking. About the bells?"

"Every day is in six parts. Midnight to four. Four to eight. Eight to noon. Noon to four. Four to eight…"

"And eight to midnight."

"Right. A bell is struck for each half hour. So, thirty minutes after midnight is one bell. Two bells is one o'clock. Three bells is one thirty. And so on until we get to eight bells at the end of each watch. The quarterdeck rings them in batches of two, so it is easier to make out the pattern. Understand?"

"I think so. Are they rung this loud throughout the night too?"

"Yes."

James finished drying his bowl and put it on the warm rack on the stove. "I don't think I heard them."

"Well, listen tonight."

"How do they stay on schedule?"

"The captain sets the noon hour with his instruments, then the helmsman's sandglass and the ship's clock are set right again each day. See, he's got a thirty-minute sandglass. When turned, he rings the correct bell to signal the time."

"I see," James said, not fully understanding.

"Watches change every four hours. Tomorrow morning, be here at four a.m. That's eight bells. Just like you got up today, but tomorrow there won't be the 'all-hands' thumping on the deck. Ask a sailor going on the 'four-watch' to wake you for the first few days until you figure it out."

"I will."

"Report here, and I'll put you to whatever work we have. Questions?"

"No, sir."

"Make that Donald. 'Sir' is for other blokes."

James shook his head, having so many questions that there was no place to start. In the days that followed, he found himself with two masters. After James had cooked all day, Jefferson called on him to dress well, serve at the captain's table, pour wine, and entertain with his violin. At first, Jefferson had offered his own violin to James to play. When he discovered that James had brought his in the trunk, he smiled, knowing that Bob did not play the instrument.

As James soon discovered, the amount of cleaning left in the kitchen after preparing the elegant dinners was substantial. He was not shy about extending his concerts past dinner and brandy for the gentlemen. For the first few nights, the bells roused James. Then he found in them a comfort that the ship was progressing night and day toward France and that his new career as a cook had started. Less comfort was found in the seamen who had regular watches to stand, of assigned four-hour lengths and had to fit in all their other chores such as eating, mending torn trousers, and crafting the carved or knotted knickknacks they sold for some extra funds in port.

Late in the morning after several days at sea, McArthur sent James to deliver a mug of tea to the captain, who was with the helmsman. The captain then invited him to linger and enjoy the ocean for a moment. Jefferson had found his sea legs by this time and was on deck, pacing its length. As the first mate passed him, Jefferson caught his elbow. "Mister Fox? These lines? There must be a couple miles of them."

He answered quickly. "Rigging is just over six miles of line, sir. Over 156 separate lines at work. The tarred ones on each side of the masts are called 'shrouds' and are permanently fixed."

"Looks like a ladder."

"That it is, as well as holding the mast in place side to side. All other lines are needed to adjust our sails or turn the yardarms to manage the sails or tighten the mast fore and aft."

"And how many are you to sail her?"

"Thirteen in this crew. Taking out the cook, carpenter and sailmaker, we have ten for the rigging."

Jefferson stood at the base of the five steps leading from the main deck to the bridge on the quarterdeck, where the captain was pointing toward something off the port side. The captain had his telescope trained on the commotion. Fox mounted the steps quickly to join the captain. Jefferson followed and saw the last of a flock of seagulls bobbing on the water suddenly taking flight. A shark made a feeble snap at the gulls, missed, and splashed hard. Jefferson heard the first mate laugh and looked toward the deck. "Captain? It is Mister Jefferson."

The captain turned, put down his telescope, and grinned. "Come up, Mister Jefferson." James backed to the rail where he could easily hear the captain. He stood behind the helmsman, who glanced at the compass inset into the binnacle atop the chest, which shaded it from the sun. Unlike the bright amber varnish on the wood trim or the cream- and lemon-colored paint on the sides of the *Ceres*, the chest was a dull black with chipped paint. When Jefferson eased past it, he shook hands with the captain and looked at the large brass-ringed floating compass. "Clever design, that, to rotate in this chest."

The captain said, "Called a binnacle. Holds all my navigation instruments." Each of the square drawers was edged in a bright Chinese red. "Clever. That bright a color."

"It certainly does facilitate access to the right instrument in any weather or light."

"Perhaps during our voyage, you would be kind enough to offer me an introduction to your navigational instruments, glasses, and sea compass. You see, as a surveyor, I have some familiarity with gauging distances on land, even substantial distances and with odd angles, but at sea, I have no bearings."

"Be most pleased to do so. In fact, just before noon today, meet me on deck. I'll have you shoot a sighting with me."

The captain left the bridge, leaving the first mate to entertain Jefferson. Both appeared to be oblivious to James's presence.

"Did he say a sighting?"

Fox smiled. "Best be there a tick early."

"Certainly, will do so."

"As to the compass. Not much different than one you would use on land, but for floating in double gimbals to let it remain level in spite of the motion of the ship."

"I have heard of an experiment placing the magnetic needle in an oil bath to dampen the gyrations at sea."

Fox said, "I have seen one, but this is dry. As it has proved reliable and the experiments with liquid mounts have been inconsistent, he plans to use his compass for some years yet."

"His?"

"Yes. The binnacle is the property of Captain Tracey. He's had the same chest since his first ship. All his instruments and charts go where he goes. See the tie-down ring on the deck and the one at the base of the chest?"

"Now that you mention it, I do. I expected to see a wheel on the bridge, but you only have a tiller."

"Captain's preference. You see, a tiller offers an ease of repair that a wheel does not. If a wheel breaks, you have to replace it and all of the connecting lines, gears, wheels, and rods from the wheel to a tiller below deck. Now, if this were a cargo ship of greater tonnage, the mechanical advantage of a wheel, and the ability for two men to muscle it in heavy weather, would be attractive. But look, we get the same advantage from a simple pulley running from the underside of the tiller, near the handle, to the far side of the deck, just under the rail. And see how the pulley lines run through this brass lever on the handle? I can flip it and lock the rudder in any position."

"Ingenious."

After tapping each of the ropes to see how they responded, Jefferson looked at the small rope mats under each pulley. "What are those for?"

"Called thump mats. First, they keep the ship from eating itself by eliminating the chaffing of continual rubbing. They also reduce the thumping of the block on the deck, which can be quite annoying in the captain's cabin, which is directly below this quarterdeck."

"Chaffing. Interesting."

"She's exceptional in how she rights. We took her to sea and into a storm to test her mettle. See if she would go under in a storm, before Captain Tracey bought her. I held a hard course. She heeled over so far that the tips of her yardarms touched the whitecaps, yet she righted fair and fast when allowed to do so. She's a good ship. Safe and sound."

A cry came from the sailor at the mast top as James was leaving the deck. Jefferson could not make out his words, but his meaning was clear as he pointed off their port bow. The first mate pulled a small telescope from the cabinet and offered it to Jefferson. "Dolphins at play, a pod of them if you care for a closer look."

Several hours later, McArthur sent James topside with a bucket of kitchen scraps. When James saw the cabin boy throwing slops from chamber pots over the starboard side, he went to the opposite railing to dump the scraps. He was about to throw the bucket's contents overboard when a sailor grabbed his arm.

"Watch the wind, lad, or it'll blow back on ya."

"Thank you, sir."

"Sir? No more a 'sir' than you."

"But I am a servant, a slave of Mister Jefferson."

"Not here, you ain't. No such animal on this ship. You be as free as that there gull."

After he emptied the bucket, James reached into the slit in his boot top and took out a folded scrap of paper, opened it, and let the wind blow away the remainder of the powder that allowed him to be here, on the way to France and a new life. He held the stained paper by a corner before letting the wind spin it to the sea.

That night, James ladled his stew from the recessed pot after the sailors had theirs and were seated and joined the cook. "Donald?"

"What?"

"Why don't we eat with the other sailors?"

He looked down but then said, "I usually do, but I don't know what to do. You're na' a sailor here or a man's servant there, so I did not know how to serve you without offense."

"There be no offense. Do you think the other sailors might allow my company?"

"Yes. I think it may be welcomed."

James picked up his bowl and followed the cook to the suspended tables. Without being asked, the men slid over to make room for both. Overhead, an oil lamp cast a pale glow about the area.

At first, they just told him their names and ate in silence. Then Rudy, a swarthy man who sported a red kerchief at his neck, asked, "Is it true you play the fiddle for them passengers?"

"Yes. Every night."

"Think you might know some tunes we'd like?"

"Only one way to find out. Be happy to." Suddenly the others relaxed and asked about where he had lived and started telling tales of past voyages. The French sailor, called only Frenchie, showed James knots and handiwork of woodcarvings. The Bristol sailor, Andrew, talked to him about how other cooks had managed their dinners. The Swede, Lars, asked about his family.

Provisions in midday for the crew were often only a thick soup or stew. And apples. An apple a day per man. So common were apples at Monticello that James was surprised that they were given such reverence aboard the *Ceres*. Later he learned from a sailor that on a prior long voyage he had contracted some scurvy disease in which his gums swelled, and his teeth came loose. Once they found land and he ate limes, his health was restored.

That night James overheard the sailors talking and was taken by the notion that the ship had changed. "Sailing from port, she was lazy. Her rigging had slacked in just a few days in port. Lazy for want of work. Like a sailor too long on land needing to earn his callouses all over again. Now she's as tight as a wet barrel and sleek as a fox."

The remnants of land left them by the third day. Dust was washed from the deck and the wet wood scrubbed clean by men on their hands and knees scouring it with blocks of pumice. James thought the gallons of varnish on the upper structures would have been applied to the deck for protection as well. But he soon came to realize that in any wet conditions, fog to downpour, a varnished deck would become glass-slick and treacherous. Soon enough it became evident that there were patterns and routines to be met every hour of every day to fend off the ravages of the sea. Brass was polished daily. The decks were to scrub.

Over several dinners, James learned that wages alone would stand them at home no longer than a month or so. Some of the captains would pay three months in advance. Hoping that it was quickly spent on family or vice, so the sailor had to go to sea again. Many supplemented their wages with earnings from their crafts. One man worked a walrus tooth with a fine-pointed awl, scoring into the ivory a scene of the *Ceres* under full sail in a tall sea. Once completed, he rubbed soot into the lines and, magically, the scene disclosed itself. A thin coat of varnish was applied to protect it. James told Jefferson of it. He asked to see the scrimshaw near the end of the voyage. Once beholding it, he bought it on the spot for a sum the sailor thought handsome enough to bow deeply and pocket the silver coins with a grin.

Soon James learned that weather defined the mettle of a sailor. Rain or shine, dry or wet, in heat or cold, a sailor had to climb the rigging to set or furl the sail, to stand lookout at the bow or atop a mast, and to adjust the lines. Not all did so with the ease of others. On a particularly calm day, the cook told James that if he ever wanted to monkey up the ropes to the crow's nest, this should be the day and promised that he could see almost forever from that spot. With the permission of the first mate, while the captain and passengers were at lunch, James went aloft. He made a slow walk to the rail. Two sailors accompanied him for his safety. One hopped to the rail to steady him as he began his slow crawl up the crossbars. Sailors on deck shouted encouragement. "Don't rely on your fingers, James!" "Hook one arm in, then the other!" Another called, "Keep three contacts. Move only one hand or one foot at a time!"

Just as he heard that last comment, one of his feet slipped off the rope. He caught himself, but looking straight down, past the web of rope to the deck below brought sweat to his brow. Slowly he continued. A sailor on deck, seeing the slip, scampered up the opposite shroud to the platform he called a crow's nest and helped James onto it when he arrived. Holding the tip of the mast like it was gold, James looked over a flat sea and saw whales in the distance. Even in the calm, the ship rolled. The height of the mast magnified this motion. James clutched the mast. Steadying himself, he started a slow and cautious climb down. Once he was on deck again, the others clapped him on the back. He grinned as he made for the kitchen to resume his duties there.

In the galley, McArthur kept a sharp eye on the pot of a boiled beef New England dinner for that evening. Mister Richards had requested it after proclaiming that the rich evening meals were not to his daughter's liking. James chuckled to himself, having seen this play out in the past. Soon enough they would be preparing two dinners, one for the pampered children and another for the adults.

After feeding the crew and passengers, the cook had restored order to his pantry and was putting away the clean dishes that James had washed and dried. James was scouring the pots and pans in silence when McArthur crossed his arms over his belly and leaned back into the railing. "Think you'll like cooking on a ship?"

"I'm learning from you. I like that. But as for living on a ship, I don't know."

"There's much to be said for the life." He held his scarred hand out for James to see. "Don't let this scare you off."

James looked up from scouring a large pot in disbelief.

"When our captain was a fisher, I was with his crew when he sailed out of Peru. One afternoon, a week out we were, the sails caught fire. It was from a hot tar bucket that touched the jib. The fire flashed through the jib, caught the mainsail, and from there, all the rigging was aflame. The captain ordered both the tenders launched at the first of the flame. They laid off, a hundred feet away, while we cut down the masts and dropped the flaming rigging into the sea. Even so, the ship burned almost to the waterline."

"With no sails, you must have been floating like a cork."

McArthur shook his head. "Captain kept the tenders in the water and in shifts we all rowed back toward Peru. Another ship found us, by the purest of luck and mercy of God, after eight days. They had extra timber for a mast. We had canvas and rigging so we were able to sail back to port."

James had stopped working. "Eight days?"

"Yes. We had provisions and a good captain. I'd sail with him to the gates of hell if he asked."

CHAPTER 9

The first days at sea, Jefferson was as jumpy as a squirrel, trying to learn all he could about the instruments of science on board the ship. Chair on deck, book in hand, he read, or pretended to read, *Don Quixote*. When James brought a plate of gingersnaps for the morning amusement of the passengers, Jefferson closed his book and turned to one of the bankers. "I've been thinking that we need a national library," he said. "Every great civilization has one."

When the banker grunted while reaching for a gingersnap, Jefferson took that as encouragement. "Indeed, one of the greatest of tragedies in the past was the burning of the Library of Alexandria. We need our truths to be preserved, ideas to be promulgated, and a place to honor such." He paused for a bite. "Even in the few years since the Revolution, I hear distortions on who wrote what or who voted for what. But for that there are legislative minutes that we need to preserve in a library, a Library of Congress, for the nation." The bald banker nodded and retreated into his own book.

James squinted in the bright sun after being below in the dim kitchen. He saw that the day was fair; light, high clouds hovered on the western horizon. The sails were all opened and full. The wind was from directly behind them. He walked along the rail to the bow and saw that the whitewater tossed up at the bow spread farther than he recalled. Looking back, he saw that the wake of their path seemed longer than in the prior days.

Three sailors marched in a line past Jefferson, who had opened his book again. Lars, the Swede, carried a walnut box by its brass top handle. Andrew and Frenchie trailed after him, but there was no slack in their step.

When the blond sailor stopped at the widest part of the ship on the port rail, he set the case against the solid bulkhead. Taking the tools from their walnut box, he placed the items on the deck at his feet.

He picked up a triangle of wood that was tied from its three corners to a thin line wrapped around a spool. Into the open center of the spool, he passed a loose rod so the line would move freely.

Jefferson had been watching the ritual and now set his book down and went to where the three sailors stood at the rail.

Andrew greeted him. "Good morning, sir."

"Good morning to you. What are you doing with that line?"

"Taking a measure of our speed, sir."

"Can you tell me how, as you do it?"

"Certainly, sir. This here is a measuring cord, and to it we ties a wood triangle, what we call a log, by its three corners. As you see, it's not so much larger than my hand, but sufficient to catch a drag in the water. Now as to the line, the first fifty feet of the line is bare. That gets it over the side and settled in the water. Then the line has a white, heavy thread knotted to it, large enough to both see and feel as the reel plays out the line."

"So, you could take a reading at night if needed?"

"Yes. It is knotted with one knot exactly every forty-eight feet, three inches. I'll let the line run through my fingers as the log gets a purchase in the sea and is pulled away."

Jefferson chuckled. "A log, indeed. Perhaps the first of this measure used a real log."

Lars held the log and passed the rod and spindle to Andrew. Then he dropped the wooden triangle over the side. It fell free of the ship and into the water. But once it took purchase there, Andrew clamped his hand on the rod to stop the line. Then he gently circled the line between his thumb and index finger until the line ran across his palm.

Frenchie held a small sandglass at the ready.

The Swede nodded, and Andrew let the line run free and called,

"Turn." Frenchie flipped the glass. Sand ran through the narrow waist of the glass and all were silent.

Jefferson watched the line run through the sailor's fingers and him nodding and counting aloud as each knot passed over his palm.

He glanced at the sand and pinched the line to stop it just as the sand ran out. He called, "Ten. Ten knots be our speed."

Lars scowled. "Ten? You certain of it?"

He nodded while looking surprised. "We take it again, for sure."

The sailors repeated the ritual and came to the same result.

The Swede grinned. "Ten, it be. I'll tell Cap'n Tracey." He sprinted for the quarterdeck and took the stairs two at a time. The first mate intercepted him. James sensed that this was not to Fox's liking as he put his hand on the Swede's shoulder and stopped him. When the Swede told Fox something, he nodded. Both walked to the captain, where Fox did the talking.

Jefferson was now handling the wet line and pointed to the sandglass. He asked Andrew, "What was the time you measured? Thirty seconds?"

"Twenty-eight, sir. Special glass that shaved off a moment at each end for the turn to be accomplished and order executed."

"So is that how you figure where we are? A compass and speed?"

"In part, sir. At noon, the cap'n takes him a reading that is a far sight better than this old way. But he be a man of certainty and holds to measuring all he can. A cautious man who might favor both belt and braces, if you get my meaning."

Jefferson chuckled. "What do you call that, how you measure the speed?"

"Measuring speed? It's called knots."

"No, that tool. The cased instrument that you are using."

Andrew slowed his speech to be understood. "Oh, that is a log and line. But we say it faster though, like 'log'n'line.'"

"And is ten knots good?"

"Best we ever made. Most ships manage between two and eight knots a day. Figuring the thirty-three hundred miles from Boston to London at this great speed is just a month, not the usual two. Be a quick run to France. Shows the ship is trimmed perfectly now."

"Thank you."

Jefferson returned to his reading in the shade of a filled sail. James knew that his master was just waiting for noon to pounce on the captain for an explanation of how his calculation was made. James decided to be on deck again to see if he was right and to find out just how forbearing the captain was with Jefferson's incessant questioning.

By late morning, James had talked the cook into letting him go on deck to peel the turnips and carrots for the dinner's stew with a knife and wooden bucket for the trimmings. The shade from the sail failed to give relief as noon approached. Jefferson's collar was wet as he remained in his coat on deck awaiting the captain's reading.

James had peeled just over half of the carrots when Captain Tracey took a brass instrument from a case that he left on the quarterdeck's cabinet. Fox followed him with a small chalkboard in one hand and the case in the other.

Jefferson looked up from his book and watched as the captain adjusted the instrument and pointed it toward the horizon. Jefferson's first impression was that it was just a small telescope until he noticed the curved base with a scale on it and two small mirrors, neither one larger than a tax stamp.

The captain held it in his right hand, loosened a screw along the curved base and aimed for the horizon. Then he adjusted the arm that tilted the second mirror and tightened the screw. Taking it from his eye, he was about to read the scale etched in brass along the lower arc to Fox, when Jefferson called from his deck chair. "Captain? Could I have a look at that instrument?" Jefferson slipped a seagull feather that he found on deck into the book and rose from his chair.

Jefferson grinned as he approached the captain. "I am interested in your instrument. Have you a moment to let me examine it? As I think I told you a few days ago, I am a surveyor and acquainted with a variety of measuring instruments, but yours is new to me."

The captain instructed Fox to ring the time and return immediately.

"The sextant is new to most mariners as well. Yet, it has changed our capacity to know our location with a new precision."

From the quarterdeck, the first mate rang the ship's bell. A crisp series of two strikes each for a total of eight.

"What's that bell now?"

"We reset noon by the sun. Take our celestial reading at the same time."

Jefferson set his pocket watch to noon as he asked, "How exactly does this instrument do such a thing?"

"The overall principle is to determine the angle between the sun and horizon. Putting that angle to our chart will tell us our position. Obviously, having an accurate calculation table and chart is essential."

"Interesting!"

"Care to take a sun sighting?"

"I would be most grateful."

"First. Get to the rail and brace yourself, as you will need both hands to shoot a sighting. Lean back so you won't drop it overboard. Now. You see how the scale is on the lower curved piece? The rod is hinged to move along it."

Jefferson took the sextant from the captain before the latter was really ready to hand it over. Jefferson released the clamp and slid it easily. The captain shut his eyes and sighed; Jefferson had lost the reading before it was recorded.

"Here, let me demonstrate." The captain then took the sextant from Jefferson and quickly shot another sighting to verify his memory, knowing it to be a minute off. Putting the sighting tube to his eye, he explained, "You see, there are two mirrors, set together. You sight through the tube and hold on the horizon whilst releasing the clamp and pulling the arm through the arc until the sun appears in the second mirror, then slowly, fine-tune it until the sun is exactly on the horizon. Tighten the clamp so the arm is held fast to the scale. Tilt it to verify the sun is on the horizon. Reshoot if it wobbles. Record the angle and time. Take your reading, then I will be pleased to show you how it is converted into our position, on our charts."

While Jefferson shot the horizon and fiddled with the clamp and knobs, the captain told Fox the reading, which he wrote on the slate. At the captain's nod, Fox quickly went to the captain's cabin, where the navigation table was maintained and left the slate there. Returning to the quarterdeck, he saluted the captain when he looked over from helping Jefferson adjust the mirrors.

"So, now that you have the angle locked in on this brass scale on the curved arm, we can go to my cabin and transfer these numbers to my latitude charts."

Jefferson followed the captain to his cabin. James moved his position on the deck to be able to look into the first of the captain's rooms and hear their conversation. The slate rested beside the boxed sea clock.

The captain's voice boomed from the small cabin, and Jefferson matched his volume to account for the older man's deafness. "We take sightings exactly at noon, and that is when I order the glass turned and the noon bell struck. At night we take a reading off Polaris, the North Star. The angles, horizon to the sun or North Star, are in a table for reference. By knowing the angle and the time we can calculate the distance we are from Greenwich, England."

"How is that?"

The captain went to a globe set in a dark oak frame to the right of the door. "Of course, you know the equator is 360 degrees. A full circle." Slowly spinning the globe, he continued. "Now breaking that number of degrees into the perfect 24-hour day, we find that in one hour, our globe travels fifteen degrees. We also know that the night falls three minutes and 54 seconds earlier each day, or later in the autumn if after the solstice. Thus, if at noon at my location, I take a reading, I know my angle and ascertain the time from my Harrison clock before consulting my charts."

"Your what?"

"Harrison clock. I have the privilege of having one of the first. Accurate to one second a day! The most accurate of any sea clock. With it, I can plot my longitude. You see, I set it to match the time in Greenwich and hold that time as I sail. I take a noon reading and compare my noon to the clock. So that if the difference is one hour..."

Jefferson grinned. "Then we must be at fifteen degrees west of Greenwich. I see how you can then plot that on your nautical chart."

When James told the cook of his observation, McArthur laughed. "Good as the captain's reckoning is, we still need soundings once we approach a coast if we aren't within sight of a lighthouse of a promontory or headland known to the captain."

"I'm afraid I don't know what you're talking about."

"It's a sample of the seabed. Old as Moses. Drop a line over with a brass fitting at the end. In it is a gob of tar. That tar picks up what's on the bottom. At Georges Bank the sand is light and white because it is all crushed-up seashells. Off Block Island it is black mud. Toward Nantucket it is dark sand. A good captain has his notes on charts and knows these things."

Over dinner, Jefferson and the other passengers recounted the wildlife they had seen that day. Petrels and gannets soaring. Hagdons skimming the sea. A pod of dolphins. Cod caught by a crewman for dinner below deck. Jefferson also watched sharks and whales from his chair on deck on those occasions when he looked up from his book. Oddly, Jefferson would recount the adventures of the mad Spaniard to other passengers over dinner as if it were gossip at Monticello, not a book he was translating.

At dinners he saw that the bottles of German hock that he had brought aboard, and shared generously, enhanced the conviviality of his fellow passengers significantly. Alliances were made. Promises given.

Arrangements secured. Mutual friends discovered and business recommendations made. It was all a small spiderweb of the wealthy and powerful. The bearded banker wanted funds from the new America. The other banker represented the interests of a Londoner who wanted to establish trade through France, as England could not trade directly with the new nation. The young ladies continued to eat earlier than the others and retire to their cabin to play games of cards.

Into the second week, the fresh stores of meats were diminished, as were the more fragile of the vegetables and fruits. A small pig was butchered below deck, the bloodied straw tossed overboard discretely after darkness to protect the sensibilities of the ladies on board. McArthur guided his long knife to separate the animal into usable parts. Ultimately, diners enjoyed pork roast, then chops, then stew while the crew had roasted ribs, then stew from the unnamed trimmings.

Seventeen days out, Henry, the oldest of the sailors, came into the galley holding a bucket of several mackerel. The black stripes against the light green of their backs glistened as the fish squirmed. He passed the bucket to James. "Seems that your Mister Jefferson got fine hits on his line just before noon. Good school of mackerel. They'll snap at anything, so he was able to put a line in several times and got a mess of three- and four-pounders. Landed them well. We gutted them on deck so's you can clean 'em easier here. Cap'n Tracey says serve it to the passengers for this dinner. With potatoes."

"Did he now?"

"Yes. Any leftover can go into the crew stew. Oh, when I tossed the entrails overboard, several gulls made a mad dash for the guts."

James looked at him. "Gulls? Are we almost to land?"

He shrugged. "Could be a couple days. What was dinner going to be tonight?"

McArthur chimed in, "Chicken and dumplings. Guess the chicken gets another day on this earth. James, pull more carrots and potatoes from the bin."

Returning with the added vegetables, James was excited but tried not to show it. "If he saw gulls, doesn't that mean we were close to land?"

"Sometimes. But I didn't smell land when I was on deck at noon to confer with the first mate about the menu. Before he caught these fish."

"Can you smell it? Really?"

"I can. Maybe I just know when we get close by the birds and the way the sea starts to shift color. Maybe I just imagine it because some gulls can be far out to sea. Or hope it when we are on the homeward leg of a sail."

As James set to work, he wondered what his life would be like in France. When he was sent topside with the scrap bucket, he tossed the potato peels and fish trimmings overboard as usual. But the gulls swooped at him, shrieking, so many and so fast that he held the bucket in front of his face to avoid being pecked by accident.

Dinner that night at the captain's table was filets of mackerel and vegetables. A plain meal that the girls attended. Jefferson declared the German white wine as perfect. The conversation centered on men boasting of hunting or fishing triumphs and scant discussion about politics. Whitehead invited Jefferson to fish for salmon at his estate in Scotland and visit him in London, when possible. The girls were dismissed as James cleared the plates.

When James returned and served the brandy, Richards was saying that just before they sailed, his Methodist minister announced from his Manhattan pulpit that anyone continuing to own slaves would be expelled from membership in the church. When Richards looked up at James, he stopped talking. Whitehead started to say something about the Quakers but stopped when Jefferson cleared his throat.

James poured their drinks into small glasses and left the captain's decanter on the sideboard. As he looked up, he was close enough to read the stitchery of a small-framed item he had noticed while playing music but had been unable to read from the distance. In red thread, with ornate capitals with trailing curled ends, was stitched "Do Right and Fear Not."

The "and" was in smaller letters and set at an angle between the two admonitions. This heartfelt message was no doubt the handiwork of the captain's wife or daughter. Later the girls were invited to abandon their game of cards and join the men to listen to James play the violin.

After washing out the crew's stewpot and taking a fast walk around deck, James went below to his bunk in the forecastle. Several of the sailors were sitting on the edge of their bunks. Some were carving on wood or bone while others mended trousers. Some made gull squawking sounds for his benefit. James ignored them and put his nose into a small book of French stories that he had purchased in Boston. After lanterns were doused, James slept briefly then awoke in a bad temper. Irritated by the ongoing chatter, James went above just as the watch changed at midnight.

The heavens were clear. The stars wove a thick blanket above them. James went to the bow, where his view of the sea and sky was unimpaired. Henry came forward, firming up a line and stopping a luffing of the forward mainsail. "You? What're you doing up?"

James answered, "Can't sleep." Henry undid the hitch over the belaying pin and the line was ready to pull. James got up, helped bring the line tight with a hand-over-hand haul. Once right, Henry slipped the line around the lower part of the pin and took a turn around the pin's top. Repeating this, he soon formed a figure eight, then snugged off the hitch and coiled the remaining rope and tied it to the pin.

Henry said, "I get that way close to land too. Sailors know."

James shook his head. "I'm no sailor. Just wanted some fresh air."

"I'm taking the tiller this watch, if you want a try at it, come on back with me."

James trotted after him. Even in the moonlight he saw that the tiller was a beautiful run of oak at least a foot wide and tall and stretching ten feet back to the stern. The varnish glowed amber in the lantern's light. Hip high, Henry's hand fell naturally to the handle.

Henry motioned to a rope running across the tiller, under a brass lever. "That's the tiller lock so I can hold a course while I take a reading or trim a sail. Usually, I steer free when I am at the tiller." He pointed to the compass, with a face larger than a dinner plate and letters all around the edge. "We hold to a course set by the captain but keep a watch so as not to ram a floating log or fail to spot another ship or read its banner to be clear about its intentions. The sails do most of the direction finding and I just make the finer adjustments to our course. Here. Take it. Hold the needle just where it is." The small lantern beside the compass illuminated the thin needle. As James moved the tiller with care, he saw the adjustment and heard the soft *whoosh* of the lines running smoothly through the wood pulleys. When the needle slipped too far off, James heard a sail snap and quickly eased the tiller back.

"You've got the makings of a good tar if you want to sign on. Good balance. Strong. Eyes and ears about you. I venture you could scramble the shrouds with the best of 'em in a day or two. Smart. You get on with the saltiest of us. And Cook likes you. He'd put in a good word with the captain." Henry took out a stub of a pipe already filled with tobacco, opened the lantern door, and paused.

James asked, "How long before land, do you reckon?"

"You mean France? Another day or so."

James nodded, thinking that he was between two minds of wanting to get to the adventure in France but not wanting the freedom and newness of the voyage to end.

"Smell it? Smoke."

James felt a spike of fear and quickly scanned the deck to see if something was aflame.

Henry laughed. "Not us. Sniff off the port side. And come back."

James went to the rail and sniffed, as a dog would test the wind for a scent of a deer, then returned. "Perhaps I am imagining it, but I think I do smell smoke."

He grinned. "The Irish smoke their fish to preserve 'em for winter. Cheaper than salt. We can smell it far out to sea if the wind's just right."

James looked at the sails, canted to use the wind coming off the land. He went to the rail again and cupped his hands to block out any hint of light from the ship's lanterns but saw nothing. He went back to the deck. "Nothing. I couldn't see anything."

"We'll have the cliffs of Ireland along our port side most of tomorrow. We'll not make land, but if you are so hungry for dirt, come back up with the next watch and check from the bow." He looked at James and smiled. "Or climb the rigging now and see if you can see any of their bonfires."

"You mean we are close enough to see land?"

"From the crow's nest, top of the main."

James felt his stomach tighten when he considered climbing the shroud lines again. "Climb it? At night?"

"I could have the lads rig a bosun's chair and hoist you up if you haven't got the stones to make the climb again."

"Now?"

"No better time. Sea's calm. Dry night, no dew on the lines. Take it slow and hold on. One hand for you and the other for the ship. Feet, one at a time after both hands are set. And fall into the lines if you slip so that you can hook an elbow." He held his pipe against the candle flame, closed the lantern door, and then drew on the stem until the tobacco glowed red in the darkness.

At the railing, James held the tarred lines running to the mast and carefully swung up, so his feet were on the varnished wood. He climbed as awkward as a toddler in the dark. The rope shifted under his feet. For an instant James thought he was falling. Hands set; he moved the other foot to the higher hemp rung up the shroud. Above the railing, he could hear the sea ticking against the hull as they cut through the water's light chop.

With the cautiousness of a cat, James advanced. The shroud narrowed as he climbed. The lines came to a point, not at the top of the mast, but just under the top royal sail. From the deck, he had seen sailors scramble up the shroud lines like monkeys and somehow find themselves on the foot ropes of the top royals, climbing out along the yard to let a sail out or gather it in, but James had no such intention.

Clinging to the top of the shroud line with white knuckles, he smelled the tar of the whipped end of ropes and nothing else. He listened for the hiss of the sea at the bow and heard only his heart drumming. At the base of the crow's nest now, he reconsidered climbing onto it but dismissed the idea. He'd had the helping hand of a good sailor before, but now he was alone.

Turning his face toward the amber dots he saw along the horizon, he smelled smoke. Not coal or wood, smoke but something richer. Almost like seaweed on the fire at the beach near Boston, but more acidic. He let his eyes find the stars and then looked down. The darkness of the horizon without stars shocked him. Then he saw a line of eight, then ten amber lights again. Fires along the coast. Land. Ireland.

James held on to the rigging until his hands started to shake from fatigue. He let his feet slide past the footrope into the rigging. He sat on the footropes and cocked his elbow around the thicker rope for support. For some time, he stayed suspended in space watching the night fires ahead.

A soft whistle pulled his attention away from the shore fires of fishermen. Henry was waving his arm at him. Once James hailed him back, Henry pointed off the starboard beam, where all the sailors on that watch had gathered. Amidships, in the opposite direction of his gaze, the sea had become a light green as though there were a thousand lanterns somehow burning below the surface. Soon James made out the forms of great fish, longer than a man's body, that shot up from the water then arced back into it smooth as could be. First a dozen then three or four times as many so that the sea churned and radiated. With each leap and dive of the fish, the water glowed brighter. The crew watched silently, reverently. Only Henry stayed at his post, minding the tiller. After a few minutes, the school submerged, and the lighted sea went dark again.

James made a slow and clumsy descent. Once down, he started for the quarterdeck to ask Henry about the fish and why the sea had been alight. Just as he started up the steps, Henry turned the sandglass and rang the bell for the four watch to come up. It seemed impossible that James had spent just shy of four hours aloft, watching stars and Irish fishermen's smoking fires, and great fish playing in a glowing ocean. His watch was called. He turned for the kitchen.

Later that day, James told McArthur about the light in the sea and the great fish. He laughed. "They was no more a fish than you or me. They was dolphins. Give birth to their young like a cow, but in the water."

"They swam so fast. And there were so many of them."

"Good omen. I heard stories about men being shipwrecked and getting pushed to shore by them animals. If true, they must have a kind soul."

James stared at him. "Do you think animals have souls?"

"I know there is an order to things beyond me. But some things just ain't right, whether you believe in souls or not." McArthur lowered his voice and came closer to James. "I know it's not my concern, and I'll say this but once. You'll be a free man when your foot hits that French dock. There is no need for you to go back as a slave, you know. France is a free country for people of color." James felt a cold stab of fear then decided to trust the man.

"I've heard that, but where would I go? What could I do?"

"Sail with us. You are liked by the men and captain. You could learn the deck work as well as galley work and become a high-share sailor."

"What do you mean by 'high-share'?"

"Every man sails for a wage or a share. On a whaler or merchant ship you usually split the profit. Captain Tracey has fifty-five percent and the crew has shares in the profit according to their agreement with him, based on their duties."

"But I could not land in America again. Runaway slaves have a bounty on them."

"Then don't go back. Sign on to a French ship. You talk their lingo. I seen you and Frenchie jawing away."

James did not answer but went about his tasks in silence.

On the eighteenth day, James was on deck when Fox called that they had arrived in French waters. The captain came on deck and motioned for James. "Now to anchor. Do you think your Mister Jefferson might want to watch as we arrive?"

"Yes, sir. I'll advise him immediately."

James hurried to Jefferson's cabin. Once notified, Jefferson came up and stood beside the captain as the ship approached the harbor. Soon the captain cut sail and slowed the approach. The docks were filled with craft loading and unloading. Within moments, the captain pointed to a man standing in the stern of a long boat being rowed out to the ship. It flew a red flag from a pole at the bow.

Jefferson pointed. "Is that a warning flag, like yellow for the pox?"

The captain suppressed a laugh. "No. He is the harbor pilot. He'll tell us when we can dock and unload. If you, or any of the others, care to disembark earlier, I am sure they would take you ashore in their tender."

The square-rigged sails were slacked as the *Ceres* drew closer to the harbor. First the top royals, then the top gallants, and finally the mains were stowed. Then men aloft bunched in the canvas and tied it to the yards and yardarms, leaving only the triangular sails. The ship slowed. The captain steered so that the wind on the port side was used to advantage.

The sailors became quiet and tense as cats sensing a mouse. When he discerned the wind was as he wished, Captain Tracey barked orders, setting the crew into motion.

"Haul down the jib!" The front sail dropped, and canvas bunched on deck.

"Haul up spanker!" The rear sail was hoisted to catch the wind from the port side.

"Hard a port!" The helmsman leaned his full weight against the tiller and the stern swung sideways.

Partway through the ship's arc, the captain shouted again. "Let go anchor!" The chain rattled through the metal-lined openings in the railing at the bow.

"Brail the spanker!" This call set the men to hauling down the rear sail that they had just used to turn the ship.

The anchor caught on the bottom and the ship spun, finishing the motion initiated by the captain's many adjustments to sail so that her nose was into the wind and the anchor chain held fast.

Without any added orders, the sailors set about squaring the deck, trimming the yards by tying up the lines holding the sail, coiling the many ropes on deck, and hanging them in proper order.

The harbormaster held the ship at anchor for three hours before medical clearance was given to land and a space opened at the dock.

BOOK II

FRANCE

1784–1790

*Wherein James discovers the most elevated of French cuisine
as Jefferson's industrial spy while apprenticing in a renowned kitchen,
cooks for royalty,
is* chef de cuisine *in Jefferson's American Embassy in Paris, and
breathes free.*

CHAPTER 10

As the ship docked at Le Havre, all of the passengers were dressed in their best clothes and assembled on deck to make their farewells and watch the commotion of tossing lines to the dock and pulling the ship tight against it. A tall man carrying a large black valise came aboard as soon as the gangplank was settled upon the dock. He made a loud announcement in French directed at the passengers. When Jefferson appeared puzzled, James whispered, "He's a banker offering to convert money into French livres, for a small fee."

Jefferson turned toward his cabin. "That could prove to be a convenience. Bring him along so I can conduct the matter in private."

After leading the banker to Jefferson's cabin, James lingered in the doorway to determine if the banker spoke English. On seeing that he did not and Jefferson's efforts to communicate were hopeless, James smoothly introduced himself in French and determined the terms of the exchange which he then explained to Jefferson. With a nod, Jefferson authorized the transaction and watched the conversion of his dollars and English crowns into French livres. When the banker went to find his next customer, Jefferson said, "You astound me. Did you learn all that just from that French sailor on the ship?"

James suppressed a laugh. "As you say, sir."

Jefferson and Patsy took to lodgings near the harbor for a week to recover their balance after the passage. James was dispatched to conduct other business for Jefferson. He immediately organized the disposition of the cargo into several wagons and sent them on their way to a warehouse in Paris selected by Benjamin Franklin. Then he secured a brace of horses for the phaeton, managed the transfer of the carriage to a stable, and oversaw its reassembly.

James was then entrusted with seventy-two livres and sent ahead to make arrangements for rooms at a small rustic inn in Rouen to provide a day of respite at the midpoint of the journey to Paris. James hired a sturdy horse, made his way, and secured the room. He stabled the horse and explored the town. To his surprise, there were several stonemasons at the cathedral working on the bell tower. *They're all darker than me.* He watched them while he ate at an outdoor table beside a small inn. They took no notice of him.

Once Jefferson and Patsy were ready to travel, James took their luggage to the carriage, hitched horses to the sporty open phaeton, and drove to their dockside inn. Beggars milled around the tall wheels of the carriage as they boarded. Jefferson tossed a few coins to the side of the dock and the crowd scrambled for them, opening the pathway.

It seemed that just as soon as James believed that he had any understanding of Jefferson, the man completely confounded him. Going to France, he took crates of German wines and read a book written in Spanish. But for Marie's tutoring and practice with her, James would have been as mute as a stone. Confusing the matter even more was the fact that Jefferson had a pause in his speech, a stutter he called it, that seemed to occur whenever he was pressed into a new situation. Poised and charming at Monticello, he became a schoolboy complete with blushing silence when confronted by the dockworkers wanting to know which cases were to go to the inn and which were to be loaded on the first wagon.

While he and his daughter were enchanted in Rouen by the cathedral and its dyed windows, he was somewhat displeased by the accommodations, which were more provincial than he desired. He seemed heedless that the funds he provided James went only so far after consideration of the lodging of the horses and also their feed.

The summer of 1784 was warmer than usual. In spite of the heat, Patsy seemed to enjoy the overland journey from Rouen to Gaillon through Vernon, Mantes, Meulan, and Triel. But as they approached Paris, the sultry heat of August made the dusty carriage ride through the rich farmland irritating. Patsy fanned herself continually while Jefferson tried to read in spite of jolting over rutted roadways. Finally, the tall stone barricade surrounding Paris appeared in the distance. Jefferson put his book into his valise and pulled out a folder of papers. He had James halt the carriage while he consulted his letter of directions and smiled. "There she is, James. That's Paris. We are on the instructions precisely. That should be the Neuilly Bridge straight ahead." As they drove closer, they found their progress slowed as they shared the narrow roadway with the parade of farm wagons and people leaving the city carrying empty baskets after having sold their goods.

As they approached the tollbooth at the Neuilly Gate its operation became clear to James. The booth itself looked like a miniature castle that he had seen in Jefferson's books about Germany. Several soldiers lingered in the shade while another stood blocking the way of those wanting to enter the city. After extracting a coin or several, he stepped aside to allow passage. When they were a few carriages away from the gate, Jefferson passed his small leather coin purse to James to pay the toll. A uniformed soldier took the toll from the several coins that James held in his palm.

Aggressive beggars in ragged, dun-colored attire surrounded the elegant carriage as James started to drive into the city. The stench from their sweating bodies and the rotting garbage piled outside the city wall exceeded any odor James had encountered on the plantation or at Boston Harbor. Jefferson tossed a few coins to the side of the carriage. As the beggars scrambled for them, James hurried the team forward onto the city's cobblestones. Just inside the gate, the buildings seemed familiar to James. Buildings were one and two floors in height, built of wood and fieldstone. The bland, earthen tones and raw wood framing echoed the trade houses at Monticello and the small homes in Boston. As they progressed, the buildings became more complex. Rough stone faces and planked doorways gave way to whitewashed walls, terra cotta–tiled roofs, and woodwork that was well crafted and painted.

Jefferson tapped James and pointed to the right. Turning onto the wider street, a new world emerged. The buildings were all three stories high and built one next to the other forming solid walls on either side of the street. The colors were as nature intended, pale limestone, pink marble, and granite in shades from light gray to coal black. Massive blocks of stone were fitted with precision. Many of these buildings had coppered roofs that had aged to a pale green.

James craned his neck looking up at the ornate ironwork on some rooflines. A shop displayed hats for ladies behind a large glass window with lettering in gold on it. The creamy limestone of the building only served to make the shimmering silk, jewel-colored ribbons and feathers on the hats more dramatic. They passed several statues of the current and former kings. The narrow side streets and shadowed walkways were filled with well-dressed men and the various trades making deliveries. A baker's boy with a basket on his back scurried along the walkway with rounds of bread stacked to the basket top. A girl with a rack on her back sold firewood door to door.

As they jolted down the cobbles, they came to an area that offered various foods. It was a banquet laid out in the windows of small shops. James could hardly keep his eyes on the street amid the swirl of pedestrians and carriages. Often the neat script of the signs above the door was accompanied with a picture of the type of food for sale. The *charcuteries* had meats, *boulangeries* breads, *pâtisseries* pastries; shops with roasted game were called *rôtisseries*. Some shops sold whole meals to carry home, *traîteurs*, and coffeehouses, where men were drinking cups of coffee.

Older men sold squares of gingerbread from small carts. A woman had a tray of apples that hung from a strap around her neck. Somehow the aroma of the gingerbread and apples and baking bread rose above the stench of the sewage running along the side of the street.

The congestion and sewage diminished somewhat as they drove

into an area with large residences and small graveled entrances, just big enough for a few carriages, behind iron gates. At Jefferson's command, James pulled the team of horses to a halt in front of a residence that Jefferson indicated on the Cul-de-sac Taitbout on the right bank of the river.

James looked at the elegant three-story residence in dark stone. Tall iron rail fencing enclosed the entire property. It was more magnificent than any home he could recall seeing in America, yet modest in contrast to the few estates they had just passed with lawns, refined gardens, and manicured hedges.

James looked back when Jefferson made some grunt of disapproval. James saw he was frowning and glaring at the gate to the residence. Suddenly, Jefferson stood and opened the door of the carriage. "I'll be but a moment." He easily sprang to the ground. He stopped and again checked his letter of instruction to verify the address before opening the gate to the graveled carriage entryway. In long strides, he passed the huge front door, around the side and in a few minutes had returned to the carriage.

"Empty! Not a stick of furnishings to be seen. And it needs some renovation before it is fit for us." His voice softened as he considered his options, then he snuffed and resumed. "And the size. I don't know if it is sufficient for the prestige and entertaining that is associated with the position George wants me to present here. It looks like the smallest of the estates we have passed in this section of the city."

Patsy took her father's hand to calm him. "Couldn't you just tell the president to rent a larger one for you?"

Her question seemed to put water on his flames. "Dear child. I understood he had already paid a year lease on it, so best we make it suffice and see how we can manage."

"It does have good grounds."

"Yes. They seem to have hidden the most glorious of its features from view. It has a courtyard and two gardens that we could easily improve with some American plantings."

She smiled. "See? I knew you would find a way to make it yours."

Jefferson patted her hand. "But not until they complete repairs and a renovation I already have in mind. James, now that we have seen it, best we go to our temporary lodging to get out of the sun and our dusty attire."

James drove to the residence Jefferson called the Hôtel d'Orléans, barely understanding his pronunciation and requiring the assistance of several different groups of soldiers they passed in their travels. Ultimately, they were directed to a large, private residence near the royal palace on the right bank of the Seine. The accommodations were shabby. Upon inquiry, they discovered that the correct Hôtel d'Orléans was on the left bank and serviceable until they located an appropriate residence.

After six weeks, they moved the furnishings and still-unpacked crates to the Hôtel de Landron on the Cul-de-sac Taitbout.

Jefferson sent for the same milliner who provided hats for the court's ladies, a stay maker, mantua maker, a dressmaker, and a cobbler to re-invent his daughter as a French gentlewoman. Thereafter, he enrolled Patsy in the Abbaye de Penthemont, a convent school for young ladies, where she remained during the week and visited Jefferson only on week-ends or other special occasions. The fact that this was a Catholic school created much consternation for many of his associates. Jefferson passed these comments aside with a casual remark that his daughter was not learning religion but French through immersion.

As was his manner, Jefferson made the residence his own by renam-ing the Hôtel de Landron as the Hôtel Tetebout, a variation of the street's name that was for some reason easier for him to pronounce. Jefferson had remodeled a room into a library by adding bookshelves, knocking down a wall to create a grander entrance, and furnishing it with the fin-est of modern French appointments.

Settling into Paris was much more than the madness that James ex-pected. While attending to his master's morning needs, James listened to

Jefferson's plans for the residence and for his new position in France, as though Jefferson were testing his thoughts aloud. Once prepared for the day, Jefferson's demands for things that were not attainable and calls for constant attention made the unpacking and settling into a new home a swirl of confusion. For almost two months, James accompanied Jefferson to the finest of salons to select draperies, to craftsmen to find furnishings worthy of the American residence, and to galleries crowded with paintings, statuary, and fine glass chandeliers with hundreds of cut teardrops that cast sparkles.

During his initial ventures with the merchants of Paris, Jefferson soon validated what James had feared upon their arrival at Le Havre. Although Jefferson had studied the language in school, his instructor was a man from Scotland who had transmitted his deep brogue to Jefferson, who now spoke a completely unintelligible form of French. Clearly, he knew some of the written language. He read what street signage there was and was the first to read any contract for his purchases before handing it off to James to verify the contents. This discovery, coupled with his occasional stuttering, put him into a mood or sulk every time they went to a new vendor.

The city was a tangle of streets. James found no pattern to them at all but for walls encircling the oldest part of the city and then another wall encircling the next layer of the growth of the city. Each wall had tollbooths. The continual extraction of tolls was bothersome to James, who had to halt frequently and to Jefferson, who was continually digging coins from his purse. At the center of the city, the streets swirled like a whirlwind. Jefferson repeatedly explained that medieval cities were constructed in a manner to confound invaders and limit their vision or arrow's flight to a short span before the street twisted against them.

Within days, the house was teeming with deliveries of all manner of things from furniture and carpets to linens and blankets. The finest of appointments in artwork, clocks, silver platters, and teapots arrived at the house and were positioned with care. Noting that Jefferson was appointing a vacant residence, a gallery owner recommended a house master who would hire the staff for his new residence. Jefferson hired him quickly.

Beyond his frustration with the language, Jefferson needed to shed his own rustic attire and adopt the foppish peacockery of the French. Seeing that he appeared the country bumpkin in contrast to the flash of those with whom he would be meeting, he consulted Franklin and found a tailor. Days became a flurry of measuring and selecting fabrics from bolts of cloth, each finer than the one before it. Shimmering silks were selected in pale pastels, velvets in dark woodland greens and the deep reds of Jefferson's favorite wine. Soon parcels arrived at the residence holding laced collars, velvet frock coats, black boots, the latest, glistening red leather shoes, and a jeweled side sword. A hairdresser powdered his hair daily and set his wig for appearances at court. Jefferson was reinventing himself in the model of the French.

After the days of going with Jefferson and translating for him, James spent his evenings opening crate after crate of the kitchen materials and stocking the pantry with treasures from Virginia. Finally, he got to the crates of books. James smiled as he removed each from the container and organized them as Jefferson had them at Monticello. James knew the order well.

When James reported that all the crates had been unpacked, Jefferson sent him to rent a pianoforte, buy sheet music for violin and pianoforte, and a music stand.

Now appointed to his liking, Jefferson was in a mood to take up residence. He ordered James to get the carriage ready and drive to his new residence on an unseasonably warm October day. Jefferson had dressed in his new French attire. As soon as the horses came to a full halt on the graveled area in front of the new residence, the tall entrance doors swung open and a parade of eight servants lined up against the gray stone face of the building with their hands clasped before them. Three pallid men and five pale women all wore various arrangements of black attire from short coats and knee britches for the men to shifts and fitted dresses for the women. After the servants had formed an orderly row, a tall man in a coat more elegant than Jefferson's made a grand sweep from the entrance to the carriage and opened the door for Jefferson.

"James. This is Marc, the *maître d'hôtel.*" Even with Jefferson's horrid accent, James understood that Marc was the manager of the house and that all servants reported to him. While shaving Jefferson the next morning, James was able to clarify that he did not report to Marc but took his instruction only from Jefferson.

Within weeks, Jefferson's daily schedule was running smoothly. Marc had the house in order to Jefferson's liking and had passable English skills. James settled into his small room in the attic with the other house servants. His room was no wider than the stretch of his arms, but tall enough so he did not need to stoop to get into the narrow bed or access the small wardrobe that was shoved against the chimney. James left the wardrobe there to insulate the room from the heat of the hearth cooking in summer but planned to move it to use the chimney's warmth in winter. Two gardeners and a stable boy had cots in the stable behind the house. Casual meals were coming on time from the small kitchen on the ground floor while elaborate dinners were catered to the residence.

During the fall of 1784, Paris seemed to James to be a city of continual disruption and contradiction. Although Jefferson had talked about training James as his chef, he had required that James serve as his interpreter while gathering furnishings, altering the building, and going to meetings to do anything to forward his plans. Throughout the winter months, Jefferson's mood lightened. He seemed to resume his attention to matters of state with interest and found a place in the social life of Paris.

Jefferson soon abandoned his agrarian schedule, ruled by sun and crops, for one placing him in contact with those in commerce. As such, his day began at ten, when the courts opened. At noon, when the *Bourse* opened for trading and financial transactions, he met with investors, trade partners and bankers. All public transactions were suspended between two and five for lunch and liaisons of a romantic or private commercial nature. After five, theater, a late meal called a *souper*, and socialization consumed Jefferson until after midnight. This irritated John Adams, who chaffed at such excesses and lectured Jefferson with some regularity on the virtue of adopting simplicity in both attire and speech.

When John and Abigail Adams sailed for London in the spring of 1785, Jefferson took their recommendation and hired Adrien Petit, who had been their house manager and whose command of English was excellent. Petit arrived on a Sunday morning, by hired carriage. Jefferson was surprised to discover this man with a gigantic reputation was a mere wisp who emerged in an elegant light blue frock coat with matching breeches. The coat's velvet collar was in the deepest blue. He took three steps toward Jefferson and bowed. *"Monsieur Jefferson, Je suis Adrien Petit."* Then he changed to flawless English. "I was the *maître d'hôtel* at the Adams residence." His bow was graceful. His hand swept just above the ground.

As he approached Jefferson, it became evident that his wig was well powdered. His face was a ghostly pale. His fish-belly pallor contrasted to the robust farmers in fields and tanned and beefy merchants on wagons drawn into the city. On closer inspection, Jefferson discerned that his face was powdered to hide deep pox scars. He scrutinized the man who he had inherited when John and Abigail Adams left for London, wondering if John had misrepresented the man's talents.

Jefferson paused and revised his offer. "I fear that position is currently filled, but I am in need of a junior houseman to assist me in the daily operation of the residence, and a personal valet once James, my servant, is no longer in residence. I understood from Mister Adams that such an arrangement would suit you. At your prior salary, of course."

Wincing, Petit forced a smile and bowed slightly. "It does." Within a week, he had slipped into the role of valet for Jefferson and left Marc to manage the house.

Life at the residence went according to Jefferson's plan for frequent lavish ambassadorial functions ranging from elaborate dinners to teas and dances during which he found opportunities for the continued improvement of relations and trade between France and the United States. Struggles about tariffs were managed and resolved. Matters regarding the capture of American vessels by Barbary pirates required ongoing attention and efforts to seek the release of American sailors and their ships. Unlike the other sailing nations, the United States had no treaty with the warlords and sultans of the Barbary region. As such, American goods were the objects of their prey. Sailors were imprisoned by the Mohammedans and used as slaves. However, those who converted to the religion of their captors were freed; the Prophet Muhammad forbade slavery of others sharing that faith.

In May of 1785, grave news arrived, conveyed to Jefferson by his friend Lafayette, who had just returned from America. He carried a letter with the particulars of the death of Jefferson's youngest daughter, Lucy, in the winter of 1784, at Eppington. Not yet three, her death from whooping cough was deeply felt by Jefferson. His loss was only partly assuaged by his deep immersion in his work and knowledge that the Eppes had done all they could for her, having lost one of their own children to the same contagion in the prior week. While briefly considering bringing his other daughter to Paris, Jefferson decided that it would be best for her to remain in the maternal care of her aunt.

When the lease expired in the fall of 1785, Jefferson decided to enhance the official residence. As the Minister Plenipotentiary to France, he moved his residence, furnishings, servants, and all manner of items to the much larger and grander residence, the Hôtel de Langeac on the Champs-Elysées, some 200 steps from the palace. It was one of the few residences in Paris to be fitted with both running water and water closets.

In less than a week at the new embassy, James had emptied all of the crates of books into bookshelves, replicating the order that Jefferson had in Monticello. Jefferson called James into his library.

James stood just inside the doorway. "You sent for me, sir?"

Jefferson turned his chair away from his desk to face him. "James, I wanted to mention how I appreciated your managing the bookcase. Perfectly matching that which I enjoyed at Monticello for these few volumes. Well done."

James was confused, as compliments were unusual. "Thank you."

"And now, about your training. I have arranged for you to apprentice with the most talented of the *restaurateurs* in Paris."

"*Restaurateur?*"

"The latest thing here. Seems this fellow offers elegant dining at his establishment, which he calls a restaurant, as well as catering to the grand houses as others do. Call themselves *traiteures-restaurateurs*. Claims his dishes are 'restorative of health' as well as elegant. Combeaux is the fellow's name."

"The caterer that Marc uses?"

"One in the same. All the best houses use him for their table at home or dine in the latest style at his lavish restaurant. Your training with him begins tomorrow at nine."

"Training in catering?"

"No. In the fine and complex art of French cuisine. This apprenticeship will be neither simple nor quick, but I expect you to apply yourself with the full measure of your effort. You will continue to live here, attend my mornings, and do as Combeaux instructs as though his directions were my own. You can leave after you shave me."

"As you wish. But I do not know where it is."

Jefferson frowned. "Do you recall when you picked up some packages from the milliner for Patsy?"

"The hats? Yes."

"That shop is beside his restaurant. You should have no difficulty finding the Restaurant Combeaux."

Only later did James realize that Jefferson neither knew the address nor had any understanding of how to find the place. However, the impression of Jefferson's mastery of all subjects let James enter this new world with borrowed confidence.

The next morning, James left the residence by eight thirty and found the city streets completely unfamiliar. The crowded avenues that he had walked the day before were almost empty. The baskets of goods in front of stores and the street vendors that had become his landmarks were missing. His sense of direction, which had been formed in the openness of the plantation's rolling hills and far horizons, abandoned him. The narrow streets of the older section of the city that lay between the residence and Restaurant Combeaux seemed to twist like a barrel of eels.

He walked faster, hoping he was on the right path, fearing a wrong turn would cast him into hopeless confusion or that he had misjudged the distance and would be late. Soon, he was sweating. He loosened the long bow at his neck and unbuttoned his vest. His heavy breeches and knee-high boots were better suited to carriage travel with Jefferson than racing through the labyrinth of unnamed streets afoot.

At last, a bridge that looked familiar appeared. James relaxed now that he had found his way again. The day had brightened in the quarter hour of his journey. Once he spotted the large sign for the milliner hanging from the building over the cobbled walkway, he discovered the small sign above a doorway of oak and etched glass. The chocolate brown sign had ivory lettering that in a swirling script declared, "Restaurant Combeaux." He stopped and straightened his attire to make a proper impression. The elegant façade had leaded glass windows. James squared his shoulders and tested the front door. Locked. He swiped away the film of sweat from his forehead.

He tapped on the door. Almost immediately a slim woman with an easy smile opened it and startled James. Her brown vest was laced tightly over a white scoop-neck blouse. Her long skirt was the same rough homespun brown as her vest. "*Shammes Emme?*"

It took a moment for him to understand that his name could be pronounced in such a manner. He smiled. "James Hemings, of America."

He glanced at her face. Smooth skin, a blush to her cheeks, and full lips. Chocolate eyes. He quickly dipped his head in a clumsy bow.

"Chef waits for you." Her English bore little of the accent he had become accustomed to in Paris.

James looked up and decided to press forward in French. "*Merci, mademoiselle.*"

"Gabrielle." She sighed and seemed relieved that he spoke any French at all. "*Vous parlez français?*"

"A bit," he said in French before he even thought about it.

He followed her through the dim tunnel of the dining area. Even in the morning light, the crystal droplets from the sconces cast rainbows against the pale silk that covered the walls. The dozen tables had four chairs each in a matching burled walnut. White tablecloths were folded atop each table and each chair had a padded seat and back covered in a fine shimmering fabric like the silk jacket that Jefferson wore.

He slowed as he imagined how dazzling the dinner service would be when the candles in each of the sconces were lit, the silver serving trays glittered, and elegantly attired clientele laughed and whispered over the most magnificent of foods and wines. When he noticed that Gabrielle was several steps ahead of him, he hurried to catch up to her. Her floor-length skirt barely swayed from side to side as she sped through the room. Her chestnut hair was tied at her neck with a ribbon and fell in easy curls to her waist. She smelled of lavender and rosemary.

When she opened the door to the kitchen, he was dazzled by the glinting row of copper pans hanging on the far wall above a long counter made of brick. A shelf holding small, tin boxes ran the length of the row of pans above the counter. The huge kitchen was at least two stories high, fifty paces long, and half as wide. Smoke sliced in shafts from the skylight to the long wooden table against the right wall. There was a side of beef on the table and men breaking it down with cleavers and long knives. Most of the pungent coal smoke vented through the skylight, leaving the raw scents of the meat and onions.

Along the center of the room was one huge worktable. Eight men were preparing vegetables on it. There seemed to be room for another eight to work as well. Platters, serving dishes, and all manner of strainers and odd contraptions he had never seen before were stacked on shelves under that table. Not one of the men peeling and chopping looked up from his work. And not one looked like him.

To the left was a small landing. Beside it was a brick wall with four large iron doors covering the oven boxes. A rack to the right of the oven held tin baking sheets and deep, ceramic baking pans. There was an open firebox below the ovens and a large coal bin to the left of them, under the edge of a staircase. Two men were shoveling coal from the box into pails. Another man shoveled coal into the smoky fire under the ovens and shut the black iron door. At least a dozen bushels of produce in a rainbow of colors were on the landing between the base of a narrow stairway and a door to the rear of the restaurant. James frowned as he searched for the open hearth for roasting meats. Gabrielle saw his concern and asked in French, "What is it?"

"The hearth? Where do you roast meats or heat pots? On a fire." He gestured with his hands fearing that the term he had learned from Marie or his pronunciation may be confusing.

She walked toward the row of pans and he followed. "We have no open-fire cooking here. Look there. See where they are shoveling in the coal? We have what my father calls a closed-fire system. Those ovens are large for roasting meats and breads. Very new and not all caterers or even the new restaurants have them, so you don't talk about it to the others. The pans for frying meats and making sauces go there." She pointed to the wall holding the gleaming copper pans and shelf of tin boxes.

James looked at the large iron plates that topped what looked like a counter made of brick. "I thought this was just a work counter." Waist high, with black iron doors along its front, he saw how it could operate.

She tapped the cold iron plates. "*Plaques de cuisson* is what my father calls this, the plates for cooking." James smiled as he saw the benefit of such a system just from the ability to work at a standing level, not stooping into the fire to cook. He was puzzled about how the plates could cook until he recalled the small Franklin stove that Jefferson had installed in overseer Miller's cabin. He could call these cooking plates a stove when he tried to describe all this to Jefferson.

She motioned for him to step back to allow a slim man to open the doors under the cooking plates. He opened all five, placed in kindling, and set it alight. By the time the last was fired, he added some coal to the first door and shut it. Evaluating how the kindling had caught, he added more coal, and closed all the other doors. Gabrielle tapped his arm. "He'll get it hot and keep it at cooking temperature all day. That's his job."

James pointed to the landing. "Use that for the wash-up?"

"Yes, and the place to do the first cleaning of food as it comes from market." James saw a huge barrel of water, wooden tubs for washing dishes, and a smaller barrel for waste. An open stairway led from the kitchen to a room above it.

Sweat beaded the faces of workers and their shirt backs were wet. They wore dark trousers and wooden clogs. Their oatmeal-colored shirts had full sleeves, which were rolled up past the elbow. The simple string closure at the shirt necks was open halfway to their waists.

James stood a few paces into the massive room and tried to imagine the use for all the new cooking tools and equipment that he had never seen. So lost in thought was he that he was startled by Gabrielle calling his name. "James, this is Chef Combeaux."

James turned and watched a barrel-chested man with wavy, silver hair and a hawk nose stride across the room toward him. James guessed his age as slightly over forty, but his vigor and presence was of a younger, vital man. He stopped beside the table piled with vegetables and motioned James to approach. James edged his way past the men chopping on a long table.

Combeaux greeted James in French. "Welcome, Mister Hemings.

Your education in the best of French cuisine will begin today. From the earth. Remove the earth and peel from these carrots. You understand French, don't you?"

James nodded and looked around. "A little, sir."

Combeaux pointed to the end of the table where a bushel basket was filled with carrots. He looked at James and asked where his knives were. James shrugged before saying he had none.

Combeaux called to the young woman to get a knife for him before he walked away. She hurried to the table holding a well-used knife with a four-inch blade and motioned to the carrots. "You know how to?"

He looked at her, not having a clue what to do, and shrugged.

She placed the empty basket on the floor. "Like this." She snapped off the green top, dropped it into the basket, deftly used the knife back to scrape the bumpy carrot to a uniform, clean surface, put the perfectly formed carrot toward the center of the table, and swept the trimmings into the basket with her palm. She handed the knife to James and walked away, wordlessly. He glanced at her as she left the kitchen, followed by several of the cooks.

James started cleaning his first carrot, badly hacking into it with the blade of the knife. The lean, black-haired young man next to him at the table was working rapidly on a bushel of turnips. Without turning from his task, he asked, "You the American?"

James stopped and looked at him. "Yes. I am here to learn."

"Keep working. We talk while we work."

James put the malformed carrot beside Gabrielle's and winced at the difference. He pulled his carrot back and started to shave it to a round with the blade.

The man chuckled and took a new carrot from the basket. "This way. With the back at an angle. Hold it against the table. You want to remove as little as possible. But make it smooth. Understand?" In the brief time it took him to tell James this, the man had prepared three carrots to perfection.

"Thank you."

"Jean-Claude."

"James."

James turned his knife over, snapped off the next top and set to work, first slowly to get the right angle to take off the least amount of peel, then to work faster. Jean-Claude got another bushel of turnips from beside the stairs and set to work on them.

James finished the bushel of carrots at the same time his companion completed his third bushel of turnips. Nearing the bottom of the bushel, James had amassed a formation of carrots like words on a page. Ten across, nine rows down. He started the tenth row, his palms stained, the scent of earth replaced by a hint of the sweetness of spring in the back of his throat. He checked his progress against the perfectly smooth and rounded carrot that she had peeled. The row to the right of that model showed an effort, but not completion. The next row was better. Almost a hundred carrots later, he peeled one and shaped it as well as the model she had left for him.

He did not push the carrots into a mound as others had done with their peeled produce, but rather he placed them with care. He saw Combeaux approaching and decided not to look at him, but to keep working. The older man simply stared and waited for James to complete his task. Sweat drenched, he looked at the imposing figure and said, "Finished, Chef."

"He speaks! *Ah bien.* Not too bad for the first try. Now do it again. Once you know this, you will learn how to cut. Perhaps later in the day."

Combeaux picked up the first of the carrots that James had scraped and shook his head. He motioned for Gabrielle, who had just returned with a pushcart full of produce. "Use these for a purée." Turning back to James, he said, "Try it again. Do another basket. I see you later."

During his work on the second bushel, James developed a routine, found the angle to the knife blade, learned how to adjust the pressure of it to skim off a high spot, glide over the low, and create a perfectly uniform carrot.

While he peeled, Jean-Claude cut and chopped his turnips into perfect cubes and got a nod from Combeaux. Other men brought a huge pot to the table and swept the turnips into it. James watched them take the pot to the iron plates and set it there. Soon steam was rising from it into the smoky haze. A man stirred it with a paddle the size of a his leg. Men were all working with incredible speed and accuracy.

Combeaux returned and looked at the new rows of peeled carrots. He plucked out only a few from the mass and nodded. "Good. We begin with the beginning. The knife. We have a precision to our cuisine that requires sizes to be specific. You see."

James said, "*Oui, Chef.*"

"So. Let me see you cut into a slice, a dice, a mince, and a julienne."

James felt his face go hot with embarrassment. He only recognized the words for cut and slice. The other words were new to him. "Chef? I do not know all these words."

Combeaux shouted, "Gabrielle!"

She came to the table immediately. "*Oui?*"

"Explain to him that I want a carrot cut in one of the four styles. He does not know the words, tell him."

Gabrielle hesitated before she spoke in English. "Take four carrots, to each apply one of the four cuts." As she pronounced each, she cut a carrot into the required forms and left the samples in small piles for him to use as a reference.

James repeated aloud in French and English. "*Couper en tranches.* Cut in slices. *Une tranche* is a slice. *Couper en dés la carotte.* Dice the carrot. *Émincer la carotte.* Mince it, even smaller than a dice. *Julienne* to make small sticks of it."

Combeaux turned and stomped away.

Gabrielle whispered in English. "You get used to him. He is mostly puff, how you say, bluff and bluster."

James resumed in French. "Show me again?"

Gabrielle took another carrot and demonstrated the cutting skills slowly and then at a speed that was breathtaking. James tried to imitate her precision and failed miserably. He tried again and again until he made a good sample.

Combeaux returned and looked at the mess of carrots. "More for the *purée*. Try it again. Again!"

James finally got a passable sample of each style. Combeaux nodded approval and tapped his index finger near his eye. "Once you finish these, help dress the fowl and then just watch the others. Observe. Understand?"

"*Oui, Chef. Merci.*"

After Combeaux moved away, the man beside him clapped him on the back, laughing. "Not too bad for a first day. My first, I nearly cut off my thumb."

His fingers stained orange and his neck aching, James sat in the corner of the kitchen and plucked the feathers from small pigeons, which another worker had pulled from the cage, strangled, and gutted for him.

Gabrielle carried baskets of herbs and raw vegetables to the worktable, where men started breaking down the vegetables into precise sizes and filling ceramic bowls with the readied produce. Waste was thrown into a basket on the floor. Scrap trimmings were thrown into a large ceramic bowl on the table. When full, this bowl was dumped into a huge metal pot on the floor near the iron cooking plates.

At the next table, men were dressing out game birds and butchering a side of beef into portions for pan-frying and larger cuts for roasting. The bones were tossed into a huge, low-rimmed baking tin. Once all the bones were collected, a worker took the pan over to the oven. Another cook opened the heavy iron door for him. A casserole dish that had been collecting the better meat trimmings and vegetable scraps was doused with water, salt, and pepper and shoved into another oven.

Gabrielle passed quickly with a refilled jug of water that she put on the end of the stove. On her way back she paused briefly by the pile of feathers swirling at James's feet. In English, she said, "Is a madhouse, yes?"

He shook his head. "No. I am starting to see how it all works."

"It is going to be very warm soon. There is wine and cider over there if you be thirsty."

"Water is fine."

"No. Only use the water to cook and wash. Not good to drink unless boiled. Remember."

"Yes. I will. Your English. Where did you learn English?"

Gabrielle said, "London. My father was a cook for an important family when I was a little girl. They taught me."

"Is he still in London?"

Gabrielle nodded toward Combeaux. "This is his restaurant. But don't expect him to speak to you in English. Ever."

James felt a shiver of fear, stood straighter, and reverted to French. "*Merci.*"

CHAPTER 11

When the sun was overhead and the room the brightest, Combeaux went to the stove and pulled a large copper sauté pan from the hook on the wall. All action and the dull noise of chatter ceased. Everyone gathered around him.

"Today. A new dish. Filet of beef with mushroom and a Madeira sauce. Watch."

Combeaux demonstrated the totally new technique of pan-frying to sauté foods. Butter in the pan was heated on the iron plate set in the brick counter. After four thin filets of beef were seared and turned once, they were removed. A knob of butter was tossed into the pan. A handful of sliced mushrooms from the large bowl hit the screaming-hot pan and jumped. Salt and pepper were pinched in from tin containers on a shelf above the stove. Thyme was added from another tin. The room smelled like nothing James had ever encountered and everything at once. Rich. Herbal. Fresh. A meadow. A woods after a winter rain. He sniffed and sniffed again. Combeaux grabbed a pitcher and poured in a splash of Madeira wine. A cloud of steam exploded and drifted over to James. A grin that he could not contain spread over his face.

As the cooks gathered closer to the chef and asked questions, James retreated to the stairs, trying to understand how this new scent was made. After a moment, Combeaux poured the sauce over the four filets and passed the plate to Jean-Claude. He took it to the end of the table and cut the meat into small bites. The others stood by with small paring knives or spoons, ready to taste. As Combeaux left the kitchen, he pointed to James, who was sitting on the stairway, and yelled, "Gabrielle?"

She went over to him. "Come, James. You must taste. This is how you learn."

James joined the others in tasting a spoonful of the meat with sauce. He inhaled over the spoon before taking the bite. He shut his eyes trying to parse the flavors into butter and sweet and savory and wine and something like roasted meat and woody. "I have never tasted anything like this."

She smiled. "He is very, very good. He imagines food and then makes something so new it has no name."

"Does he cook everything tonight?"

Gabrielle laughed. "Oh, no. He demonstrates so that the others replicate. The others will do most. You will see."

"Will they really eat all this? Your restaurant only has so many tables. Do all the rest go to catering like Jefferson uses?"

"Oh. We make platters of food for much more important residences every night, and for larger dinners. Don't you have caterers in your cities?"

"I don't know. I live on a..." James struggled for the French word for plantation, then offered, "a great estate in the country."

"Most of our money comes from the night platters. They send their servants over to fetch them. In a city this large, few have cooking facilities. It is not like in the country where anyone can cook over their hearth."

James looked at her, confused. "Could someone cook like this in a private home?"

"If they have a chef and staff, and equipment and space. But having all that is like being at court."

"But that is what Massa Jefferson wants."

"Then you better be the best student ever."

Combeaux marched to the oven, opened the iron door, and shouted. "Gabrielle! The casserole is done. Bring our new student."

Gabrielle stood and motioned James to follow her. "Like they say, if you are a cook, you never go hungry."

Combeaux stepped aside to let Jean-Claude pull a large, glazed baking dish from the oven using his heavy apron to protect his hands. He rushed to the end of the table. Pierre brought over a stack of glazed bowls and placed them beside the casserole. Jean-Claude filled bowls with the braised meat and vegetables in a thin broth. Workers eagerly took them to their places along the long worktables. Maurice rushed in with four round loaves of bread and dropped them along the table where others ripped off a chunk. Gabrielle fetched a large pitcher of wine.

The richness of the meat married the freshness of the carrots and density of the potatoes perfectly. Each gained from the other what they lacked. The broth carried hints of each. James mimicked the others, dipping his bread into the broth and eating quickly, emptying his wine glass with his last bite of meat, and letting their flavors become one.

As each person finished eating, they moved into the afternoon's work without prompting. Someone pulled the deeply browned bones from the oven and another gathered vegetable scraps while a third worker dumped buckets of water into a huge pot on the end of the stove. Stock was made from the browned bones during the next hours. Conversation in the kitchen was minimal now.

When James finished eating, Gabrielle pointed to a bushel of onions that remained by the stairs. "Now, those onions are for you to peel and slice into rings, across the onion. Understand?" She motioned the desired thickness by showing a distance between her thumb and forefinger.

He carried the basket to his station on the worktable and dived into the task. Tears streamed down his face as he finished the last of the onions. Combeaux walked past the mound of onions and nodded.

Gabrielle loaded the onions into a large pot and whispered, "He nodded to you."

"That's good?"

"That's very good. Carry the pot with me. We start the soup for our dinner now."

She threw in a fist-sized lump of butter and stirred the huge pot with a paddle more suited for a boat while the onions softened, then browned.

Later she poured buckets of stock on top of the browned onions.

The action in the kitchen that afternoon became a blur of interrelated movements from which James tried to sense order. Diced onions were dropped by the handful into large skillets and danced in butter while they became translucent. Some were taken out when barely cooked while the remainder were browned. Both were placed into pottery bowls.

Mushrooms sizzled in copper pans until reduced to shimmering chips, then stored in yet another bowl. Pounds of butter and an equal weight of flour were measured on a balance scale then kneaded together into a thick paste in yet another large ceramic bowl. Knobs of it were taken out to thicken sauces at the stove.

Sauces were made in high-sided pans by the quart.

Filets of beef were sliced from a tenderloin, pan-fried, and stacked in a large side platter. Just before adding to a serving platter, the steaming sauce was poured over the filets of beef.

James assisted in carrying the completed platters with square covers to the long counter at the front of the kitchen. Liveried footmen from noble houses entered through the rear door of the kitchen carrying large, square baskets. Some baskets were the size of trunks and required two servants to carry them from the kitchen. Others just placed one or two platters in small baskets that they carried on one arm.

About the time that the rush of cooking for the servants to carry to their estates was completed, the restaurant opened for the service to diners. This only intensified the work in the kitchen.

Unlike the platters of rich and elegant food that James had seen prepared, these platters had additional ornamentation on them and became artful displays with vegetables cut into fanciful figures, or fronds of dill draped across fish wrapped in thin dough.

Four hours later, by the light of oil lamps hoisted by ropes above the workspace, the men scrubbed the tables and floors. The gleaming copper pans and pots were placed back on their hooks and the last of the scraps were removed. The men gathered at the table for a glass of wine. They dipped brittle shards of now-stale bread into large bowls of onion soup. They were bent with fatigue and ate in silence.

As they finished, they took their empty bowls and dropped them onto the table beside the washtubs and left. Gabrielle poured another glass of wine for James and pointed to the stack of remaining dishes. "Your last chore for the night."

James washed the bowls with the tepid water as Gabrielle wiped off each of the worktables with a cloth soaked in vinegar. When he finished, he rolled down his sleeves and waited for her at the door.

"It is dark. Can I walk you home?"

"You have. I live here, in the room above the kitchen. Brave enough to come back tomorrow?"

"Yes, as soon as I shave him."

"Oh. We start at dawn but come as you will. Good night, James."

He left by a door at the rear of the kitchen and found himself in a dark alley. He heard the bolt on the door slide into place. He waited a moment for his eyes to adjust before he started toward Jefferson's residence.

James walked alone down streets lit only by a few flickering lanterns, dodging the occasional horse cart, steering clear of drunken men arguing on street corners, and whores servicing men in the dim alleys. It was minutes before midnight when James passed the grandfather clock in the entryway and climbed the stairs to his room. He plopped, fully dressed, on his bed. Exhausted, he fell asleep immediately.

James barely woke in time to attend Jefferson the next morning. He poured the basin of water for Jefferson's foot bath and stropped the straight razor on the side of his knee-high boot. His rhythm was distinctly his own: two short strops up and down then two long strokes and a pause to test the blade against his thumb before giving it two more short strokes. Jefferson slouched in a chair with a towel over the chest of his nightshirt and his feet in the basin on the floor. His hair was tousled.

Jefferson glanced at James as he brushed on the shaving lather. "None the worse for wear, I see. How was it?"

"Like nothing I ever imagined. They were well underway when I arrived."

"What time do they start?"

"Someone said dawn, but they may have been testing me. Men do all the cooking. All rushing to do different things. Some cutting up meat. Some chopping vegetables. Some grinding spices or chopping herbs. Get lots of little parts ready. At first it made no sense, then the chef used some of this and some of that to make his new dish and by the end of the day, a dozen kinds of food platters were finished and went out the door. And there was a dish I'd never seen before."

"What was this new dish?" James brushed the lather onto Jefferson's cheeks and throat.

"A filet of beef was cut thin and each slice fried in a pan over some kind of hot box I've never seen before, then a brown sauce of mushrooms and thyme and wine got made and poured over it. It sizzled in the pan and gave off the most attractive smell when the pan sent up this cloud of vapor." Without pausing in his report, James made two careful strokes from Jefferson's collarbone to chin.

"I'll make a point of dining at his restaurant soon so I can taste this new creation myself. Tell me more."

James stopped and wiped the lather on a towel. "Nothing is wasted. Scrap bones got baked off then boiled up with vegetable scraps into what they call stock. Tasted like a good soup to me, but it did not stop there."

"How so?"

"They used it to make the sauce. Boiled it way down. Put in a knob of butter so it shined like ice on Christmas Day."

Jefferson frowned. "They baked off the bones over a fire in the hearth? Didn't they scorch?"

"No. No open fires there. Got a coal fire under a big closed box they call an oven. Not like our little hollow-outs in the fireplace. Got four built into a brick wall. Each big enough to hold a big hog. Heavy iron doors on the front. There's one man, Pierre. His job is to keep the right heat in each oven and the stove plates by stoking and adding coal or banking a fire as needed."

"Why?"

"They got flat-bottom pans made of bright copper that catch the heat quick. Then if it is too hot, they just pick it off the iron plate and let it cool. Called *plaques de cuisson*, cooking plates. They resemble the top of Mister Franklin's stove, but larger by twentyfold."

Jefferson held up his hand for James to pull the razor away from his chin. "Can you make drawings of these inventions for me?"

"Certainly." James paused long enough for Jefferson to turn his head toward him.

"What?"

"As I worked, I found that my attire was impractical for the labor. They wear plain shirts and long trousers…"

"Have Marc get you what you need. Two sets. What time did you get in last night?"

"About midnight." James worried that he had displeased his master. "I came home right after we cleaned up."

"I am certain you did, but you smell like an onion patch."

"Chopped a whole bushel of 'em, at least."

The blade nicked Jefferson's chin. They both flinched.

James finished shaving him and handed him a wet then a dry towel that he ran over his face. "This schedule. Leaving as soon as you finish with me and getting in after midnight, might be too much for you to be attending me in the mornings."

"But—"

"No. Your apprenticeship is important. I will have the French staff attend me. Make detailed notes on the manner of cooking and ingredients without raising their ire. I will expect you to become my *chef de cuisine* here at our residence upon the completion of your training, so study well. Plan to meet with me every Sunday to apprise me of the week's events while you shave me."

Before James could answer, Jefferson bolted from his chair. "Follow me!"

James hurried after Jefferson to his study. There, he handed James a small, wooden box without a top. James looked into it and saw several booklets formed by papers cut into two-inch squares and sewn together on the side and a dozen wood sticks. "Today, it occurred to me that during this apprenticeship, we will not be seeing each other as frequently as we have in the past, but I want to know what you are learning. To that end, I want you to record what you learn. At night, use the quill and ink that I will have Marc provide in your room to record your observations of that day in detail. During the day, note key observations in these small booklets with what the French call a *crayon* so nothing slips from memory."

Jefferson reached into the box and removed what James thought to be just a wooden stick and held it at eye level. Jefferson continued, "It is an improvement over our pencils. See? There is a tube of graphite glued between two thin pieces of wood to make a solid rectangular unit. Easily slipped into a pocket. When the graphite is worn away, you just shave back the wood ever so slightly with your penknife. But you must be inconspicuous."

James looked puzzled.

Jefferson whispered, "Understand, you should not be discovered as you write this private intelligence on the cuisine. Your notes are for my eyes alone."

"But a knife, I don't have one. I'm not allowed."

He opened his desk drawer and pulled out a well-used quill knife. As he handed it to James, he said, "We are not in Virginia anymore."

So began the daily practice of James Hemings observing and recording the secrets of French cuisine for his spymaster, Thomas Jefferson.

It was barely light when James left the residence for Restaurant Combeaux. The cool air carried the heavy scent of late-blooming orange blossoms from Jefferson's garden. A few streets away, the city began to awaken. He dodged men, still in their nightshirts, who were emptying piss pots into the gutters before returning to their small apartments. The narrow streets were devoid of carriages or carts, yet there was an increasing population of men in workers attire walking ahead of him.

When a piss pot was emptied from an upper floor, its contents sailed over his head before splashing into the gutter. He realized that he needed to join the others walking in the center of the muddy street. After another ten minutes, he approached the district where the restaurant and a small bakery were located. A crush of women in tattered dresses grumbled at the doorway of the bakery as they waited for it to open. Through the stink of mud and freshly emptied chamber pots, James sniffed to find the hints of bread fresh from the oven, bright wood smoke, and a scent almost like caramel.

James entered the restaurant kitchen through the rear door as previously instructed. The harshness of coal smoke had not yet entirely cleared. The initial rich smell of meat browning mingled with the sharpness of raw onion and sweat. Combeaux paced with his arms crossed over his barrel chest. James glanced around the kitchen. Against the far wall, cooks had their heads bent, fully engaged in chopping piles of vegetables. On the long wooden table, Marcel was at work breaking down a quarter of beef with a long, thin knife and placing similar cuts of meat into piles.

Gabrielle translated her father's words to ensure James understood. "Today, you learn about spices and herbs. You need to know the names and scents and how to prepare each."

James nodded. "*Oui, Chef.*"

Combeaux spoke directly to him. "*La feuille de laurier, la marjolaine, le carvi...*"

James grimaced. "I am sorry, I do not know."

Combeaux muttered to himself in French and stomped away. "*Merde!* Perhaps he should just read *Les Dons de Comus, ou, L'Art de la Cuisine,*

Réduit en Pratique, and leave me in peace!"

James said, "What…"

Gabrielle spoke to him in English. "He wants only to speak French. A secret is that his English is not so good. Perhaps it is best if you know the names of the herbs and spices in French before he tells you about…"

"Can you write them? I'll have someone read them to me. By tomorrow, I will know them. I know some already."

Gabrielle looked skeptical but named the herbs and spices in English and French as she wrote them. "*L'anis* is anise. *Le basilic* is basil. *Le carvi* is caraway."

"What was that he said I should read? Is it about spices?"

"It is a book on how to cook by François Marin. The first in French."

"Can I borrow it? I can have one of the servants translate it and read it to me."

Gabrielle laughed. "No! It is three books long and no. Let me talk to him. I have an idea."

The next day, James woke early and approached the restaurant hesitatingly. When he opened the door, no one looked at him. Those standing closer to James chopped herbs and ground spices in tall brass mills. James was soon beside Combeaux at the scarred oak table looking at an array of whole spices, including sticks of cinnamon, whole peppercorns, threads of saffron, and dried bay leaves.

Combeaux spoke slowly. "Here we have the primary spices, dried and brought here from all over the world. We begin with this…" He pointed to a dish holding the sticks of cinnamon.

James quickly answered. "*La cannelle.*"

Combeaux grinned. "*En Français! Bien.*"

"*Merci, Chef.*"

Combeaux pointed to each on the table in almost an accusatory manner. He barked the name of each spice for James to repeat.

"*Le sel.*"

"*Le sel.* Salt."

"*Le poivre.*

James echoed the name of each spice and translated it into English to verify his understanding, watching for Gabrielle's confirmation.

"*Le poivre.* Black peppercorns." She nodded.

"*La fleur de muscade.*"

"*La fleur de muscade.* Mace. The husk of the nutmeg."

When Combeaux pointed to saffron threads, James took the lead. "*Le safran.* Threads of saffron, for color and flavor."

Pointing to a bowl of whole nutmeg, he said, "*La noix de muscade.* Nutmeg."

James continued rapidly as he walked past each spice. "*La moutarde.* Mustard seeds. *La non...*" He stopped and corrected himself. "*Les clous de girofle.* Cloves. *La feuille de laurier.* Bay laurel leaf."

Combeaux smiled his approval as James named each of the remaining spices correctly. "*Demain, nous appredrons les noms des herbes.*"

Gabrielle had moved to the corner of the kitchen to wash a baking pan. She glanced at James and smiled. There was a large crock next to her and a dipper for rinse water. After Combeaux left, James went over to get a short drink from the earthen pitcher of cider. He was sweating.

Gabrielle whispered, "You survived his examination, eh?"

James drained a small glass of cider. "Barely. I think he said we learn the names of plants, herbs, tomorrow. Isn't that when '*demain*' is?"

Gabrielle said, "Yes. You are learning very quick."

"Not fast enough for him. Our colonial kitchen had only clove, nutmeg, allspice, and cinnamon besides salt and pepper. The array of new fragrances arising from all manner of dried buds and berries, peels and husks is a new universe."

"Wait after the others go. I'll tell you the names and show you the herbs he likes best."

"And write them for me again?"

She smiled and nodded.

After the others had departed that night, she brought paper from her room and wrote the name as she pointed to each of the herbs. James sniffed each and rubbed some between his fingers to get a stronger scent.

He was leaving by the back door when he saw Pierre, the man who stoked the stoves during the day. He saluted him as he approached.

Pierre returned the greeting with a nod. They walked side by side for almost a block in silence. At the doorway to a small inn, Pierre stopped. *"Faites attention.* Caution, my friend."

James frowned. "Sorry?"

"Gabrielle." He raised an eyebrow.

James shrugged and opened his hands to express his confusion.

"Look, my friend. There is something nobody is going to tell you."

"What?"

Pierre tipped his head toward the smoke-filled dining area. "Join me for a drink?"

James felt in his pocket to see if he had any money with him.

"Let me pay tonight. You another. I'd like the company."

James smiled and followed him out of the dark into the crowded room. They shouldered their way through men to the bar. Pierre motioned for two drinks. Almost immediately, two short glasses of rough brandy were shoved toward them across a wet bar. Pierre handed two coins to the barman, who put them in his vest pocket.

"I don't always come here, but the baby is getting his first teeth." He raised his eyes to the tinned ceiling and mimicked a scream. "I can barely sleep."

"I didn't know you had a child."

"This is the third."

James hoisted his glass. "Congratulations."

Pierre looked into the glass and thought before he spoke. "You know that Gabrielle is the daughter of Chef Combeaux, don't you?"

"Yes. She told me."

"If you anger her, you will be on the street in a moment."

"Oh. I see. But I am not an employee. He doesn't pay me. My master has paid him for me to apprentice."

"Still. Be careful. She had a man, a very talented cook, last year. When she tired of him, he had to leave. You see?"

James choked on his drink and laughed. "She has no more interest in me than in that." He pointed at a stuffed deer head on the wall. "That poor animal."

"A trophy? Perhaps you could be a trophy, so different you are."

James shook his head and raised his eyebrows in disbelief. "I have no money, am not French, and have to go back to America."

"Still, use caution. You might be of interest to her." Pierre finished his brandy and clapped James on the shoulder. "Sleep well, tomorrow comes fast."

James followed him into the chilled night.

The next day, Combeaux was standing with his arms folded over his chest when James arrived, now wearing the same attire as most of the others. The practicality was evident in the dark trousers, black wooden clogs, and beige pullover shirt with a string to tie at the neck and long sleeves, which were full enough to push or roll up easily. James rushed to the table and stood facing the chef.

Combeaux began slowly. "*Les herbes sont—*"

James interrupted him by reciting the names of each in French, properly identifying rosemary, thyme, sage, and a dozen others.

Combeaux pointed to a man in a pale blue shirt and black pants who was chopping herbs and smiled as he handed James a knife and ordered the man to teach James how to chop herbs. James prepared all kinds of herbs throughout the day. By handling the herbs, their textures as well as their scents became a part of him. Imagining how each could contribute its individuality to a dish made the work go faster.

Late in the day, the soup pot was brought to the long table and bowls set beside it. Once James sat at the table and relaxed, waiting for the soup to be served, his fatigue showed as he massaged his wrist and forearm. But rather than leaving his staff to eat, Combeaux motioned to

Jean-Claude to delay in serving the soup and walked to the table holding a large baking tray covered with white napkins.

Gabrielle laughed. "Are you ready for another examination, James? He wants you to tell him the spice or herb."

James stood. Combeaux took his shoulders and turned him away from the tray. He then blindfolded James with the napkin and turned him back. Other workers watched the ritual they had all endured.

Combeaux took one small dish after another from the tray and held a sample of each herb or spice in front of James. After sniffing each, he properly identified each and stated its name and use. One of the workers stopped smirking and looked at James with awe.

James continued in French. "Thyme is for the brown sauce with beef. Sage goes with fowl. And black pepper, which makes me sneeze."

Combeaux snatched away the blindfold, laughed, and clapped him on the shoulder. "*Bien,* James. *Bien.*"

Everyone in the kitchen applauded. He discretely nodded to Gabrielle, who was dipping a huge ladle into the soup pot and filling bowls for their dinner.

Exhausted, James made his way to Jefferson's residence that night, passing ragged people who walked aimlessly. Carriages jolted past them carrying well-dressed men from one late-night amusement to another.

The next day, James approached the kitchen with confidence. However, as the new cook in training, he was given menial chores. He was directed to separate eggs, placing whites in one small bowl and yolks in a large one before he transferred the one egg white to a larger bowl. The cook was clear that no yolk could get into the whites. James started to suggest that the process could be faster by cracking the egg over the bowl of whites. Scowling, the cook said, "Any yolk in the white would spoil it all. It would not beat to foam or hold a peak." With that, James resumed the exacting process for the next five dozen eggs, transferring each egg white to the larger bowl only after he was certain there was no yolk in it. That way, the yolks could be used to thicken sauces and the whites beaten into frothy meringues.

James looked up when he heard a clattering of large pots being tugged from the racks. He stopped and glanced at the cooks stacking one pot of meat and vegetables inside a larger pot with water in it. After Combeaux laid a rope of thick dough around the rim of the smaller pot and seated a lid on the dough to seal it, two cooks hoisted the heavy pots onto the stove to simmer.

Once James finished separating the eggs, the bowls were removed to another table and examined by the chef, who nodded and said something to the worker beside him. Soon two cooks carried in a sack of pecans, as big around as a man and half as tall. After dropping the sack on the floor beside James, the taller man rattled off some instructions in rapid French. James did not understand him and scowled. Shrugging, the man opened the sack and pulled out a handful of nuts. He rapped the shells on the table with a small, wooden mallet. He swept the shells to the floor, separated the nut into two pieces, and removed the woody portion between them. He then gestured that this was how James was to proceed with the whole bag.

An hour later, Combeaux walked by and noticed only a third of the nuts were whole; he quickly made two piles, one of whole nuts and the other of pieces. He sent Gabrielle over to James. "He wants at least half of the nuts to be left whole. The pieces he will crush with sugar for the filling of a dessert." She whispered, "The trick is to get as many whole ones at the start while your fingers are strong."

"Thanks. What is he doing with that set of pots?"

"You know the *bain-marie*, that saucepan over one of simmering water?"

"That keeps the sauces warm without burning?"

"Right. This is the same, but huge. The long, slow cooking of beef and vegetables with his spice mix distills its essence into a broth only made here. Be close when it is opened. It is the richest aroma you could ever imagine."

By four that afternoon, James wondered if he would finish before his quivering fingers bled from the pecan shells digging into his flesh. He could barely hold the mallet anymore, let alone separate the nuts with care. He stopped to massage his fingers and palms. Fearing Chef's disapproval, he quickly resumed shelling the pecans. By five, a third of the bag remained and his fingertips were raw. Seeing his distress, Gabrielle hurried to finish her tasks and came to the end of the table. She dropped the armful of unfolded dinner napkins and took the small mallet from him.

"Enough! Soon you have *du sang* blood on the *les noisettes*."

James translated from her clear French to English. "Nuts?"

She nodded and picked up a napkin. "Watch me." She folded it into a complex pattern resembling a swan and handed him a napkin to fold. She nodded approval at his first attempt. They traded positions, he wiped his hands on his trousers, and folded each of the napkins. She scooped up all of the intact pecan halves and took them to another cook. When she returned, she said, "He says he has enough. The rest can be broken pieces."

Across the room, the butcher was finishing his last lamb.

James had seen stock killed and broken down into cuts for the smokehouse. But he found himself stealing glances during the day as the butcher broke down sides of beef and several lambs that had been drained and skinned at Les Halles. This was the last one. He gently placed it, spine down, on his worktable. After a few deft cuts below the ribcage, he slid the rear of the lamb until the butt was off the table. After one deft cut through the spine, he snapped off the rear quarters and placed it on the center of his table. Cutting chops and roasts, he was finished in what seemed like mere minutes. Loin, neck, ribs, tenderloin and leg, all cuts were perfectly symmetrical. All bones were cleaned and tossed in a large pan to be baked before making more broth. After the last lamb was prepared, the butcher rinsed his bloody hands in the dish water and sauntered to the table where James was folding napkins. He stood waiting for James to look up from his task.

The butcher was a man of middle years, barrel chested, and big bellied. His hair was a pale brown and fine, like the fur of a mouse, and drawn back by a string at the nape of his neck into a horsetail falling to his waist. To no other of his kitchen staff would Combeaux allow such long hair, but the butcher had a gift of finding the line on any muscle, of drawing his long knife with such skill and clarity that each cut resulted in the perfect sectioning, cut of roast, filet, or dice.

James had watched the man's deft movements with admiration. James had seen cattle and sheep, lambs, and chickens all moved from field to table, but never with such skill. When James did not look up from his chore, the butcher untied his brown-flecked apron, folded it carefully, and let it drop beside James. He looked at Gabrielle. "For the sugar paste?"

She nodded. The butcher pulled the other large marble mortar and pestle off the high shelf with one hand and dropped it on the table across from James with a thud. When James looked up, the butcher smiled. "André." He shoved his bear paw toward James, who shook it.

Surprised by the lightness of his touch, considering his size and the brute strength needed for his work, he smiled back. "James."

André scooped a double handful of the nut pieces into the bowl and in four crashing blows, dispatched them into crumbs. As soon as he finished, he clapped James on the back and left before the latter could thank him.

When he looked at Gabrielle in confusion, she smiled. "They do not think to see you come back tomorrow."

"Why not?"

"Most quit after the nut assignment."

James laughed. "I will be back tomorrow. Even earlier."

"You're not finished yet. Go put the crushed nuts on the balance and get an equal weight of sugar, then bring both back here to blend."

He did this and blended the nuts and sugar into a smooth paste. Once he had done so with all the available nuts, he took the mallet from

Gabrielle and motioned to the napkins. "All done. Let me finish here."

She brought the napkins to the dining room and returned to carry the nut paste to a cook who was making a layered dessert.

Soon, the cooks began completing dishes for the restaurant by finishing sauces and plating platters. Roasted beef was shredded and put into hollowed bread bowls, topped with sweetbreads cooked in butter, crisped bacon, and a shaving of black truffle. The special broth was served in a cup to the side of the bread bowl. For those grand houses that had requested catered meals, James ascertained that the last of the assembly would occur in the kitchen of those mansions. The dinner service had ended. The kitchen staff cleaned up after they ate. Each worker departed as they finished, leaving James and Gabrielle alone washing dishes. "I talked to my father. He gave me the books he said you should know."

"I am sure I can get someone at the residence to translate if I don't know a word."

"No. He said for me to tell you and explain. We start tonight for an hour."

"Now? I'm not finished. There are still nuts."

"Those few pecans can wait to morning. Leave the mortar there. If you want to be a *chef de cuisine*, you start by knowing how to cook for a simple household, to be *le cuisinier*."

James scowled at her. "But aren't most of them women?"

"Yes, that's *la cuisinière*, but you must start by knowing what they know. And stop looking like that. Many of them are as talented as the men here."

He put away the dishes and rubbed his stiff wrists. Gabrielle took the last of the oil lamps from the kitchen and led James up the staircase. He followed her tentatively into the small afterthought of a room built over the kitchen's storage area.

Only the two interior walls had been plastered. Those formed by the building's exterior remained as rough stone and mortar. A small window faced the street. But unlike the kitchen's rough male scent, the aroma in this room was somehow familiar, feminine, and safe. When she put the oil lamp on a small table beside her bed, James noticed a sheaf of dried lavender stalks as big as his forearm. It was tied with a string and suspended by a nail above the head of the bed. He smiled and relaxed into the lavender scent of laundry day at Monticello, of the freshness of the big house from sachets of lavender seeds in cloth bags the size of pinecones hidden in the linen trunk and butler's pantry.

Beside her small bed, there was a stack of papers more than a foot high. When he noticed it, she tugged the blanket on the bed to hide the papers then lit two oil lamps on the wall. She sat on the sofa made of rough slats covered by a thin down cushion. Books were stacked inside a crate beside the sofa, as were pencils and a sheaf of paper.

James looked around the room. "Your father allows this? Being with me? Alone?"

"He wants you to learn fast so he can get paid."

"Come. Sit by me on the sofa."

"Here on the floor is fine."

Gabrielle patted the sofa, "I want you to see the words too."

As she pulled a thick book from the crate, she handed him a sheaf of papers and slab pencil like the one Jefferson had given him.

"Will you write another list for someone to read to me?"

"It is a good thing for cooks to read and write, so why do you pretend not to know?"

"It is against the law for a slave to know how."

"But you make quick writings when you think no one is seeing you. You have a pencil and paper in your pocket at all times." James held his breath as she continued. "My father knows that you go home again to America and will not bring any problems to him. But he would cut your throat if you started a new restaurant in Paris and stole his secrets."

"Cut my throat? Truth?"

Gabrielle laughed. "Maybe not, but he would be very angry. How did you know so much about the herbs?"

"My mother tends the sick at Monticello, that's where Jefferson lives. She is called a root doctor."

"What?"

"She mixes up dried roots and plants. Makes doses for people. Puts it in folded paper so you know how much to take. More for big men. A little bit for a child. She knows potions to make a child throw up if he eat some poison, and powders to make you sleep if you real sick and need quiet time to heal. Pokeweed berry salve on open sores to make them scab up. She got tonics so ladies can have their babies without all the fuss and pain and special teas when ladies don't wanna have no babies."

"So, she is like a doctor?"

"Sort of. Maybe even smarter than Jefferson's doctor."

"Your Jefferson lets her attend to him?"

He laughed a deep, robust laugh. "Not usually. Most owners are afraid to let their slaves dose them. Fear they be poisoned."

"That true?"

James nodded, thought of how his mother had calibrated Bob's purging perfectly, and slipped into French. "*Vrai.*"

Gabrielle tested him. "What would she give for a stomach indigestion?"

"Sage or ginger tea. Peppermint tea if you feel like you gonna puke."

"I believe you."

"Do you believe the right foot of a mole hung on a baby's neck keeps it safe or the left foot of a graveyard rabbit protects an adult?"

"No."

"Me neither, but I know some who do." James tapped the book. "Where do we start?"

"First is how to select the proper foods in the market. I don't read this to you now but tell you when we go there tomorrow. Be here just before light."

"But the nuts?"

"James!" She laughed. "That was just his way to test you. To see if you wanted this. Nobody's ever finished it. Go home. We start before the sun tomorrow."

James barely slept that night. They met at the restaurant at dawn, finished preparing the nuts, and hurried to the food stalls and barns of Les Halles. Gabrielle marched at the head of the parade of six cooks from the restaurant. Each carried two large canvas sacks with handles at the top. James followed behind the cooks, pushing a large wooden wagon, trying not to lose them in the crowd. Buyers for the inns and great homes elbowed each other to get the first look at fresh vegetables and meat. It became an ever-more crowded crush of men arguing over crates full of the bounty from the farms outside the city walls.

Gabrielle stopped often and bargained with vendors. A few were dark-skinned. When he asked about them, she called them Moors or Algerians. She pointed to the vegetables or other produce that she wanted. Then it was handed to her helpers to carry. Each purchase included a great deal of arm waiving and yelling; often she elbowed her way past men of greater bulk and stature to claim a prized specimen. Once the negotiations were concluded, the vendor bowed his head as she extracted coins from her small purse in the pocket of her apron. She called James to her side and directed two cooks to push the wagon with its ever-increasing bounty. After each purchase, she explained to James why she selected each item and rejected others for a bruise on a cucumber or brown spots on lettuce, an irregularity on a melon or some almost-invisible flaw.

Vendors called for her attention and often maligned their competitors. Occasional shoving ensued. A valued client like Gabrielle garnered great attention and favor over the men from other establishments or the housewives who came later in the day for the meager leavings. As most homes had no hearth for cooking, breads and the occasional roasted meats came from shops. The lettuces, radishes, cucumbers, and other specialties of summer were purchased first. Bushel baskets of mushrooms and truffles were added to the wagon.

Past the freshness and earthiness of the vegetable stalls were the birds. The stench from their droppings would have allowed James to find them if blindfolded. Crates of live quail, pigeons, chickens, geese, and ducks all added their voices to the commotion of the market. In huge covered pens were two swans and in another, three fully plumed peacocks and two plump peahens. Gabrielle pointed to several crates of smaller birds; these were immediately handed off to the cooks, who stacked them on the wagon. Passing a barrel of live eels, she bought eight. The bucket smelled of the sea. From the next vendor, she took a basket of fish that were bright-eyed, silvered, and squirming. Once she had paid, she nodded to the cooks, who left with one pulling and two pushing the heavily loaded wagon. She turned to James. "This may seem odd to have everything removed so quickly, but Papa does not want others to know what specialty he is cooking."

Empty handed, James followed her as she walked quickly to the butchering section, where whole sides of beef were being lugged on the backs of men from a barn-like building to open tables covered with flies. The odor of hot iron and rust was so strong and reminiscent of a bloody nose, that James put his hand to his lip. Butchers had both smaller cuts and sides of beef, swine, and lamb. One yelled that he had fresh venison. Blood ran into the gutters of the brown-stained cobblestone street. Fresh hides were stacked beside the barn door. Gabrielle glanced at the offerings but made no move toward the tables. When James looked confused, she explained. "I'm waiting for Jacques. He has the best beef." James ventured to the barn and looked in to see men hoisting pigs by the rear feet, flashing a knife, and leaving them to swing and finish bleeding out. Other men were skinning and gutting bled-out cattle that had been killed hours before. The hot smell of blood and rankness of guts and excrement being shoveled into barrels was nothing like what he recalled from Monticello. This was different. Pigs to pork, cattle to beef. Massive in scale. Battlefield cruel.

Soon a slight man left the barn, passing James, and glanced toward the crowd of shoppers. His blood-spattered blue coat hung to his knees. He saw Gabrielle and nodded to her. She held up her right hand and extended her thumb and two fingers. He nodded and returned to the barn. Several minutes later, a boy emerged from the barn leading a dogcart pulled by a massive animal with a shaggy black coat. On the cart were three sides of beef. She paid the slight man, who then sent a boy off. The boy tugged the dog's rope halter to move through the crowd and toward the restaurant. Gabrielle and the butcher smiled at each other. He turned and sauntered back to the barn. James was astounded that the costliest of the purchases was consummated wordlessly. Then he thought of the trust and relationship that must have been developed over years to allow such a pivotal aspect of the kitchen to rest with one vendor.

As they retraced their path through the marketplace, James thought that he had seen every fruit and vegetable that the earth could offer and any animal that could fly, swim, or walk. By the time they left, more than half of the produce had been sold.

She pointed back to the marketplace. "It will be abandoned by this afternoon. As though none of this was ever here. Then around midnight the wagons start in from the fields. In summer, there are almost three thousand of them. Then the fish and cut meat arrives. The cattle and swine are driven in about three, slaughtered before daylight, and dressed out during the morning. That is the most expensive."

Later that day when the kitchen was running at full speed, pan sauces were being made. Butter sizzled and flour was added to make *roux* before milk was beaten in with a wooden spoon to make gallons of the basic white sauce. Then portions were taken and made into unique sauces by the addition of spices or other ingredients. The sturdier sauces were held in *bains-marie*. Lumps of flour and butter were kneaded together and then added by the spoonful to thicken the fragile sauces that were made at the last minute. Brandy was flamed in a pan before cream was added. James now understood what Combeaux meant when he said that cooks were in the service of the food. It is the cook who must adapt and create to let the food find its full glory. James looked at the bounty and creativity and thought, if, as Jefferson had said, Versailles was the head of France, then certainly Les Halles was the belly of Paris, and Combeaux its soul.

CHAPTER 12

As the fall of 1785 deepened into winter, Jefferson showed greater interest in his Sunday briefings with James. The varieties of vegetables changed. The cooler weather called for thicker sauces and more robust game and braised meats. James offered new detail on the processes that would be more understandable to Jefferson than James's abstract notions of the flavors. "Herbs and spices of the most enormous array. And how the chef combines them is in a way that is magic. He makes a completely new aroma and taste each day."

Jefferson said, "Well, it is up to you to record these formulas for duplication at Monticello. Be precise on weights and measures. If you can't, then use ratios."

"Ratios?"

"One thing to another. Like one measure of this to three of that."

"I see."

"No one will have your depth of knowledge."

Shortly after James began his apprenticeship, many changes were made to the household. Marc hired his friends. Legrand, a rotund man who was once valet to a duke, replaced James as Jefferson's *valet de chambre*. An older man named Vendome became the coachman. Marc also hired a woman from the country to cook the everyday meals, while Combeaux sent platters for special dinners. He retained the staff of lesser importance to him, including the gardener and several house servants, called *frotteurs*, whose only duty was to put rags on their feet and slide over the floors of parquet wood and travertine tiles to make them shine.

Benjamin Franklin decamped to the United States for the Constitutional Convention to review the Articles of Confederation.

This left Jefferson to the task of negotiating treaties of trade unaided. Jefferson often told his dinner companions that his was the laboring oar and he had to press on. This required long hours and many social events. In this new role, James spoke less frequently with Jefferson. But when the two did talk, James saw that the melancholy that had hung like a fog about Jefferson's shoulders in Monticello had lifted. The man's enthusiasm for new projects lit him aflame. In the heat of this newfound vigor, he designed the capitol building for Virginia and drew up plans for a comprehensive national educational system, suggesting it as a prerequisite for an informed electorate. He calculated an eclipse, posited a theory on how seashells came to be atop the Swiss Alps, and began to dine with philosophers.

William Short was summoned from Monticello, arrived in November, and easily slipped into his role as Jefferson's personal secretary and confidant. As others established new housekeeping routines, James spent long days learning from Combeaux. Sundays when he had moments to meet with Jefferson and attend to his laundry and other matters, he noticed ongoing changes in the residence. Jefferson continued improving the house by knocking down a wall here, adding a door there, replanting the entire garden in his design, adding plants from Virginia, and planning when to plant the corn and peas from the seeds that Short had brought with him. At the outer sill of his study's window, he installed the latest in weather-measuring instruments including two brass-bound thermometers and a rain gauge consisting of a glass tube with calibrations etched on the side.

He proceeded as though there were no cost to such things and money grew in his garden. Seeing his interest in weather-predicting instruments, Lafayette sent the newest barometer for a gift. It was a yard tall and crafted in walnut as fine as furniture. It looked like a banjo, with a round, lower enameled plate in cream with delicate black lettering on a dial. It marked the inches of mercury in the tube and had simple predictions such as "wet weather" when the mercury dropped, or "dry weather" when it rose. Lafayette had smiled broadly when he saw that Jefferson had installed his gift in the study adjacent to the outdoor thermometers.

In late November, James marched down the gleaming hallway to Jefferson's study with several papers in hand. Then he stood before Jefferson, as usual for their Sunday exchange. "Sauces. I've spent the whole week making different sauces to pour over game or fowl or fish. I write down what I can recall at night. It is not complete, but I know there are five mother sauces. Perhaps more."

Jefferson frowned. "'Mother sauces'?"

Nodding, James counted off the names on his fingers. "*Béchamel, velouté. espagnole, holandaise,* and *tomate,* that he calls *Pomodoro* as the French don't trust tomatoes."

Jefferson looked puzzled. He muttered the new word under his breath, then asked, "Are they like ours?"

"Similar." James continued his report. "Chef says the names of the sauces come from the style of cooking or to pay honor to the house making it first."

"Like the Prince Soubise's sauce?"

James nodded again. "I made notes each night after learning how to make the mother sauces. Each of the mother sauces has daughters. To help me remember them, I drew a tree, with all daughter sauces as branches. Five trees each with five branches. Suddenly there are twenty-five sauces at your hand. I still don't know what they're all used for."

"Let me see your diagrams."

James handed Jefferson one page. On it, a stark tree had names and lists of ingredients hanging off bare limbs like Christmas ornaments.

James tapped the page as he explained the illustration. "First is the white sauce called *béchamel.* Made of butter, flour, and milk. He adds clove and nutmeg sometimes. But when you add cream to a *béchamel,* it becomes a *crème sauce.* Add Parmesan and Gruyère cheeses, and you have a *Mornay* sauce, used over vegetables. To make a *Soubise* sauce, add slow-cooked onions and beat it smooth. Perfect on eggs or chicken dishes. The *Nantua* sauce is just adding shrimp-butter and cream to go over seafood. And if you add cheddar cheese, mustard, and a dash of the English Worcestershire sauce, it becomes a cheddar cheese sauce. That is quite nice over the larger of the Italian macaroni. I must make that for you soon. But as much as you love mustard, I think that the mustard sauce would be your favorite. Now that is what may be made from just one of the mother sauces."

James passed the next page to Jefferson. "Second is the brown sauce called *espagnole*. Roasted bones and vegetables make a dark stock that is thickened by *roux*, a flour-butter mixture. And then tomato puree is added, but that is a secret. This is further refined by slow boiling to a dense sauce called a demi-glace. The demi-glace is the tree from which branches off the *marchand de vin* sauce by adding shallots and red wine."

James closed his eyes and counted on his fingers as he named the other sauces. "*Robert* sauce, *lyonnaise* sauce, *chasseur* sauce, Madeira and Port wine sauces, and the *charcutière* sauce."

Jefferson reached for the remaining pages that James had carefully written. James watched him examine the illustration with anticipation. "What is this *velouté*?" Jefferson stumbled over the word.

James pronounced it with precision. "*Velouté*. Means velvety. A white stock, made from fish, veal, or chicken, thickened with *roux*. A chicken *velouté* plus cream becomes *Sauce Suprême*. A veal *velouté* thickened with cream and egg yolks, and I think perhaps lemon juice, becomes the *Allemande Sauce*. A fish *velouté* thickened with cream and white wine becomes the white wine sauce."

Jefferson tapped the page. "Not unlike Haydn's violin pieces. It is all theme and variation. You are making it all quite logical. I commend your scientific rigor on this, James. But you just list ingredients. Have they no measures or are you supposed to just guess at portions?"

James shrugged. "There is no standard for any measure at all. A liter in Paris is a great deal different than a liter measured by a cook from Lyon, where they call it a *litron*. I am trying to gauge the amounts and will be adding those to my notations as I learn more. This is a challenge; there are no set measures for anything, except tea."

"Excellent start, James. Excellent. One thing we need to do as a new country is to develop our own standard measures. A knob of butter or an egg's weight of flour is simply not consistent with the scientific method that we need to expand knowledge. What is the weight of an egg, after all? A goose egg? A chicken egg? A duck egg?"

"Exactly. That is the problem in replicating what Chef does."

"That is one of the matters I will have Franklin bring forth at the Constitutional Convention. We need to have a federal government with the authority to fix a standard of weights and measures as a part of the regulation of fair trade, so your observations and ideas are helpful." James lingered. "Was there something else?"

"Yes. About my supplies."

Jefferson was studying the first illustration and appeared annoyed at the interruption. "See Mister Short for any added paper or new pencils or your attire…"

"It's not about that, sir. Chef wants me to buy my own knife. In Virginia—"

Jefferson was irritated. "Yes, I know. You could not own property let alone carry a knife on your person. We've been over that. I think it best to adopt the local customs, as we did with that penknife. We can see what still fits once we are home."

Jefferson reached for a bell on his desk and rang it in three short bursts. In a moment, Mister Short appeared in the doorway. He gave the impression of being even more confident than he had been in Virginia. He had adopted the French attire and looked somewhat the dandy. "Sir?"

"Mister Short. Please convey to Chef Combeaux the funds necessary for James to have the rest of his equipment issued to him. Today, if possible."

James motioned for Short to remain. "With your permission, sir. I would prefer to buy it from the wages you pay me. Chef says it will have my initials burned into the handle and nobody else should use it."

Jefferson nodded. "Very well then. If that is what you desire."

"Thank you, sir." James backed out of the room.

Jefferson motioned to the seat beside his desk. "William, James has brought a matter to my attention that should interest Congress. That of weights and measures. Take notes for a proposal on a uniform system of measures for weight, volume, and distance. This is essential to advance commerce and science. I intend to give Congress two systems for their consideration. One is a modification of the familiar British measures. The other is a decimal-based system. The first in the world to be completely logical. So, start your draft of this report with this introduction. Tomorrow we will discuss the details."

During the following week, James found the arguments in the streets to be more and more reflective of the turmoil that he was hearing in the kitchen. Rumors of food shortages had become true. Cooks were only eating a part of their evening meal in the kitchen in order to take scraps and leavings home for their families.

As James was about to exit an alleyway and enter a larger street one night, he heard shouts in the distance. Soon a mob of ragged men ran in his direction. He ducked behind a wagon, reaching for his new chef's knife. He held the handle but left it in its leather sheath on his belt. He listened to the crowd shouting for freedom from the oppressive taxation and decrying the lack of bread. The mob rushed past him.

Walking between the marketplace and the restaurant, he saw flimsy paper notices pasted to the walls of main streets and on several of the fountains in the squares where people from different neighborhoods met to draw drinking water. It was at these locations that the few who could read, met, and shouted the announcements of meetings and called for rebellion.

The next Sunday, James reported his unease in the streets. Jefferson dismissed the activities as part of normal political growth but remained concerned for James and his safety during his late hours of travel.

James paused before his next topic. "While I continue to collect the formulas for the sauces, let me report on beverages. Now of tea. They drink it, but in a brew a bit different than what you were accustomed to. The measure used by Combeaux is in grams. Three grams of tea for a cup. And he uses a balance scale to do his measures so he can brew tea for five or fifty with the same accuracy. He has it steep, as odd as it seems, for one-third of a quarter of an hour."

"One-third of fifteen minutes?"

"Yes. There are no clocks in the kitchen. Chef has a pocket watch that he seems to consult occasionally. But there are a few hourglasses and smaller sandglasses that are used for timing specific periods. The hourglass turned three times for a covered pan on braise in the oven. The smallest of the glasses is for a quarter-hour, although how one can determine when a third of the sand has run to the bottom is beyond me."

"Do they actually watch the sand run through the glass?"

James laughed. "Not at all. They seem just to know when it is ready. Some sense that becomes built in over time. But regarding tea, that is not the oddest thing of all."

Jefferson looked up from his notes. "How so?"

"They smoke it."

"In a pipe?"

"Precisely. Moistened with a bit of brandy."

"And you have tried this?"

He smiled. "In the interest of science. And it is a horrid taste. It does smell rather fine, however, best noted from afar."

"And does he have a coffee?"

"Yes. Strikingly similar to that of Mister Petit."

"Other beverages?"

"Hot chocolate. Usually made with water, rarely milk. But seasoned with sugar, cinnamon, vanilla, and occasionally fine black pepper. Now here is how it is different. In a four-cup pot, he adds one egg yolk and whisks it to a froth with a thin wood rod that has rings on it."

"Wouldn't the egg cook?"

"Of course, if the two just met. But by cooling the liquid slightly and adding it slowly while beating rapidly, it tempers and thickens smoothly. And the odd thing is that he makes this a day in advance then reheats it slowly."

James had completed his report and started to leave. He paused, wondering if he should disclose that his notetaking had been discovered, then decided against doing so.

Jefferson asked, "James? I want to return to something you mentioned. Did I understand you correctly that he uses tomatoes?"

"Yes. Mostly flesh, few seeds, and so sweet."

"But I have not seen any in the market. Nor in gardens, as we might see at home in Virginia."

"Many people here and in England think they are poison. He got seeds from Milan and has a farmer grow them just for him. They add a density and a new flavor that his customers admire."

Jefferson smiled. "Yet, they know not what they eat. Bring me some of those seeds. I can dry them here and germinate them at Monticello."

In early December, Gabrielle reached for the earthen pitcher of wine that was on the floor between them. A torn boule of bread sat on the nearby crate. James held his small glass for her to fill. "Jefferson ate here last week. You know what he said?"

"What?"

"That it was better than anything he has ever had at *La Grande Taverne de Londres*."

She pushed back her hair. "Beauvillers has a better location at the Palais-Royal, but we do cook better. Besides, he still uses the old name, his is just as much a restaurant as ours. Tavern indeed!"

"Jefferson said he was chef to a Count."

"He's right. He is as famous for that as his cooking." She looked at James for a moment before continuing. "Papa says you are a good student."

"Good? I am better than good."

She laughed. "He tries to keep his employees humble."

He ripped off a crusty chunk of bread. "I am not his employee. I can't be."

"You could. He says in three months you have learned what should take a year. You are already better than most country cooks. And he admires them. Especially those in Lyon."

"Why?"

"He was born there. Anything that grows there is superior. Just ask him! It is halfway to the Mediterranean Sea. The Rhône wines are gentle in a way that the wines of the north are not. I must take you there."

"How? Except for my chef's knife, Jefferson owns me and everything else I have. I even had to have his permission to buy that. A slave owns nothing and can't even carry a knife or sword, let alone a gun, without written permission in his pocket. Even these clothes are his to burn tomorrow if he takes a notion."

Gabrielle paused, then sipped her wine. She took a deep breath and put down her glass. "Leave him. You can petition the admiralty court."

"To do what? Starve in the streets? Stand in line for bread that is not there? You know he has to take his own bread rolls to dinner parties now."

"I know. The harvest is late and the last one was poor. It will not always be so."

"How could I support myself?"

"Cook! Cook for my father. You are that good already."

"And trade one master for another? No, thank you."

Gabrielle leaned over and kissed him. He pulled back in shock. She reached for the string at the neck of his loose pullover shirt. He remembered the cook's warning and grabbed her hand to stop her. When she tugged against his hand, he grinned and pulled his shirt over his head. She straddled his lap and kissed him.

It had only been a few months, but she saw a difference in him. His shoulders had broadened, chest hardened, and the lean boy she had met that late summer morning was now a muscular man. She stood, extended her hand, and led him to her bed. He sat on the edge and watched her undress slowly. When he shed his breeches and reclined, she went to her dresser and then handed him a sheath.

"What's this?"

"A lambskin. You don't use them in America?"

"Looks like a sausage casing."

She fell on the bed laughing. "It is! Sheep intestine but called a lambskin. Here, let me show you."

When she gently slipped it on him, he shuddered as his desire intensified.

After they made love, she ran her finger over his forehead and whispered. "Like *café au lait*. You are not like the others."

James opened his eyes and smiled at her. "Your other lovers?"

She swatted him. "*Gèns de couleur*. Other dark men. Cooks. Merchants."

He rested on one elbow. "You know that I am not from Africa. I was born in Virginia. On the Wayles Plantation in Cumberland County."

"Are all the men born there lighter, like your beautiful color?"

He chuckled. "Just me. I am the only one who looks like me. Not white. Not African. Just me. My grandfather was a redheaded sea captain, but my grandmother was not always a slave. She was a free woman in Africa who was kidnapped and taken to the colonies. So my mother was born a slave. My father was a white man too, Mister Wayles. So, I'm a slave. You see how it happens?"

Gabrielle frowned. "But if the father was a slave and the mother white?"

James smirked. "Law say that child be free. But if that happened, it be a good bet that they'd sell him off right fast and pretend he never happened."

Toward the end of December, the kitchen was shutting down for the night when Combeaux called everyone to the worktable in the center of the room. James was the last to be cleaning his work area with a rag soaked with vinegar. Combeaux spoke slowly so James understood him. "Finish that later. I want to show you all how to make a new dessert for the celebration of the New Year. How heat transforms sugar into something wonderful."

"*Oui, Chef!*" By the time James had walked the few steps to the big worktable, Combeaux had whisked eggs into a deep saucepan of hot milk. "This is the start of my new dessert. First, make a milk custard as you know, but now I add gelatin to it. I demonstrate. But with double the usual vanilla." He strained the hot mixture through a fine metal sieve into a large pitcher. "Marcel! Butter a dozen ramekins. Quickly."

As the stocky man buttered the interior of the small dishes, Combeaux explained his plan. "First, we make a custard. The use of the gelatin is essential for a good set, but it must be strained so there are no bits or lumps to interrupt the silken texture." He poured the warm custard into each of the ramekins. "We will bake them off in a water bath." He then poured hot water into the rimmed pan until it was halfway up the sides of the dishes. He pointed to the oven, and Marcel carried the deep pan to it. James opened the heavy door for Marcel to slide in the pan.

Combeaux pointed to the cooling room. "James! Bring out the set custards. On the top of the rack."

James hurried to the room, found the pan, and quickly brought it to the table in front of Combeaux. "Now we put plenty of sugar on the top of the custard. And then." With that, he topped the custards with clumped, tan sugar and pulled a red-hot iron from the coal fire under the cooking plates. At the end of the long metal handle was a thick disk, just smaller than the top of the ramekin.

James watched the process as a normal lesson until the red-hot iron was held above the sugar and it started to bubble. Suddenly, he smelled not the sugar but flesh being burned. He closed his eyes and again saw a slave being branded with a letter R. He was an older man who had run away from Monticello and was returned in chains.

James leaned against the end of the worktable for support. Another cook turned and grabbed his arm as he started to slump. When he looked back at the ramekin, he saw that the sugar had melted from a dark, bubbling caramel into a glassy surface. There was no smoke, no burning flesh, and no branding

Combeaux shouted, "Gabrielle!"

Gabrielle ran over to James and took his other arm. They steered him to the bottom step of the landing. After sitting, he let his face fall into his cupped hands and leaned his elbows against his knees. A few of the cooks patted his shoulder as they walked by him and left for the night. As Combeaux passed them, he told James to try the *crème brûlée* that he had left for him on the table. James nodded while still holding his head in his hands.

When everyone had left, Gabrielle pulled his hands away from his wet face and brushed the tears from his cheeks. "What?"

He leaned his elbows back into the stairs, shook his head, and took a deep breath. She got up and brought their ramekins over. With a spoon, she cracked the brittle sugar crust and gave him a taste. "Better?"

"Better."

After they each finished eating the new dessert, she put her arm around his shoulder. "Come upstairs?"

Gabrielle helped him to the edge of the bed. He fell back as if punched. She felt his forehead. "Are you ill?"

James shook his head slowly.

"Have you eaten today?"

James covered his eyes with his forearm and sobbed. "The iron. I seen that iron before. Smell how it is when it gets red-hot. Old man, Tommy his name, a runaway. Third time when Massa went away. The overseer copped him when he was just two days gone. Built a fire in the middle of the dirt road by the slave cabins at suppertime so all the field hands was in. Lay an iron into the fire until it come out glowing like the sun. Just like today. We all had to watch." James rubbed his eyes. "He takes up the iron with the letter R on the end and laid it into that old man's cheek. He did not scream or nothing. Smoke come off his face. Two grown men holding him got tears down their faces and can't do nothing. That's the only letter most slaves know. R for runaway."

Gabrielle barely made out the words through his sobs. She sat beside him. She stroked his forehead until he relaxed and seemed to be asleep.

She whispered, "*Dormez bien.* Sleep well."

James shook his head as he sat up on the edge of the bed. "I gotta go now."

Gabrielle put her finger to his lips. "Rest a minute more. I understood enough. How could someone?"

"A slave got no say in their life. None. I hear them in the street yelling for *liberté*. But they got more liberty today than I'll ever know."

"Does not your Jefferson see that?"

"He sees what he wants to see. I hear him tell Petit and Short how good the King is to keep the streets clean of horse droppings. That is what he sees from his carriage."

Gabrielle laughed. "Doesn't he know people are too poor to buy wood, so they burn the dried droppings? But my father says he is a philosopher who has written a plan for freeing those enslaved."

James shrugged. "He thinks we can go step by step from slavery to bond servitude to a freedman for wages. But he doesn't say how or when. He says his friend the Marquis de Lafayette has a notion to make the slaves in your French colonies into tenant farmers. But when I go home, I become a slave again."

"Until then, will you still come here? Even after you complete your lessons?"

"Yes. Of course."

"Then stay tonight." She kissed him, stood, and tugged his shirt over his head.

The pace at Restaurant Combeaux intensified for the winter holidays. Although the dishes were lavish in both the abundance and the extreme ornamentation, James found himself bored. There was nothing new to discover in the methods of preparation or ingredients. Now it was all variation on a theme during the day, no matter that the pace and quantity of production was physically challenging for the most seasoned of the staff. James found himself secretly pleased at his skills in the kitchen. In some ways, he regretted that he was apprenticed for a limited time and not an employee so he could try to extend what he had learned into new methods and dishes.

As he mastered his work, Gabrielle had become more than a teacher and lover. Theirs became a relationship with easy silences and robust laughter in her room. Then they started going out on Sunday afternoons. Coffeehouses sometimes, the few that allowed women to enter, or coffee from a street vendor that they sipped on a bench in the park. A glass of wine at an inn or tavern on other days. Soon James was able to relax in spite of the scrutiny or whispers of others and often was absent from Jefferson's residence for days at a time.

During his Sunday mornings with Jefferson, James found it difficult not to share his joy at knowing her. He struggled to find new things to report. His account of finishing off dishes made by Combeaux that he delivered to great houses seemed to bore Jefferson, while the report of who dined with whom did amuse him. James filled the silences by revisiting processes or dishes or some obscure aspect of cooking in more detail than was necessary while he shaved Jefferson. James chuckled when he noticed that his replacement, Legrand, had left unshaven patches under Jefferson's chin.

In the spring of 1786, Jefferson set a new line of inquiry for James during one of their Sunday meetings, asking if he were acquainted with how the house staff should be organized regarding the kitchen once they returned to Monticello.

Some weeks later, James arrived for his usual Sunday meeting particularly well-dressed. As he lathered the shaving soap, Jefferson took his chair and asked, "You look the picture of a man on his way to the... what do they call that place where people walk?"

"The gardens, the arcades?"

"That's it. An arcade. Do you go there on your Sunday afternoons?"

"Occasionally for a coffee at an outside table. This afternoon Gabrielle and I will be going for a walk. There is much to see if you look for it in this city. But now that there are shops at the Palais-Royal and pavement, you need not just stroll the muddy streets. In fact, they have a name for that aimless stroll, *flâner*, and a man strolling in this certain way is a *flâneur*."

"And what have you stumbled on that might interest me? I will be going to do my sketch of the cathedral's buttresses tomorrow and then meeting a friend. What is of interest near it?"

Near it? James fought to hold the clean stroke of his blade as he shaved Jefferson. *What could compare to the cathedral?* Notre-Dame de Paris was itself all that he needed to clear his mind, find his peace. The incense-heavy interior was where he stood for hours one Sunday, hidden behind a pillar, watching the hues from the stained-glass windows cross the stone floor, where he found something greater than himself that had no name. This was a holy place. Gabrielle said the Romans had a temple to Jupiter there before there was a Christ. And what was worshiped there before the Romans? The majesty Jefferson found in how the stones were arched into a flying buttress to hold high walls was what James found in the quiet interior. Jefferson could rattle off that the cornerstone was laid by Pope Alexander III and King Louis VII in 1163, the number of bells in the towers, the catalogue of relics the King had collected in his treasury, but could he feel its power? Find its solace? It was the sense of the eternal, of being more than this moment that held James in its grasp, brought him back nights to stand in the candlelight and receive its gift.

What would interest him? Everything interested him yet nothing held his attention as he flitted from project to project, meeting to meeting, person to person. Could he actually be still long enough to watch the sun move the colors across the cathedral floor? He could tell you the story of the carved figures above the center portal of the west façade, but what faith had he in such matters as represented by the artwork? He explained on their first visit how the carvings told the Biblical tale of the Last Judgment to a population unable to read. He even had a name for that: *libor pauperum*, the poor man's book, yet did he believe the story or was it only that to Jefferson, a story without meaning?

Who were those people who believed with such force that they hewed a forest of oak to build the cathedral's rafters, built the cathedral over generations, and read from a Bible made from pages of parchment from a whole flock of sheep? How was this faith found? How could this symphony in stone speak so lovingly?

James wiped the blade. "What would interest you? The challenge of a chess match at the Café de la Régence? You can play for hours."

"No. I want to entertain a companion. She heard of a wax works that is supposed to have Franklin's head in it. Have you found such in your wanderings?"

"Yes. The Cabinet of Doctor Curtius. They call Mister Franklin the Commissioner for the Free America. Looks quite like a younger version of him."

Jefferson chuckled as he squirmed. "Doctor Franklin a Commissioner! Where is it?"

James paused to visualize the area. "On the Boulevard du Temple. Number twenty, I believe."

"Take particular care today; I want a very good shave. What intelligence have you for me this week? A new recipe? A new instrument of measure?"

"Not this week. As you requested, I have the report on the organization of the household as to the kitchen. First, I was referred to two books on the organization of a home. *La Maison Réglée* by Audiger details how to operate a home with one servant."

Jefferson chuckled. "One servant? Heaven forfend we should ever fall to such depths! Go on."

"The other book is by Menon, *La Cuisinère Bourgeoise. The Household Cookery.* Now while it is more rustic than the finest of foods you are encountering, it does explain how a simple *potager* operates."

"Who is that?"

"It's a what, and a who, sir. Remember when I first went to the restaurant, how I explained the cooking plates to you?"

"Similar to the top of Franklin's stove, you said."

"Yes. There was an early version that just heated one soup pot called a *potager*. Combeaux has expanded the idea to allow twenty pots and pans to be on heat at any one moment, without exposure to an open fire. This is the arrangement that I strongly recommend you employ at Monticello. Safer. Smarter. More economical."

"*Potager?* I have heard that before. It means a cook's garden, things to make a soup of."

"Chef said the English had appropriated the French word. In his kitchen it also refers to the cook who makes soup. Although he has room for twenty pans at once, at Monticello, you would need only half that size."

"I see. I would expect you to direct the construction, James. The kitchen shall be your domain, unchecked. Combeaux already is singing your praises, now that you are approaching the end of that apprenticeship. It seems to have gone very well."

James ignored the compliment and cleared his throat. "The organization of the kitchen in a great house is complex. But here is what I have gathered, and I use the French terms as I don't know of equivalents for many of the words in English."

"Oh, my, are you forgetting your English? Are you that immersed in your cooking with the Frenchies?"

James chuckled and shook his head. "Large homes, as yours, have two kitchens. The main one is the *cuisine* like the large one at Monticello, where all the main cooking is done. Then there is a smaller one, usually adjoining it, called an *office*. In this one, the more delicate work is done."

"Somewhat like our butler's pantry?"

"It is for the final preparation of food, garnishing, and the like. But it also is where they make the salads. During the daytime, it is the place for sugar work, pickling, and preservation of foods, and making infusions, or distillations. Those tending to these specialized duties are the *officiers d'office.*"

Jefferson smirked. "Bit redundant, isn't it?"

"That's what they call it. Now, there are underlings in the main kitchen called *aides,* and *garçons de cuisine.* The *écuyer* is also an *officer de cuisine.* The *rôtisseur* is a cook specializing in roasting meats."

"That's all he does? Stand around waiting to roast something?"

"I am certain there are other duties to which he can be put. But they have a new way to roast over an open hearth. They have added glazed ceramic tiles to the back of the hearth. This increases the heat, reduces cooking time. It makes for a better browning, and also speeds the cleaning of the soot from the hearth. But you asked about organization. These are the positions in a grand house. Now, how many and how deployed is a matter I am still exploring, but from my observation, a staff of eight to ten would be needed at Monticello to conduct your entertaining in the manner and frequency you have here."

"Well, soon enough you will finish with Combeaux and join the household again. Then we can see what is really needed in a practical way."

"Of course. But in the meanwhile, shall I continue my investigation on staffing in other grand homes?"

"Please."

James wiped lather from the razor's edge. "Sir? There is another matter."

Jefferson's eyebrow rose. "And that is?"

"The *batterie de cuisine.*"

Jefferson sighed, wanting the discussion to end so he could return to his papers. "And who is that?"

Without correcting him, James continued. "The cookware. The array of pots and pans all stored on hooks. The tools to cook with. I recommend that you start gathering those for your use back at Monticello, as they are specialized and not always available."

"Thank you, James. Start a list for me. And, have a good stroll. And James, we will not be meeting for several weeks as my schedule has become overly crowded. I'll have Petit inform you of our next meeting."

"Certainly. Thank you, sir."

In the following weeks, the hints of spring were followed by huge swings in the weather, from sleet to brilliant sunlight within a span of a few days. The sun was just warm enough to fend off the light chill in the air when James and Gabrielle strolled through the Jardin des Tuileries and admired the budding flowers before stopping at a coffeehouse with outdoor tables.

Over the remaining months of his training with Combeaux, James continued to learn more and more in the kitchen. His relationship with Gabrielle deepened. When fall arrived, there was intensity to their meetings as though all their future had to be compressed into long nights together.

When James returned to Jefferson's Paris residence in October, he became the under-cook to Sophie, *la cuisinière.* Sophie ruled the kitchen and its menus with a force and assurance that was as firm as her training of James was caring and tender. She had no use for the shouting and drama that James had seen in the kitchens of the great homes where he had delivered catered meals and provided the finishing touches to elegant dishes.

Only occasionally did Jefferson alter one of her announced menus. Her only frustration, which she did her best to hide from James, was that Marc had tasked her assistant to do much of the provisioning of grains and staples for the house. She balked and refused to let Marc interfere with her daily trips to Les Halles for fresh foods. On these journeys, she had James accompany her to use his skill and relationships with vendors to secure the best items and bargain for the best price. During these private moments, Sophie confided how much she missed her family and their farm. James nodded silently, not disclosing how he longed for Gabrielle every night.

By late January, James was making many of the selections, with Sophie only coaching him with a wink or a nod. So positive was the relationship between the two and James's enjoyment of working for her that he was shocked when Jefferson announced he would be leaving the kitchen.

James stood beside Jefferson's desk while Jefferson searched for the words. "A *boulangerie* and a *pâtisserie*. Yes, a bakery and a pastry and confectionary shop. That's where Marc said you should work to complete your training. Once you have mastered those crafts, you will be able to do anything at Monticello."

"A bakery? We buy our bread here and as for sweets—"

"I think Marc has a point. But it is Petit who has the craft and connections to secure such positions for you. See him for the details."

"But Sophie?"

"Managed before you arrived and can struggle for a few months while you finish your training." Jefferson frowned at the challenge to his directive. "Petit is waiting for you." He returned to reading his dispatches and ignored James, who stood looking at him for a full minute before stalking off to find Petit.

CHAPTER 13

At Jefferson's request, Petit had negotiated something of an apprenticeship with both a bakery and a *pâtisserie*. Breads and sweets were all that James needed to complete the most extensive culinary education in France. Petit had a nose for bargains and struck one with two of the vendors used by the residence. The trade was simple: James would be trained just to the point that he could function in the craft at no cost to the residence, then James would work a month for each employer without a wage. Underlying this arrangement was the tacit agreement that they would continue to be the exclusive purveyors of goods to the residence of the representative of the United States of America in Paris.

When Petit advised James of the details related to his new assignments, he took the news poorly. He wanted to be in the residence and at liberty several evenings a week to see Gabrielle. The night before starting at the bakery, he was having coffee in the kitchen when Petit arrived with Jefferson's empty sherry glass on a tray. As he washed it, he glanced at James. "So? It begins tomorrow?"

"With a baker!" James could hardly disguise his frustration. "I'm a chef, not a baker!"

"James. This was not my idea. Marc went to Jefferson with this notion, because he wants you to be away. But there is actually good that can come from this."

"What could that possibly be?"

"There are many chefs in France. But there are almost none who also know bread and confectionary. If you have those three talents, you could work anywhere in the world. Anywhere."

James put down his cup and stared at him. *What is he saying? Does he suspect that I planned to stay?* "Why do you say that?"

"Because you may not see the truth yet. France is changing. The very rich have too much and the poor too little. This will change."

"But you live off the rich. Without these grand houses, how could you survive?"

"I know my life and my country. But in you I see something larger. If you stay as a free man, your life would be your own."

James lowered his voice. "Have you said anything to him?"

"Of course not. What you do with your life is for you to decide. But I saw an opportunity to offer you more choices while I get this house in order. It is not ready for you to be its chef."

"I am ready!"

"I know that. I was not clear. There must be corrections made in the staffing before you are the *chef de cuisine*, or you will fail."

"Why would I fail? I can do Sophie's work now!"

Petit motioned for him to be quiet. "Marc will make certain that you fail if you remain here now. He fears you and is jealous of you as well. Go. Learn your new skills as fast as you can. The arrangement is that you work a month for them after your skills are acceptable."

"A month? That's two months plus the training time!"

"If you apply yourself. Now James, there are two things to these agreements that might interest you. First, both shops are well away from here. Second, I have informed Monsieur Jefferson that you must find lodging near them to be able to perform well. So, you must spend nights elsewhere."

His shoulders slumped. "Where are they?"

"By coincidence, both are quite near Restaurant Combeaux."

James stared at Petit and slowly grinned. "You did this? For me?"

He shrugged. "Remember, no work is beneath you unless you do it poorly. Make the best of this opportunity. When you are ready, this kitchen will be yours. I promise." Petit raised the wet glass to James in a mock toast before drying it.

Petit's directions were clear and James found the bakery with ease. It was on the Seine, twenty minutes from Jefferson's residence but only five from Gabrielle's room, although in a decidedly less affluent section of the city. Dray horses crowded the street, moving produce or materials. The stench of their droppings filled the chilly January air.

It was midday when James presented himself at the bakery. As he approached it, he saw an unimposing brick façade with small shops on either side. One made candies. Another made infused spirits with such oddities as a clear cherry brandy and orange-flavored liqueurs. The third shop offered dried fruit peels or fruits preserved in sugar syrup for use in baking. This allowed cake makers or bakers to add orange zest or candied bits of lemon, cherry, or other dried fruits to their goods throughout the year. To the side of the building was a sign, *Moulin à Grains*, a grain mill.

When he entered the Boulangerie Boutin, the young woman beside racks of the rounded *boules* looked up from the sales table. James introduced himself. She went to the doorway and called into the back for the owner. In a few moments, Jean-Paul Boutin came through the doorway and smiled as he approached James. He was a tall, thin man with wispy white hair that was close cropped at the sides and rear while it fell forward in front almost to his eyebrows. He gave little impression of his strength or vigor but appeared similar to the monks James had seen walking in pairs throughout the city.

Unlike Combeaux, Boutin did not put him to work immediately, but instead took him to the mill and made a cup of coffee for each of them. Sitting on the dock overlooking the Seine, James watched the striped cats prowl inside the flour mill for mice. Jean-Paul told James of the history of his establishment. He had a small bakery and was proud of his breads but did not like the reliance on vendors of flours that were never quite the same.

Boutin held his cup aloft to make a pronouncement. "Inconsistency in baking is flirting with ruin." He explained that he needed to control the process from the field to the final boule, roll, or loaf which he sold in the shop or delivered to his subscription customers. To manage this, he convinced other family members to join him. Boutin found an abandoned brick warehouse that had a dock on the Seine. It had been used previously for shipping tanned hides. He placed an option on it and had his relatives come to Paris to see it. With sweeping gestures, he told James how they came to share his vision and trusted him to proceed.

They sold their three family farms to become his partners. He bought the empty warehouse and partitioned the building into several businesses. In the front third, facing a large street, he built his bakery and three stores beside it. He installed ovens behind the bakery but held the area behind the shops for his warehouse. But the brilliance of his plan was in reserving the rear of the space for a mill.

He hired a Dutch millwright who drafted a plan to harness the power of the Seine to turn his millstones. He ordered millstones quarried, cut, and faced even before the construction began. The millwright fabricated the waterwheel and the interior gears and pulleys to move the stones at whatever speed and pressure was required. Boutin pointed to a series of support beams attached to the waterwheel. "You know what those can do?"

"No."

"Because there is none like it. I can pull my wheel above the water if I need to. I think of the future and how I could lose it if the river ran too fast or if there was a flood and logs floated down."

"Does it work?"

Boutin grinned. "It did two years ago. Trees were swept away by a flood and every mill in Paris took damage, except mine. Although it is cold now, it is not so cold I need to stop milling. To bake, you need to think ahead, that is the skill I applied in this planning." James smiled as he thought how Jefferson would appreciate Boutin's planning and craft.

The baker told him that it took only four months from the start of the project until he milled his first batch of flour. He stood. James followed him as he walked to the end of the dock. "The river gives us the power of the mill, but also immediate transportation to buyers downstream." As they spoke, the waterwheel groaned and splashed, reminding James of his sea voyage. Boutin tossed the remainder of his coffee into the river and used the empty cup as a pointer as he walked toward the enclosed building. "Here is the shaft that the waterwheel drives; now come inside and see the gears and pulleys it powers."

James quickly finished his coffee and followed Boutin. "By adjusting these, we can hold the millstones to the perfect rotation speed for any grain, no matter how fast the river is running."

"Do you run the mill overnight?"

"Not yet. The dust from the milling can explode if conditions are just so. Dust to flame." He made a gesture with his hands, flinging them out from his chest to the sky. "That is why I put in the glassed areas in the roof, to let in daylight."

James looked out of the sliding door to the river. "What if you put lanterns outside and glassed windows on the riverside of the mill?"

Boutin nodded and smiled. "A thinker. I like that. First, let's have you work in the mill to get to know flour, then we bake."

James hoisted fifty-pound sacks of wheat to the hopper that fed the grain to a hole in the center of the upper grinding wheel. Each of the gray granite stones was five feet across and weighed over five hundred pounds. When the grain was ground to flour, the white powder and darker chaff fell from the sides of the grinding wheels into a slanted tray. From there, it fell into a bin.

Next, James shoveled the blotchy flour onto a screen that held back the bitter bran husks. As soon as the mill stopped grinding new wheat, he refilled the hopper and began the process again. It seemed easy at first, but after three hours of lifting sacks and shoveling, his arms and back started having small spasms.

As he was stretching to calm his muscles, Boutin walked over to him and patted the top stone as it turned. "These stones? They are French quartz from La Ferté-sous-Jouarre, near the town of Châlons."

"Do you do only wheat?"

"No. We can mill any of the variety of corns. Rye, wheat, buckwheat, millet. Some farmers want us to grind and let them screen it, others not. Bakers have their own blend of grains and specific requirements on how many times the flour is screened. We have even ground some dried American maize for a man, I cannot say his name, who became accustomed to your American corncakes, he called them."

James suppressed a grin wondering if that man was Franklin or Jefferson and who had fried up the corncakes. "So, you grind more than your own flour?"

"Yes. Some pay us a fee to mill their grains, and for some they keep the type of wheat and other grains a secret. Others bring in their rye or wheat and let us take a portion of their product in payment. And we charge to dress the millstone for a new type of grain as each has its own best way to grind."

James looked at the far wall of the mill that had huge shelves running to the roof. Each shelf was filled with three or four huge sacks of flour. Several cats were asleep in a pale shaft of winter sun. James thought of the rumors that he had heard of bread shortages yet hesitated to ask about the matter directly. "You seem to have a lot of bags of flour here. Are those waiting delivery?"

"No. We hold a reserve so if the river runs too fast to mill in winter or the spring rains are poor and there is little crop, we still can bake."

After a month of hard labor in the mill, James was finally assigned to the bakery. Above the ovens was a hand-lettered page in a frame. Although the ink had faded, James was able to discern that the words were Spanish, and the attribution was to *Don Quixote*. He asked Boutin to translate it. He grinned. "With bread, our sorrows are less."

The hours at the bakery were suited to the bread, not to James. Baking started at three in the morning and ended after nine at night—as soon as he had completed his tasks. He was grateful that Petit had arranged for him to room away from the residence during this part of his internship. James found it unusual given Jefferson's attention to detail, yet a relief, that he never inquired where James was sleeping.

His first job was simply to move the racks of yeasty dough to the baker, who then knocked the dough out of the round willow baskets onto a floured peel and slid it onto the brick floor of the blazing-hot oven. The racks of raw dough smelled like a brewery. Once the bread was done, the baker pulled it out onto a large table. The caramel scent of browned crust that filled the afternoons seemed an impossible transformation from the morning's aroma. James then picked up each of these rounds weighing about two pounds apiece and stacked them on racks to cool and move to the front for sale to individual customers or deliver to restaurants or homes with bread subscriptions.

Cleaning up sticky baskets and then mixing the dough were his duties for the next month. During the third month, he progressed to weighing the dough on the balance scale before folding it upon itself until the dough became a ball that he then dropped into the flour-dusted baskets to proof. Once that was mastered, he was taught to measure and form the small loaves and rolls favored by the taverns and inns.

The physical labor of baking was more than he had imagined. Working long hours in the flour-filled room left him with a consistent shallow cough and red eyes. Mixing the dough with long paddles in wide-mouthed tubs tore into his shoulder muscles as if he were doing fieldwork on the plantation. Most days, fifty sacks of flour were blended with water and the buckets of yeasty starter. Somehow the bubbling, runny starter that Boutin called *levain* smelled like old beer would cause the thicker flour and water to become alive and expand over the course of several nights.

Throughout the winter, the dance became obvious to James. The starter held the magic of the yeast that gave the flour life, so the dough rose in its willow form and again in the oven. But what happened in the span of forty hours from mixing to baking astounded him. The slow development of the dough was in sharp contrast to the fast pace in Combeaux's kitchen that transformed raw ingredients into a finished platter in minutes, not days.

After his work on either side of the actual baking of bread, he was allowed to bake off rounds for a day under the eye of the master baker. He only burned one round, which he was sent home with as a reminder of the need for continual attention and precision in the baking. As usual, the restaurant had been closed for almost an hour by the time he arrived.

Gabrielle laughed when he gave her the burned bread. He ripped away the blackened bottom crust and tore off a piece for her to dip in her soup. She grinned at him. "What can't you do?"

"Seems I was thinking too much on you and not enough on moving the ones in the back of the oven."

Soon James had the skills to manage any of the several duties that were rotated between the bakers. One day he had to clean up. Another day he only mixed new dough from the starter, water and flour. He most enjoyed forming the dough into the prescribed shapes to rise in baskets for the big round boules, or on pans for rolls or loaves. Handling the dough was tactile and sensual in a way that surprised him. Holding the dough, he learned to test its strength, to add a bit of flour when too wet, to knead it longer if it was flabby, and to fold it to develop the strength to retain its shape in the oven. This was the moment in the life of a bread that could make a difference between it being just bread and perfect bread.

Most of the boules used a blend of wheat, rye, and buckwheat flour. The loaves and rolls rarely contained buckwheat. Soon, James learned that the main diet of most people in Paris was a boule or two a day, supplemented by vegetables and rarely by meat. In his last week with Boutin, several men had charged the delivery cart, two stopped the horse while others took bread from the baskets. The next morning, James was relieved of his baking duties and tasked to ride on the back of the wagon with a small club.

By the time that he had completed his work for Boutin, James had strengthened his body and lived as a free man. He also discovered that he had the luxury of working in a heated building while many residents did not have firewood. The cooks that Combeaux had fed daily ate better than most shopkeepers. Seeing Jefferson infrequently had hardened his resolve to be free one day.

James knew that he was due to start his new apprenticeship in pastry and confections upon the completion of his baking experience. Without informing Jefferson that he and the baker had met their obligations, James invited Gabrielle to go away with him for three days in the countryside. This escape was over all too soon. They returned to Paris without any resolution concerning his future plans after completing his pastry apprenticeship.

When Short discovered that James had taken leave without permission, he raged at Marc for the lapse and stormed into Jefferson's study. Short arrived out of breath and flushed. "Sir? I need to discuss James."

"Please close the door."

Jefferson motioned toward the chair. Short continued to stand. "He's gone on his own accord. A few days in the country with that woman."

"Yes, Marc told me."

"He's acting as free as if he'd gone to the Admiralty Court."

"Yes. Yes. I know that, but I presumed his bonds of loyalty ran deeper than they may actually be."

"Why so? Have there been other incidents?"

"He as much as confronted me before he went to that baker, stating that he was free here. Do you have any idea the embarrassment it would cause me to have my servant go to court against me? I've spent considerable sums to train him as my chef. How would I replace him? That money was spent, invested, and now I need my return on that investment."

Short regained his composure. "Certainly. Sir, if you will permit me to speak honestly?"

"Of course."

"You have engaged in discussions with him that have allowed him license to speak freely to you in a manner inconsistent with a servant, let alone a slave."

"But he is an exceptional Negro."

"That aside, he has associated with who knows what types while living away from the residence. I fear the flame of freedom has flared in his imagination. I have tried to warn you."

"You think me too easy on him?"

Short paused. "No, sir. But he takes liberties, like going off with that cook's daughter for several days."

Jefferson smiled. "Well, he is a young man."

Short continued the idea. "Who needs to start his pastry education this week."

"Agree."

"If I may suggest," Short said, "he needs an anchor to hold him fast to America."

"What are you thinking?"

"He always was particularly protective of his little sister. Your girls liked her. What was her name?"

"Susie? No. Was it Sally?"

"Yes. Sally. By my reckoning, she should be, what thirteen or fourteen by now. Old enough to serve Polly here."

Jefferson thought on that a moment. "We do seem to be entrenched. Yes, bringing Polly over is a fine plan. Logical. Polly's not even ten years of age, a bit young to travel unattended on a voyage. Frees her aunt of her care and that of the slave girl as well." Jefferson nodded and turned back to his papers. "Draft a letter for me to Missus Eppes to ready Sally with letters and news of Monticello, and attire for a spring crossing to accompany Polly. That should reset James's sights."

"Certainly, sir."

"But there is no need for you to make a copy of the correspondence."

"Sir?"

"I want it to appear as though my sister-in-law has made the decision to send Sally in opposition to my desires. I shall kick up some dust claiming that I wanted an older companion and have no need for contrary documents."

In April, James began his work at the *pâtisserie*. Unlike the bakery, which was nestled in the working district, the *pâtisserie* was not more than three streets from the Restaurant Combeaux. The wealthy would arrive in grand carriages as much to be seen as to shop. Men of renown would arrive for the fitting of a suit or sword. Ladies visited the perfumeries, bought hats, and browsed for fine linens for their table. The pastry shop was ideally located to offer delicacies to revive the wealthy after the arduous work of shopping or for a later moment of indulgence. The window display was arranged as though it were a jewelry case.

Before James entered the *pâtisserie*, he gazed at the samples on glass stands, topped by thin glass domes. Each item was an exemplar of delicacy and precision. There were bite-size replicas of palaces or art pieces. Crusts as delicate as a dried oak leaf held perfectly symmetrical, paper-thin slices of apple glazed over with a substance that made them look like they were glassed paperweights. Other tarts were the size of a dinner plate with a full array of summer fruits displayed in a pattern like an artist's pallet.

Small cakes, one bite at the most, were frosted in one color and decorated with another. A stack of *profiteroles* fascinated him. The small creampuffs formed a tower within a net of strands of caramelized sugar. He glanced past the display and noticed that the woman inside the store was staring at him. Embarrassed, he straightened up, adjusted his coat, and entered the shop.

The short, slim woman of his age stood at the polished oak counter and dropped a coin into a basket. He stepped aside as a man held a creampuff in one hand and walked out to the street to eat it. James waited behind a woman who purchased a small box of the bite-sized cakes. When it was his time to be served, he asked to see Pierre DuBois.

The clerk looked offended. "You don't want to buy a pastry?"

"No. I'm the new apprentice."

She pointed to the end of the counter. "Stand there." After she helped another customer, she turned and pulled back the curtain covering the doorway to the work area. "Papa? He is here."

A burly man whose shirt and trousers were a stark white swept the curtain aside and stared at James. "So, you want to learn the finer arts, eh? Cooking is one art, but pastry is the combination of many arts, as you will see."

James just nodded and followed him to the rear of the shop. This room was small. Everyone seemed to be working alone on some project without assistance. Unlike the camaraderie that Combeaux encouraged, each person in this kitchen seemed engaged in their own solitary endeavor.

He was first tasked to do the hard labor that everyone hated. Hauling buckets of coal from the basement and learning how to stoke the coal-fired ovens and maintain an even heat was all he did for a week. During that time, he felt as if his eyes were on fire from the coal dust and heat.

Next, he was tasked to make puff pastry. First, he made a dough with a sturdy, bread-like texture, but without any leavening. Then, he used a huge rolling pin that was almost three feet long to form a large, flat rectangle. Thinking he was finished, he reported to DuBois and thought how simple that was. DuBois carried a pail of cold butter to the table, used a large scoop to cover the right half with butter and then folded the sides over it to make a square. Covering the middle third of this square with another layer of butter, he folded each side over it and told James to flatten it.

DuBois crossed his arms and let James struggle while trying to compress the cold butter by rolling the pin over the top. Others glanced at his futile efforts and snickered. Finally, DuBois took the long rolling pin from him and used it like a pickax to flatten the cold butter between two pastry sheets. Using the rolling pin again, he beat the butter and dough into a flat rectangle. DuBois then folded the left third over the center before turning the right third on top of the folded dough forming a tall rectangle. Then he turned the dough sideways and folded the right half over the left, as if he were closing a book and told James to pound it flat again. After repeating this process four more times, James created a multilayered dough that rose in the oven from the expansion of the butter and created paper-thin layers of a flaky pastry. After ten hours of batting dough flat and rolling it, he felt like he had been hoeing row crops in a field.

The next day, he made puff pastry all morning. In the afternoon, he was partnered with Paul, who was noted for his *canelé* cakes. These individual servings of a caramelized rum-flavored cake were unique to the shop. They were made in a mold so that they had a lacy crust on top and a soft interior that was more like custard than cake. While others mixed the simple batter, which resembled a *crème anglaise*, James was tasked to coat the interior of the fluted copper molds with beeswax. This allowed the deeply browned cakes to slide out as soon as they emerged from the oven and were turned out of the mold. The wax also gave a shine to the baked cake. Each mold was copper and just deep enough for his long fingers to reach the bottom and run along the fluted sides. His attention to detail and ability to make this simple batter had him making these desserts exclusively for a week.

A last-minute order for a *croquembouche* rescued James from *canelé* production. DuBois knew that James had made *profiteroles* before. Combeaux often had the simple creampuff filled with a liqueur-flavored whipped cream to offer as an ending to a meal. Once hearing that, James was relegated to the production of a hundred walnut-sized puffs. Making the *pâte à choux* was easy for him. Melting butter in water in a pan, then beating in flour was so engrained that he did not need to measure his ingredients. After beating it for two minutes in the pan, the batter pulled together into a sticky mass. Once it had cooled, he beat in the eggs. The feel of the hot dough in the pan was as much a part of him now as was its history as related by Combeaux. Popelini, the chef of Catherine de Medici, introduced it to the French court. Then it was called *pâte chaude*, hot dough. Once the dough pulled together, dry but not browned, James took two small spoons and dropped the dough in small balls on a huge pan and baked it off in a hot oven for twenty minutes. The dough swelled, left an empty center, and browned into perfect globes.

As the treats cooled, he made the filling of cream, milk, and vanilla bean. These he heated in another deep-sided pan to a boil. Leaving it for a moment, he beat egg yolks, flour, salt, and sugar. He drizzled this into the hot mixture, beating furiously all the while to prevent the egg from cooking into lumps. He set this aside to cool. Once both were at room temperature, he filled a pouch of canvas with a tin tip at the end, punctured one of the pastry globes at a time, and filled each with the vanilla pastry cream.

His instructor then took over, melting sugar in a pan until it developed a golden glow, then removing it from the heat. The residual heat took to the sugar to a rich brown.

The pastry chef took puff after puff and dipped the edge of each into the molten sugar. Quickly, these were affixed to a silver platter provided by the mother of the bride. This creation was to be the centerpiece on a wedding table. Building a base two feet in diameter, the pastry chef proceeded to add level upon level of slightly smaller layers while James heated pan after pan of sugar without burning any of it.

Ultimately, the tower came to a point three feet above the platter. Now the chef draped the outer edge of the platter with napkins and reheated the sugar to a boil. Then he took a fork, dipped it into the molten sugar, and drizzled the strands of liquid sugar over the tower. It cooled instantly, making a web of sugar over the creampuffs.

Three days later another order was placed for a similar item. James was tasked to make it. He did well, until DuBois passed near his workstation. Distracted, he dipped too deeply and hit the melted sugar. The sugar clung to his right thumb, burning away the top layer of skin. He jumped back and knocked the pan onto the floor. A thin rope of the molten sugar hit his left forearm and stuck. He lunged for the water bucket and shoved his arm into it. The sugar solidified and burned off a swirl of skin, leaving a ruddy, raw patch.

As DuBois found butter to put on his arm, he smirked at him. "Perhaps you might prefer making the *pièces montées*." He went on to explain that these were small, intricately designed mounted pieces. When James looked puzzled, he explained that these were composed scenes or geometric shapes with one piece of chocolate, cake, or some other pastry balanced on another. Elaborate. Inventive. With a level of detail not unlike watchmaking.

James finished wrapping the length of sheeting around his burned arm. "Do you eat it all?"

"Not necessarily. We may need to have a piece of wood or wax to hold a part in place. Think of these more as flower arrangements than confection and your imagination will soar." From his sideways glance, it was clear that he thought that at least James wouldn't harm himself or others during his time there by avoiding the boiling sugar.

James found that his imagination for arranging mounted pieces did not soar but ran elsewhere. To Gabrielle and a farm or country inn. To living in France as a free man. Living with her. Hearing her laugh every day. Knowing the future would be theirs and that her intelligence and tenderness would make their lives together rich and loving.

For his next assignment, James brushed honey and sprinkled ground nuts on a rectangular sheet of puff pastry, then rolled each of the longer sides toward the center, forming two logs. He cut across them and put the slices on a baking sheet. When browned, they looked like palm trees. Later, he filled the front counter with trays of intricately frosted cakes, creampuffs, chocolate-frosted éclairs, *beignets*, and rows of palm frond-shaped *palmiers* sparkling with grains of sugar. He pocketed two *palmiers*.

As he walked to Gabrielle's he thought of the ease with which he learned to make complex pastries. He was now certain that he could work in the finest of the mansions in France. Jefferson no longer had to rely on Monticello's rustic shortcakes, simple pound cakes, or sponge cakes sopped with custard and sherry. Complex desserts like snow eggs of meringue floating on custard or ice cream inside a hot puff pastry and all flavors of ices and ice creams were simple for James. He chuckled to himself as he decided never to offer to make a *croquembouche* again.

Gabrielle greeted him at her door with a hot bowl of pea soup. He put the treats on the dresser and sat beside her. As had become their practice so others would not understand them in the kitchen, they spoke English.

"Thank you. You made these?"

He nodded and finished drinking the soup.

"You enjoy this work?"

"I like learning."

"No. Do you enjoy making pastry for the rich? So they can top off a full belly?"

He pulled back as if slapped. "No. I think to myself, *Why should I use the finest of flours to make a dessert for someone who has already eaten enough to feed a family for a week?*"

"Are you becoming a revolutionary, like me?"

"Perhaps. Perhaps just practical. Today, Anton, one of the bakers there, told me about his village toward the ocean from here. In Poitou."

"I know it."

"He says that they make a *broyé du Poitou*, a large cookie for weddings. Just one big cookie that the groom taps in the center. When it shatters, all the guests take what they want. Large or small."

"Cookie?"

"Biscuits, in English you'd know. Baked into a sweet disk."

"Biscuit."

"That is the kind of place I want to live. Where we share food and care for each other, like we did at Monticello, but doing that as a free man with you would be a dream."

"Want to go to Poitou?"

"Not really. It's not about a place. I want to make my own life. One of community and cooking. I think that is possible."

"You are as much a dreamer as I am."

"Want your horribly decadent *palmier* now?"

"If it came from your hands, yes."

She nibbled it. He picked a crumb that fell to her chest. He ate half of his and gave her the other half. "I said I would finish this apprenticeship. I must. But I don't know if I will go back to America with him, if you won't come as well."

She reached up and pulled him closer. "Then quit."

He chuckled. "A slave? Quit?"

CHAPTER 14

By July of 1786, James had returned to the residence and again worked under the direction of Sophie. Although Petit continued to serve as Jefferson's valet and Marc oversaw the household staff, there were occasions on which Jefferson interrupted this plan and requested that James attend him. James found it amusing that after his extensive training in bread and confection, Marc still purchased bread and sweets.

In August, Jefferson was introduced to the Cosways, an English couple in the middle of the city's social whirl. Enchanted by the wife's beauty and engagement in the arts and intrigued by the husband's political connections, Jefferson often invited the couple to dine at his residence. Some weeks later, he met with James for his usual Sunday intelligence report, which now included rumors from the street and household intrigues. After half-listening to the latest, he let James finish shaving him. Toweling his face, Jefferson watched James putting the room back to order. As James turned to leave, Jefferson called after him. "Oh, James?"

"Sir?"

"Have a seat." Once James was sitting across from him, Jefferson smiled and casually asked, "I have been meaning to inquire how your romance with the chef's daughter is proceeding."

Stunned that he would ask, James barely found his voice. "Gabrielle?"

"Is there another daughter as well?"

"No. I see her when I can."

He lowered his voice. "Where do you meet?"

"She has an apartment, rather a room above the kitchen. Small, but private. Some days she returns to the family home not far from your first residence."

Blushing, Jefferson asked, "Have you an idea how one may find such a room or a modest apartment?"

James paused and decided that this was no mere inquiry about his doings, but a far different matter of which Jefferson did not want his staff to attend. He selected his words with great care. "How discrete must such a transaction be?"

"Very."

James folded his arms across his chest and looked directly at Jefferson, sensing a rare vulnerability. "Would someone reside there or merely visit on occasion?"

"Oh, just visits."

"Daytime or night, so I could judge the sector of the city best suited to the occasion."

"Not far from the palace. A quiet street. One that would not attract attention, day or night, if I were to be seen upon it." He blushed again. "Or someone of my standing or in fine attire."

James nodded. "And would it serve to have a large courtyard or a carriage house behind, so that a carriage could arrive and depart with discretion?"

"Indeed! Have you a thought?"

"If you could suggest when and for how long this might be used, visited. And the cost you are willing to bear."

Jefferson sat taller. "I didn't say it was for me."

"Of course not. But would it be of assistance if I took it in my name and provisioned it for entertaining a guest?"

"Why, yes, it would."

"With your permission, I would be pleased to make inquiries and report next week."

"Or sooner if at all possible."

"Of course."

By the following Thursday, James submitted a listing of addresses and monthly costs for small apartments near the palace. Jefferson selected one and provided James with the cash for rental to the end of the year. As he walked toward the apartment with the funds secured inside his coat, James wondered why he and not Petit or Short had been entrusted with such a delicate acquisition. Perhaps they were too publicly associated with Jefferson. Or perhaps he feared their use of such knowledge as it was more than just another one of his notions.

While Jefferson spent fewer evenings at the residence, Petit undertook a private examination of the household. He had the force of personality and craft to sense that it was being mismanaged by overspending and hiring persons ill-suited to their duties. In a bold move, he requested to see the household account books and audit them on his own time. Jefferson agreed.

Once Petit had reviewed the entries, he set a meeting with Jefferson. Petit stood before Jefferson's desk and waited for him to finish reading a letter. Once he had Jefferson's attention, he said, "Marc is simply shoeing the mule."

When Jefferson looked puzzled, he calmly explained, "Fabrications! Many of the entries in the household ledger book were for 'shoeing the mule,' that is to say they were simply false. You see, mules are not shod, and even if they were, there are no mules in your stable." He then explained how other entries in the monthly household accounts had been inflated and the difference skimmed into Marc's pocketbook. Petit was soon promoted to head of the household. Marc was dismissed without letters of recommendation, and his friends replaced with skilled servants.

In September, Jefferson was with Maria Cosway when he broke his right wrist. Although he offered various accounts of how and where the injury occurred, the only fact of import was that it healed poorly and was a source of continual weakness and pain. While he taught himself to write with his left hand, he relied on Petit and Short to pen letters for him and hid this infirmity from all but his family and trusted staff.

On a Sunday afternoon, James and Gabrielle took their walk in the *Jardin* and stopped for a coffee at an outdoor table. Then he saw them.

Jefferson and a slim woman were walking arm in arm. Her blond curls shook when she threw her head back in joyous laughter. They stopped at a bookstall. While Jefferson looked over the titles, she crossed the street to explore the weekly bird market, looking at finches and lingering by the parrots.

Gabrielle motioned with her head. "Isn't that your Jefferson?"

"Indeed." He lifted his cup and hid behind it.

"Who is she?"

James whispered so that Gabrielle had to lean closer to hear him. "Maria Cosway. She and her husband have been to dinner parties at Jefferson's when I helped serve."

James watched. When the woman returned to Jefferson's side, she pulled a tinned cage from behind her back and presented him with a small green parrot with a yellow head.

The next week, Petit requested James to attend Jefferson on a late Sunday afternoon. Jefferson was still in a silk dressing gown, unshaved. The window was open just enough for the slightest breeze to bring in the scent of orange blossoms from the garden. "I waited for you for my shave. I want a particularly close one today."

James followed Jefferson to his bedroom. Once there, James silently wet the new cake of lavender-scented shaving soap by dipping the badger brush into the basin already poured in Jefferson's room. James then whipped the soap into a thick lather. He held the brush in front of Jefferson, who then slid back in his chair to expose his neck.

As James lathered the ruddy stubble, it was evident that Jefferson was deep in thought and not inviting conversation. James opened the straight-edge blade from its ivory handle and stropped it against the top of his tall boot. Jefferson was uncommonly disinterested in any gossip. "New soap? Lavender scent to it is nice."

Jefferson smiled. "A gift from a lady."

"Missus Cosway?"

Jefferson sat up and turned to him. "Why did you suggest her?"

"It is her scent. A distinctive blend of lavender and rose, a light citrus high note, not lime but bergamot orange. Her maid told me the perfume house where she has it blended when I asked what it was."

"You astound me some days."

James neglected to mention that it was also the scent that trailed after her husband.

The yellow-headed parrot from the Amazon chuffed into a dish of seeds on the stick above a platform. Suddenly, it flapped its wings stretching toward the cloudless blue sky past the open window.

Jefferson flinched at the commotion and splashed water out of his foot bath. James had drawn the blade away in time to avoid nicking him.

The thin chain from the perch to the band on the parrot's leg held. The bird slammed into the far edge of the platform scattering seeds. A lone green flight feather spun to the floor. Gathering some sense of dignity, the bird stood on the platform and started preening by drawing its beak over its crimson tail feathers. It flapped its wings and settled its ruffled feathers. Once resigned, it stomped across the platform and climbed back onto its perch.

James put the blade low on Jefferson's neck, almost to his collarbone, and drew upward, slower than usual. After a moment of silence, James took a deep breath, finished shaving Jefferson, and walked to face him. He blocked his exit from the chair as he wiped the razor on a towel. He folded the razor and mopped up the splashed water. Suddenly he stood, clutching the towel, and looked Jefferson in the eye.

"*My* chains are not real anymore, Mister Jefferson." The latter frowned without speaking. "No. I am a free man in Paris. In all France. All I need to do is apply to the Admiralty Court for my freedom papers. And then they post it in that newspaper."

Jefferson drew a deep breath and finished wiping his face. "You would go to the Admiralty Court against me?"

"Not against you, sir. Never. But against my condition. And for my liberty. You yourself called slavery an abomination."

"And it is. Haven't I tried to change it?"

"By proposing laws that have no support?"

"But they will someday."

James stood back a step and glared at Jefferson. "How did the French so easily assume the mantle of the freedoms you wrote of in the Declaration? How did they see the necessity of freedom when you couldn't?"

"A moment! Get your facts straight. The French have abolished slavery here, where it is economically feasible, where they have no dependence on it. It remains in their colonial plantations, as it does ours."

"But that should change."

Jefferson sat straighter, his face flushing. "Agreed. That is why I am shifting crops from tobacco to wheat and other crops that take fewer hands to manage. I see a time of transition, from slave, to indentured, to free hired hand."

"Over how many generations? How long will Virginia rely on the labor of many for the comfort of the few?"

"Would that I could answer that, James. But that is also why I proposed that our westward expansion be into new free states, with new names, not merely a westward extension of Virginia, Maryland, and other states. I drafted that in '84 before we left and now we can watch its progress in the congress."

"Which does nothing for those brought by force or born into bondage by a law that imposed constraints by dint of their mother's condition."

"Progressing. We are progressing. The ordinance will open a new door of opportunity for the brave of heart now that we have secured the land from England by war and the treaty of peace."

"And how does that change my life if I go back?"

"If?"

"If." James started to leave when Jefferson stood and blocked the doorway. Casually, Jefferson ran his fingertips over his smooth cheek. "Well done, as usual. I want my guests tonight to experience your special biscuits. Please tell Petit to adjust the dinner menu and make them before you go." Jefferson moved aside and searched for his stockings without waiting for any reply from James. As soon as he met with Petit, James made the biscuits, and left the residence without changing his clothes.

It was after nine when he let himself into the rear of the restaurant with the key that Gabrielle had given him and climbed the stairs to her room. When he entered, she put down the pamphlet she was reading and hugged him. She turned down the oil lamp and poured red wine from a pitcher into two stubby glasses. They sat on the floor and leaned against a wall.

Gabrielle took a sip and turned to him. "You're late."

"Sorry. He was locked in his study all morning, so I had to shave him late in the day. Then he had me make my special biscuits for his party."

"Doesn't he know there is a flour shortage?"

"He wants what he wants."

"So that's how they do it. Not enough bread in a bakery to buy, but enough for here and your Jefferson's party. When *les regrattiers* buy the leftover meat from the plates of stuffed diners in mansions and sell those scraps to the poor, don't you see the injustice of it?"

"Of course, I do."

"Do you want to spend your life working for the rich?"

James almost said that was what her family did but held back. "No. I'd like to be in a kitchen with you. What joy it would be to see you out of the corner of my eye any time I wanted to."

"Better to see your face at night when we can be ourselves. Can you stay?"

"Yes, Petit is serving tonight."

"No. When your Jefferson goes back to his Monticello?"

"I don't know yet. He made me promise I would cook for him after all the training he paid for. Just a year."

"But what choice did you have? It is not a fair bargain."

"Maybe not, but I gave my word."

"Give *me* your word."

James paused.

Gabrielle shrugged. "At least you can stay tonight."

James nodded. "He has taken to dining at Lafayette's on Mondays. Especially since that Cosway woman joined their group. He is smitten with her."

"The one who gave him that parrot?"

"Yes. He laughs now, for a change."

"Is he usually dour?"

James nodded slowly. "He has lost too many of those he loved. His wife, several babies before she died, and then there was little Lucy. It weighs on him. But this woman, she makes him laugh."

"Do I make you laugh?"

"You make me dream. That's even better."

Gabrielle laughed. "Your Jefferson must love the kitchen."

He chuckled. "The kitchen? No. Just food and wine. The only time our cook ever saw him at Monticello was when he'd wind the clock once a week, same day, same time."

"The same time?"

James smiled. "He is a man of science. He counts and measures and sums anything he can and then writes it down in innumerable notebooks. He says science combats the chaos of experience."

Gabrielle frowned. "Is experience chaotic? I find it exciting."

"He is complicated. The other night, I was serving a platter of beef filets with a mushroom sauce while he was agreeing with Rousseau that a simple life and simple foods, mainly vegetables, are the key to a life of reason."

She laughed. "Doesn't he realize that his dinners rival the King's?"

"I know. He reads several languages but is hopeless at speaking French, which he learned from a Scottish tutor."

"But your French is getting better every day."

"I have a tutor now, named Perrault, but he has me confused about how to say goodbye."

Gabrielle pouted in a teasing way. "Are you saying goodbye to me?"

"Never. But I see a time when I may be able to say it to Master Jefferson."

"That's better. What is your confusion?"

"Can you tell me the difference between *à bientôt, au revoir,* and *adieu?*"

Gabrielle paused to find the words in English to explain. "*À bientôt* is to 'see you soon,' a casual way to say goodbye. *Au revoir* is more formal. 'Until returning,' it means. But *adieu* means 'to God.' We will meet again only with God. It is final. *Fini!*"

James nodded. "I understand now."

She teased him. "Why are you paying this man if he does not explain? I can teach you."

"What would you charge?"

"A story. Tell me another story about where you lived in America." She snuffed out the oil lamp and sat close to him. Moonlight provided a dim glow to the room.

"I've always lived on plantations. I was born on one and sent to Jefferson's Monticello when I was a small boy. That's been the only real home I knew."

"What is a plantation?"

"It is like a big farm, an estate that makes or grows most of what it needs. Sells crops to support it. He grows all means of crops for use and sale. Has his own trades to make cloth and nails and a dairy for his family."

"How many?"

"His family? It is now just him and his two daughters. But I count his slaves at about a hundred, his white tradesmen at about ten, that's free and indentured, and then there are two, no, three free Negro men working in the trades."

"That must be like a small village."

"It is."

"And where do you live? In his house?"

"No. My sister did when she tended his girls. I live in a frame cabin close by. Boards on the sides, a door in front. Steep roof." He put his hands so that his fingers formed the pitch of the roof. She kissed his fingertips and drew him to her. James kissed her. "How can I finish the story if you interrupt?" She laughed as they slid to the floor and embraced.

The next morning, James awoke with a gasp. Patting the bed beside him, he turned and saw that Gabrielle was dressing. "Time? I need to go."

"It is early still. Not yet fully light."

He dressed in haste. "I don't want to embarrass you by being here."

"He knows. I told him. He is quite fond of you. Misses you working here. In fact, he might offer you a position."

"Here?"

"Yes, here! But he won't tell you. He fears Jefferson could speak against him."

James shook his head. "He'd really let me work for him?"

She winked. "Perhaps it was an idle comment. A compliment. But, would you?"

"I don't know."

"You confuse me."

"When you addressed me by my full name, that first day, I did not recognize it. Hours later I came to realize that I had never in my life been called by other than my first name. James or Jamie or Jimmy or hey, or boy. Here, I was no longer invisible. That first day, when your father looked me directly in the eye when he spoke to me, I could not imagine he would want to hire me."

She frowned. "And why wouldn't he? Stay and live free here."

"How? My family is there."

"And I am here."

James ran both hands over his hair in frustration. When Gabrielle reached for his face, her sleeve fell away from her wrist and he noticed a black smear. "Give me your hand." He took a clean handkerchief from his pocket and tried to blot the smudge.

She pulled away from him. "I must have rubbed against the press yesterday."

"What press? The menus are written by hand."

She drew her sleeve over the stain and set her jaw.

His shoulders dropped. "My God!" He pulled her to him and whispered, "You are printing pamphlets, aren't you? If they catch you…"

"They won't. I just pick them up and give them to others to hand out or paste on walls when there is a meeting to announce."

"Gabrielle?" His hand trembled as he reached for her.

She took his hand. "You could be freed here and still return, if your family is that important to you."

"How could I?"

"I know *un avocat*. A lawyer. He works on the rebellion, but mostly he is at Admiralty Court with petitions to free blacks from the colonies who are here with their masters. I could have him talk to you."

"I have no money to pay for such."

"A talk is nothing. He would talk to you as a favor to me. But for you not to know, that is a disservice to yourself."

"I don't know."

"If you do not do this for me, then talk to him for yourself. You are blinded by loyalty to a man who sees you as just another of his many possessions. Say you will meet with him."

James held her in a long embrace then left, wordlessly.

The next morning, Jefferson passed through the kitchen and asked James if the order for the dinner the following week had been placed.

"Yes. I did it myself this morning."

"And visited your Gabrielle, I assume."

James grinned. "I learned a great deal from her father. Not just how to cook, but the idea of getting as close as you can to the origin of the food. That makes you free to create. And…" He stopped himself.

"And?"

James felt sweat trickle down his back. He looked at his boots. Then directly at Jefferson. "He talked about offering me a position but fears it would anger you."

Jefferson paused before responding. "Even after being gone for months? You must have impressed him."

"Yes, I believe so."

"You do know that your training has been quite costly. I would think as a matter of honor you would be obliged to work off that cost, at the very least."

"I would expect you to take my wage as you did when you hired out my brother." James almost argued that the fee was already more than met by his lifetime of unpaid labor.

Jefferson agreed but found the loss of James's industry in his service to be both troublesome presently and a threat in the future. "I had considered added training for you. But now..."

"You hesitate."

"Yes. I do. I have no intention of throwing good money after bad if you are tempted by Combeaux to stay here."

"I thought if I worked for Combeaux, you would be entitled to my wages. I would like to continue learning there at no cost to you."

Jefferson paused. James was no longer the unsure provincial boy who had replaced Bob. He had become a man unto himself. Confident, perhaps overly so, to speak to him in that manner. "Don't you want to be even more skilled than you are now?"

"Of course."

Jefferson's neck was flushed. "I'll not agree to a mere return of your wages in payment for all the training I have afforded you. Or find new opportunities if this is your attitude. Understand?"

That night Gabrielle searched his face and knew. Her smile faded. She extended her hand and held him in silence until he pulled away, took her by the shoulders, and walked her back to sit on the bed. He stood in front of her and shifted from foot to foot. She looked up at him. "I know. Your face told me he won't let you work here."

"No. He won't."

"When will we see each other? On the occasional night as now?"

"I will find a way."

"What if there is no way?"

James sat beside her and wrapped her in his arms. He inhaled the rosemary and lavender scent of her hair. "I will make a way."

During the early days of fall in 1786, Jefferson often had dinner plans away from the residence, in addition to his standing evening with Lafayette. Some days, his appointment diary was left with merely the notation "occupied." Whether Mister Short was aware of how Jefferson was occupied or not, he gave no indication, but attended to scheduling matters of state around such days.

Jefferson seemed to blossom as summer ended and gloom fell over the city. He acted as though spring had come into his very being. His step was livelier. His wrist, while still a nuisance, seemed to bother him less. His quest for invention and discussion with his associates of science over dinners was exuberant. His laugh was robust. His time with his daughter, Patsy, was more intimate and caring.

One evening, when the temperature was more moderate than it had been for weeks, Jefferson hosted a dinner party that included both Maria Cosway and her husband, who had considerable influence in matters of trade. As Jefferson dressed, James reported that the quail and truffles which she favored were featured predominately in the evening's offerings. Jefferson smiled, splashed on his new cologne, and turned to select a jacket. When James returned to the kitchen, he thought that Jefferson seemed dangerously oblivious to the risks of having his lover's husband to dinner as a cuckolded husband could be a powerful political enemy.

During the meat course—boar—was served, Richard Cosway began making puns that were base and inappropriate. He became louder and more challenging as he drank.

That night Jefferson had dressed in a new silk suit of a deep ruby color. During the aspic course, Mister Cosway hinted at assignations rumored at court. Not naming names but offering details and hints of who the parties were, his comments caused obvious discomfort in several diners.

When James saw Jefferson heading into the snare set by Cosway, James spilled a drop of wine on Jefferson's cuff. Apologizing profusely, he begged Jefferson to step into the other room so that he could repair the damage.

Once around the corner, James stopped and motioned Jefferson to come closer. He whispered. "*Caveat*. He intends to reference your apartment. One of his men said he saw you nearby."

"What day?"

"Don't know. Claim it is mine and you were coming to find me."

"Thank you, James. Well worth the price of my jacket."

"Here, let me dab it off, I can repair it easily in the morning. Burgundy wine on burgundy silk is not too difficult. At least you did not select the light blue for tonight."

At the table, Jefferson fended off any barb or hint of impropriety, but his world changed that evening. Usually, a party was reviewed, and jibes were recounted for sport while James shaved him. The next morning, however, there was silence. He worked quietly in his study all day, not pausing for any nourishment, and only taking a tray for dinner while he worked. By candlelight in his study, he was sketching a domed roof over the classic square face of Monticello when James entered carrying a small silver tray with a glass and small decanter. "Your Madeira, sir."

Jefferson did not look up. "Particularly fine dinner tonight, James. More suited to a well-appointed table than a tray. But I have had a thoughtful day."

"Thank you, sir. Fresh ingredients make for fresh thinking and the most flavorful of dishes."

Finishing the sketch, he glanced at James. "Indeed. Pour my glass, will you?"

"Can I fetch something from the kitchen if you are going to be up late? A coffee?"

"No. Come look."

Jefferson slid his chair aside and pointed to the sketch he had made of the main house at Monticello. Beside it was a small enamel portrait of his late wife, Martha.

James asked, "That Monticello?"

"It will be. Look here. If I replace the classic columns on the second story with a rounded dome, there could be the most magnificent room under it. None like it in all the United States."

"Can you do that?"

"Of course. It is just a little reconstruction on the upper floor. I came upon the idea when I was walking along the left bank on my way to a meeting with some importers of our whale oil. The Hôtel de Salm is almost finished, and its dome is stunning. I am violently smitten with the design. I asked who the architect was and by chance was able to meet Pierre Rousseau. After this change, I want to extend the garden."

James pointed to an area by the kitchen designated as the herb garden. "Could you put in a fish pond?"

"Rather odd for this garden design, don't you think?"

"If not there, nearby the kitchen so we can hold the big fish the boys catch in the river. It would keep them half a day fresher for dinner. Maybe even raise fish."

Jefferson looked up in wonder. He reviewed his plan for the grounds, nodded, and drew a pond near the kitchen.

Throughout the remainder of 1786 and into the start of the following year, James continued to work under the guidance of Sophie, gaining greater responsibilities in the kitchen. Jefferson's dinners became smaller parties for intimate discussions with policy makers and philosophers. The intellectual challenge and stimulation of Paris was perfect for Jefferson. Sophie and James managed these smaller affairs. When there was a matter of state requiring a lavish display, he again called on Combeaux to cater it and James to finish the dishes and serve.

In January of 1787, James was presenting a dinner menu to Jefferson in the study when Short interrupted them. "A dispatch, sir." James started to leave but stopped when Jefferson motioned for him to stay.

Jefferson tapped the document on his desk. "Mister Short. This report on the shipping losses presents a dilemma. I want to bring my daughter Polly here as soon as possible, yet our current maritime conditions give me pause. Barbary pirates kidnap our sailors and impound our ships. It has become the most vexing of my duties here to negotiate the release of men and ships. Yet, Washington deems it not in our interest to pay the ransom. Still, they need to be freed."

"Are intermediaries of assistance?"

"To some degree of success. But our best approach will be a treaty of peace with them."

"Them? Isn't there a bundle of them? Moroccans. Those in Tripoli. All sorts and manner of Arabic tribes. How will you get them all to come around?"

"Good question. We haven't the funds to pay a tribute or ransom at every demand, yet they can capture our ships at will. We lost the protection afforded our ships by the British agreements when we severed ties with them in the Treaty of Paris in 1783. The French won't protect us now as we are no longer at war."

"But isn't it in our interests to find our own agreement?"

"Certainly. Our ships pay over twenty times that of British ships for the same cargo insurance. That puts us at a significant trade disadvantage. But my prime concern at this moment is how to safely transport my daughter to Paris. Let me know your thoughts tonight at dinner. Lafayette is coming. Just we three. Tell Sophie. And tomorrow I shall dictate another plea to Washington to let me negotiate."

Jefferson turned to James. "Help Sophie and serve tonight. And play for us."

The dinner was simple and easily served. James played his violin softly throughout the meal. Discussions of the development of a democratic process consumed most of the conversation. When Lafayette asked about his daughter coming to Paris, Jefferson turned to Short. "Have you given consideration to the question I posed earlier?"

"How best to transport her? Yes. I suggest booking her on a ship flying a British or French flag so the pirates will not harm her or the ship. Second, I would look for a new ship, not older than two or three years, so the rigging will be tight, and she will not have suffered any damage in the war."

"Good suggestions." Jefferson turned to Lafayette. "Your ships are more frequent. What about booking on one of them?"

"I know you would prefer not to trade with them, but I think his idea of a newer British ship without any possibility of war damage is sound. It may delay passage a month or so, but it is a prudent approach. Our merchant fleet has suffered in recent years having been used in battle as often as commerce to the colonies. You know, in one of the slave rebellions in a colonial holding, they actually took a merchant ship as their own."

"I think I heard of it. That is a growing concern in our southern states as well. A slave rebellion, once started, could catch fire easily now."

"Which takes us back to our usual discussion. How do we sever this rope of slavery in our colonies?"

Jefferson inspected his wineglass. "Strand by strand. It is easier for you here in France; your reliance on their labor is less. You were able to cut the cord with one swift swipe of a sword. But you have the same dilemma in your colonies as we have in America. What is the pathway between God-given freedom and the current laws of man and our economic dependence on slavery? As I have said, it is like holding a wolf by the ears. Holding on or letting go, each is fraught with peril."

Short interrupted Jefferson. "But sir, you never bred your slaves like others did, and you respected their families, when such existed. I know you reduced the labor-heavy crops like tobacco to plant other crops."

"True, I intend never to buy another slave, so that over time, there should be an abolition of that most horrid practice at Monticello. But understand, if I were to just free the slaves at Monticello with a wave of my hand, it would impoverish both the slaves, who were unable to be self-sufficient, and my family." His volume and tone to Lafayette suggested that wine was winning the night and Jefferson's reserve was slipping.

"So then, my friend, how would you release the wolf in a manner that did not harm your family?"

Without pausing, Jefferson sped into his plan. "At each cabin, I would install a garden plot and chicken coop so slaves could become self-reliant. Many have such already to augment their weekly ration. Miller, my overseer, had a simple formula: a peck of meal, a pound of bacon, and a pint of molasses for the field hands. Eventually, they could indenture and work for wages, as a way to freedom might be bought. A trade, perhaps."

Short asked, "Wouldn't those learning a trade opt to go into the open marketplace?"

"Hmmm. It is a slow pathway. Maybe not in my lifetime, for all, but some of the brightest and most productive. Perhaps a long indenture or a lifetime with freedom for their oldest son. Perhaps."

Jefferson held his glass for Lafayette to refill. James continued to play a simple tune, as though invisible to the men at the table.

In early February, Petit interrupted James who was washing glasses in the kitchen. "He wants to see you in his study."

"A new dinner menu?"

Petit shrugged. James had his sleeves rolled up and was wiping his hands on a towel as he entered the study. "Sir?"

Jefferson pointed for James to sit in the nearby chair. "A dear friend of mine has discovered an opportunity for you that is exceptional. He has found an apprenticeship for you to develop your skills to even a greater level. And in the royal manner." James felt dizzy. What was he saying? "Do not misinterpret what I am about to tell you. Your skills are superb, but there is a manner of presentation at court that I want you to learn."

"At court?"

"The King's relative, the Prince de Condé, is going to be traveling for the next few months. The demands on his kitchen will be reduced but not ended during his travels. I have heard that his chef will be both in Paris at his estate here and at the Château de Chantilly to cook for the members of the royal family and other nobility as they wish to come to Chantilly to hunt or just to travel. This presents a rare opportunity for you to discover the operational methods and means of that most ornate and complex manner of preparation and service. Not that we would adopt it regularly at Monticello, but for special occasions it would serve well."

"You want me to spy on the royal household?"

"To inform me of your discoveries, of course. I have a friend who is now arranging for you to train there."

James felt short of breath. "Where again?"

"In Paris or at his château in Chantilly, as needed."

"But I was to cook for you. Here."

"Yes, but this is such a fine opportunity. Besides, I will be traveling for much of the next few months myself, so the timing is opportune."

James forced a small smile. "Of course. When will this begin?"

"Petit will let you know the details as they unfold."

As James walked to Gabrielle's apartment that evening, he wondered what this next level in his training could be. Cooking for a Prince. That would involve even more costly and exotic ingredients, more complex presentations, and possibly new tools and techniques. He felt a rush of excitement, then a cold recognition that he would be away from Gabrielle. He stopped on the way and bought a bottle of Côte Rôti wine he knew she loved. On arriving, he held the bottle in front of him.

"What? You arrive with a great wine but no smile. What is it?"

He shook his head. "Jefferson has some idea that I should learn the royal presentation methods under the Prince de Condé's chef."

"At Chantilly?"

"You know it?"

"Everyone knows it! It is a massive estate. Only the King's Versailles is larger. Just his stable can hold hundreds of horses for his racetrack. In hunting season, his gamekeeper flushes birds and deer for the hunters. Royals from all over Europe come for the hunts."

"Game? I haven't done much game."

Gabrielle was suddenly wide-eyed with anger. "James? Think! It's a day away by horse, longer by carriage. When will we see each other?"

"He has an estate in Paris too. I'll be working here as well."

"When? Once a week, a month, a year?"

"I don't know." He poured two glasses of wine and handed her one. "All I know is we are here now, and I don't want to waste a moment with you." That night was sleepless and the morning tearful.

CHAPTER 15

Barely warmed by the pale February sun, James slept atop the sacks of flour as the wagon bumped toward Chantilly. When the driver shouted that the Château de Chantilly had come into view, James scrambled forward. "Did they really build it in a lake?"

Laughing, the driver said, "No. That's what they call a moat. Kept invaders away long ago. You will see in a moment when the road turns that there is only one approach."

A horseman in the King's colors galloped past them and left them choking on a swirl of summer dust. A pride of peacocks honked like geese at the horseman then took flight over the wagon to roost in a nearby grove.

The wagon jolted over the cobblestones toward the massive entrance, then swerved to the kitchen door to the side. James was tasked to transfer the sacks to the storage room as though he were the deliveryman. As he stacked the last one, he heard shouting and went toward the noise, which he assumed to be coming from the kitchen. Familiar sounds and smells greeted him as he turned the corner. A rotund chef was standing on a small stool just inside the doorway to the massive kitchen and shouting orders to more than two dozen men and a handful of boys. His meaning was clear: King Louis XVI was arriving with a retinue of thirty for dinner in less than six hours, to be followed tomorrow by a light breakfast, field baskets for the men at hunt, and a formal lunch for their ladies. At the end of this tirade, the cooks scattered to a frenzy at their workstations. The silver-haired chef mopped his brow and stepped off the stool.

"Chef?" James called.

Chef spun and challenged James in French. "And you are?"

"James Hemings. Mister Jefferson's chef. He made an agreement for my training in your kitchen."

"I don't care about that tonight. You know how to peel carrots?"

James held back his laughter and said, "I apprenticed with Combeaux."

"Combeaux! *Bien.* Then you go to the sauce stove. Maurice will instruct you. We talk tomorrow."

"Oui, Chef." Over the next hours, James fell into an easy rhythm, similar to what Combeaux had required when the restaurant was overbooked with royalty requiring special dishes or unexpected demands for catered platters.

Almost all of the dishes were similar to those he had made with Combeaux, but the number that were served at one time was astounding. Only one dish was new to James. A huge platter of roasted peacock had been carved, reassembled, and dressed in all its original glistening feathers. A dozen roasted quail surrounded it. Cooked asparagus was fanned into wheat sheaves and bands of golden Hollandaise sauce glistened across the center of the stems. Thick slices of black truffles were layered between slices of chicken breasts. It was as if a month of work at Restaurant Combeaux had been compressed into one evening.

By eight, liveried servants started carrying the ornate platters from the kitchen. James asked to see the dining area and was denied. He then suggested that he could make an interesting dessert that was known only to Combeaux and Jefferson. Chef agreed. The dessert that surrounded chilled ice cream with a warm pastry was received with admiration. When he returned to the kitchen, Chef started weeping. The dessert was such a success that the Prince's chef claimed credit for its creation.

The following week, James was taken back to Paris to cook for guests of the Prince's at his Paris residence. Quickly, James discovered that the promise of learning new techniques was merely a ploy by the Prince's chef to pad his purse. Over the next few months, James was randomly shifted from town to country as the chef's whim dictated. James was asked to do tasks more challenging than those of the usual kitchen helpers, yet far below any stretch of his talents. Only the scale of the kitchens and the volume of production were new to him. The only redeeming aspect in this chaotic arrangement was the opportunity to see Gabrielle while in Paris.

On June 10, the gardener banged open the front door and shouted that Jefferson was home. By the time Jefferson's carriage stopped, the gardener had taken the horse's bridle and the driver had jumped down to open the carriage door. Short rushed through the front door followed by several of the housekeeping staff.

Jefferson was tanned and in good spirits. He greeted Short with a hearty clap on the shoulder. Petit emerged from the shaded carriage and brushed dust from his shoulders before bowing to Short. A wagon of crates rattled into the courtyard and stopped behind the carriage. Without added instruction, Petit supervised the unloading.

Short tipped his head. "Welcome back, sir."

"Has Polly arrived?"

"Not yet."

"Good. Have the small trunk on the carriage rear taken to the kitchen and have James meet me in the kitchen at four."

"He's not here, sir."

Frowning, Jefferson asked, "Has he run off?"

"Oh no. He is still with the Prince's chef. They were in the city a few days ago. Want me to see if he is still here?"

"Send a runner. I want him in the kitchen at four."

By late afternoon, a freshly dressed Jefferson made his way to the kitchen. James was taking inventory of the dry goods pantry. Jefferson took a chair at the small side table and motioned for James to do the same. "James! So they did find you. How is it with that chef?"

"Not as challenging as I would have imagined." James waited for Jefferson's reply. Although his hair was combed and a new ribbon tied at the nape of his neck, he had dressed in the homespun shirt and work trousers which he usually wore when fussing in his garden. His cheeks sported two days of stubble while fatigue rounded his shoulders. "Was your journey as you had hoped?"

"More than. My notebooks are filled with farming inventions, crop rotation plans, and new plants." Jefferson rubbed his wrist as had become his habit.

"That water cure give your wrist any relief?"

Jefferson shrugged. "While that was the intent, I was much more successful in finding new foods of interest. In the Grand Duchy of Tuscany, I found a wealth of vineyards and wines of depth and resilience that paired with the local food. I also discovered new vegetables, tomatoes, and lettuces that I had never encountered."

"Bring any with you?"

Jefferson laughed as he went to the trunk. "The fresh vegetables would never withstand the heat and distance." Wood shavings scattered on the floor as he dug into the trunk and the strong scent of pine resin filled the room. "I did find a seed vendor though." He pulled out a small box filled with paper packets of seeds and handed it to James. "I intend to plant these at Monticello."

"Think any might grow here?"

"It is too late in the season, according to that fellow."

Jefferson handed two small cloth sacks to James, who laughed as fine white powder sifted through the cloth.

"Let me guess, it's flour." He started for the pantry.

Jefferson put two more bags on the counter. "Leave them all here. It is a special flour from Naples. A very fine grind, talc-like, in fact. When I was in this crowded part of Naples near the waterfront, there were vendors on the street selling these flat breads, almost like large crusts. But the bread was not alone, it was topped with anchovies, garlic, or other foods that would adhere to the sauced tomato that they slathered on those thin crusts."

"Sauced? How thick?"

"Cooked down to almost a paste. A slight bit runny but cooked drier on the flatbread. Some were cooked on flat stones right out on the street, but most were made in ovens, fired by wood. Cut to a hand-size piece, they were easily carried by workers and eaten while they walked, not like the staid foods of Tuscany. I know Combeaux had travelled into those regions and you said he makes a tomato sauce, but I have never seen a tomato in the markets here as is common in Virginia."

"One theory that I heard from Combeaux is that the tomato is a poor person's food. Eaten off wood trenchers or by hand on baked flat-breads as you saw. It is amiable and digestible. But he said when served on pewter trenchers or plates, or eaten with pewter tableware, it is in-clined to etch the metal and on occasion make the diner ill, if it is a con-sistent portion of the diet."

"Did that kitchen girl from New Orleans... What was her name?"

"Marie."

"Did she mention that tomatoes were used there?"

"She did. Mostly in a stew with other things."

"Hmmm. I might plant a few seeds here next spring and see if we could have some for our next Independence Day celebration. That would shock our French guests, wouldn't it?"

"Combeaux has a grower, I could ask him if he has any extra."

Without answering, Jefferson dug into the trunk and put several notebooks on the counter. "Notes on farming and implements I found. There is a new plow that cuts through turf faster than any before it. I took sketches for our blacksmith to make once we return home."

Brushing aside the last of the wood shavings, Jefferson exposed a half wheel that was a foot thick, three feet across, and wrapped in cloth.

"What's that?"

"A new cheese that is called Parmesan. It is a key ingredient in a rice dish I discovered in Milan. *Rosotto alla Milanese*, it is called. They spelled it both as *risotto*, with an 'i' and *rosotto*, with an 'o,' so I am not sure which is proper."

"What's it made of?"

"A special type of rice that gets almost like a pudding, it is so smooth. I brought some back, but do not tell anyone."

"Why not?"

"They are very protective of this strain. Wouldn't sell me any. Actually, I had to smuggle some out in the lining of my coat. Petit hid small bags in each of the flour sacks. I want you to make the dish while my memory of it is fresh. It is most agreeable."

"What do I need to have?"

"Saffron, beef stock, bone marrow, lard, and cheese." James imagined how he could combine these ingredients in several different ways. That range, those decisions, the pleasure in presenting the final product to the diner, their enjoyment, all these things were what James loved about cooking. Then he paused to consider what cheese could compliment this unique blend?

"The cheese? What is like it?"

"Nothing like any French cheese I have yet discovered. It is a dry, hard cheese." Jefferson started to lift the wheel. His wrist gave way. He grimaced and let James hoist the cheese up to the counter.

James untied the cloth. A yellow wax protected it. Where the wheel had been cut in half, a crusted, dry cheese was exposed. "Could I try a piece to taste?"

"Yes, and a bit for me as well. And open a bottle of something white."

James quickly retrieved a bottle of white wine from the cellar, poured a glass for Jefferson and placed it in front of him as he returned to the small table at the edge of the kitchen. "James! Get yourself a glass. You need to see the pairing."

He wedged off shards of the cheese, placing some on a plate for Jefferson before tasting the new cheese. James watched Jefferson as he tried to name the new flavors. "Salty. Nutty. I see how it could blend with rice. Do you have the time to explain the dish and how it is made so I can think on it?"

"Of course. The final dish is flavored and colored a bright yellow by the saffron. The instructions I took to be fairly straightforward. Heat the lard and cook the rice in it, not to golden but to the start of a transparency, not all the way through. Then add the broth, a ladle at a time just as the previous one is absorbed. At the end, the bone marrow and cheese are stirred into it, giving it an intense density and astounding flavor."

"What is the consistency or texture?"

"Slightly toothy. Moist, like porridge. It seems to thicken as it stands, so it is eaten immediately. I watched how it is made and can instruct you as to the manner of its making."

"What is served with it?"

"Nothing. It is so rich that it becomes its own offering for the evening meal."

"Is the bone marrow poached and sliced or melted into it?"

"Sliced. After it is pulled out of a baked bone."

James grinned. "As I imagined it would be."

"Splendid! We'll have it tonight."

"Perhaps the dish could benefit from some diced onion at the start and perhaps a splash of white wine before the broth is used to bloom the rice."

"Didn't I mention the onion? I thought I did."

"And the cheese? How is it added?"

"At the last. In small bits like a snowstorm."

James closed his eyes and sniffed as though to experience it. "The color? Do you mean a light or a deep yellow from the saffron? That will tell me how much to use."

"Light. The chef at the estate where I stayed told me a story, true or not I'll let you decide. When they were building the cathedral in Milan, this would be in the mid-1500s, the artisan making the stained-glass used saffron to tint the glass. It was golden and superb. I saw the glass and can attest to this personally. His fellow glassmakers called him 'Zafferano,' that being the word in their language for saffron." Jefferson paused and then continued with the rest of the tale. "But here is the best part. They mocked him, saying he would put saffron in his risotto next. Well, when his daughter was married, he did. The risotto was golden at the wedding celebration and has been copied in that region ever since."

James carefully dug the packets of rice from the flour bags and assembled the ingredients while Jefferson sipped a white wine and watched James cook it perfectly without additional instruction. When he tasted the rice dish, Jefferson swore that it was even better than the original he had tasted in Milan.

As James spooned the last of his *Rosotto alla Milanese* into his mouth, Jefferson put his bowl on the counter and sighed. "Excellent. Write up your process and portions for my records. That was perfect."

"Thank you. It is a pity that there isn't enough rice to make this for your next gathering, but I don't think our American rice or that in our French pantry would combine in this fine a manner with the cheese."

"I agree, best I reserve the remainder as seed stock. But I would like to have a special small gathering when the weather cools. A reunion of my closest friends. Something they could not have experienced. Have you an idea?"

"How small?"

"Under a dozen. Themed."

"Themed?"

Jefferson looked to the ceiling. "Regional food or a specific time, I don't know."

"What about an ancient Roman dinner?"

"I wouldn't know where to start." He grinned. "But then, neither would my guests. What are you thinking?"

"Would they have read Pliny?"

"The Elder or Younger?"

James shrugged. "The one who wrote the book I bought at a stall near the Pont Neuf a month ago. I don't know which, but he wrote on cooking, or at least described their banquets."

"You found an English translation? Here?"

"No. It was Latin."

Jefferson paused before asking, "You read Latin?"

"I taught myself."

"How?"

James took their plates to the counter and wondered if he had blundered but decided to confess. "Your library was available that time when you and Bob were icebound and were away for so long."

"Pliny? You really read Pliny?"

At Jefferson's grin, James nodded and relaxed. He leaned on the counter; his hands spread wide. "First, there is the number of guests. Pliny said it was usually nine, one for each of the muses. Most diners brought their own napkin and spoon, just as Paris now expects diners to bring their own bread. You could mention that practice in your invitation."

"Interesting. The food?"

"Roman food for the elite was complex and abundant, often with game or unusual meats. The killings in the Coliseum were highly prized, wild bears and tigers. And crisped flamingo tongues were a true delicacy."

"I think that is a bit much for this dinner. Who even could find such a thing?"

"Game, we have in the market. Deer, boar, large and small birds. Peacocks occasionally. There's some of the exotics in the King's own collection, his zoological park."

"I doubt if he would spare one for my dinner. How did they dine?"

"They had scissor slaves to cut the meat on a plate for a diner…"

"Impractical, as you know how many of my guests cherish their privacy."

"Practical for them, though, as it required the guests to be unarmed during dinner. They reclined on couches as they ate."

"Impractical, for the ladies in particular with those big skirts," he said with a laugh. "Is there a signature dish of renown?"

"Of course. One of the more unusual is the use of a sow which has recently given birth. Stuffing an udder with sea urchins or its own meat, chopped and seasoned with eggs, pine nuts, pepper, anise, and silphium."

"What's the last thing you mentioned?"

"Silphium? A leafy herb that was in short supply then and unobtainable today."

"Why?"

"They never found a way to grow it. Only picked it in the wild. Picked it into extinction."

"Do we know anything about it?"

"Pliny described it as a spice with great powers, like a recently plucked fennel. He said they often substituted asafetida for it in the recipes, suggesting a leek-like flavor when cooked."

Jefferson chuckled. "I think a stuffed udder might be off-putting. What else would capture the flavors?"

"Meatballs seem eternal, of pork or game. The tapenade of chopped olives you like was popular in Roman times as well. Mustard sauces, rabbit, lentils, and a type of *foie gras*."

"*Foie gras?*"

"They fattened the liver in hogs by feeding them honey, wine, and figs."

"Not geese or ducks?"

"No. Pigs. But we could use the goose liver or duck liver *foie gras*."

"Interesting. Draw up a menu and budget for my review. And suggest wines."

"Of course."

Jefferson refilled his wine glass, motioned for James to do the same, and settled back into his chair. "Now, tell me about the Prince. What interested him? Who was with him?"

"He was never there. The King did come, unannounced for some hunting, throwing the chef into a fit. I do know the Prince is related to the King in some way but is not his son. A relation. His real other title is Louis-Joseph de Bourbon. I think Petit knows the connection, if it is important to you. A huge table was set, all as a display for the diners to pick at, not really dine, judging by what came back to the kitchen. A strange way to treat such beautifully prepared food, but so it was."

"You have now cooked for the King of France. Quite an accomplishment."

James shrugged. "I did a dessert. A pastry with ice cream in it. The same one I made for you."

Grinning, Jefferson asked, "Now, tell me about the grounds of the Château de Chantilly."

"It is huge. I think you would be intrigued by the style of the construction. I have never seen a drawing that did it justice. The château itself looks like it was two castles that were joined. One had rounded corners, turrets I think they are called. It is of gray stone and the other part has a steep roofline. And there was this large expanse of water surrounding it on most sides. A moat. Swans were in it. Huge white swans. There is game on the property and hunting."

"And the interior?"

"I only got to see the kitchen."

"Oh. How was it?"

James thought a moment before responding. "In function, not unlike the one Combeaux has. Larger by ten or more times in the scale, mostly for more tables needed for the elaborate final preparations. Nothing new to me. Well, maybe one dish. Several hearths are still used for spit-roasting game."

"No new tools? Invention? Technique?"

"Not really. But I did find it of interest that the Prince's favorite items on his own menu included *foie gras*, made many ways, and fried potatoes, split into sticks the size of your little finger and boiled in duck fat until browned. Most flavorful."

"What else?"

"Chef boasts about the fame of their desserts, and in particular concoctions of ice cream, whipped cream, and meringues."

Jefferson frowned. "But you made those with Combeaux when we first arrived."

"Not that I told him. He is quite taken with himself."

"I am not getting the impression that you are really learning anything new or useful to building a store of grand dishes to entertain our guests."

"To the contrary. I learned how to skin a whole pheasant, leaving every feather in place. Once the game bird was cooked and dressed in a layer of white truffles all over it, the skin was reattached, and the bird was presented as though alive. I have no idea how it was served."

"Is it worth your while?"

James chuckled. "If you want to serve game birds in their original attire."

"Any other value?"

"I heard a story about a chef that might be useful for you to recount at one of your dinners."

"Tell me."

Jefferson listened intently. "When Louis XIV was at the château, that is in the mid-1600s, his chef was so concerned that the fish course would be served late that he threw himself into the river. Drowned."

Jefferson looked amazed. "Who would do such a thing?"

James mistook the comment for a question. "The chef's name was François Vatel. He is renowned still for his attention to excellence."

Jefferson shook his head and shuddered at the thought. "But let us speak of better things. Do you have more information or observations about the grounds?"

"The estate must be massive if what I heard there is to be believed. There is a racetrack. The stables are supposed to be the largest in all France, if not all Europe. Oh, there is a small village, a pretend village, made just for there. Someone said that Marie Antoinette copied it for her own village at Versailles."

Jefferson raised an eyebrow. "I would not share stories like that with our French hosts, James."

"Of course not. But I want to tell you all I hear."

"I appreciate that."

"And, sir?"

"Yes?"

"As valuable as you seem to think this training might be, I fear that they are taking advantage."

"How so?"

Digging into his vest pocket, James pulled out a folded sheet of paper. "They just presented me with an invoice for my working there."

Jefferson snatched the paper from James. "Let me see that." After reviewing it, he handed it back. "Have Mister Petit look into it. And tell the chef you are needed here for a few days until we settle this matter."

For the next week, James assisted Sophie in routine kitchen matters. James was cutting herbs in the garden near the study window when he overheard Jefferson and Petit arguing. Moving to the wall beside the window, James strained to hear Jefferson. "That cannot be a correct accounting! Seriously, Petit? How could we have spent that much on truffles? They are as common here as corn is back in Virginia. I think your accounts must be in error."

"They are correct, sir. There is an issue, even if I am able to cancel that charge from the Prince's chef. I reviewed each invoice and every cash draw by your cook to market. There is pilfering by the cooking staff. Sophie's assistant who does the marketing, Marc made an arrangement with him. Sophie is doing her best. But she has family that is tugging at her to return to Provence, so we may need to replace them both."

"Let me know."

Petit nodded. "When you dismissed Marc, I thought we had resolved pilfering in other areas, but some of the suppliers clearly had other arrangements with him. Unless you let me stop it in all areas of the household, you will find yourself in a pecuniary embarrassment. I can say it no other way: your cook is a fine woman, but her assistant is a thief."

"But then how will we manage if you terminate them?"

"James can assume her duties as well as those of her thieving assistant."

"Now? He is still under that agreement with the chef of the Prince de Condé. He's very prestigious."

"And very costly. Now that I have had the opportunity to discuss the invoice with the Prince's man, I am of the opinion that the invoice is an insult! Your friend Philip Mazzei did you a favor by finding the position but failed to consider or advise us of the cost."

"Why would I have to pay? Why? He is getting free labor."

Petit pointed again to a page. "I have the invoice that James brought. For his training and lodging at the château, they want twelve livres a day or 100 livres a month."

Jefferson stood, grabbed the paper, and shook it at him. "The entirety of the year with Combeaux was but 150 livres, how can he think that I should pay such a sum?"

"I fear Mister Mazzei cared more for your appreciation for placing James than for any of the details."

"Seemingly."

Petit took the invoice back. "Let me review the demand and see what terms I can reach. It is simply too costly to continue."

Jefferson sighed. "What do you propose?"

"My first concern is to stop the outflow of cash. Sophie has been excellent and taught James well. I recommend you give her a bonus and send her off to her family in Provence. Then pay him half of her wage."

"But he still has not completed his training with the Prince's chef as agreed. Although I thought it to be at no cost."

"I will tell the Prince's man there was some confusion on the length of the training, and that James is needed here now. A few livres across his palm should resolve the matter."

"Good. Best we keep him on a shorter leash. Bring him back. Tell him that he is promoted to the position."

"As *le cuisinier*, the head cook?"

"No. As *chef de cuisine*. Better title but at lower pay. Now. as to the matter of the wine…"

James leaned his back against the wall and closed his eyes. *Chef de cuisine* for Jefferson. He could not have imagined such a day.

He heard Jefferson continue in an irritated tone. "What about the wine? I know you are a good butler, but this?"

Petit's voice rose in pitch but not volume. "I am much more than your butler, sir. As your *maître d'hôtel*, I manage all aspects of this residence. From arranging with kitchen staff how to implement your most elaborate dinner parties to when staff should polish the parquet or travertine floors and what flowers should be cut for the vases in the dining room. And I tell you that you are headed for ruin at this rate. Ruin! The billings from Bondfield and Girandeau alone were outrageous."

Jefferson was exasperated. "But they are the best wine merchants. How can we be so overspent?"

"I asked Mister Short to review the accounts with me. It seems that your allowance from President Washington barely pays the lease on this residence. The rest is coming from your private funds. And your frequency of hosting large dinner parties here has created a deficiency."

"Well then, have Mister Short draft a letter for my signature to my overseer. Have him sell off fifty cords of wood to the town, send the proceeds here, and yet again delay the interior plastering at Monticello until I return. That should free up some funds."

"Very good, sir."

James quickly gathered the cut thyme and rosemary into a basket and walked past the study toward the kitchen. Petit motioned for James to stop.

James forced a grin, set the basket on the floor, and pulled his pencil and paper from his vest pocket. "Good to see you. The Prince's chef asked if I could provide him with your instructions for Mister Jefferson's coffee. He says he heard from one of the Prince's guests that it was the best he has ever had."

James could see that Petit was seduced by the flattery. "Simple enough. Into one measure of roasted coffee beans ground into a fine meal, pour three measures of boiling water. Boil it on hot ashes until the meal disappears from the top. Pour three times through a flannel strainer. This will make two and a third measures of clear coffee. One ounce by weight of coffee makes one and a half cups of clear coffee. Be certain to rinse the flannel after each use."

After quickly scribbling these notes. James picked up the herbs and started for the kitchen. Over his shoulder, he called, "Thank you."

Petit paused before calling to him. "James?"

He turned and walked back to Petit. "Monsieur Jefferson and I would like you to assume full control of the kitchen. He knows that you are not quite completed with your studies with the Prince's chef, but you are needed here."

"When?"

"As soon as you can retrieve your belongings."

"But Sophie?"

Petit raised an eyebrow. "She will be leaving us at the conclusion of tonight's dinner, as will her assistant. Mister Jefferson wants you to be his *chef de cuisine*. I will expect to see you tomorrow morning to review the menu for the week."

James removed his belongings from the Prince's Paris residence, and went to Gabrielle's for the night.

CHAPTER 16

The celebration of the Independence Day in 1787 was modest. Jefferson and Petit had only recently just returned from their extensive travels. Most of those guests Jefferson would have liked to have entertained had fled the city's heat for the countryside. Jefferson had sent Petit to London to retrieve Polly who had been in the care of Abigail Adams since landing on June 26. The last-minute invitations were extended to the dignitaries of other embassies and vendors. Jefferson's daughter brought a French friend from school to enjoy the buffet featuring Virginia ham and play card games. Most guests seemed oblivious to the meaning of the event but enjoyed Jefferson's cellar and the chilled lemonade.

A full week after Petit left for London, the dispatch case contained two private letters for Jefferson. Short recorded the correspondence before handing Jefferson the unopened letters. He ripped open the envelopes and read their contents before saying, "Petit's letter of the fifth reports that he had arrived, and Polly and her young companion were fatigued but in good health. The letter from Abigail Adams that she dated July 6 prattles on that Polly's sea voyage from Norfolk was a hard five weeks before transferring to a smaller craft, the *Robert*. She continues to say that although Polly found Captain John Ramsey charming, she is fearful of another voyage; therefore, she wishes to remain in London."

Short suppressed a laugh. "Is she really telling you that your own daughter has *declined* to leave the London home of Ambassador Adams?"

"That is how I take it. She concludes by saying that she and her young companion are most welcome to remain there until I can fetch them."

"But Petit is already there!"

Jefferson tossed the letter toward Short to file. Noticing James in the doorway awaiting his attention, he said to Short, "She actually complains to me that Polly's companion is but a mere slip of a girl, that Sally Hemings. Not at all who I requested. Was I not clear in my letter that an older servant was to accompany her!"

Short took his intention and emphatically nodded agreement. Jefferson turned to James before saying, "At least you will be pleased by this error. It's your sister who will be joining us."

James felt a shiver in spite of the trickle of sweat that ran down his spine. Sally? Could she really be coming to France?

Paris was in the final days of a breezeless heatwave that had all but wilted Jefferson. As much as he wanted to escape to the shade of the countryside, he was tethered in town for meetings. Windows open full, he heard the plod of horses and crunch of carriage wheels on the courtyard gravel. He stood, welcoming the distraction and wondering who was calling unannounced. He rolled his sleeves down and tied the loose bow at his neck to receive any caller of note.

Jefferson arrived at the front door in time to see the driver pull the team to a halt. Petit opened the door, jumped to the ground, and helped Polly descend from the covered carriage. Jefferson remained in the cooler doorway as Petit offered his arm to Polly to cross the gravel. Once they reached the foot of the stairs, Petit bowed and stepped away from her. Polly bobbed a curtsy to her father.

As she walked up the steps, Jefferson barely recognized his daughter. She was tall and slim for her nine years and comported herself with poise. He suspected that Petit had offered an admonition to curtsy on arrival in the French manner. When she reached the top step, she said, "Papa."

Jefferson extended his arms and held her by her shoulders. "Welcome to your new home, my dear." He turned to retreat from the sun. She paused, watching one of the house servants offering his hand to assist Sally in leaving the high carriage. Polly waited on the step of the residence for her companion. At fourteen, Sally had developed into a young woman. Once joined at the step, Polly slipped her arm into Sally's and entered the house. Both girls were dressed in equally fine attire.

In light of the arrival, Jefferson sent Petit in a carriage to bring Patsy home from the convent school for that night's dinner. Upon seeing her sister, Patsy tried to be lady-like at first, then squealed with delight. Soon all three girls were hugging and chattering to each other as though they were sisters.

James heard the girls and came to discover his sister was with them. After greeting her briefly, James left to prepare the informal evening meal for Jefferson and his daughters. While he and Sally ate in the kitchen, James asked after his mother and news of Bob. Sally shared what news had come to her at Eppington of their family and of her time at the Eppington Plantation as Polly's maid. James marveled at his sister's transformation into a young woman, yet one who was so provincial in her bearing and views.

After dinner, Jefferson gathered his girls in the music room, pulled several pages of sheet music from a drawer, and handed them to Patsy. "Play whichever selection you prefer on the pianoforte."

She leafed through the options and selected one. Jefferson put his arm around Polly. "Did your aunt instruct you in music as I asked?"

"Yes, Papa. I can play a few pieces on the pianoforte."

"Do you read music?"

"No, Papa."

"Then your sister shall assist you, in addition to your lessons at the convent school."

Polly clutched his hand. "I don't want to go away from you and Patsy, not ever again."

Patsy got up from the bench and hugged her sister. "You will be with me at nights. I am sure they will allow that at the convent, and you will see how kind the nuns are there. It is going to be fun for you. And on weekends, we get to come here and see Papa."

Once Polly stopped crying, Patsy began to play. Polly sat on Jefferson's lap and whispered, "Aren't you going to play your violin, Papa?"

He rubbed his wrist. "Not tonight, Polly. Some other night."

Patsy stopped and looked at her father. "I rather enjoy this piece as a duet. It's that *Canon in D* that James knows. Do you think he could come and play it with me?"

"Certainly." Jefferson left his girls alone for a moment and went to the kitchen.

Jefferson watched the brother and sister in easy conversation as though there had not been a gap of years between their meetings. As James washed pans in a wooden tub, Sally dried them. Their backs were to the door.

"I still do not believe my eyes that you are really here. Massa said Polly was coming with a nursemaid who'd been inoculated."

Sally chuckled "She's having herself a baby and was too far along to travel. So, the Eppes sent me."

"You get inoculated when you were at the Eppes?"

"No. They didn't hold with that. But Massa already say I gotta get the cowpox inoculation."

"Don't be scared. I been inoculated and it is nothing to fear. Just a scratch on the arm and a couple days of a fever. See, they didn't do it here and lots a folks got sick. Some like Petit got scarred real bad, but most of the people who got the sickness here died."

Jefferson interrupted by scuffing his shoe. "James, the girls would like for you to play the violin tonight."

"Certainly. I'll get it."

"No. Don't bother going up to the attic, use mine."

James was shocked that Jefferson would allow another person to play his favorite violin.

While they played, Sally and Polly whispered to each other and Polly would elbow Sally and giggle. James found it disturbing to see his sister acting more like a playmate than a maid to Polly. Soon the soothing repetition in the music and fatigue of travel hit Sally, who started yawning. When Polly saw her yawn, she followed with a yawn and a dramatic stretch. Jefferson laughed. "I think you two are losing your audience. Patsy, show your sister to her room. It's beside yours. Sally, I've had a bed put in your brother's room in the attic."

Polly then started to cry. Jefferson looked confused. "What is it?"

"I can't sleep without my Sally," she whined. The remainder of Polly's thought was lost in a long wail.

Jefferson summoned Petit to move a bed into Polly's room.

By the end of the week, Jefferson had enrolled Polly in the abbey school, where she boarded with Patsy. Sally assisted James in cleaning in the kitchen until Petit set her to sewing new clothes for the staff and mending their older attire.

During August, Jefferson and Short were consumed with dispatches from America. Over meals, they debated and drew up proposals to offer to the convention which would resolve thorny issues of trade policy and apportionment of powers between states and the federal government. James overheard snatches of these conversations. At lunch toward the later part of the month, Short arrived at the residence with some letters. "New dispatches. Congress of the Confederation." He shook a page at Jefferson. "They did it! Adopted your proposal."

Jefferson put down his fork. "Which one?"

"Free state expansion. Listen." Short read slowly from the dispatch. "On the thirteenth of July, the year of our Lord 1787, the Congress adopted the Northwest Ordinance. Formally titled now as 'An Ordinance for the Government of the Territory of the United States North-West of the River Ohio, an act of the Congress of the Confederation.' They adopted much of your proposed Land Ordinance of 1784. All new land is federally controlled; the federal government installs a magistrate and establishes schools. Once their population is large enough, statehood is granted. The central government gets revenue from the land sales and controls the legal formation of the new states."

"On slavery? Did they adopt *all* of my free state proposal?"

Short paused before answering. "In large part. All new states will be free states, but to get the southern states to agree, they bargained in a fugitive slave clause."

"So that a runaway slave could be returned to slavery from the new free states?"

"Yes."

James folded the towel, threw it on the counter, and left while the men discussed the additional dispatches.

Later that day when James brought a coffee to his study, Jefferson was dismissing Short. The lawyer stood, papers in hand. "Certainly, sir. I will redraft that letter to Madison on the need for a Bill of Rights to be attached to the Constitution."

Jefferson pointed at Short. "Strongly emphasize it. Without it, a citizen may never know where he stands in relation to his government. We need to knuckle Madison into agreement on that point. And start a letter to Franklin on the necessity for a unified federal authority to set import tariffs. It is impossible for me to negotiate any treaties of amity and commerce when each state can alter its tariffs at a whim. I'll tell you which parts to cipher when we have a final draft." James sensed the tension and silently left the coffee.

In early October, Jefferson called James to his study and motioned for him to close the door. His mood was grim. A crumpled letter leaned against his inkwell.

James frowned. "Was there a problem with tonight's dinner?"

"No, James. It was excellent, as usual. No. There is another matter."

"Sir?"

"I will no longer have need of that apartment."

"I see."

Jefferson flushed and made every effort to control his voice. "You see what?"

"I understand your direction, sir. I mean no disrespect."

He calmed and reached for the glass of sherry that had become his evening companion since Maria Cosway ended her summer visit to Paris. She had returned to London, apparently for good. Jefferson's temper had been shorter, his diary no longer had pages blocked out as "occupied," and his time in his study had lasted late into most nights.

"There is no need for that expense any longer."

"I will cancel the rental tomorrow, if that suits you."

"It does." Jefferson paused and sighed. "Thank you, James. It was always provisioned to perfection."

"We can only control so much, sir. As they say, the two most important things in life are beyond our control."

Jefferson tilted his head, puzzled.

"*Eros et thanatos.*"

Jefferson nodded slowly. "Love and death."

CHAPTER 17

After several dreary months, the spring of 1788 was welcome. James served the last of the salted cucumbers as an imitation of fresh food and checked the market for any hint of spring crops. Combeaux's wintertime reliance on turnips, cabbage, scallions, and leeks for decoration was boring.

In the farmhouses, there was a rush to slaughter a hog or two as Lent began. Forty days of not feeding a pig while it was in the smokehouse and having a fresh ham for Easter was a winning formula for increasing a farm's bounty. As the earth warmed, the spring crops began to arrive at Les Halles in order of their harvest. The kitchen at the Jefferson residence was no longer reliant only on the ever-present leeks, spinach, turnips, beets, cabbage, carrots, fennel, and garlic. The menu came more alive month by month.

Asparagus seemed to herald spring to all the caterers and the few fine restaurants in Paris with a wide array of presentations. This year, however, Combeaux steamed stalks and then arrayed the buttered stalks like shimmering sheaves of wheat tied at the middle with the wilted long green tops of spring onions. Later in the season, he steamed and chopped asparagus before baking it in an egg mixture in a crust with copious amounts of nutmeg and pepper. Then celery and peas entered the market, followed by eggplant, cucumber, and squashes. Soon the market was overrun with the bounty of the fields surrounding Paris. A delicacy of flavors emerged as if from under melting snow, and pantries were freed from the prison of their reliance on dried beans and baked bones, onions, and broth.

Early in the spring, James visited Restaurant Combeaux to place an order. A simple vegetable soup was nearly ready for the cooks' noon meal that day. Combeaux was about to demonstrate something. When he saw James, he motioned for him to join the cooks. Chef then proceeded to make what James discovered to be a universal seasoning for a broth-based vegetable soup. He called it *pistou*. He dispatched one cook to chop basil and parsley. Heads of garlic were diced and then swept into a large bowl while another cook grated a mound of hard Gruyère cheese. As soon as all the ingredients were arrayed in bowls, he spooned portions of each into a mortar, added a fine olive oil, and made something of a loose paste.

For serving, he added a hefty spoonful of the paste to a bowl of vegetable soup. The scents exploded in the heat of the soup and filled the kitchen with a most welcoming and robust aroma. James asked the chef for a taste of the sauce alone and found it complex, layered, garlicky, green, and fresh. He could not put a name to the new taste. When he ate his soup, he discovered how incredible the addition of the paste was in marrying all the diverse flavors of the new vegetables and converting a thin broth into a rich meal.

James reported the soup discovery to Jefferson, who asked that he make it soon.

Continuing his report, James added, "He made a confection, one he claims is from antiquity."

"What is it?"

"A taffy, he calls it. To make it, he boils sugar and water, adds minced pistachio. That's a green nut about the size of a garden pea. This is stirred with vigor until the clear, melted sugar gains an opaque nature and goes from water clear to eggshell white. He pours this hot mass onto trays and when cooled, cuts it into shapes such as diamonds or strips. These he may serve as is or dust with sugar even more powdered. It is sticky and horribly sweet."

"Did you like it?"

"Not really. But the other one I did. It is an almond paste made of crushed almonds boiled with sugar, rosewater, honey, starch, and musk, if available. This forms a sturdy paste that he pressed into wood molds shaped as any number of fanciful characters. But he also makes it in molds of loaves and fishes for the church."

"Buy some of the latter for us to try."

"Of course."

By fall, Sally's influence had increased. When the girls were in the residence, she was at the table with them for meals. One night in late September, Jefferson's daughters were away visiting a local shrine, not more than a day or two distant. Their travel guide substituted for Sally's services. Sally and Jefferson dined together. When Jefferson finished eating, he left for his study. Sally brought their plates to the kitchen, where James was drying the last of the pans. He looked up at her. "Think he wants a coffee tonight?"

She shrugged. "He's gone back to his papers again. Maybe ask him later."

Sally leaned on the wooden counter and idly twisted a lock of her long hair as she watched him clean the dishes.

As he leaned forward to take the dishes from the counter, a cloying scent smothered him. He blinked and recoiled to consider it. *Gardenia? Half-rotted gardenia? Mossy? Earthy? A hint of lemon.* He sniffed again. "That you?"

She brought her wrist to his nose. "Bought it for me today. Called it a *mugget.*" She emphasized the "t."

He corrected her. "It's *muguet!* 'Moo-gay.' It's that little white lily of the valley flower."

She sneered. "You think I don't know that! Oh, by the way, how's your lady-friend these days? Still pasting up them pamphlets?"

He clenched his fists and struggled to keep his voice low. "What do you know about such things?"

"I know enough to know that she could get you into a world of trouble."

"Or get me my freedom. We're still talking about filing my papers. You know that I can file for you too."

"I am going back. I already made up my mind."

"That's crazy. Why? Tell me why."

Sally stood taller and lifted her chin. "I gonna be his *châtelaine*. You know what that is, mister chef man?"

James frowned. "That's someone who owns a castle. You're not making any sense."

She smirked. "Mam said it means key carrier. That what she was for Massa Wayles, like his *maître d'hôtel*. Like Petit is here. But more. I'll be in charge of the whole house when we get back home. You'll see."

James slammed the dishes into the water. "You think you gonna 'carry his keys,' be in charge of anything? You really think so? You are a silly girl. And how did that turn out for Mam? She never really ran his plantation, only decided some chores in the house. He just visited Mam at nights Then, she gets sent to Jefferson no better than the rest of us."

She smirked. "But I am better. I know that. Why you think I look so much like his dead Martha? We's sisters, just with different mothers. Sisters!"

"I know who fathered us. But he was no father, just our owner. Just like Jefferson is Massa to us back there."

She fanned his concern away with a flick of her wrist. "He looks at me. I see it in his eyes. He can behold his past and future all at once. I's like when his Martha loved him."

"You don't have a future with him back there. He won't let you ride sitting next to him in a carriage to go to bookstalls or the opera. Not in Virginia. You going to be sleeping back in the cabin with Mam, eatin' off wood trenchers, not fine china plates."

"No! I ain't."

She started to leave. He grabbed her shoulders and held her facing him. "Soon as the girls grow up, they are going to see how much you look like them. You can't be around them then. They won't have it. You gonna be in the kitchen or go to the trades if you go back to Monticello. Maybe he trade you away if they ask."

She shook free of his grip. "Can't you see what's in front of your face, brother?"

He stopped and looked at her, his head pounding. She had grown into a woman.

She laughed at him and jutted out her chin. "You don't know everything. I gonna be better than Mam. In control of the plantation and the owner both. You'll see."

"Mam was still a slave when he died. His protection died with him when we got sent off to Jefferson. You're an amusement now that his lady-friend's gone."

"You mean that Cosway woman? She be married to a rich man. She was just toying with him."

"You think so? Isn't he just toying with you?"

She almost spit her words at him. "No. It's more than that. We're…"

He shouted at her. "We?"

She laughed.

He leaned toward her. "Is he visiting your bed at night?"

"No. I sleep in his. All night. He is gentle. I soothe him."

He started to respond, but she held her fingers to his lips. "James. He has my heart. All I know is I want to be with him and go home again. Monticello is the only home I know. Not here. Not Eppington, but Monticello. Can you understand? It's what I want."

He let his chin fall to his chest. His anger left him.

She took a breath and took his hand. "Brother? Tell me true. You going back?"

"I don't know. Mam is there. Our brothers. But here, I am free. He'd let me work in his kitchen, but here I am a chef in a great house, not some backwoods plantation kitchen cooking with black pots on a hearth."

She paused. "In a way, you are freer than he is. He's bonded to his work. He does more for others than his family. Them girls barely knew him after his leaving the older one with that woman in Baltimore and the younger ones with their aunt. He never sees them. Stuck away in the school. Paraded out for occasions."

"And doesn't he just parade you for attention?"

"He likes me on his arm. Riding in his carriage. People notice. I flatter him."

He laughed. "Yes, you do. But he won't do that when he goes back."

"Back to Congress? I can travel with him. Nobody knows who I am."

"Back there, everyone knows *what* you are. Here, they don't mind him going around with you, young enough to be his daughter. Maybe they even find it interesting that the great man has his dead wife's half-sister on his arm. His light-skinned slave in finery."

"You're no better. Got yourself a fine coat and a little French whore."

He raised his hand to stop her.

"Brother, I didn't come back here to argue. Listen to me. I seen her with you. I was coming back with him from the opera. You and her was pasting papers on a wall. Lucky it was dark. I had him look at me as we passed so's he didn't see you."

"When?" James struggled to hold his voice down.

She ignored his question and continued. "Best she stay away from that printer man."

"Why?"

"They know where he is."

"Where did you hear that?" He grabbed her elbow as she turned to leave. "Is she in danger?"

Sally smirked. "We all in danger here. Just like the English was in danger once Thomas set his mind on freedom for our country."

"*Thomas?*"

"Your nose is either in the kitchen or up her skirt so you don't even see what is happening around you. France is gonna explode. Men like

Thomas will pull power from the King, and people gonna go crazy in the streets. It be just a matter of time."

"Who says?"

"I hear things."

"You make up things."

"Not this. Best warn her. Tonight."

"Did Massa put this into your head? Try to *scare* me back to Virginia when he goes. Stop me talking you into your freedom?"

Sally looked deep into her brother's eyes. "You both so headstrong that you will get your way or die trying." Hands on hips, she leaned close enough for him to feel her breath. "Gonna leave your family for an idea you can be free?"

"An idea? It is like I just got born. Here is the first time I ever..." He stopped himself.

"You what? Got to bed a white girl?"

He started to slap her but turned away. James sprinted from the residence, from the mansions surrounding it, toward her. They had been lovers for two years. Now James knew that he wanted more. He wanted them to have a life together. He slowed to appear inconspicuous to the nearby soldiers although his pulse hammered in his temples. He passed clusters of a few men and women as they shared the latest news. Most discussed the posters depicting the King in some bawdy or ill-disposed state. The cartoons and sketches were clear and needed no translation.

But the pamphlets, printed at risk, were another matter altogether. They explained, reported, and emboldened. Common enough was the supposition that James heard in the noble houses that the poor were incapable of understanding or running a country. But he knew better. Inability to read was not an inability to think. And think they did. Debate and robust discussions followed the distribution of pamphlets that called attention to yet another outrage, a food shortage, or an increased tax. Often over the past several months he had lingered to listen and try to measure the mood of the citizens.

At most of the gatherings, someone was reading a pamphlet aloud while others reported on posters they had seen. Women often led the marches, James discovered. Judges were lenient on them. James chuckled when he heard this, knowing the innate ferocity of both his mother and Gabrielle. The soldiers feared the men, and often just turned away from a march of women if they disbanded in a reasonable amount of time. Knowing this, many men attended marches or attacked the soldiers while attired in dresses and bonnets.

If, as Jefferson often said, George Washington was the father of the United States, James thought that certainly some woman was the mother laboring to give birth to a new France. How did Gabrielle have the courage to carry sheaves of pages from the printer and slap them against the walls of the city in the middle of the night with a paste of flour stolen from her father's kitchen? How did she embolden him to accompany her? Yet, how could he still hold to such fear of grabbing his own freedom and staying with her in France when she was the very soul of courage?

In her room at nights, he helped her sew the small rosettes in red, white, and blue that the revolutionaries pinned to their lapels. No larger than a lime, these *cockades* became the symbol of the Revolution. He puzzled at Gabrielle's obsession of knitting what she called liberty caps. A brimless hat, like a cone, tapered to a narrow but not pointed top, pulled forward. Such caps, she said, represented the glory of ancient Rome, which freed its slaves as the French citizens must be freed of servitude to the King.

He vaulted up the stairs. The small oil lamp beside the bed cast the only light in the chilly room. She was in her nightdress and reading. He slumped when he saw that she was safe.

"Thank God."

She frowned and closed the book. She stood and embraced him. "What is it?"

"Sally. My sister, Sally said your printer is known."

"We thought so. He left for his family's farm last night. The press is being moved tonight."

He glanced around the room. "We should take away any posters."

"All gone."

"And the rosettes you made."

"Gone."

"Caps?"

She pointed to a basket of yarn. "None here. I am not careless, James."

He closed his eyes. "I was so afraid. I know what the revolution means to you. I think that way too."

Gabrielle had him sit beside her on the bed and held him.

"Then it is time to petition for your freedom."

He sighed. "I know it is, but Sally is here now. She's family."

"You need to tell your Mister Jefferson to read what he wrote and free you both."

James laughed until he coughed. "I'll do that. What if he turns me loose; how can I leave my baby sister with him? She's still young, but she all filled out. I think he looks at her and sees his dead wife."

"What? That's impossible."

He shook his head. "They got the same daddy. I see Mister Jefferson looking at this little picture on his desk that he had painted of his wife when they got married, and then he looks at Sally. It's like they are the same in his mind. Truth."

"Oh, James. I know you feel the pull of family just like I do. What do they want of us?"

He drew her close and kissed her. She pushed away. "No. We must face it. My father is going to leave the city. Our hope for you to work here with him is now gone." She gestured quickly, her fingers thrusting toward the ceiling. "But you still could be a free man here. Weren't you angry all the time knowing his power over you?"

"Angry? I never knew I could be angry. It just was."

"But you knew there were free Negro men in the north."

"But I never knew *how* they came to be free. If I had considered it, the thought of freedom would have festered like a boil and come to some fatal eruption. But as it happened, I found my way to you and to new dreams." He paused and held her. "Once, you said I should talk to a lawyer and see about getting my freedom papers."

"Yes. Jefferson could not take you back then."

"If I was free, would you come to America with me?"

"What?" She turned. The nightgown fell from her shoulder. "And leave my family?"

"You see my problem. I need to be near Sally, at least until she is more grown and can fend for herself. But, if I went back free, you and I could open a restaurant."

"With what money? This is my father's place. Not mine. He'll need everything he can sell it for just to return to Lyon and start over there."

"I have money."

"You do?"

"Yes, I've saved enough to buy my freedom if he won't honor the French papers."

"And he would do that?"

"He might."

"Opening a restaurant is expensive. Fitting out the dining room is why there are so few. Caterers just need a kitchen."

"But we could. I know we could. I can dream it."

"And can horses fly in your dreams?"

"Perhaps they can, if you are with me." He kissed her shoulder.

The winter of 1788 went from cold to the coldest in living memory. Outdoor labor was suspended, making matters worse since without in-come, neither food nor fuel could be purchased. Water froze and so was in short supply. As though nature had conspired to make a miserable situation even worse, the temperature continued to drop. At one point it was all Jefferson could do to keep a livable temperature in the mansion by closing all the draperies and restricting fires to the interior rooms for both his family and staff. He abandoned his foot bath and shaving. The heavy scent of the lily of the valley seemed to hover in his bedroom and study now that the house was as tightly closed as possible.

The convent school sent its students living in Paris to their homes and cloistered the few remaining ones with nuns in one large room with a fireplace to conserve both heat and funds.

When bread and firewood became scarce, the government was consumed with the provision of both. Huge bonfires were set and tended by soldiers at the major intersections. Citizens huddled around them to keep from freezing to death. Cattle froze standing in fields. Winter crops failed. Snow covered fields and blocked roadways. Carriages drove over the frozen Seine. What bread was obtainable by the government was distributed to the people who mobbed the back of the wagons that delivered it. Bakers stretched what flour they had with fine sawdust. This slowed the starvation and fanned the hope for an early spring.

All hope of festivities for Christmas or in celebration of the New Year were dashed. Only those who absolutely had to venture into the cold did so.

When Short came into the study in late January to review the plan for the next trade meeting, he was wearing gloves as well as a muffler at his neck. Jefferson got up, letting his lap robe fall to the floor and went to the heavily draped window. Parting the drapery to examine the thermometers that he had installed outside the window, he rubbed the frost from the glass to read the mercury in the brass-bound tubes. He called to Short to record his reading. Short grabbed a pencil, as the inkpot had crusted with a light film of ice.

"First, the Reaumur." He muttered to himself as his breath clouded around him. "Or as some call his scale, the *octogesimal division*. Ah! There it is. The mercury is right at twenty below. It's fifty-two degrees below freezing on the Fahrenheit scale, which, as you know marks freezing at thirty-two degrees whereas Reaumur, like Celsius, marks freezing at zero, a more scientific measure, I believe. Easier to calibrate."

Short repeated the measurement to verify it. "Minus twenty and minus fifty-two."

Jefferson rubbed the glass again and squinted. "Perhaps it is minus fifty-three. Hard to read it."

Short suddenly snapped at Jefferson. "What's the difference? I saw a horse frozen solid in the street on the way over. The haunches had been chopped off. Hacked apart for the meat before it froze to a solid block. Shoved over the fire on a stick. Now an axe couldn't chip off any flesh. Crap from the chamber pots is piling up in frozen mounds. Going to be a horrid stink in the city come spring."

Jefferson let the curtain drop and tossed another log on the fire. "With this cold, there won't be a spring, not when we expect it. The ground is frozen deeper than it has been in the lifetime of anyone I have talked to. The winter wheat crop has failed, and spring will be delayed. The bread shortage will worsen. What reserves bakers have is about to be depleted. I sent James to get flour from that baker he worked for so he could bake for us here. All he could get was two fifty-pound sacks. This was the man with a mill and a full warehouse in reserve! All gone now."

"At some inflated price, I suspect. Between the removal of price controls on the grain market and this confounded weather, the price was destined to elevate to unreasonable heights in this shortage."

"Of course. The market demands it. The King has impounded much of the available flour from the countryside, which is only making matters worse. Between that and the taxes on farmers that the nobility is freed from, I sense a genuine anger."

"He thinks handing out wood and bread will stop the Revolution?"

"Revolution? It is a natural *evolution* in a government. From slave to free, from monarchy to democracy. But not an easy transition, I grant you. Haven't you listened to the arguments around my dining table for the Philosophy of Enlightenment?" Short pulled his coat tighter and shivered. "William? I want you to live here until the weather breaks. It is safer here."

"Are you certain?"

"Yes. Let's put aside the trade strategy for now and work on a letter to the President. We need flour here as soon as possible. I thought there was a more varied diet, but James told me that most people here subsist on a boule or two a day and little more."

Short broke the ice on the inkpot with a quill. "You think the shortage is that important?"

"It will fan the flames of rebellion for those who live through this winter."

Jefferson rubbed his wrist as he dictated his letter, which described the crisis and explained the need for as much flour as could be shipped as soon as possible.

Short sighed. "An admirable sentiment, sir, but sending it in the winter sea is dangerous."

"I know. It is fraught with peril given the fierceness of the weather. In that regard, we'll send copies of the letter on three separate ships, mark each as one of three copies."

For the remainder of the winter, people hibernated in their homes, pooled firewood, burned furnishings for heat, and rationed their food to wait out the weather as best they could. Those isolated in the countryside were held hostage to the cold and feared taking their horses from their stables. In the city, blanketed horses drew carts of wood, only as absolutely necessary and did so with woolen feed sacks over their noses to heat their air with their own breath. Those horses that fell in the streets from the cold were set upon by men with long knives, skinned, butchered on the street, and slabs of meat rushed into homes before it froze. For most, it was the only meat they would have that year. Carcasses littered the streets.

The extreme weather forced changes in the great houses as well. During this time, Combeaux closed the restaurant and housed the families of his cooks there. He restricted his kitchen to making stews, which could be carried easily in the cold and heated again in the better homes. The ovens burned continually both stewing and giving what heat there was to those in the kitchen and on cots in the restaurant. On evenings that Jefferson wanted dinner to be brought into the residence, James went to Restaurant Combeaux and helped with the preparation. He peeled carrots and assisted in any way that was needed. He worked in his heaviest coat with a long wool scarf tied over his ears and around his nose and mouth.

In this time of peril, the church solicited weekly subscriptions of food and funds for the indigent. Once a week, James was sent to buy one pot of stew for the household. With his own funds, he bought a second one and left it at the abbey on his way home.

CHAPTER 18

Spring came late in 1789. Melting snow flooded fields and ravens clouded the sky. There continued to be food shortages, as Jefferson had feared. At Jefferson's urgent demand, President Washington sent 21,000 barrels of flour, which arrived at France's Atlantic ports starting in March. Shipments continued arriving until May. Added supplies were shipped to the French colonies in the West Indies from the United States, thus relieving the drain on resources from France.

As the stunted crops started arriving in the market, James saw a new vigor in the citizens. Their quest for governmental change had not been hampered by the devastation of the winter. If anything, the flames of revolution burned brighter. By June, those who had lived through the horrible winter took as their mission to speed the Revolution onward. Anger in the countryside and cities grew from watching half the children under the age of ten die of illness and starvation, and the weak or infirm wither.

Sharing their grief and wanting to make France his home, James agreed to let Gabrielle contact her friend the lawyer. Her annoyance was clear when, a week later, she told James that the lawyer had left the city on a family matter until the end of June. James replied that he was too busy at the residence making wine jellies and other last-minute requests by Jefferson to see either her or the lawyer until after Jefferson's Independence Day celebration.

As he cooked, it seemed to James so obvious that there was serious trouble afoot. The marches and mobs were growing and the vegetables in the market were minimal and costly. But Jefferson was intent on having his party on the Fourth of July as though he were at Monticello. The menu was classic for Jefferson. Ham was from his own smokehouse, so he could explain the smoking process to anyone within earshot. Dried beans were soaked and sauced in the Boston style with chips of bacon and dark molasses, hearth baked all night under heaped coals. Plantation foods of beef stew and apple dumplings were made in the American style. Sole in butter sauce with capers was served in the French style. Asparagus from the Netherlands was smothered in Hollandaise that James made by the gallon that morning.

Once the sauce was set aside to remain warm until it dressed the platter of asparagus, James then made his mixture for the ice cream in plenty of time for the blend to chill. First, he beat the egg yolks and added sugar until a fluffy light yellow was achieved. He reserved the whites for omelets for the kitchen staff. To this egg blend, he stirred a good pinch of salt into the mix. Then in a heavy pot, he warmed the cream with several vanilla beans until it was almost at a boil. At the first hint of bubbles along the pan's edge, he removed the pan, scooped out the whole beans, split them lengthwise and scraped out the tender insides, which he returned to the pan. He beat fine grains of sugar into the mixture, stirring vigorously and letting the pan cool only slightly. Once combined, he put the pan into a larger one filled with simmering water, making a *bain-marie*. Over this more temperate heat, he stirred until the mix thickened. He let the mixture cool on the counter for an hour. After straining through a towel into a large bucket, he nested it in a barrel of ice to chill. For the rest of the morning, the mixture chilled as did the tinned cylinders of the five *sorbetières* James would use to churn ice cream for Jefferson's many guests.

Just before the guests started to arrive, James set five hired lads to preparing the ice in the half barrels that would hold the filled *sorbetières*. "Mind the balance!" James shouted. "A layer of ice, then salt, then ice and salt again. Leave enough room for the canister to fit in and be covered once the mixture is in and the lid secured. And only fill the canisters a bit over half to get the right chilling."

The first of the helpers had made ice cream for James before and knew what to do once the mixture was in the tinned containers. James started him making the first batch under his supervision. Once he saw that his helper had recalled the process and the other four boys were watching carefully, James left him to make the first batch and start the next four half an hour apart. He served it in a chilled silver bowl, not the molds that James would have used for a smaller group on a cooler day.

James left a ten-minute sandglass with the first helper and trusted him to open and scrape down the sides of the *sorbetières* as the mix froze to the walls. By using a long wooden spatula and scraping every ten minutes, the iced brine converted the mixture into ice cream in about thirty minutes. As he had planned, a new batch of ice cream arrived at the buffet table every half hour for the final two hours of the party. James enjoyed witnessing the amazement of Jefferson's guests, who had never seen the dessert prior to that day. Many of them had multiple servings of the treat.

A buffet had been laid out for guests in the rustic colonial style. Finely attired men and women piled their plates high and drank through all of the cases of deeply cellared wine that had survived the winter. There were eighty guests on the hottest summer of their time in Paris, yet it all worked perfectly.

After the cutlery, dishes, and glasses were all washed and returned to their cabinets, James excused the additional hired help and lingered in the dark kitchen, alone. He poured a tall glass of brandy from the last of a small keg brought by one of Jefferson's French guests. Sitting on the counter, he slumped against the wall. He glanced at the recipe that Jefferson had written for ice cream for his notebook of things to take back to Virginia when their time in France was over. The portions and processes were correct, but he had spelled the containers as *sabbottieres*. He shrugged and let the paper drop to the counter. *Who would know? How would he even pronounce it?*

James heard Petit's brisk pace in the hallway. He came into the kitchen. "Oh, I did not mean to intrude."

James lifted his glass. "About to have a brandy. It's the last of the keg the Marquis brought."

Petit retained his formal demeanor. "That is an excellent Cognac."

James smiled and reached for a second glass and poured in half. "Join me?"

He tipped his head. "With pleasure."

James handed it to him. They each took a sip. After some silence, Petit turned to James. "You did well today. It will be long remembered after your Mister Jefferson leaves France."

"You think so?"

"Yes. Did he tell you about packing?"

"Packing what?"

"The household goods. I ordered the crates today. They should be ready in a month. I cannot believe Monsieur Jefferson failed to mention it to you."

"I've been so busy here. Before today, I had not seen him for over a week."

He paused and looked into his glass for the longest time. "James, I have come to admire your skill."

"I have learned much from you."

"Thank you. But since I pay all the food bills, you may not be aware of how some things are changing."

"I know the party today cost a lot."

"Not just that. Money buys less each day. The King simply mints more livres or Louis d'or coins or prints *assignats* to cover his debts, but soon your money will be worthless."

"Does Jefferson know this?"

"I have told Mister Short so he can transfer funds out of the country before the collapse. I know he has given you chef's rights to sell fat, bone, and excess foods."

"He did."

"I would like to recommend that you take whatever you have saved and convert it into an asset that is easily moved and of consistent value."

James frowned. "Such as?"

"A gemstone. A ring. A watch."

"What would you recommend?"

Petit studied his glass for a moment. "A watch. The most expensive one you can afford with a chiming repeater."

"I don't know what that is."

"It is a watch for your vest pocket that can ring on the hour and quarter hours. The chime adds significant resale value."

"And would you know of such a dealer?" James laughed at himself. "Of course, you would. A relative, perhaps?"

"No. But our families have known each other for many years."

"Would you go with me?"

Petit nodded. "I will ask for the family courtesy. A reduced price."

"Why would you help me?"

"You are a good person and…"

"And?"

"Life is short. You never know where it may take you."

James tipped the edge of his glass toward Petit and smiled.

The following night in bed, Gabrielle ran her fingertips over James's forehead. "He can see you tomorrow, at noon."

Half-asleep, he mumbled, "Who?"

"Roget. The lawyer. There's a small tavern on the rue Saint-Honoré across from the *Palais-Royal*. He'll be there."

The next morning, he made his excuses to Petit so that he could leave the residence for the meeting. As James hurried past *Cirque du Palais-Royal* and the young men selling political tracts in front of the *Palais-Royal*, he wondered when the soldiers or police would arrive. Looking for the small bar, he failed to see a sign but after noticing a few tables against a wall of irregular stone, James walked in that direction and finally saw the small sign for the bar. He checked his new pocket watch and noticed he was a few minutes early for his noon meeting. Nonetheless, he went into the bar to escape the sun.

Avocat Jean-Claude Roget had taken a table for two against a bricked wall as far from the door's hot draft as possible. He hunched over papers scattered across the entire tabletop. His empty beer glass was on the floor beside his scuffed leather portfolio, which had a powdered wig draped over it like a dead animal.

When James entered the small tavern, several men glanced up from their glasses or plates of cheese, more in response to the blast of hot air than his presence. As soon as he shut the door, the musty smell of spilled beer and old cheese surrounded him. The patrons quickly returned to their conversations or food. Gabrielle had said just one thing: the lawyer had brown hair, and he tied it back at his neck. To James, they all looked like they had hair in shades of brown, but only the man against the wall failed to look up when the door opened. James started toward him slowly, then gained confidence when he saw a powdered lawyer's wig under the man's chair.

As he approached, James took his measure. He was deep in concentration. Ink-stained fingers shuffled the papers. His hair was indeed brown but a mussed mess, no doubt from the wig, but without any of the vanity to which James was accustomed. When Jefferson had occasion to remove a wig, he immediately returned each hair to its proper location and tied a fresh ribbon at his neck. James put his hands on the back of the chair facing the man and waited to be noticed. After a moment, he cleared his throat. Without looking up, Roget asked, "Monsieur Hemings?"

By now, James had become accustomed to his name having lost its American pronunciation and sounding more like "Emmie." "*Oui, Monsieur.*"

The lawyer struggled to find the English. "Sit you in that chair. *Un instant.*"

James thanked him and asked in French if he could buy him another beer. Roget nodded. The conversation resumed in French once he had put his flimsy papers into his portfolio.

As he took the glass from James, the lawyer smiled easily. "This beer. It is in payment for my consultation. I am now your *avocat* and what you say to me is only for us. Understand. Gabby is not a part of our conversation. No one else is."

It took James a moment to connect "Gabby" to Gabrielle the way he had said it. He nodded. "How do you know her?"

"No. We talk only of your situation."

James frowned as Roget held his hand out, not to shake hands but expecting something, rubbing his thumb against his fingertips. "Gabrielle said there would be no cost for a consultation."

"There isn't. The beer is an unexpected compensation. Let me see your papers." He waggled his fingers impatiently.

"What papers?"

"Your *cartouche*."

"I don't understand."

"You know of the *Police des noirs*?"

"No."

"Possibly because you are light of skin or travel at very early or late hours for your work, you have not encountered them. The law allows the police to stop you, a person of color, and require a showing of your papers proving you are a free man, otherwise you can be arrested and deported or sold as a slave. Resold, as it were in your case, if I understood your legal position as still enslaved to Mister Jefferson."

James leaned forward and lowered his voice. "My God. I had no idea."

"You have never been stopped?"

"No. Never. But I have no freedom papers. Nothing for here. When I travelled for my master in Virginia, he wrote me a travel note saying where I was to go and that he owned me."

"Until you have your own freedom papers, have your master write an ownership notice with his address here on it to bridge this gap in your identity."

"Certainly. But Gabrielle said I should meet with you."

"This is about you. If you want to be declared free, I can do that. Write the petition to the Admiralty Court and process it for you."

"How much for that?"

"Nothing. There is a group that supports my work."

"Is it the *Société des Amis des Noirs?*"

"No. A smaller group. But related in philosophy. When Jacques-Pierre Brissot de Warville founded it, he opened the eyes of many. Several smaller groups are like the Friends of the Blacks in seeking freedom declarations and finding work for them. But in the city, there are more people than jobs. Farm boys come to be porters or houseboys. Now many girls come from the provinces here thinking to be housemaids or tavern girls. Too many. Many end up selling only themselves on the street, so there is resentment of freed blacks competing for any work. But for you, we are posed with a practical challenge."

"What is that?"

He downed a quarter of the beer and wiped his mouth with the back of his sleeve. "I can process your petition for freedom. This court is most favorable to such, and your owner will be assessed the costs of court, and my fee. But then, where do you work. How will you support yourself?"

"I am a cook. Soon I will be a chef in a great house."

"The call for that skill is now rare. Look around you. As the rebellion moves apace, many noble families are departing Paris for their country estates. They sense the sparks of rebellion are coming closer to their dry tinder." His voice lowered to a whisper. "They know the days of ninety-nine Frenchmen supporting one nobleman are almost over. Small attacks on a gilded carriage or dandy in an alleyway have terrified many. Two, three years ago, such a thing would be unknown. Now many of the police and guards feel the winds of freedom surging in their breasts as well."

"My master expects that I would return to America with him and cook in repayment for my training here. And that is where my family is."

Roget huffed. "There was no contract to that promise. No consideration or manner of your agreeing to a task in which you had no free will to agree. If you feel a loyalty, that is to your heart, but not the law."

Outside the bar, a sharp report of an explosion rattled the small windows. James was startled, but no one at the bar looked concerned. James whispered, "Police?"

Roget laughed as he took his watch from his vest pocket and tugged on the stem. "Hardly. It's the big noon cannon. Better than that small one that relied on a sundial. Don't worry, they just stuff in paper to hold the powder in place when it is fired like the old one. A fine piece of science it is. It has an ingenious firing device. They load it as I said with powder but without a projectile. The fuse hole is primed with gunpowder. Now here is the interesting part. It is set alight when the sun is directly overhead, and its rays are concentrated through a looking glass that is focused down the fuse hole. When the sun is in the highest position, bam!" His hand slammed into the table and their glasses jumped.

James checked his watch and did not reset it. He finished his beer and took a deep breath. "What if I were to be freed here and return to America as a free man?"

"I do not know how your America would rule on our legal order. We have relations, our countries. But things are changing in both our lands. The matter of jurisdiction is uncertain in this new area of the law, even between countries here in Europe."

James stood, squared his shoulders, and bowed crisply. "Thank you for your time. I must think on which path to take. I may have been born enslaved, but I will not die a slave."

"Certainly. If I can be of service, let me know. And thank you for the beer." After James left the bar, Roget lifted his glass and muttered. "Goodbye, Mister Hemings. Good luck."

That night, James left Gabrielle's room just before midnight. As he cut along the alleyway, he heard the swearing of a disorganized mob before he saw the ragged men cross the street. There looked to be about twenty people; some held torches that sent off sparks.

James pulled back and crouched behind a large wooden crate until they passed. Looking around the corner, he saw them stop and surround a statue above the fountain in the small plaza where five streets converged. The tallest of the men threw a rope over the head of the marble statue. Others grabbed the rope. They pulled the statue off its pedestal. The cheers of the crowd drowned out the shattering of the stone and seemed to energize them. One of the men on the edge of the group tossed his torch on top of a passing wagon that was filled with straw. It flamed quickly. The horses snorted at the crackling of the fire and bolted, their hooves skidding on the cobblestones. The driver jumped free of the burning wagon and fled. The men ran away. James remained hidden, choking on the acrid smoke from the burning straw, until their shouts faded. In the distance he heard more shouting and pistol shots as the mob next came upon a carriage. When night fell, he sprinted toward the residence, passing a scarecrow, dressed as the King, hanging from a lamppost.

James rushed in the kitchen door and stopped when he saw Sally mending a dress by the light of an oil lamp.

She nicked her finger with the needle when she jumped. "You gave me a fright. What on earth?"

He wiped the sweat from his eyes with his palm. "I gotta see Massa, now."

"He's not home. Had one of his dinners somewhere."

"Then I'll tell Petit. We ought to be ready to leave."

She sucked the small drop of blood from her finger then laughed. "Leave? You crazy? Why'd we leave?"

"Because there is a rebellion brewing. I told him that I hear it on the street when I'm out buying provisions, but he ignored me. Says it just a 'healthy expression.' Tonight, when I was coming home from Gabrielle's,

I saw them burn a wagon and hang a straw man dressed almost like the King." He stopped to catch his breath. "I saw them beat a man they pulled from his carriage. Maybe shot others. Even Jefferson says the die is cast. He says he expects a civil war."

"So what if they are mad at the King? I hear the visitors here grumble about the tax too. No one likes the King right now. But we are safe."

James splashed cider into a cup and downed it quickly. "I don't think so. The great houses will be overrun. We have food, and the beggars on the street don't. Bread accompanies our food but is their only food and they can't get it. Do you understand? There is talk of looting. Get an old dress from one of the maids if you need to pass."

"Why'd I want an old one? I got new dresses."

James shook his fist in front of her to get her attention. "If a mob comes here when he is away, you slip into a maid's dress and go to Restaurant Combeaux. Wait for me in the alley behind the kitchen, hear?"

Sally went back to sewing. "You just being crazy. Nothing's wrong."

"That gang I saw tonight would just as soon hang someone from one of these fine houses as that straw man. I just want you safe."

"He'll keep me safe."

"Like a caged bird. You think carrying the keys makes you free? It just makes you another kind of slave to him. You're not his mistress, like some rich woman here. They got a choice who they bed with. You don't."

"He don't force himself."

"Doesn't matter if he did or didn't. You couldn't say no anyhow. Not back there."

Sally turned away from her brother.

"What are you now? Sixteen? Trust me. All I need to do is file a paper and we are free. Slavery is not legal here. I even hear Count Mirabeau telling Massa that he's gonna push for voting by *gen de couleur*. Voting! That is being free!"

"He treats you like you free. Pays you a wage, don't he? Pays me for looking after the girls when they're not in school and for sewing their things. He even keeps my wages under lock for me so's no one can take them."

"Even you!"

"Stop!"

"He may be legal, but he's not living up to his ideas. Stay here in France with me. We could be free."

"Free? What's that really mean? So we could starve here?"

"No. So I could live according to my will, not his. My will to say yes or no. To say *no!*"

Sally shrugged. "Say no to what? What could I do here? I can't talk French like you."

"I could teach you. Women are paid to cook here. You could be my assistant. We could work together."

Sally shook her head at the idea. "For wages? How'll I know what tomorrow bring? They can let you go for no reason at all. At Monticello, I know that he will be there today and tomorrow and the day after that. Even if he travels, Monticello will always be there. He will take care of me, forever."

James grabbed her shoulder. "And if you have him a baby, it'd be a slave just as bound as you and me. *Partus sequitur ventrem*, they call it. Your enslavement bleeds onto your child. You displease him or Miss Patsy, and you'll get sold off to wherever. With or without your baby. That be that. Besides, he's going broke. He's gonna have to sell off some slaves, break up families he's been good enough to keep whole or he'll lose the plantation."

"You're wrong. Even spouting them words. He promised me." Sally dropped her mending and fought for composure. "You can believe what he say."

"Really? In public, he say, 'Shame on fellas what sniffin' after a married lady,' then he romances that Cosway woman over dinners that I make and she's married. And then he beds you."

Sally stood and slapped James.

He put his hand to his cheek. "Go tell Petit I saw people rioting in the street. Tell him about the burning wagon and the straw man. Tell him I heard gunshots. He'll know what to do."

He took his hand from his burning cheek and started to say something. But then, he turned to the door. She shouted after him. "Where are you going?"

James ran toward Gabrielle's. He was covered with sweat by the time he was only a few streets away from the residence. He slid to a stop and pressed into a doorway when he saw a dozen men gathered in the middle of the road. They were shouting at each other, arguing. James heard that one of their group had been shot when the mob overran the Bastille, tearing up cobblestones to throw at the guards and trying to release its prisoners.

A tall man said they should go back with bats. A slim man shouted that bats were no match for the guards' muskets, and they should tear down another tollhouse instead.

Another man ran toward the group and shouted that men had broken into the armory at the Hôtel des Invalides and had muskets and canons for them. With that, the mob turned and ran.

As soon as they had moved toward the river, James sprinted to Gabrielle's. Once in the alley behind the restaurant, he noticed the door was slightly ajar. Feeling a cold stab of fear, he shoved the door open and bolted up the stairs. "Thank God you're here!"

"What is it?"

"They're tearing down the tollhouses. Fighting with guards at the Bastille."

"Anyone hurt?"

James wiped his forehead with his shirtsleeve and continued. "I don't know! I could only hear what they were yelling at each other. Sounded like they were tearing the place apart stone by stone."

Gabrielle took his hand to calm him. "Then we stay here until it is quiet."

James noticed her leather valise on the bed and clothes scattered nearby. "Are you leaving?"

"Just to father's apartment. He's closing the doors next week. Then we go to family in Lyon."

James pleaded. "Come with me to America. I'll just need six months to train someone to take my place there."

"And another three months each way in travel. That's a year, James. That is a lifetime now." She said softly, "I'll be in Lyon. If you return."

"*When* I return."

"Papa says that if our clients are going to their country estates, so must we. Without the great houses buying platters from us, we cannot sustain the restaurant."

"Does your father have employment in one of the estates?"

Gabrielle folded a blouse. "Not yet. Come with us."

"And peel carrots for your father for the rest of my life?"

"He treats you like a son."

"But I'm not. And my sister needs my protection."

Gabrielle cinched the leather strap on the case and turned to face him. "From what? From the rich man who wants her? I've seen her in his carriage at his side. She has what she wants. That is clear. You should have gone to the Admiralty Court when there was time. You should have as much faith in yourself as you have in your Mister Jefferson."

James flinched as she shut the bag. "I will find you, if you have to leave."

"No, James. It is you who have left me."

Jefferson was oblivious to the requirements to meet his demands for specific social events and regularly underestimated the duration of time or magnitude of effort to acquire and prepare his menu. In August, when James had started packing the kitchen for their return to the United States, Jefferson had an even more difficult request. Coming into the kitchen, which was littered with open crates into which James was placing the new copper pans, Jefferson stopped and looked at the mess with his hands on his hips.

James glanced up from packing. "Almost finished with the cookware. I thought I'd pack the foods you wanted to take last. It's already over fifty crates."

"Hmmm. That's a good idea. Foods last. But I need you to cook tomorrow night."

James tried unsuccessfully to hide his concern. Jefferson paused, only now discerning the difficulty of his request.

James leaned back against the counter. "How many?"

Jefferson said, "There should be twenty, perhaps a few less. Not all have replied to Lafayette."

"Is this *his* dinner?"

"No. I am hosting it for his benefit, not mine." He adopted the tone that James had heard him use so often with political opponents, most of whom were swayed. But not James. He crossed his arms and watched as Jefferson tried to change the reality of the moment. "You see. It is important that the competing factions get together and resolve their main differences soon, or the rebellion will get out of hand. It is a situation much like I faced in drafting the Declaration of Independence."

James raised an eyebrow and laughed. "And you think my cooking is going to stop the Revolution?"

"Well, your dinners are renowned. Most are coming for that experience rather than any hope of finding common ground, but that is what they must do. I hope to facilitate that."

"Sir? The kitchen is in no shape to do this. I can build a menu and cater it through Combeaux."

"Fine. Fine solution, James. I knew that you would provide."

Jefferson smiled the smile he used when he had won and did not want the other party to feel defeated. And he was right about the need for adjustments between the warring positions of what they wanted and what was possible.

The next morning, James grabbed his satchel with the funds and menu for Combeaux and hurried using only side streets. When he turned out of a small passage near the restaurant, he stopped, disoriented. The smoldering building beside the restaurant had been the hat shop.

The sign above Restaurant Combeaux was charred and hanging only by its left edge. The front windows were cracked and sooty. James pushed open the front door, which scraped against a mound of broken crockery and fine china. As he shouldered the door the rest of the way open, the top half splintered away. Ash swirled at his feet. He scrambled over the mound of crockery shards into the burnt shell of the dining room. Table linens were gone, not singed, but stolen. The cupboards hung open, devoid of their glasses and plates, silverware and vases.

He spun and sprinted toward the kitchen. At the doorway, he crouched and listened for looters. Nothing. He entered the charred cave that had once been the magnificent kitchen. His universe. His new beginning. The smell of men and cooking had been replaced by acrid ash and char. Huge gaps in the roof now opened to the sky, and James heard birds and a distant hum of people and carts. When he looked up, ash stung his eyes. The bricks holding the iron ovens had crumbled. The oven doors had toppled to the floor. The brick stoves slumped, blackened and cold. No copper glinted on the wall. The worktables were scorched. The place had been stripped of pans and knives and hope.

Slate roof tiles and splintered beams littered the stairway to Gabrielle's room. Although he knew she had intended to leave, he felt his chest tighten. He dropped his satchel and clawed aside the smoldering debris. Taking the stairs two at a time, he slammed into her door. A step into the blackened room, he froze and spun around. Most of one wall had collapsed into the kitchen. The room was stripped of furnishings and papers. No hint of her remained.

A sound from below echoed in the starkness. He started to lean toward the gaping hole in the wall but retreated at the groan of the timber beneath his feet. He listened again and heard only his breathing. He picked his way down the stairs and tried to understand what he saw. He swept debris from the table where he had first worked, then something caught his eye. He reached for it and saw that it was a small copper skillet, no larger than his palm, now deformed and tarnished by the heat. He threw it against the wall and blinked away ash and regret.

He looked around the kitchen once, slowly, to sear it into his memory. The edges of the shattered skylight sparkled and sprinkled light over the center tables. He leaned against one and dropped his head. This was where his life had started. *His* life. Not someone's idea of what he should do. This was where he had become his own man.

A rasping sound came from the dining room. James looked toward the door and called, "Who is there?" He instantly regretted doing this, anxious that it might be looters. He slid his sweaty hand to the knife on his belt.

When Combeaux turned the corner, he felt the fear drain from him. He ran to the chef, crashing into him and holding him in a tight embrace. "Gabrielle?"

"Safe. On her way to Lyon. I still own a small home there. You are welcomed there and to wherever I find to cook." James blinked, realizing that Combeaux spoke to him in English. Clearly and perfectly.

"You speak English?"

"Of course. But why should I when you were the student? You had much to learn."

James smiled, bowed his head, and said softly, "*Oui, Chef. C'est vrai.*"

Combeaux looked around the cavernous room with an impassiveness that startled James. "The fire seemed to have been set in the shop of the milliner. To the side of the restaurant. I wonder what they intended. Are you still with Mister Jefferson?"

James held up the satchel and laughed. "Yes. He wanted your dinner tonight."

Combeaux responded with a belly laugh. He wiped his eyes. "Tell him we are indisposed this evening."

"He wants me to be his chef at his mansion in Virginia."

"Is that good for you?"

"He promised to set me free once I train my replacement."

"Do you believe him?"

"I do not know. But I do know that I owe you everything. You have given me a skill and a confidence. A life. I do not know how I can repay your kindness."

"You have a unique talent, James. Not just for cooking, you go beyond what can be taught. You can surpass me. You have already, in some areas. That is how you repay me. Be better than I am. Wherever you go. Whatever you do. Excel. Bring joy to others." He paused. "As you have to my daughter." Combeaux shook his hand, turned, and walked toward the fallen ovens, kicking away the charred timbers. Ash clouded behind him.

James went to another caterer which was guarded by armed men. He ordered, and had the platters delivered to the residence. Once home, he scrubbed the gritty soot from his body and found clean clothes.

Over a fine dinner that night, Jefferson forged compromises between his French guests and bridged their political chasms. That six-hour meal was Jefferson's last formal dinner in Paris. The wines were all from Burgundy. James took the remainder of the last bottle to the garden and finished drinking it in the moonlight, wondering when Jefferson would realize that his life in France was over.

CHAPTER 19

In the oppressive September heat, James packed the last of the wide spatulas, the copper pans, and *bain-marie* pots. Jefferson entered the kitchen with a smile. "Almost done?"

"Yes."

"Good. I have invited a few intimates for tonight. Just a few. Nothing fancy."

James took a breath and looked up from packing the last of the small items. "How many?"

"Let's see." He started counting. James looked annoyed, then smiled. "There is the Marquis de Lafayette. His kindness to us cannot be overstated. The Duke de La Rochefoucauld, always a fine dinner companion. He is a scholar and chemist, and I always learn something from him. Then the Marquis de Condorcet, one of the first supporters of the American Revolution, a polymath, mastering many fields of knowledge. And finally, Gouverneur Morris."

"Governor? From what state?"

Jefferson laughed. "None at all. Just an odd family name. But he is a statesman. Helped draft the Constitution with Franklin. He is here on his own and quite interested in business opportunities. Should spice up the conversation."

James sighed. "Five. Plates for five. You know the kitchen is already packed so if you want to serve more than an omelet, I will need to use a caterer again."

"Combeaux? I heard they might leave the city."

"They have. Weeks ago, but you were too busy for me to tell you then."

He shrugged. "Whoever you select, James. Tell Petit to plan on French service."

James nodded.

Unlike his celebration of Independence Day with the ridiculous number of guests and their uninvited attachments, Jefferson's last dinner in Paris was an intimate and quiet gathering. James contacted the closest caterer and ordered several dishes that he knew were favored by Lafayette. As he walked the short route to retrieve the platters, he felt a longing, an emptiness that had no name but pervaded throughout his being. He was between two worlds that he loved. In some ways he felt that the city was in the same turmoil. He pressed past a clot of men that smelled like an ill-kept stable. One was reading a notice that had been pasted to the wall. James hurried.

The dinner was as Jefferson had planned. Platters were left on trays beside diners who served each other after the servants were dismissed. There were fond goodbyes. Promises and hopes were expressed. James only overheard the end of the conversation when he brought in a pastry for dessert and a bottle of sherry.

Morris was a businessman and blunt in his inquiry. "Who is replacing you, Thomas?"

The Marquis de Lafayette pulled a lace handkerchief from his sleeve and flourished it as a flag of surrender. "There is no replacement for our Thomas. He is a *sine qua non*."

"Essential? Hardly!" Jefferson laughed and raised his glass in acknowledgment.

"But you are, you see. Essential to the liberty your country is living. You gave voice to what was in the..." He tapped his chest searching for the word. "Heart. The heart of man."

Jefferson smiled at him and bowed his head quickly. "You are too kind, my dear friend."

"*Non!* Not enough can be said of your accomplishments. We will be using your declaration as a model for our government in the future.

It offers a compromise by giving up some of our power and retaining the King as a figurehead, which should prevent losing everything to the mobs."

Across the table, the Marquis de Condorcet slapped his bulging vest and raised his glass. "To the most brilliant statesman and the best host, our Mister Jefferson from America."

After the kitchen was put back in order once again, James hoped to find Jefferson in his study attending more to the decanter that he had left for him than to his papers. James wiped his hands on a towel as he walked to the study. He stood in the doorway until Jefferson noticed him.

He flipped the towel to his shoulder and dug his fists into his hips. "I am not returning."

"You what? What did you say to me?"

"I am not returning with you."

Standing to face him, Jefferson flushed. "You ungrateful whelp. After all I've done for you. I committed substantial funds for your education. You knew my expectation."

"None of that was for me. It was for you and your table. And that is why I can recommend to you my colleague, Claude, to serve in my stead. He is as schooled by Combeaux as I was, and longer in his service."

"But he spent no time in the Prince's kitchen."

"I learned nothing there. Nothing, unless you plan to serve peacocks! Claude is also adept in all manners of cuisine and pastry."

Jefferson's eyes were moist. "But he is not you, James. He is not you."

"You still see a slave boy for your kitchen. I am a man now. And here I am free." Jefferson started to reply but was stopped by James holding his hand in front of Jefferson's face. "Consider my recommendation. Claude is superb. I can arrange an interview tomorrow."

"I can have the police detain you."

James shook his head. "You won't. Do you want the embarrassment of my going to the court for my declaration? The scandal?"

Jefferson fell back in his chair and stared at James. "You are set on this?"

"Yes. You yourself have written about the wrong of one person owning another. On that we agree. I must do as I will in support of that right, a natural right. But I intend to do so in an honorable manner. I expect someday you will do the same. The interview?"

"Is there nothing I can do to convince you?"

"Free me, now. Write my papers now."

Jefferson flicked his hand as if to end the matter. "Tell Claude he is hired. Arrange for him to meet us at Le Havre. Give him directions and funds, if you are intent to abandon us."

The next morning, Sally was folding a light summer dress on the top of her small traveling valise when James came into her room. Sweat beaded on his forehead. "The carriage is here to take you to the convent school."

"Wait a minute and you can carry my bag down." She then whispered, "You staying here?"

"I told him to hire Claude."

"It'll break Mam's heart if you don't go back."

"Wouldn't she want me free?"

"What if you get both? I can ask him to give you your papers as soon as you train our brother Peter to be the chef."

"He hasn't said that to me. Besides, that's another year at least. Here we can walk away any time before the ship sails."

Sally put her hands on her hips. "You really think some grand house is gonna hire you—some high-toned fella from Virginia—when they got their own?"

"Yes. Because I can cook better than anyone. Anywhere."

She buckled the valise. "You just a dreamer boy, always been such."

"And you? You think because he goes between your legs, you own him? He uses you just like you use him. You ain't got no life a your own."

"Do you? Who do you love besides your damn kitchen? Gabrielle?

You let her go."

"You think that having his red-haired bastard baby someday is going to seal you as his wife?"

"He promised me."

James lowered his voice. "Promised you what? He'd let you sneak into the big house some nights?"

"Stop."

"When he says he loves you, are you still in bed? You think he's going to have you live in the big house after his girls are grown up and gone?"

"Stop it, James. Now."

"That man needs love. More than you can ever give him. He lives for the idea of everyone loving him, even people he don't know. He'll go off again and he's not taking a dusky gal with him. He won't stay on his little farm now that he seen how big the world is."

"Come back to Monticello. Train Peter. Then leave. I can make him see your way."

He slumped against the doorway and looked past his sister. She reached for his arm. He pulled back, picked up her valise, and looked away. He barely had the strength to speak. "Hurry. Petit is taking you to stay with the girls at the convent for a couple of days until we get the house crated and shipped. Don't make him wait."

While the promise of liberty was in the air, so too were the sounds of pillaging mobs setting great houses to torch and the crack of musket shots. Jefferson spent his last days visiting those few friends who had remained in the city. After a light supper, James packed Jefferson's few remaining belongings to be able to leave Paris on a moment's notice.

During the prior week, James had inventoried and packed the most modern of all the French culinary inventions and tools to equip the kitchen at Monticello. Long, covered pans for cooking fish and copper pans of all sizes and shapes joined the kitchen equipment and foods that Jefferson had listed for transit to the United States. What he learned of cookery, he had written for Jefferson's records, but had retained a copy for himself intending once to use the guide to train Peter. Now that Claude would accompany Jefferson to Virginia, James decided to keep the copy for his own use.

As crate after crate was built, Petit packed the artwork and furnishings. Jefferson seemed more concerned about his plants than the household effects. He paced in the formal garden of his design and pointed to the crated olive and cork oak seedlings. Four men strained to move the half-barrel containers that held the trees. Once all four had a grip on the base, they staggered under the weight but somehow got the trees onto the bed of a wagon. Following the olive and cork trees were smaller tubs holding cuttings of a poplar from Lombardy and bushes to plant at Monticello.

James checked off items on the written inventory as crates were hauled past him. The first of the many wagons carried a dozen crates of foods and preserved items that would be shipped on a slower freighter. A crate held hundreds of varieties of vegetable seeds and the bag of rice Jefferson had smuggled out of Milan. Another crate was filled with a case of Maille mustard, bags of dried figs and dates, the foods he had sent up from Tuscany and Umbria. A waxed wheel of Parmesan cheese. Casks of vinegars and olive oil. Truffles from France were submerged in olive oil in five-gallon crocks and sealed with wax and string. Petit said the truffles would last a lifetime in this manner and that the infused oil itself would be invaluable in America.

Equipment unknown in America included copper pans, a new coffee mill, and a press to infuse greater intensity in the ground coffee, tins for baking and gelatin molds, and pots designed to fit into an iron indentation in the brick stovetop, and that iron plate itself. Most astounding was the macaroni press that Jefferson had Short acquire on a visit to Naples. The macaroni press had arrived only weeks prior to Jefferson's decision to leave France. Although Jefferson had wanted to serve macaroni at his Independence Day celebration, Short persuaded him to keep the press safely in its packing crate, which was as tall as a man. However,

Jefferson provided James with the formulation for the dough that would be pressed through the machine's die to form many different shapes of the pasta. Jefferson had written the formulation in his own hand during his trip to Naples, when he convinced the cook in a local tavern where he first encountered the macaroni to divulge his family's manner of combining the ingredients.

Jefferson found this note in his desk while packing and directed James to slip it into the crate with the press. Before doing so, James copied it for his own collection of kitchen information. The heft of that crate required six men to hoist it onto a wagon.

James shook his head thinking of Jefferson traveling to Naples, having macaroni for a meal, then buying the huge machine that made it so he could make it to amuse his guests at Monticello. It was almost the size of Doctor Franklin's first printing press. He recalled Jefferson's grand gestures as he explained how he convinced the cook to show him how a firm dough was put into a chamber, then a long arm applied pressure to a plate from above so that the machine extruded the most wondrous variety of shapes of what he called pasta. By changing the die through which the dough was pressed, Jefferson assured James that he could make the long strands, or tubes like the dried pasta that he brought back in bushels from that journey. James checked off the crate from the inventory list.

Once the last of the wagons had departed for Le Havre, James gave Petit his inventory sheets to place in the folder of Jefferson's traveling desk. In all, they had packed and shipped almost ninety crates of the best of the treasures of the field and vine, a few paintings and some furnishings, over two thousand books, and all manner of gimcracks. Within a few days, Jefferson and his family would be leaving Paris. James looked at the departing wagons and for the briefest moment wondered if he should be on the ship with them.

The hollow sound of his boot heels echoed on the tile of the kitchen. After a last look, he walked down the main hallway and out of the empty house. Only the servant's quarters remained furnished. Once it had been a home, then Gabrielle became his home and his heart. Then Sally arrived. Now he was torn between what was and what might be. James knew that Short planned to remain in Paris, to conclude several business matters despite the unrest and Jefferson's invitation to sail back with him. After Jefferson paid off the last of the staff, he went to dine and spend his last night in Paris at Short's spacious apartment. Petit and James were left alone in the residence. They ate together at a tavern near the Seine.

The September morning was humid when Petit put the traveling valises and Jefferson's portable desk in the covered baggage boot at the rear of the carriage. Once Jefferson arrived and said his farewells to Petit, he climbed into the carriage and opened a book. James shook Petit's hand and clapped him on the shoulder. Petit turned to lock the empty house as James mounted the driver's elevated seat. James paused. Petit turned and offered a deep bow as James clicked the team forward.

The drive to the convent was slow. The streets were crowded with empty wagons leaving Les Halles and returning to their farms. Polly and Patsy were red-eyed from their farewells with their schoolmates and the nuns. After retrieving their three traveling bags, James helped Polly into the carriage to sit beside her father. He was relieved when Sally assumed her proper role and sat beside Patsy. Once the baggage was lashed to the rear of the carriage, James snapped the leather lines and the horses responded smartly. Jefferson held his closed book in his lap and was silent as James held the team to a trot through Paris for the last time. Only after they had passed the city gate did he relax and begin to chat with his daughters. The country air was sweet. Jefferson smiled as though he were responsible for it.

In the ensuing days of travel to the port, Jefferson's conversations turned to Monticello and the improvements he intended to resume, the visits they would have with old friends on the way home from the harbor at Norfolk, and how dinners would astound those visiting the plantation.

Unlike his prior journeys to the countryside beyond Paris, Jefferson found none of his prior associates in residence or available to lodge or entertain them on their journey. The simple dining in taverns and inns and the Spartan accommodations soured his disposition. Lodging the girls in one room, Sally and James in another, and sleeping alone in a third seemed to strain his temper as well as his purse. Once in transit each morning, his mood lightened. He resumed conversing with his daughters about their schooling, the natural beauty of the countryside, and plans for their Virginia homecoming.

At the dock in Le Havre, James reviewed the inventory, checking what trunks should have arrived to accompany the passengers aboard the *Clermont* and which were destined for the larger but slower freight ship, while Jefferson and the girls rested at a local inn. In addition to verifying the correct shipping arrangements for each of the ninety-some crates, and crated trees of fig, cork, larch, and olive, he insured that Jefferson's phaeton and a closed carriage he bought in France were lowered below deck and secured. One flat-topped trunk, Jefferson insisted be placed in his cabin although it cramped his space. By late afternoon, all of Jefferson's goods were accounted for and the traveling party retired to their nearby lodgings for an evening meal and a last night of sleep on land for a month or more. Claude, the cook from Restaurant Combeaux, arrived and took a cheaper room in a nearby tavern. James confirmed his arrival and returned to his own lodging in a light rain.

That night, James had just drifted into sleep when he heard a small crash in the room. His sister was leaning on the washstand retching into the basin. He rushed to her.

"Sally!"

She pushed his hand away. "Water?"

James found the pitcher of drinking water, poured a glass, and handed it to her. Once she rinsed her mouth and spit into the basin, she leaned against the wall.

James took the glass from her and stood facing her. "You in a family way?"

She nodded and smiled. Reaching for his hand, she pulled him to sit beside her on the bed. "Brother? You can't tell nobody. Promise?"

"Is it safe for you to sail like that?"

She sighed. "Think I'm gonna throw up just the same if I'm on land or sea. But on a small ship, his daughters might wonder. Can I stay in your cabin?"

"We should stay here. We don't know if he'd sell us all off or go away and send us to the fields or trades."

"He won't let me come to any harm. Not now."

"Why should he care for a moment about you back there?"

"He's happy about the baby. He promises to set all my babies free when they get twenty-one years of age. Wrote me a paper such." James stared at Sally. After all Jefferson's promises, he wrote *her* a paper!

It rained heavily the morning they were set to sail, which only made the heat more unbearable. Jefferson had Sally and his daughters board early during a brief break in the weather. He and James stayed on the dock, under a canvas cover that seemed to make the rain even louder. While Jefferson was talking to the captain, James found a nearby ship's chandlery and inquired after a store selling hard biscuits that settled the stomach. They had two small boxes and he bought both, returned to the ship, and smuggled them to Sally.

James saw Claude leave his lodging and hurry toward the dock. He called to him and they talked briefly in the covered doorway of the tavern at the foot of the dock. James asked him to wait there and gave him coins for a beer. He found Jefferson on the forward deck watching the loading of the produce and livestock for the voyage. Water ran off the tip of his tricorn hat. "Is everything in order?"

James motioned toward the foot of the dock. "Yes. Claude is here."

Jefferson shrugged. "Is there nothing I can say to change your mind?"

James looked directly at Jefferson. "Sir. I will sail with you on one condition."

Tipping his head, Jefferson asked, "And that is?"

"I respectfully request that before we sail, you place in writing your promise to release me when my brother, Peter, is trained. Like you wrote your promise to Sally to benefit her children."

Jefferson clenched his fists at his side and leaned closer to James, his face flushed. "That is a private matter not to be spoken of again. Am I understood?"

"Yes. But a letter…"

"Or?"

James pointed down the dock. "Claude is ready to serve your kitchen. I'd like to help Sally, but I can make my way here perfectly well as a free man."

"But we had an agreement."

"No. An agreement is between equals. I've heard you say so when talking about treaties and contracts. We are not equal. I understand that and respectfully request this."

Jefferson's face had turned ruddy and a vein on his neck pulsed. "When?"

"Before the plank comes off the dock. That's at noon."

"Best we get this matter behind us. Let's go to my cabin."

Jefferson threw his wet coat on the bunk and wiped his hands on a towel before he opened his portable desk and snapped the silver cap on the inkwell. Taking a pen with a gold nib, he scratched out a promise to release James after a replacement had been trained. Barely breathing, James held his hands to his sides to stop them from shaking. Jefferson blotted the ink, folded the paper, and thrust it at James. "I think I need some air, if you will excuse me." With that, Jefferson reached into his pocket and gave some money to James. "Give Claude this with my thanks." He left James and went on deck. James felt lightheaded and sat on the bed, leaning forward. He held the paper in front of him. After reading it, he sobbed.

A few minutes later, James composed himself, carefully secured the paper in the inner pocket of his light jacket and went on deck. The rain had become a drizzle as he left the dock and turned toward the tavern. Crossing to the other side of the street, James hurried into the tavern where Claude was nursing a tankard of cider.

James sat across from him. "Claude, there has been a change in Mister Jefferson's plans. He no longer requires your services."

Claude started to protest, but James stood and reached into his pocket. "He bid me to extend his thanks and in appreciation for your efforts, offers you this sum." Claude accepted the money. After counting it, he smiled and shrugged. "You going with him?"

"Yes. Will you go back to Paris now?"

He chuckled. "No. Paris is not Paris anymore. A farm in Normandy with my family, that's where I will go next." He offered James his hand. "Safe travels."

"And to you."

The *Clermont* set sail in a light rain after noon on the last Sunday in September. Once the ship was well underway, the captain invited the Jefferson party and the other three passengers to his salon for a modest reception. James went on deck and watched the coast of France. He patted his coat pocket where Jefferson's promise resided.

He held fast to the starboard rail and watched a gray curtain of rain sweep between the ship and land. He thought about what he had gained and what he had left behind. He did a quick calculation. They entered the Neuilly Gate to Paris on August 6 of 1784 and left September 26 of 1789. Sally had grown from a girl to a young woman. He had learned to cook in a way that no one else could. No one in America had his skills. Those few in France who had almost the range and depth of his knowledge and experience lacked his familiarity with ingredients unique to the United States or his ability to merge the intense flavors of rustic colonial cooking with French techniques and presentation. Cooking for a King. Imagine! He chuckled to himself. It was all too much to understand in a moment like this. He would teach Peter and return. The madness of the Revolution would be past, and the great estates would want his services.

By then, Gabrielle would have missed Paris and him. They could return to the city together and eventually open their own small restaurant.

He had lived free for just over five years. Jefferson had honored his freedom and now had given him a written promise of freedom in America. James also knew that Jefferson's baby was growing inside Sally when they sailed. She had that lady sickness but would hide it from Polly and Patsy by nibbling the hard biscuits and eating light at meals. The only other time James could recall her being this sick at night was after she got her inoculation of cowpox in Paris. Jefferson rightly feared smallpox, which had no cure, and the infection of cowpox stemmed that greater evil.

The *Clermont*, an older, slower ship plowed and bucked through the increasingly stormy weather.

After crossing the channel, the captain made for the Isle of Wright to let the storm pass. Taking to shore for a walk, in spite of the ripping wind, Jefferson roamed the hills above Cowes. Upon his return to the ship, he had a sheepdog that he called a *chienne bergere,* on a rope lead. The dog was big with pups. Although not amused by the acquisition, the captain ordered the dog lowered below and crated for the voyage.

When the weather cleared, they resumed their voyage. At night, the oil lantern on a brass gimbal gave just enough light for James to hold the bucket for his sister. Soon, taking meals with the girls was out of the question as any hint of fat or spice brought on a paroxysm of vomiting. James attended to her in his small cabin although she had been booked to sleep in the spacious cabin with the two girls.

James wondered if the Jefferson girls understood the complex relationship between their families. Their grandfather, Mister Wayles, had fathered Sally and James as well. That made Sally and Jefferson's wife half-sisters. He wondered if that also made Sally their aunt. Now the baby that Jefferson and Sally were having would be a half-brother or half-sister to the girls, and maybe a cousin as well. He shook his head to clear the complication. He hoped that the girls might be innocent enough to simply attribute Sally's illness to the rough seas they were bound to encounter on the way home.

During the days of inclement weather, the Jefferson girls read, embroidered, or played at cards in the salon while their father rooted through his papers from Paris. Diaries, logs, accounts, and papers on science as well as his official reports. All were reviewed and put in order during the voyage. Using his traveling desk, he added to the records by offering an account of the travels from Paris and drafted letters to the President on other matters for his consideration. These were to be dispatched by messenger upon their arrival in Norfolk in the coming weeks.

James ate with the crew and brought back what would stay down for Sally. Porridge started each day. A clear soup, weak tea, and the hard biscuits sustained her throughout the day. Neither saw much of Jefferson or his daughters during the return voyage except for the few minutes a day when James shaved Jefferson when the sea was calm enough. During these moments, Jefferson's longing for Monticello was paramount in his comments. Plans for expansion, speculation on how French and Italian seeds might grow in his garden, and his relief at being released from public service all seemed to bring a new spark to him. A spark that had died two years earlier when Maria Cosway left for London.

The voyage home was neither fair nor fast. Increasingly, those drawn-out days filled James with thoughts of those he had left in France. As they approached the Virginia coast, the weather worsened, putting all hands on deck to manage the sails. Off the Virginia banks, the ship lost its topsails. Approaching the harbor, the ship was met with only light rain, but an outbound brig almost rammed them in a freshening wind.

Not knowing if the dock had space for his ship, the captain set the crew to the anchor wheel. Once his ship was anchored, the captain put on his freshly brushed frock coat and his best three-cornered hat for the November arrival.

Within an hour, the harbor pilot in the bow of a tender drew close and shouted for lines. After the pilot verified with the captain that there was no illness aboard requiring a quarantine, the pilot signaled for the tenders to approach. Quickly fixing lines, they towed the ship between other ships at anchor into a berth at the crowded dock. In a quick consultation with Jefferson, they agreed to delay unloading his goods until the next day when the rain had passed.

On the wet dock, thirteen esteemed gentlemen were assembled to greet Jefferson. Patrick Henry and the mayor of Norfolk were at the front of the welcoming party. A band struggled to hold a tune in the cold rain. The banners made for the special occasion sagged. The mayor doffed his hat and bowed before he greeted Jefferson as "Mister Secretary."

Jefferson's face showed an uncommon confusion. "Sir?"

Patrick Henry took a folded newspaper page from his pocket and handed it to Jefferson. "Sir? Are we the first to inform you of your appointment by the President?"

"As what, Patrick?"

"As his Secretary of State. Here, read for yourself. I thought one of the ships you passed nearing shore would have conveyed the news to you. Or a government tender would have met you with the dispatch from the President. I apologize if we had but known."

"Not a concern. We've known each other too long to stand on formality."

Jefferson's face firmed and showed no emotion at this news while the mayor escorted his party to a closed carriage to convey them the short distance to the inn. However, by the time James and Sally arrived with the sheepdog, her four surviving pups, the parrot, and traveling luggage, he was raging about the affront and swore he would reject the position. Secretly, James was relieved to know they would continue on to Monticello.

Shortly after James had changed into dry clothes, a runner came from the dock announcing that their ship had caught fire. James knew that Jefferson's treasured papers remained on board. He sprinted the three blocks to the dock, grabbed the largest sailor he could find, and bullied him into accompanying him through the smoke to Jefferson's cabin. James threw the traveling desk on the flat top of the trunk. With each holding an end handle, they moved it to the dock just as Jefferson arrived. Jefferson looked at the sooty trunk and laid his hands on it and the travelling desk that was balanced on it as though they were living things rescued from peril. By then, others had contained the fire and set about quenching the few remaining embers and removing cargo.

The harbormaster rescinded his order to tow the ship away from the dock and scuttle it to put out the fire and protect the other ships. Within hours, the ship was emptied, and its cargo moved to a nearby warehouse for safekeeping. The next day James saw their crates loaded and sent off toward Monticello. The phaeton was carried on a wagon with the crated trees. The French closed carriage was removed to a stable. Jefferson bought two older chestnut horses, which were reported to have worked as a team for several years. This proved to be untrue; they were stubborn and unwieldy for their first several days in harness.

Travel back to Monticello was slow by any measure from both the impedance of foul weather and the unceasing number of house calls Jefferson made on friends along the way. While Jefferson's visits were welcomed, it seemed to James that the distance from friend to friend approximated one day of travel and eliminated the cost of rooms or food in any of the inns or taverns they passed. Such was the hospitality that Jefferson extended to others. He assumed that all acquaintances maintained as generous a policy.

Clearly, by taking a month to traverse the 170 miles from Norfolk, Jefferson was in no rush to return to Monticello and accede to the new demands that President Washington had placed on him. The heavily laden wagons with the phaeton, the parrot and crated dogs took only a few days. By the time their closed carriage reached Monticello, it was two days before Christmas. James felt half frozen from driving the large rig.

By then, Sally's belly was evident to all but the blind.

When the coach came within sight of the big house, there was a joyous shouting from Jefferson's slaves, who ran toward the carriage all at once. They surrounded the carriage and unhitched the team. A dozen men grabbed the long traces to pull the carriage the last few yards of Jefferson's journey home. Children, some of whom had been born after Jefferson's departure for France, ran in circles around the carriage.

Christmas at Monticello that year was the homecoming that all had wanted. Within days, Jefferson had sent his objection to the appointment to President Washington and settled his household. Sally lived in the big house tending Polly. James returned to his mother's cabin and the kitchen by helping Lizzie and teaching Peter the fundamentals of poaching chicken. The kitchen had not been readied according to his plan, so they were still limited to hearth cookery.

In mid-January came the President's reply, which James overheard Jefferson reading to Patsy. "And here he says that it is not for me to select my post in the government or refuse to serve. Here, listen to this." Jefferson took on a deeper voice in imitation of the President. "It is not for an individual to choose his post. You are to marshal us as may be best for the public good."

Patsy almost wailed, "The public good? Haven't you done enough?"

"Be clear, I shall not leave for my post until you girls are all settled." And so it was. Jefferson received leave to delay his posting until March, having arranged the wedding of his older daughter, Patsy, to Thomas Mann Randolph, whom she had known since childhood, on the twenty-third of February.

Thereafter Jefferson organized his household and belongings for travel and his new position. Sally was delivering an afternoon plate of shortbreads to Polly when Jefferson was telling her that he planned to take James with him since there was no need for a chef at Monticello when he was not in residence. Sally hurried to the kitchen and called for James to follow her outside.

James frowned. "What you coming down here for? I got a lot to do for dinner tonight."

"I heard him say he going to go like the President said and he's taking you with him."

"No. That must be wrong. He promised when I trained Peter, he'd give me my papers."

"Well, that ain't gonna happen just now." She huffed. "And, he's leaving me here with Polly. Me! Swelling up like a melon on account of him!"

Jefferson and James were not at Monticello to greet Sally's baby. Some said the boy died after a few days. Others said he came out bright as a snowflake with copper-red hair—and that Sally gave him away to be raised as a white child. Sally never answered James when he asked her about it years later.

BOOK III

AMERICA

1790–1801

Wherein James gains his liberty,
earns his way, and
discovers himself.

CHAPTER 20

The journey in March of 1790 from Monticello to the new capital in New York was long and laborious. James and his older brother, Bob, both drove wagons of essentials. James now understood why so few slaves tried a northern journey in that season before crops were ripe for foraging. Roads were either bogged with mud or crusted with dry ruts that imperiled wheel rims. Upon arrival at the capital, James found himself scurrying throughout the city to gather the craftsmen and furnishings that Jefferson required for his residence while Bob tended to their master's needs in the boardinghouse and accompanied him to meetings to carry his papers and run his errands.

After several weeks of venturing forth into the extreme reaches of the city, James came to several conclusions. The orderly New York streets, which almost formed a grid, were easier to navigate than the randomly twisting streets of Paris. Although the buildings in New York were not as elegant as those in Paris, even the poorer sections of the city had taverns and shops filled with food. Jefferson's interest in the new crops in this northern state pushed James to new inventions and experiments.

James marveled at how Jefferson reconciled himself to his appointment as Secretary of State and the unpleasant but necessary proximity to Vice President John Adams. Once Jefferson fixed his mind on how he would conduct his office as the first Secretary of State, he set about managing it as a draftsman and architect rather than as a policy maker. He established rules and processes and created an impartial structure that would bear the weight of debate, of argumentation even, yet hold firm.

Jefferson drafted objective parliamentary processes that were adopted by Congress. This required a series of dinner meetings with all the colleagues he had worked with in drafting the Declaration as well as reliance on his experiences in the Virginia legislature. Unlike Washington's brief afternoon events that he called "levees," Jefferson thought that longer, more intimate conversations were needed to address the more vexing issues such as the respective powers of the national and state governments. Soon a routine was established in his residence. Bob tended to the home and Jefferson while James created elaborate dinners. Within a few months, the household routine smoothed. Jefferson returned Bob to Virginia, where he took employment and paid a part of his wage to the plantation's caretaker, as before. James assumed the full duties for the home and tending to Jefferson in addition to his position as chef.

In contrast to the complex dinners he had James prepare, Jefferson's simple manner of service and ease at table made for an exceptional experience for his guests. Ultimately, the discussions lasted long enough for James to overhear much of what was said as he presented and cleared dish after dish in the small, rented home that did little to separate him from the conversations at the table.

What path the new nation would take and what role he would have in directing its course under Washington was the center of Jefferson's attention. He knew how little assistance he would get from Adams, from whom he was progressively estranged, so Jefferson used his home strategically for entertaining and forming alliances to overcome the administrative issues domestically and to foster relations with those representatives of foreign nations who happened to visit, taking particular delight in French visitors. Through these discussions he initially found the information he needed to write the operational rules of order for the new Congress and develop clear lines of authority for the new government.

The management of foreign interests through their envoys and Washington's appointments abroad seemed scattered at first. Soon, the pace of the dispatches and patterns of the emerging international issues took form and became manageable. Jefferson also smoothed the pathway for the administration of both the executive and legislative branches by clarifying roles and establishing lines of formal communication. At home, he instructed James that dinners should demonstrate the largess of his cellar and the wide array of dishes that James could prepare. He could elevate the tastes and flatter the guests with riches and share ideas unknown to them. He could craft alliances that would otherwise be impossible from his mountaintop in Virginia.

Jefferson was intent on expanding the culinary interest of those in the capital city. James was tasked with inventing new dishes featuring local seafood, the plantation's preserves, and treasures from France. Jefferson ordered new French wines to complement those from the cellar at Monticello. James assembled new creations that he paired with wines to expand the colonial palate well past beer, applejack, and hoecakes.

As he served Jefferson's guests, James overheard the bickering and controversy about where the capital of the new nation should be located. Northerners wanted New York. Southerners didn't. It was on a rainy day late in April that Jefferson called James into his study while he plucked papers and maps from his worktable and slid them into a leather portfolio. Without looking up, he said, "No dinner tonight, James. Washington just called me over to discuss the siting of the capital; I'll eat there."

"Certainly."

"It might behoove us if you were to meet his chef and see what you can learn from him."

James stiffened his back. "As you wish."

Jefferson glanced up after tying the leather portfolio. "Don't find insult where none was intended. See what you can garner about his interests, style, oh you know."

"Again, you want me to play the spy in the kitchen. Is that it?"

"You know me too well." He handed the portfolio to James.

James accompanied Jefferson to the President's House on Broadway ostensibly to carry the heavy portfolio. While waiting for Jefferson, James wandered into the smoky kitchen in hopes of meeting Washington's chef. He saw none of the newer cooking implements. There were only three cooks working at an open hearth, and none of them seemed to be of exceptional skill. Several servers in dark coats were present, waiting to deliver food. He looked at a slim, young woman walking by and asked, "Excuse me, but is the President's chef here?"

"No. Just cooks here but not Hercules."

James guessed her age at about sixteen. She had a calm presence and an easy smile. "You aren't kitchen help, are you?"

"I'm Missus Washington's personal servant, Ona Judge. She's at her dinner now, so I have a moment to catch a breath. And you are?"

"James Hemings. *Chef de cuisine* for Mister Jefferson, your dinner guest."

"If you a chef, why're you here?"

"He had me accompany him, carry his papers, and be at the ready in the event he needs anything."

Her eyes crinkled as she said, "So you're his personal servant too?"

The lightness of her laugh brought out his chuckle. "It seems I am. You sound like you're from Virginia too. Am I right?"

"Yes."

"How long have you been with them?"

"I been with the Missus ever since I was a little thing and she was still Missus Custis." She nodded toward the dining room. "Married Mister Washington after Mister Custis passed."

"I was inherited too. I was born on the plantation of Mister Wayles. When he died, I went to his son-in-law, Mister Jefferson."

"Ain't that just the way? Pass us along or sell us off like an old mule." She ran her hands over her short, bushy hair then smiled broadly. James noticed the band of freckles across her nose and upper cheeks and looked again. Paler skin. Eyes the color of almond husks. Slim and moved like she was strong and with a will of her own.

"Miss Judge?"

She laughed again. "Judge! That's my father's name. White man working in the sewing shed, Mama say. Never knowed him. Call me Ona. They all say 'Oney' in there, like they know me and can say my name any way they want, but that isn't my name."

"Ona. That's a pretty name."

"It's a plain name. One that suits me."

"You are nothing like plain. You got your ideas on things, don't you?"

"Don't you, Mister Hemings?"

"James."

"Hemings. That your daddy's name?"

He shook his head. "Mam held on to her daddy's name." He chuckled. "I couldn't rightly use my daddy's." The way she looked at him, he felt the need to continue. "He owned us."

"That where you got your lightness?"

"Mam's half white too. My mother. She's where I got my dreams."

"What you dream on?"

He paused and looked at her. "Being my best. Doing right."

"I heard the Presid'nt say you're the best chef in all America."

"Just talk."

She laughed. "When you meet Hercules, you don't want to make him jealous."

"He's here now?"

"No. He's back at Mount Vernon. Don't know when he's coming up again."

"I look forward to meeting him."

"Well, you come back anytime for a visit. I'll be standing in the hallway waiting for Missus to ring her little bell so's I can fetch a glass of water or pick up a dropped handkerchief or hold the crying grandbaby."

"We got it better than most."

"Most slaves. Not most. I gotta get back by the door in case she calls for something." A bell rang, and Ona shrugged and scrambled toward the dining room.

Throughout his initial months in New York, Jefferson had been plagued by the disharmony that he found in the members of government, once so united in spirit, if not entirely in philosophy. James, however, found delight in his task of carrying the heavy case with Jefferson's briefing papers to President Washington's office several times a week and occasionally encountering Ona.

The June day was warm. Jefferson tarried slightly in the heat, pausing occasionally to converse with acquaintances he met on the street. But as they approached the President's House, Jefferson stopped and muttered something. James strained to hear what he had said, and then saw Alexander Hamilton standing outside Washington's residence. From overhearing prior discussions from the dining room, James knew that there was a rocky relationship between the two. Hamilton waited for Jefferson to pass. Hamilton doffed his tricorn hat and bowed to Jefferson. Looking at Hamilton, James was astounded to see that his attire was shoddy and manner somewhat disheveled, in contrast to Jefferson's impeccable attire and grooming.

"Thomas, how good to see you."

Jefferson failed to smile. "Alexander."

"While I know we have had our differences, I feel we must unite on the matter of the state debt, but we are at an impasse on how. Additionally, Madison is as bound as I on the need for a permanent location of the government's seat, but we disagree about where. There is disagreement on how to manage financially as well. Is there a way that you could host a private dinner for Madison, you, and me? I feel your vision may lead us to a better conclusion. I would not impose, but I truly fear the nation is at peril."

"Aren't you overstating the matter?"

His voice rose. "Thomas! Fiscally, we are unsound. If we don't alter the revenue relation between the states and federal governments, we shall falter. No one will trade with us." He stopped. "Thomas, I implore you. I feel that your skill in bridging differences and the privacy of your home may pull us out of this mire."

"Consider it, I shall. You know I am not yet settled into my new home on Maiden Lane, but you will hear from me shortly. You will excuse me; the President is waiting on these reports."

James had never seen Jefferson be so curt with anyone, of any station in life before. Once the briefs were delivered, Jefferson had his meeting. James went to the market and then returned home, thinking how similar the market was to Paris in its vendor's attitudes but how much smaller the range of offerings were. Basics were plentiful, but there were few surprises such as a penned peacock.

Jefferson was in a better mood when he arrived home at about three in the afternoon.

"James? What have you for dinner tonight?"

After suggesting a simple meal of fresh greens and a pork chop, Jefferson nodded and smiled. "What would you need for a dinner for three?"

"Tomorrow is possible if you wish another simple meal or a few days away if you want to really demonstrate our finest."

"Draft a finer menu and see me in a few minutes."

"Could I ask who will be attending and if they have preferences?"

"Hamilton and Madison will be joining me."

"Hamilton?"

"I know. It shocks me as well. Orphaned bastard born in the British West Indies. Educated in New York, so he is eclectic in dining experiences, likes spices. Good financial head. He has an interesting idea to fund revenue cutters, fast ships, to intercept the smuggled goods that are now evading taxation. Northern in his leanings, he is a nationalist unlike Madison, who is a supporter of the rights of the state over those of the nation." James frowned as Jefferson continued. "Madison is all his opposite. Well turned-out, civil, and a fellow Virginian."

James grinned. "That shall be my starting point."

"Good. I'd like to dine at about four tomorrow. Need to strike while this iron is hot."

"Let me create a menu for you right away. I still am settling into this kitchen so I need to figure what I can even make here."

Within the half hour, James met again with Jefferson. "The first of the courses will be a green salad dressed with a tarragon vinaigrette accompanied by a wine jelly. Made from boiling off calves' feet then adding milk, sugar, lemon juice, and Madeira wine."

Jefferson shook his head. "Really, James I need not know by what magic you achieve your results."

James ignored the interruption and continued. "Capon, roasted. Common enough in Virginia, but it will be stuffed with truffles. To the side, braised artichoke hearts, and a firm chestnut puree. Next, Virginia ham with a Calvados sauce from the apple brandy brought back from France."

Jefferson nodded as James continued. "*Boeuf à la mode,* a top round of beef braised with onion, carrots, bacon, and spiced with thyme and parsley. By adding a veal knucklebone I'll give it a silky texture and substance to the sauce. It needs to braise in a Dutch oven for at least five hours."

"I want it."

"Good. The macaroni and cheese?"

"No. Too warm a season for it, just the meats and lighter items. Some side vegetables of your choosing with the ham course."

"Finishing with sweets. Locally purchased pie or tarts."

"I would prefer your special dessert. You know the one."

"Ice cream inside a warm puff pastry shell?"

"That's the one. They will be puzzled and amazed, as I always am."

"It is complicated. Can you delay the dinner until this Sunday?"

Jefferson reached for the menu. "No! I need to invite them for tomorrow. Buy a pie or make a tart instead. Now the wines." After reading the menu again and pondering a moment, he handed James a pencil to amend the menu by adding the wines to pair to the courses.

"Now, I'll start with a Hermitage white alone as an *aperitif.* A white

Bordeaux with the salad. A Montepulciano with the capon. Chambertin with the ham, then a second with the beef. Finishing with a Champagne with dessert."

The next day, James felt the dinner was cooked to perfection. Each dish was served in the proper form, at the precise temperature, and in the most attractive style. The conversation flowed from distant to heated to calm to genial and, as midnight approached, to agreement. In August, after the Assumption Bill and Residence Bill both had passed, Jefferson joked to James that it was his cooking, not Jefferson's skill as a negotiator, that allowed the compromise. The federal government assumed state debt and the financial collapse was avoided.

More contentious was the residency of the seat of government.

Both Jefferson and Madison were angered later by the discovery that Washington had favored the Potomac location. He held this position secretly, as did several others who owned riverfront land, which rose in value many times over when the Residency Act created a federal city on the banks of the Potomac and assigned the temporary capital to Philadelphia. At least the seat of government would be in Philadelphia for a decade to allow time for the federal buildings to be constructed properly.

Some weeks later, James was disappointed to learn that Ona had been sent back to Mount Vernon to accompany an older servant who had fallen ill.

When the capital moved from New York to Philadelphia in December of 1790, the presidential residence was established at 190 High Street between Fifth and Sixth Streets. Jefferson found a temporary lodging and then moved into a commodious house in the spring. The location of the new residence was advantageous for James, as it was only a short walk to the President's House, the statehouse, and the market. On a particularly inviting spring day in 1791, Jefferson made an effort to acquaint himself with the environs outside the city and hired a carriage and driver. With James accompanying him, they visited a prestigious cider mill and distillery. Jefferson purchased a large jug of hard cider that he knew would please the President. He also bought a second, smaller crockery jug. Walking back to the carriage, Jefferson said, "You might take this occasion to introduce yourself to Washington's chef, Hercules. He just arrived from Mount Vernon. Give him that smaller jug."

"Should I leave it for him if he is not there?"

"No. Make it personal, from you. Stay and chat. I'll release the driver once we are at Washington's. I'll be in more frequent contact with the President here, so I want you to strike a friendship. Be clear: I want you to draw information from him, not pose a professional threat. Ask for his advice on current American cookery. No need to be off-putting by flaunting your superior culinary skills and knowledge." He laughed. "As if he would even know the meaning of the word *culinary*."

After Jefferson entered the President's House, James took the jug to the rear of the mansion. Through the open door to the kitchen, he saw one of the cooks piling shortbread on a plate. As he entered the sweet-smelling kitchen, a husky man rushed past him, and shooed the cook away.

Hercules carefully arranged the shortbread squares on the plate. James stopped and waited for the chef to invite him into the kitchen. Instead, the husky man in an elegant cranberry red frock coat and fine tan linen britches never looked up until the plate was perfect and he handed it to a young, light-skinned boy who departed quickly.

The large man then removed his dress coat and donned a simple, unstructured white jacket. Discovering James, he said, "You the new boy or making a delivery?"

"No. My master is visiting yours."

He buttoned the jacket. "Never know when some new face is going to appear here. We come up with just a handful of us, from Virginia. No way that ever be sufficient for this large household. Got all manner of helpers for the President and guests most all the time. Had to make the stable out back into more quarters for *servants*, as he likes to call his slaves."

James laughed. "Like that changes anything."

"So? Who's your owner?"

"Thomas Jefferson, the President's Secretary of State. I expect they'll meet a lot more here than they did in New York, so we might get a chance to talk sometimes."

"You cook?"

"Some." James paused. "But mostly we were in boarding houses there."

James held out the jug. "A gift."

"For the kitchen?"

"No, for you. My master says you are the finest American cook. I wanted to meet you. I tried to in New York, but found you were not there."

Uncorking the jug, Hercules sniffed it. "Have a tot?"

"Glad to."

Pouring a generous portion into two cups, Hercules raised his cup and drained it. James quickly looked away. He cleared his throat and made a show of glancing around the kitchen. "Nice size. Got much help in the kitchen?"

"Have to. The General serves up some thirty guests at his Thursday dinners. 'State dinners,' he calls them. Fancy food. A few other large meals occasionally. They good on giving me planning notice. Feeding the staff of thirty all their everyday meals too."

While spacious and immaculately clean, this kitchen lacked the better copper pots and pans that James had used in Paris and which now graced Jefferson's kitchen. Without the capacity for heat management, this kitchen could not make any of the delicate sauces favored by Jefferson.

James noticed a slim woman passing by the open door of the kitchen that led to the sitting and dining rooms. "Was that Ona?"

"You know her?"

"Met her a couple times in New York."

"Don't get no ideas about her. Her brother be in the house now. Austin's handy with a blade."

"Oh? Is that so?"

"You don't talk like you from a plantation."

"I'm from Virginia. But I've been away for a couple of years. Travelling with my master."

"If you know cooking, maybe you can help me when you visit instead of sitting around bothering the housemaids."

"Sure. I always like to learn from other cooks."

"Chef! I'm Washington's chef. That be a French word I heard from one of his guests. How old are you, James? Twenty, Twenty-five?"

"About."

"Well, I got ten years on you. If you try hard, I might just learn you a thing or two about cooking."

James tipped his head in deference and also to hide the smile that was escaping. "I'd appreciate that and any recommendations you might have for when the President dines at Mister Jefferson's home."

He laughed. "'Dines'? You mean when he *eats* at your house. Wanna know what makes him happy?"

"Sure."

"Anything soft. He don't got much of a taster or care for food like some. Lady Washington does, but he don't. Maybe because he got poor teeth. Lost most the top ones during the Revolution and hates them…" Hercules made a swirling motion in front of his mouth. "You know. Them false teeth."

Ona hurried into the kitchen. "Hercules? Lady Washington says send out some gingerbread too. Them ladies eating everything in sight." She noticed James and tipped her head in his direction. He returned her notice with a smile.

After rolling his eyes, Hercules pulled a pan of dense gingerbread off a cooling rack, cut neat squares, and arranged them on a platter. The rich scent of the cake filled the room. James tipped his head and closed his eyes. It was more than the usual gingerbread scent of ginger, cinnamon, and allspice. Heavy on the allspice, James thought. And cloves. James thought the dark cake would look better with a dusting of fine sugar or a crown of heavy cream whipped to a peak.

James smiled at Ona and started to say something when Hercules pushed the plate of gingerbread squares at her. "Have Austin get the small plates with the gold rims and small forks from the butler's pantry to set out with these."

She nodded and took the platter away. When she returned some time later, Hercules looked up from his freshly refilled cider cup. "That cake went fast enough."

Ona laughed. "Gonna be busting their whalebone stays if they keep on it."

Hercules frowned at Ona. "Best keep her happy. Don't want her in a snit."

When Hercules went to the counter to prepare another plate, James said, "Ona, it is good to see you again. How you getting on in this big house?"

"Fine. Got a passel of us up here from Mount Vernon now, not like in New York. You?"

"Massa Jefferson got him a bigger house here too. I don't have too much to do with the house help. Just cooking for him is a full-time thing." He continued. "All your family up here?"

"No. Just my brother Austin. He's a waiter and helps the butler in the house. My favorite is Moll, she an old lady seamstress who keep Missus in the best of clothing. She like a second mother to me. There be nine us here what know each other from the plantation house."

"You really still her personal servant? You're no bigger than a mouse."

"Well, this mouse tends to her all day and minds the grandchildren at night. Sleep on the floor right by Washy and Nelly in the room right by their door."

He grinned at her as if he had a secret. "You know, I think I've seen you before."

"Of course, in New York."

"No. Before that. At Mount Vernon when you were just a little thing. Maybe when we were on our way to France. Mister Jefferson did pass by that plantation."

"You funning me?"

"No. It's on the Potomac River, right?"

She took the plate from Hercules. "True." She turned and was gone.

James reached for his cider. "Someday, I'd like for you to teach me some of your dishes. Can I help this evening? I'm sure my master would not mind."

"Naw. They'll just want a cold plate after her guests leave, and that could be anytime from an hour from now until ten tonight."

During his remaining time in the kitchen that afternoon, James flattered Hercules into divulging many of his better dishes and techniques. James paid attention to his lecturing as if it were all new to him. When Jefferson's meeting with Washington ended, the houseman was sent to collect James. He grabbed the cider cup and drained it. "Nice to meet you, Hercules. Hope to see you again soon."

When they arrived home, Jefferson asked, "Well, what news?"

"His cook is a man of supreme confidence. If asked, I believe he would confirm that the sun rises each morning only to shine upon him. Ten years older than me and as I said, cocky. Fancy dresser. Tidy kitchen but lacking our improved equipment. He has airs about him."

Jefferson laughed. "Reserved on his cooking?"

"Hardly. Wanted to brag on all he does, did, or imagines he does. I asked him to tell me how to make a gravy, saying mine was plain."

Jefferson laughed. "You didn't!"

James shrugged and grinned. "Nothing new there. But here is what I learned about schedules. President Washington opens the President's House every Tuesday afternoon from three to four for socials that he calls levees, like in New York. Men only, as you would expect. During these small receptions, anyone could talk to the President on any topic.

No food or drink items of any significance are served, as it is limited to an hour. Hercules said that usually it is a tea service and a few short-breads or other items that could fit on a saucer."

"Seems a waste of time to me: having random gossips and favor seekers wander into the President's House."

"Hercules said it is his intent not to have the residence be removed from the people. Yet, it seems to irritate him. He most often asks for a whiskey afterwards."

"I see the point of the levee, yet with the type of intrusion it must present, I fear it may take away from his time to consider more important matters."

James continued as though not interrupted. "Thursday evening is always a formal dinner hosting someone of importance. Legislators. Foreign folks."

"Ambassadors? Merchants?"

"Perhaps. Hercules said that the President's wife spent a great deal of time deciding who to seat where."

Jefferson shook his head and puckered his lips. "Absurd British custom for a democracy to continue. I suspect a livelier exchange of ideas would come from seating diners at random in whatever seat was unoccupied rather than a forced subservience to rank. So, Thursday is a long night for the old man. I shall keep that in mind when presenting new ideas to him, so I catch his attention properly. What else?"

"Friday evenings at seven, Missus Washington invites her female acquaintances to come and sip tea or lemonade and eat ice cream. The gossip and chatter continues often to ten o'clock. After that, her personal servant would ready her for bed, then help the house servants tidy up."

"Did George participate?"

"I had the feeling he did not or did so only briefly. I had the thought that his health might be poor."

"Yes. He has been ill."

"Every Saturday, by eleven, they take the carriage for a ride around town. Most often with the two grandchildren of hers. Seems they developed that custom while in New York. Hercules made reference to some carriage drive into the countryside they make to visit friends. He failed to mention a name but was quite clear that this was of Lady Washington's doing, not her husband's."

"*Lady* Washington?"

"'That is what they say she wants to be called."

"Well, that is somewhat better than the 'Madame *Presidentess*' that a Boston paper called her. Unpronounceable. Undemocratic. Very well done, James. I think you're *almost* better suited to gathering intelligence than cooking. And as you are the best in the country at the culinary arts, you must know what a compliment I intend."

"Thank you."

"Please, let me know the most opportune times for you to meet Hercules by 'accident' to continue this friendly exchange, and I shall adjust your duties accordingly."

"Well, for sure the Wednesday-morning market." He paused only briefly before adding, "and a Saturday morning?"

Jefferson nodded. "As the occasion arises. He has such liberty?"

"Yes. He is free to walk the streets without restriction from that household—or so he says. They must have written some pass. I can test that idea by asking in the marketplace. He must be well known from his excesses in dress."

"What do you mean?"

"He carried a gold-handled walking stick and was dressed in a fashionable, no, flamboyant dress coat, fine breeches, and buckled shoes."

"Even in the kitchen?"

"Yes, but he was just back from the weekly market. But then, in place of the type working attire you might expect, he just exchanged his frock coat for a white jacket, front buttoned to the neck, square hemmed at the hip. Spotless, as was the kitchen."

"That seems at odds with George's effort to be plain in his attire and republic in his entertaining. Or to put it bluntly, he is frugal to a fault."

"Hercules buys these items from his earnings."

"Washington pays him?"

"Not that I know. But he is allowed to sell the slops from the kitchen, just as I was in Paris."

"And his income? Have you a guess?"

James smiled. "Not a guess! He is quite boastful. He says he expects a hundred to two hundred dollars a year from the sale of fats and trimmings alone."

"And how much is a cook paid here? Have you an idea?"

"About that much, but few have his talent or reputation. He could no doubt find a higher wage if he were free to market his services."

"Could you find such?"

James flinched, paused, then decided to be candid. "Easily. But he might be overstating his value; Washington has to rotate him out of the state every so often to avoid the six-month emancipation rule."

Jefferson looked shocked. "You know about that?"

"Yes. And I am sure you do, but you have not had me leave you at all."

"Because I trust you."

James stared at him. "I promised you that I would serve until my replacement was trained. But I expected we would return directly to Monticello."

"So did I. But I am a man of my word. As are you."

"But when?"

"I need you to manage this residence and cook for me."

"Bring Petit over from France to assist you, so that I can train Peter now."

Jefferson clenched his jaw, spun on his heel, and walked briskly into the sultry summer evening.

CHAPTER 21

Several months later, when James was slowly sautéing onions, he was interrupted by Jefferson's arrival in the kitchen. Without looking up, he said, "Your dinner should be ready in about an hour."

"I just heard that Hamilton is dining with the President tonight."

"I have menu ideas for his visit tomorrow."

"Nothing could be as fine as your dinner in New York. He still talks about it. What are you cooking now?"

"Starting the French onion soup. I find that it improves with a day of mellowing."

Raising his hand, Jefferson said, "That can wait. I want you to accompany me and find out what Hercules is making for the state dinner tonight."

"Now?"

"Yes. I'm meeting with the President. I'll say my wrist is acting up again, so I wanted you to carry my case to the meeting. Once we know what he is serving, we can adjust our offering, if necessary."

Holding his voice level, James said, "Certainly."

"He should be in it up to his elbows by now."

"I can drop in and offer to help. Would that suit?"

"Yes. For the hour or so during our meeting."

"I can leave in about five minutes, once I the onions are browned and into the stock."

"Perfect."

As they approached the presidential residence afoot on the crisp November day, Jefferson walked ahead of James, who carried his large leather portfolio. When they were at the heavy mahogany door, he turned to James and whispered, "See what you can find out about Washington's schedule for the next week as well. Go home when you are through with your visit."

When the door opened, James handed the leather case to the houseman and stood aside while Jefferson entered the long, carpeted hallway. Once the door closed, James walked to the back of the house.

Hercules motioned for him to enter. Before he greeted James, he turned a fifteen-minute sandglass, put a closed pan on the hearth, and covered it with coals. "Got another jug for me?"

James glanced around the kitchen, which was strangely calm and empty. "Wish I did. Thought I'd say hello. I had to tote a lot of papers here for Mister Jefferson. Like he can't carry them himself."

"Ain't that the way. I hear your house keeps a less formal table than President Washington does."

James laughed as if embarrassed. "You hear right. No hostess to do the seating plan is part of it. Wish he'd step it up to your level. He has three laws that govern his table: no healths, no politics, and no restraint."

Hercules frowned. "Healths?"

"You know. After the meal, when the cloth is removed, and the nuts and apples are put out. Someone takes a bottle and pours a bit, then toasts to the health of another. Then that man takes a pour and toasts somebody else. After several hours, they're all drunk as skunks."

"The General call that toasts."

"Healths or toasts, Mister Jefferson disapproves. Says it's a waste of time and good wine to let folks blather on and get drunk."

"He liked the glass raising when he was at Mount Vernon, but now, he is more reserved. Last week, a passel of Englishmen was here for his state dinner, expecting to have a long round of toasts. They was sorely disappointed when the General took but one glass of wine, toasted everyone with it. Then he gave only one glass to them for their reply. After that, they retired for tea and biscuits and talked late into the night. The English guests seemed to miss their custom of toasting until all were well 'toasted' and not one of them was able to stand."

"But the food? How did the English respond to your food?"

"Well enough. Not a drop of gravy or morsel of the roasted beef returned on plates. Duck, quail, ham. All vanished. The potatoes was new to 'em."

"How'd you do 'em?"

"Peeled, sliced, and baked in butter. Were remarked upon as the sweetest they had ever encountered. Secret is to put both salt and sugar into the butter sauce. Just a hint of each."

"Brilliant. And the dessert?"

"A crumble. Apple for the General, to avoid seeds in his, you know." He swirled his hand in front of his mouth as he had during their first meeting. "Blueberry, if I recall, for the rest of the table. He always makes some joke about loving apple trees in Virginia, but really it's those false teeth."

Hercules glanced at the sandglass and started for the hearth.

James stood as if to help. "What're you bakin'?"

"Cornbread. Lady Washington is in bed with a chill. Says she just wants cornbread and potato soup for her dinner. He'll have a cold plate."

"I thought Thursday was a big dinner."

"Not when one of 'em's sick."

As Hercules took the cover off the pan of cornbread, the air filled with a sweetness of both new corn and the richness of baking. There was the faintest tinge of browning on the top of the cornbread. James whistled. "I'd say that's about perfect. Smells like fresh corn, not dry meal."

"Meal sure enough, middling grind from his own gristmill. But this year's grind. Cream. Cream's the secret. Make it with water and it's just a pile of crumbles. Try to bind it with more egg; it just gets tough and dry. Ever used cream?"

"No. But I'll try it soon. Thanks. Best be on my way. Hope they get better soon. No pleasure in making bland sick food." James left and found his walk home to be relaxing.

When Jefferson returned, the evening breeze caught the door and slammed it shut. He hurried into the kitchen, where James was pulling out a tub of flour to make a crust. "Well? What did you find out about their menu for tonight?"

He took the butter crock from the cooler box and put it on the worktable. "Cancelled. Your menu is fine." Then he began blending the butter and flour with a fork.

But Jefferson did not leave as James expected. Instead, he picked up a piece of the crumbly dough and rubbed it between his fingers. Looking at it, he spoke softly, as to himself. "When you have time, prepare the smallest of the guest rooms for Petit. He will arrive sometime in mid-July, if he has a fair sail."

Speechless, James stopped blending the crust and stared at Jefferson, who smiled as he looked at him. "What's going into that crust?"

"App…apples. Making apple tarts for dessert. Didn't think Hamilton deserved my good pastry dessert, after he made you mad about that vote."

"He was less than honorable."

"He is not you." James looked away and blinked back tears. Snuffing, he looked down to his worktable and resumed blending the dough. "Making individual ones. There will be extras in the kitchen if he merits a second serving."

"Or for your breakfast?"

He chuckled. "Or yours. I thought a Sauternes with the tart would finish the meal well."

"Agree. How about a fish and braised meat dishes? Your choice. I'll leave you to select the wine as well. Why did they cancel the dinner?"

"Lady Washington is ill."

Jefferson's shoulders dropped. He shook his head. "Stop calling her that. This isn't a monarchy!"

By September of 1793, the well-ordered Philadelphia household had settled into Petit's routine. Jefferson's immediate dismissal of a coachman and his wife who disobeyed Petit's directions offered a lesson that the household took to heart. James now tended exclusively to matters of the kitchen and to Jefferson's morning shave. The only exception to Petit's complete rule of Jefferson's kingdom was that James continued, at Jefferson's specific direction, to make the menus. Occasionally, Petit reminded Jefferson that in France menus were traditionally the function of the *maître d'hôtel*. Jefferson always reminded Petit that they were in America and that the kitchen belonged to James. Usually both shrugged and went about their business.

When James arrived at the doorway of Jefferson's bedroom to shave him one morning near the middle of the month, he paused. Jefferson was reading dispatches. Once finished, he stood and went to the window. After a few moments, James cleared his throat. Jefferson look at him quickly, blinked a few times, and went to his chair, leaning back to let James drape the towel across his chest. "Do you ever think of Paris?"

As James worked the brush over the shaving soap, the scent of lavender perfumed the room. "Daily. Maybe the fall leaves remind me of the colors there."

Jefferson smiled. "And what else?"

"The men at the restaurant. The beauty of the city."

"Thank you for that. Today's dispatches are a misery. Just look at this year. The King was beheaded in January. They called him 'Citizen Louis Capet.' Men who dined at my table became martyrs for liberty." Jefferson spoke as if to himself. "Lafayette was imprisoned as a traitor. The Duke de Rochefaucauld stoned to death and gutted by a mob in Gisor. The old man I bought seeds from went to the scaffold with his family. Malesherbes was his name. Even the cathedral suffered at the hands of the mob. Statues beheaded, interior pillaged. Disgraceful."

"You were right to leave when you did. Protect the girls and remove your belongings."

"We missed that insanity by a cat's whisker. Petit should have come with us then. At least he is here now and managing the house well. You two are a treasure to me. There is never a moment that I doubt your honesty and fidelity. Never. Do you know what a rare find you are?" He shook his head as if to erase the past. "Guests tonight, James. There will be five gentlemen joining me for dinner. I want them to dine in our new style. French sauces illuminating familiar Virginia tastes. Some ham to be included."

James stropped the straight razor against his tall bootleg. "Then may I suggest an oven-roasted beef with brown peppercorn sauce and glazed carrots? And that macaroni with a cheese sauce."

"Excellent. They won't have seen macaroni before. Add a bit more mustard this time. And for dessert? I want something sweet. Sauternes to drink, but with what?"

James smiled. "*Crème brûlée*. Custard with a glassed sugar on top."

Jefferson answered immediately. "*Crème brûlée*. You have brought it all back so perfectly. You outdid Combeaux and that pastry chef."

"We had some astounding dinners there, didn't we?"

Jefferson smiled. And slid off into silence as James shaved him.

When James wiped the last of the lather from the razor and toweled off Jefferson's face, he took a deep breath. "As you say, sir, the house is running well under Petit. Could we bring Peter up so I can start his training?"

"I don't see any need to do that. He is such a superior brewer that he is bringing in significant revenue for the estate. I don't want to interrupt that."

"Why not? There's room for him here in the residence. I will happily share my wage with him—or forego it."

"A wage that I need not pay you."

"In Paris, you paid me half what you paid that French woman. Here you pay me no better, but still I am good to my word. When will *you* be?"

"Let's not squabble, James. I provided you with a complete education in French cuisine. Stood you to your room and board, clothing, and anything else you needed."

"I could have petitioned for my freedom. Sally's too."

Jefferson snapped. "Then why didn't you?"

"Because she needed me. I gave you my word."

"You did. And I respect that."

"And you said you would sign a deed of manumission once we returned. We are now in a free state."

"But you are not free under the law here. Pennsylvania respects the laws of Virginia on such matters. And you still need to keep your part of our bargain."

"My part?"

"Yes. To train your replacement."

James was almost vibrating with anger at Jefferson's trickery. He clenched his hands behind the small of his back. "With all due respect, sir. How could I? We've been back to Monticello for but a few days occasionally. And here? There was barely enough space for me to cook by myself in our last residence. But it is past time."

"Be patient. We'll be home soon enough. Anyway, why Peter?"

"He's smart." James paused a moment to weigh his words. "He and Sally are devoted to you and want to live at Monticello forever."

"And you do not? Be candid. You owe me that."

"Sir." James gathered his words with care. The ice was thin. He knew Jefferson's passion for Monticello was limitless. "Sir. In Paris, I discovered that I loved being my own master. I understood the longing for freedom of those French men and women at those bonfires in the streets. It echoed in my chest."

"But they were repressed by nobility." Flabbergasted, James shook his head in disbelief.

"Have you even listened to yourself? Not one person alive or any of those Greeks or Romans you quoted to Lafayette, not one of them has written so perfectly on freedom as an inalienable right as you. I listened to you. I read what you wrote. I believe it."

"James, you shock me."

"That book you had printed in France, *Notes from Virginia*. You left a copy in your library in Paris. I read it. I read your speeches. I believed you. You understand the essence of freedom." He held his breath for a moment, then continued. "If I can't train Peter, let me buy my freedom."

"The way your older brother wants to? I never should have sold Dolly to that doctor. But I had no idea that Bob and she were a family. I further erred in letting him work for wages for the doctor. Now he wants to buy his freedom, says the doctor will stand him the cost for an indenture in return. Wants to live with her as a freedman in that household."

"And will you allow this?"

"Let the doctor buy him? Perhaps. But to unconditionally free you? That is another matter. I don't think you realize how that would be seen by those who I need to support me once I return to Virginia."

"So, you won't let me buy my freedom or stand by your word?"

"No! The time is not ripe for such a bold move." He struggled to calm his voice. "Besides, you will need every bit of your savings to make a new life once your replacement is trained."

James shut his eyes and clenched his jaw. He thought that saying more was not going to make the days go by any faster. But he knew that insolence could change Jefferson's mind—and his agreement.

Jefferson watched James struggle to quiet himself. He lowered his voice and assumed the honeyed tones of negotiation. "James. You know, I need a plan, a drawing. I am as much an architect as a lawyer and statesman. Draw me a plan for a proper kitchen. Not that hearth-roasted pot-boiled country fare of the old Monticello. But a proper kitchen like you had when you worked for Combeaux. Make a list of any cooking pots or implements that we did not bring back with us, and I will get them ordered forthwith. Design the kitchen that will serve my need for entertaining many in grand style. I will renovate ours to that standard so it shall be ready on our return. Do you agree?"

"Year after year, you promised to make a suitable kitchen and let me train my replacement."

"This is different. I've given the President my notice. At the end of the year, we return to Monticello. Believe me."

"I need more than the promise that you made in France to entice me back to America. More than a few lines of intent scribbled on a piece of paper."

"James, you shock me."

"I have learned from you the difference between a promise and a written, enforceable agreement."

"Then would you train Peter on the best equipment in the best kitchen in the country, starting in January, if I write it?"

"With pleasure, sir."

Jefferson picked up a quill and turned to lean over the small desk in the bedroom. He started to dip the pen with his right hand and winced. He transferred the pen to his left, sat, and started again. He muttered under his breath as he wrote, then handed it to James to read.

"*Having been at great expence in having James Hemings taught the art of cookery, desiring to befriend him, and to require from him as little in return as possible, I hereby do promise & declare, that if the said James should go with me to Monticello in the course of the ensuing winter, when I go to reside there myself, and shall there continue until he shall have taught such person as I shall place under him for that purpose to be a good cook, this previous condition being performed, he shall thereupon be made free...*"

James returned it and clenched his fists behind his back. Jefferson looked relieved. "Bring in Petit. This needs a witness."

James hurried to find Adrien Petit. Once the three were together in the bedroom, Jefferson returned to writing as he spoke. "*Signed this fifteenth day of September in the year of our Lord 1793.*" He signed with a flourish and handed the pen to Petit. "I'll need your signature there, Adrien. Just means you saw me sign it, nothing more."

"Certainly." He leaned over and signed under Jefferson's signature, and returned the quill to Jefferson.

Jefferson cleared his throat, dismissing what had just taken place. "Oh, Mister Petit. At the end of the year, we shall be returning to Monticello. Edmond Randolph will assume my duties here in January. Start making arrangements for transport of the unessential goods before the weather goes foul on us."

Without any show of emotion, Petit bowed and said, "Of course."

Jefferson left the document on his desk, gathered files for a meeting, and paused by the doorway. "It's yours, James. Do with it as you please."

Alone in Jefferson's study, James carefully folded the document and slipped it into the inner pocket of his coat. Feeling faint, he leaned on Jefferson's desk and was surprised to feel tears on his cheeks. Brushing them away, he returned to his duties in the kitchen with a new sense of promise.

An hour later, Petit joined him and started to make a coffee.

James reached across the counter and took the mill from him. "Let me. I learned from a master."

Petit smiled. "Who could have imagined our journeys, eh, James?"

"*Moi? Jamais.*"

"Never! Is he really leaving to go to his farm?"

"Plantation. It is beautiful."

"Could he be done with politics?"

James poured hot water over the milled coffee. "His distaste for Mister Adams is deep. Look, Washington and Adams are just starting their second term. He loves Monticello. It needs his attention, and yours, before it falls further in debt. He needs to go back to planting tobacco. He'll need more slaves, but it will bring in more money."

"I am glad you are returning. I know it is complicated for you both."

"I gave him my word in Paris. I never thought it would take so long."

Petit shrugged. "No one did. But the President called upon him to serve."

Carefully pouring the coffee into a flannel filter, James said, "After I train Peter, then I will be free. At last."

"Will you go back to France?"

"Perhaps. But there is a woman here that interests me."

"The one you meet in the market?"

James handed the steaming cup to Petit. "Of course, you'd know that. You know everything."

Later that day, James found Ona in the marketplace and hurried her to a bench behind the flower stall and bins full of late-summer tomatoes, onions, leeks, and potatoes, both smooth skinned and red jacketed varieties. He showed her the agreement and read the words to her as he traced each character with his finger for her to follow. As she leaned forward to watch, her hair brushed his cheek. She smelled of rosewater and soap.

After he finished reading, she said, "He promised you in France. Now he promised you here in Philadelphia. Nothing's different. He's gonna work you as long as he wants. Can't you see that?"

"He is a man of his word. I believe this." He folded the paper and returned it to his inner pocket. "We're going back in December."

"That's what he say today. He's gonna do what he want to do. He needs you more than you need him."

James looked hurt. "But there is no better cook."

"That's not all you're worth to him. You're his eyes and ears. I see that. How you listen to what's being said in the parlor, how you smooth-talk Hercules into telling you things he ain't supposed to say."

"I just make conversation."

She looked at him, tipping her head.

He fidgeted. "Is that why President Washington sent Hercules back to the plantation?"

"Maybe. Never know. But I think he was getting too full of hisself, like a bullfrog listening to his own croaking. Maybe he figured the trips to the plantation and over to New Jersey to reset the freedom calendar were easy enough to jump. He talked about running a couple times, but worried that his daughters might get sold off or worse."

"Never thought he cared about anyone but himself."

"I saw him when we went back to Mount Vernon. The General's done put him to labor, making bricks and doing farmhand work. He may be short, but he's strong as any man on the plantation."

"That has to be hard for him to be just like anyone else. He's a proud man."

"Vain, you mean."

"I'm going back to Monticello."

She squinted at him. "Thought you had big dreams of living free."

"I do. He says he'll let me go soon as I train Peter."

"Who's Peter?"

"My brother. Smart as a whip. Shouldn't take more than a half year, maybe less."

She cocked her head. "How long did it take *you*?"

James paused. "Three years. At a famous restaurant for almost a year. Then a pastry chef and a baker, then for French royalty and then for Jefferson as his chef."

"And you think you can somehow squeeze three years into half a year?"

"Yes. None of that training had a plan. None of the information was written for me. I've written it all down for Peter. It's just showing him how it's done."

"And you think he's gonna let you scoot out the door once your baby brother can cook an egg?"

He took her hand. "Wait for me. I'll come back afterward."

"And then what? I won't be free."

"He's going to pay me full wages like a cook he'd hire. I can save enough."

"She'll never let me go, James. Even if she was who owned me. You know that, sure as day."

"No. I'll be back for you. I'll figure it out."

"There's only one way for me."

"Then I'll go with you."

Ona shook her head. "So the blackbirders can find us easier? Take you back to Jefferson's plantation or put you in jail? No." She leaned over and kissed his cheek. "Goodbye, James. God bless you."

CHAPTER 22

Shortly after 1794 began, they arrived at Monticello. James greeted his mother and hurried to the kitchen. Lizzie was leaning over the hearth, stirring a pot. She turned as he called her name. "James? You've changed since you was here last."

"I guess. But the kitchen hasn't."

"What'd you expect it to look like?"

When he told her about his detailed drawings and plans for the construction of the new kitchen, she laughed. "That builder man who sneaks by here for a shortbread or crackers told me ain't no changes gonna be made to my kitchen until the last of the work is done on that connecting walkway. Months and months away."

After several weeks condemned to cooking over a hearth and being unable to demonstrate to Peter anything he had learned in France, James was able to cobble together a bank of several cooktops by trading coffee beans for partially broken bricks and mid-afternoon cakes for mortar and the labor to build waist-high bricked boxes. As he could not find iron plates to match his desired plan, he installed a metal grate a foot below the top and a metal trivet above the coals to hold the copper pot or pan. Ash fell into the open space below and was easily removed through an opening at floor level. With this arrangement, as coals lost heat, new charcoal could be fed from the top with ease. James felt it was a compromise, but one made of necessity.

Once the stoves were functioning, Peter took to his training in the kitchen at Monticello with the skill and zeal that James had anticipated. Lizzie soon became comfortable in her new position assisting Peter and James. However, the need soon arose to find new words to describe the

French methods as teaching French to Lizzie and Peter was an added burden that James sought to alleviate. Thus, the *plaques de cuisson* became stew stoves, and all sundry implements and techniques were named anew.

In spite of Peter's rapid acquisition of abilities Jefferson demanded two full years of his efforts before he began to consider Peter sufficiently skilled to meet his needs without James. During that time, James rarely spoke to Sally, due to her residence in the now enhanced big house and his extended time in the kitchen. When they did see each other, they were cordial, more for their mother's sake than anything else.

On the first of February 1796, Jefferson summoned James to his study. Waiting in the doorway until Jefferson finished writing a correspondence, James wondered what change in menu or new troop of visitors would be announced. As usual, Jefferson motioned him to the front of his desk. "James?" He stopped himself and started again. "James, what is your assessment of Peter's progress?"

Having heard the inquiry before, he steeled himself for the usual argument, yet he persisted in professing his brother's competence. "I find his craftsmanship *suitable* to your needs, sir. He has become a good cook."

"I am inclined to agree with you. Not that he is nearly the chef you are, but suitable, as you say, for my needs."

It was as if the air fled from the room. James heard only his heart pounding. Steadying himself, he nodded.

Jefferson laughed and crossed his arms. "I thought you might agree with me. On both counts."

"I do, sir. I think he is most suitable. A good cook."

"Well then, have we reached that moment when our agreement has been fulfilled?"

His mouth felt dry as he spoke slowly. "In truth, I do believe so."

"Well then, I suspect you have matters to conclude in the kitchen and with your family before you leave. How soon do you believe that might be accomplished?"

James shook and barely controlled his voice. "By tomorrow, sir."

Jefferson laughed harder. "That quickly? I might need another day or so to conclude my portion of the agreement. Writing up the matter. Filing it. Let's say the sixth for your departure."

On that frosty February morning, Jefferson tossed aside the blanket and glanced at his plantation from his bedroom window. It was a day he had feared coming. He took a quick piss in the chamber pot, pulled trousers on over his nightshirt, and slipped into boots. He went to the window and watched for James to crest the hill from his cabin. Jefferson paused when he saw Petit, impeccably attired, intercept James, offer him a handshake, and present a gift, that looked like a leather wallet. When he saw that James carried a small valise and a violin case, he felt a pang of loss, of memories of France, and of how much had changed. Jefferson shrugged into a leather jacket and picked up an envelope from the bed stand. He ran his hand over his mussed hair and stubbly chin. As he passed the mirror, he noted that his copper hair had faded to a sandy gray.

James waited at the east portico of the big house, dressed in a boxy jacket, long trousers of dark brown homespun, and his best French shirt with a bow at the neck. He put down his valise and violin case when the door opened.

Jefferson held the envelope and looked at it as he spoke. "I made a copy of your manumission papers for you to carry. Signed and sealed. The original is on file with the Commonwealth office if you ever need another copy." He took a half sheet from the envelope. "Let me read it to you. *'This indenture made at Monticello in the county of Albemarle, Commonwealth of Virginia, on the fifth day of February one thousand seven hundred and ninety-six witnesseth that I, Thomas Jefferson of Monticello, aforesaid do emancipate, manumit, and make free James Hemings, son of Betty Hemings…'* And of course, the signatures. There's thirty dollars travel money in there as well."

James stared at the document as Jefferson returned it to the envelope, then retrieved a small parcel wrapped in brown paper and string from inside the door. "Open it," the former master said.

James untied the string with shaking hands to reveal a new shirt, trousers, and an overcoat.

He opened his valise and slipped in the shirt and pants. He put on the overcoat. It had a high, stand-up collar. He saw a burn on the left cuff and recognized it as Jefferson's coat from France, marred by an ember from a street bonfire.

"A man can always use an extra."

James buttoned his new coat which smelled of smoke and lavender. "Thank you. The inventory of the kitchen equipment is on your desk. I finished it last evening but did not want to disturb you."

Jefferson had a catch in his throat and paused before speaking. "You will be missed, and not just in the kitchen." When James did not respond, Jefferson continued. "Where will you go?"

"Perhaps to France or the Grand Duchy of Tuscany. And then, I do not know."

"But you will let us know where you are. Sally would be beside herself if I did not make that request."

He nodded.

"James? Why didn't you take your liberty when we were in Philadelphia or in France? Why didn't you just walk away when we were in New York?"

"I gave you my word. And I expected you to hold fast to yours as well."

"But no one would have known."

"I would have."

"James."

James shook his head to stop him. "Mister Jefferson. I am no longer your James, or Jamie, or Jefferson's boy or hey you. My name is Mister Hemings."

Jefferson handed him the envelope. "Safe travels, Mister Hemings."

James turned to go then spun back to face Jefferson, his fists gone rigid on the handles of his cases. "Sir. You have only granted me what was always mine, by the laws of nature, as you so eloquently said. But there is another fact of history that you ignore. My *grandmother* was torn from her family, kidnapped from her home in Africa. She was raped by a white man. That's my mother's roots. She was the daughter of a slave, so she was born a slave here. My *mother* was raped by Mister Wayles, your father-in-law. Raped, whether by force or not is of no matter as no slave can consent to anything. She turned that shame to her advantage. But she never consented. She couldn't any more than my *sister* can. The law does not allow it. Your law books in your library say so, calls it 'incapacity,' treats us like children or the infirm of mind."

"Wait a moment—"

"No! You wait. You freed me and pass that off to your friends because I am *exceptional*. That's your excuse, but not the truth. What was *exceptional* was your choice to educate me and give me the opportunity to grow. Hell, half of the men chopping your timber could do what I did, given the same chance."

"I don't know what to say."

"Don't say anything. I thank you for your kindness to my family and pray that you may kill this evil at its root. Stop the importation of slavery and then find a way to free those now in bondage. That is the promise of freedom you wrote about for this nation, and you alone have the wit to craft it. That could be your legacy. That would brand your name on hearts forever."

And with that, James Hemings turned and left Monticello.

Jefferson watched until James had walked past the bare orchard and was lost from sight. Jefferson left the kitchen inventory on his desk for almost two weeks before he dated it and filed it with the plantation papers.

By the first week in March, James had travelled to Richmond, found a modest lodging house by late morning, and located the residence and medical offices of Doctor Stras by late afternoon. Once on the street in front of the imposing three-story brick building, James paused. He was reading the brass plaque beside the door when the door opened. He was startled by a burly Negro houseman in a long, black coat who barked, "Deliveries in back."

James blurted, "I'm not making a delivery!"

"Then move along; the doctor does not see patients like you."

"I'm not here to see him. I want to see Bob. Robert Hemings."

The man relaxed. "You James?"

"Yes."

He looked up and down the street before saying, "Go 'round back."

"Much appreciate."

The rear of the home was welcoming, even on a chilly spring day. The manicured garden and trees made a sanctuary away from the clatter of wagon wheels on the cobblestone street. Soon James felt the chill of the day and began shifting from foot to foot to stay warm. A few minutes later, the rear door opened. James looked up expecting to see his brother, but instead saw the butler again. This time he grinned and motioned him into the home. "Doctor just left for a house call out of town, so he won't be back for a couple hours. Bob ought to be here soon. Warm yourself by the fire."

"Dolly here?"

"No. Doctor took her with him. Going to see an old lady. Dolly needs to help him sometimes. Took her baby with her."

James moved toward the open hearth, where a large kettle was boiling. Two chickens and a few carrots were swimming in a broth. He sighed as he put his palms toward the heat. If only they knew what could be done with those few ingredients. But even this simple, home-cooked food was better than the tavern meals he had relied on since leaving Monticello. Those eighty miles seemed to be almost farther away than

France. He unbuttoned his overcoat.

"Got some coffee, if you want a cup. Take the chill off."

"Be nice. Thanks."

"Name's Samuel. Bob said you might visit sometimes if you were on a job for Mister Jefferson. Where you going for him?"

"Nowhere, *for him*. I'm my own man now. Got my freedom papers." James patted his chest pocket.

For a big man, Samuel looked as excited as a little child. "He let you buy out? That's what I'm saving for. City folk don't need so many slaves."

"No. I worked my way out."

"That's impossible. Nobody'd go for that deal."

Just then, Bob came in by the back door and stood in silence for a second. The butler left the brothers alone as Bob grabbed James in a bear hug. James recognized the rosewater scent that Bob always splashed on when he was serving dinners in the big house. Mam boiled up the dried rose petals at summer's end and made a quart of it for him. Closing his eyes, he could see his big brother marching up to the big house in his finest suit, smelling like a cloud on a summer day.

"Been too long, little brother. Too long!"

"Came here directly." James paused, almost to tease Bob. "Just as soon as he give me my papers."

"He finally did!" Bob grinned.

"Yup. Hopped rides with wagons when I could. Paid for a seat in a coach when I couldn't."

Bob motioned to chairs at a small table and both sat. "How're Mam and Sally?"

"Good. Mam is slowing a bit, but still doing her potions and some sewing now. Peter is cooking and living with her. Sally's living in the big house."

"And Jefferson's girls?"

"Patsy's got another baby on the way."

"Polly?"

"She's what? Thirteen or fourteen now. Anyways she's gettin' herself to dances, eyeing the boys. Sally goes with her."

Bob frowned. "What?"

"Nothin'. I need your thoughts on a matter."

"Sure. You in some sorta trouble?"

James laughed. "Well, sorta. There's a woman I met."

"In France?"

"No. Got to know her in Philadelphia. I think she likes me. I have almost enough to buy her out. But I don't know how to approach her."

"What's bad about being forward about it?"

"I ain't seen her for two, almost three years now. I know she's still there, because I ask after her when a courier comes from Washington's office for Jefferson. She's there."

"With the President?"

James nodded. "You bought out your freedom, Bob. Why couldn't I buy out hers?"

Bob leaned back and shook his head. "I was lucky enough to have Doctor Stras advance me sixty pounds, backed by an indenture to him."

"You mean dollars?"

"No, pounds. Jefferson accepted payment in pounds. Wrote my freedom paper Christmas Eve 1794. That's a day we celebrate more than Christmas. I'll be working off my indenture to the doctor until ninety-nine, then I'll be as free as you."

"But your woman? How's Dolly?"

"The doctor's not given any sign he's willing to let her go, or our children either. But he's a good man to work for and I'd consider it even after I work off the indenture just to stay close to Dolly."

James paused before asking, "How did you approach him?"

"Straight out. Remember, Jefferson had hired me out to him. The doctor knew me."

"Just go in and ask?"

Bob slapped his knee. "You think President Washington is going to let you buy out his slave just 'cause you're sweet on her? Hell, boy. He just knows you as Massa's cook."

"I could try."

"Never happen. He's a Virginian! He needs the support of other planters here. Can't you see that? Doctor Stras won't let me buy out Dolly. Lets me live here, yes. Work for him for wages. But buy out? Ha."

"What'd you think if I find some white lawyer to ask to buy out my lady friend?"

"Who'd do that for you?"

"I might find someone."

"Careful, James. She ain't yours to buy and own. Even if she feels grateful to you for her freedom, would that be enough to bind her to you for a family?"

"I know that. I see wildness in her. I'm afraid that she'll run free, to her peril. Like a horse that ain't really broke, she got that look."

"Had that look yourself, but you haven't left Monticello, even to visit us here, for two years. That can be a forever, even if she has feelings for you."

James looked at his boots. "James? Take off your coat and stay for dinner. Dolly'd love to see you. Want you to see our baby. Doctor won't mind."

"Thanks, but best I be going. Got miles to make."

The stagecoach jolted as it left the rutted dirt road and skidded on the cobblestoned street at the edge of Philadelphia. The eight passengers inside were packed like salted cod in a barrel. So tightly confined were they that even with this abrupt jolt, no one shifted in their position.

Seating had been taken with the greatest attention to the social rank of the three gentlemen and four ladies inside the coach as soon as James slipped into its left-rear corner. The servant of the oldest of the women, a girl of no more than fourteen, was assigned to the exterior shelf on the rear of the coach with the woman's trunk.

A minister in a stained black suit pressed against James. His brandy breath filled the coach with a smoky stench that made the draft from the ill-fitting windows welcome. Two men in worn, homespun trousers and long coats sat across from James. The four ladies were seated as far from James as possible, two on the other side of the minister facing forward and the other two facing them, but with their gazes firmly fixed out the scratched isinglass window.

The minister had wedged James even further into the corner of the coach with each jolt during the past five hours, so that by the time they arrived in Philadelphia, James felt a numbness advancing in his left leg and his neck. When the coach stopped at the stage station near the City Tavern on the docks near High Street, the ladies quickly disembarked. As was the case most Saturday evenings, the City Tavern swarmed with visitors and guests.

It was a large and commodious building that spanned five levels. It included the second-largest ballroom in the colonies, a bar room, two coffee rooms, three dining rooms, and two kitchens with the capacity to serve hundreds and well-appointed rooms for half that number. Additionally, it had small rooms for the servants of lodgers. James had lived here with Jefferson during their first days in the city before the home Jefferson had leased was ready for occupancy.

James brushed dust from his coat and shifted from one foot to the other to keep warm and get the feeling back in his leg while the driver untied the luggage from the roof of the coach and handed bags to the passengers. All but one walked away into the dark city, having family or friends or other lodging for the night. James took his valise from the driver and booked into the smallest of the servant's rooms in the tavern, paying cash for a week of lodging.

During the last leg of the crowded carriage ride, James had formulated his plan to see Ona. Late Saturday would be too risky. President Washington might be entertaining, or she could be out with Lady

Washington. Recalling that they were regular in their attendance at the Sunday service at Christ Church, the next day he stationed himself at a diagonal across Second Street from the entrance. Once he spotted Washington's carriage and determined that Ona was not there, he hurried to High Street then turned inland and ran past the market stalls. Hurrying past Mrs. House's Boarding House where he and Jefferson had frequently lodged, he slowed himself for the rest of the block to catch his breath, all the while watching for Ona, hoping she had not gone out during these few hours of Sunday liberty.

Once in front of the President's House, he stopped to marvel that here he was a free man, not Jefferson's man carrying his papers or spying on the chef. He stood taller and proceeded to the rear of the house. Although the door was shut against the cold, he had seen smoke from the chimney, and knew the fire would be tended. He knocked.

The man answering the door looked familiar to James, although he couldn't immediately put a name to this white face. The man looked down the steps at James as he knotted the white cloth at the neck of a white jacket in the same style that Hercules had adopted. James thought it an affectation that Washington required, but upon reflection, saw the practicality of the attire. The man was bulky as a butcher and had a ruddy complexion. "Yes? Do I know you? You look familiar."

"We met after Hercules left. I was here before, with Mister Jefferson. I'm James Hemings."

"Are you on business for Mister Jefferson?"

"No. I'm a free man now."

He put his hands on his hips. "Are you really?"

"Yes. I would appreciate it if I could talk with Ona for a moment. Just say she has a friend to see her."

"Guess there is no harm, seeing as Lady Washington is off to church for the morning. But she's the lady's maid, so don't leave the property."

James nodded, perhaps too fast or too much. All he could imagine was her excitement in seeing him again. Then a fear washed over him that she might not even recognize him. Although hoping to be invited into the warm kitchen, he was not surprised when the door was shut. He jumped off the stoop onto the lawn and tugged his jacket straight.

When the door opened again, Ona stood there, in a lavender dress, a dark wool shawl over her shoulders and knotted in front. Her hair was shorter than he recalled, like a black halo. Her face, still winter pale, had the freckles he could map as he could the stars at night. Her face was blank when she had opened the door, but when she recognized James she smiled, and the sun seemed to shine on him again.

"My Lord. It really is you!" She ran down the steps and hugged him. Hooking her arm through his, she said, "Come in."

He shook his head. "Get your coat. I saw them go to church, so we have a little time. Can you?"

"Yes."

"I'll wait here. Tell him you're going."

Moments later she was at his side, grinning. "It's really you! Imagine."

"Let's walk. I got lodging at the City Tavern. They'll serve us in the side room."

"No. I don't want talk to start that Lady Washington's maid was out and about."

"Sorry. I didn't mean to cause harm."

"Gossip seems to fuel the city."

He motioned this comment aside with a flick of his hand and then looked around. The steeple of the statehouse where the Declaration had been signed dominated the horizon. "Still got benches by the statehouse? Think we could go there?"

She nodded. "Let me get permission. I can see their carriage returning from church from there and can run back before she figures out I'm gone." Ona opened the door and spoke quickly to the chef. She came back with a smile. James put his arm over her shoulder while they hurried down Sixth Street. He breathed deeper when she let his arm rest easily and moved even closer.

There were several benches on the edge of the small green in front of the statehouse. The grass was still winter brown. The chill left the square empty, at least until church was over. They sat side by side.

James felt tears forming and blinked them away. "I didn't know if you'd remember me."

"James! Of course. I remember you. So smart and sweet to me."

"I said I'd come back, but I didn't know it was going to be so long."

"But you're back. Mister Jefferson here now?"

"He is at Monticello."

She pulled closer to him and whispered, "You run?"

"No. He signed my papers. Like I told you he would."

"You a free man now? Really?"

James patted his side. "Got a copy of my freedom paper on me right here."

"Lord be praised! That's so wonderful for you."

"Maybe for us?"

"You thinking of trying to work for President Washington?"

"No. I was thinking of seeing if he would let you go."

She laughed, then looked him in the eye. "You serious?"

"Yes."

"That's crazy talk."

He knew their time was limited and spoke faster, his pulse racing. "I'd do anything for you, Ona. If I could get you freedom papers, where would you go?"

"North. I hear there's a place in New Hampshire that's welcoming."

"Could you go there alone? I mean, on your own?"

She frowned. "I don't know what you are asking."

James squirmed then turned to face her. "Ona, I got money and want to hire an attorney to go to Mister Washington. See if he'd let a slave get bought out. Wouldn't say who or if it's a man or woman, so's nobody know it's about you."

"Why'd he consider it?"

"I heard that he is in a hard way for funds, with all the costs he got here. Just like Jefferson, he don't get paid enough and his plantation's not doing all that well."

She looked horrified. "What if they think it be me that's mentioned?"

"No! I wouldn't say your name, even to the lawyer."

"You're in dangerous territory, James."

"I know, that's why I'm gonna get me a white lawyer to do my asking. One of the fellows from the Abolition Society."

She shook her head as if to clear the cobwebs. "You have any idea how much I'd cost? You crazy?"

"I said I have money."

She drew back. "Why're you telling me this?"

"Because I don't want you frightened or feeling beholden to me. If I could get your papers sold off to the lawyer, he'd release you right away. But I couldn't do that unless you knew so you wouldn't be afraid and then run."

"Oh, James. It seem like a dream that ain't gonna come true."

"Look. Times change. Jefferson was good to his word and signed my manumission paper. Finally. Sold my brother, Bob, to a man who's letting him work off the sale price as an indenture. He's living in Richmond. Works in the house of the doctor who owns his woman. Got him a real family now."

"And your sister? You talked about her and how in France she took up with him."

He looked at the ground. "She's living at Monticello now. She won't ever be free of her feelings for Mister Jefferson. If he signed her papers today, I doubt she'd move an inch from him."

She chuckled and looked away.

"What is it?"

"Something's happening here that you ought to know. Miss Eliza, Lady Washington's daughter, gonna get married soon to a Mister Law."

"That should be good news. Didn't you say she's a hard woman to please when they were at Mount Vernon?"

"Here's the problem. Missus say she gonna gift me to her for a wedding present."

"Oh no."

"I'm no wedding present. I am a person with my own feelings. I'm not going to live in that swampy Federal City."

"Why's she going there?"

"Her no-account man done bought up over five hundred parcels of land. Think he gonna make a fortune selling 'em off once the capital moves there in a few years."

"Might just."

"Seems to me like he courted her mighty fast. Him an Englishman and all."

James frowned. "Who is he?"

"Just overheard parts and bits, but the man scares me. Got sons. Mulatto boys."

"Got a slave mother?"

"He say she's in India, far away. But if he had relations with one-dark skinned woman…"

"You afraid?"

"I know my father was a white man with a taste for color. He come to Mount Vernon to make clothing for the entire plantation. My mother worked the sewing hut. She couldn't do nothing."

Ona started to cry.

James held her and felt his own tears rise. He could not let her be in harm's way or let her leave his life. She alone felt the pull for freedom as deeply as he did. He felt her presence enriched him in a way that had no words. As excited as he was to see her, something calmed in him, and some unnamed fear subsided.

CHAPTER 23

On Monday morning, James dressed in his best French suit of fine wool. The breeches and jacket were a dark blue and his stockings a pale cream. He adjusted his tricorn hat in the mirror of his small room. After he buttoned his overcoat, he went to the front desk of the huge inn. Dining halls on the first floor and meeting rooms above it gave way to individual rooms typical of most rustic inns. But the City Tavern had been built on a large scale in anticipation that there would be assemblies of representatives to form the government and that Philadelphia would be the nation's capital for at least a decade. Its builders had envisioned civic engagement, meetings of hundreds, banquets, boarders, and short-term visitors, not just the occasional traveler. This was a place for ideas, not just food and shelter.

He asked the deskman if he knew the location of the Abolition Society. The lean man with a red vest gave the location and described it as a small home converted to its new use just past the ship's chandlery on Front Street. The March wind off the water along Front Street was brisk. James located the office and was amused that its sign was wider than the weathered doorway under it. "Pennsylvania Society for Promoting the Abolition of Slavery and for the Relief of Free Negroes Unlawfully Held in Bondage and Improving the Condition of the African Race." He noted that the last phrase was in fresher paint.

The offices of the Abolition Society consisted of one large room. At each of the four desks, there was a man writing letters or legal briefs with cheap quills. An older man with a sallow complexion and half glasses looked up as the cold wind from the open door threatened to scatter his papers. James shut the door, harder than he intended, and everyone looked up from their work. The man with glasses asked, "Yes?"

James was quick to say that he needed a referral to a lawyer to assist in making a transaction that would result in emancipation and that he could pay a fee. He also requested someone who had dealings with the newly formed government. He was provided with the names of three lawyers. Later that afternoon, James paused before the door of a two-story brick building on Second Street, three blocks from Christ Church. He read the brass plaque beside the newly painted white door. *Franklin J. Broadhurst, Esq*. He knocked.

The eight-year-old boy who answered the door looked at the dark-skinned man in a high-collared coat and tricorn hat, turned, and retreated into the hallway of the house. Moments later, a stocky man appeared and removed his round spectacles to address James. "May I be of assistance, sir? It seems my son was too in awe of your attire to find his manners or his tongue."

"Mister Broadhurst?"

"Yes. How may I assist you?"

"I am in need of a legal consultation relating to a sale."

Opening the door wider, he pressed against the hallway wall to allow James to enter. With a graceful sweep of his palm, he pointed to the open door of a small room. The cramped office had windows on two sides, making it bright and inviting. Although the desk and client's chair in front of it consumed most of the space, it was orderly. Both men settled into their respective seats.

Broadhurst smiled, but before he could say anything, James asked, "Do you do business matters?"

"Yes. Contracts and negotiations are typical."

"And if I wished you to be my agent in negotiating a purchase?"

"Can you legally transact this matter? Are you a free man?"

"Hemings. James Hemings. Yes, I am free."

"What is it you wish to purchase?"

James blurted, "I would like to buy a slave."

After staring at him, Broadhurst laughed, and then found his composure. "Sir? Do you know that I am a member of the Abolition Society? I find the institution abhorrent to the degree that it is my intent to end, not to support, the enslavement of humans." He tossed his spectacles on the desk. "No sir, I will not be a party to such a transaction. I am sorry you have wasted your time and mine."

"Please hear me out. I said that badly."

He sat on the edge of his chair but looked as though he were about to stand and show James the door at any second.

"There is this person who is enslaved. I wish to buy that person's papers and emancipate that person immediately."

"Interesting. And why do you come to me for this transaction and not the owner?"

"To speak plainly, sir. Your face is white, and I was informed that you know the owner."

"Who might that be?"

"President George Washington."

Broadhurst sat back in his chair and crossed his arms. He tipped his head and stared at James. After a moment, he put his hand to his mouth as if trying to find words. He leaned forward, elbows on his desk. "While I do know him, it is in the context of my lobbying for legislation for the betterment of free Negroes and the emancipation of those enslaved. He has listened, but progress has been slow as you are obviously aware."

James nodded. "Would you make the inquiry to see if he would sell this slave now in his residence, and if so, the cost?"

"You do understand that Pennsylvania is a free state and slaves may not be bought here. Emancipated, yes. Purchased, no. Is there a name attached to this person of interest?"

"I fear bringing any undue attention to the slave."

"Of course. I see no impediment to making that inquiry in the abstract. I have a meeting set for tomorrow morning, on a legislative matter.

I may be able to approach him privately then, or at least set another meeting time."

"The terms?"

"Of the sale? Well, it depends on the nature of the transaction. If there is a willing seller and the terms are clear, it can be a modest fee for the drafting of documents."

"What are *your* terms for making this inquiry?"

"Normally, I require a retainer of some half of the projected cost of the matter to draw from. But this interests me and should be resolved one way or the other easily. Say a dollar as a retainer to make it legal. We can meet tomorrow late afternoon, about four, to see what progress I have made." After putting his freshly minted Lady Liberty silver dollar on the desk, James nodded and left.

The next morning seemed to James to drag on for weeks. He paced along the waterfront watching ships and fishermen come and go, ate a tasteless clam chowder for his lunch, and walked again. The spring day was bright, too warm in the sun with his coat, and too cold without it when the clouds blocked the sun. He found himself back at the same, small inn lingering over a cider at three o'clock when a light rainsquall brushed along the harbor. James checked his pocket watch eighteen minutes later and again, at the half hour. He left the small waterfront inn at five minutes before four o'clock.

The streets glistened gray and silver when the clouds thinned. James unbuttoned his coat and fidgeted with his vest after he rapped on the door. In spite of the chill in the air, he was sweating. Broadhurst answered the door and showed James to the office as he had done the day before.

Without any preamble, James leaned his hands on the back of the chair rather than taking the seat. "Well? What say you, sir?"

"None of the slaves in the President's House can be sold."

"Yes, I understood that. You said that Pennsylvania is a free state. No sales. But emancipation?"

Broadhurst shook his head. "It's more than that. I did see the President privately. It is actually a simple matter. He does not own any of the slaves now in the President's House; his wife has a widow's dower interest in them."

"I don't understand."

"Please. Take a seat while I explain. All their slaves up here are owned by the Custis Estate. When Missus Washington's first husband, a Mister Custis, died, those slaves belonging to him and his land came to her, not in fee simple or clear title, but under dower. That grants her the use and income of these properties during her lifetime. Upon her death, it all goes to the heirs of the Custis Estate. Her grandchildren, as I understand it, will inherit clear title to all lands and property. So, whoever you are interested in is not theirs to sell."

"And won't be until she dies, and if the new owner is so inclined?"

"Unfortunately, you are correct."

"Thank you, sir." James felt dizzy when he stood and reached for his pocket. The light leather sheath holding his two knives peeked from the edge of his vest. He leaned against the back of the chair. "May I settle my account?"

"No. My time was nothing on this matter. Save your money for when it can do someone some good." James started to leave, but Broadhurst took his arm. "Sit for a moment, Mister Hemings."

His face contorted with frustration. "What?"

"I want to offer you some free advice, in the abstract, of course. Have you heard of the Overseers of the Poor?"

"No."

"Many Northern cities are instituting this office to manage payments to the poor. Free Negroes coming to towns are now being required to post a sum of money in order to stay. The idea is when they can no longer support themselves, their deposit will support them. Those under eighteen can be indentured to their twenty-eighth birthday by the city, with their wages held for their future support."

James recalled Ned telling him of this in Boston years before but hoped it was not still the practice. "My God. That's just trading one master for another."

"And James, I want you to be aware that if you assist her, I assume it is a woman..." James nodded. "Or if you fund her running away, or pay her tariff to some City Overseer, the President could easily set charges against you civilly and have you arrested for criminally aiding her. So please be cautious in your consideration of your next action."

"Thank you."

He motioned for James to wait. "Just a moment. Are you aware of the six-month limitation on her stay here?"

"Yes. But Washington removes them all to their plantation or to New Jersey just shy of six months and then returns them."

"We have a law against that removal."

"He would argue that your law does not apply as he is not a resident, but merely here on government business. I heard him make it one evening when he was dining with Mister Jefferson."

"You know Mister Jefferson?"

"I was his personal servant before I was emancipated."

"I wondered at your fine attire. Congratulations."

James ignored his comment. "But Washington was firm on the matter."

"Poppycock. He's wrong. The statute specifically exempts only 'members of Congress.' There is no mention of the executive branch. We could apply to the court."

"No. He'd just send her back to Virginia."

"But the law is the law."

"What judge is gonna tell the President what to do?"

"I could file—"

James sighed. "It may be hard for you to see, but sometimes what the law says is not what's gonna happen for people who look like me. And sometimes, what the law says is not what is truly right."

"But—"

"I thank you for your effort and counsel."

Broadhurst extended his hand. James shook it and walked toward the marketplace as though he wore boots of lead.

He found Ona near the rice bins, holding a small bag of chocolate drops. When she saw him, she held out the bag for him to take one. "Missus Washington's favorites." He shook his head. When his face gave him away, she began to cry. He gently put his arm over her shoulder and walked her across the street to a bench near the dock. Sitting close enough to have their shoulders touch, they looked over the harbor both comforted by the moment of shared intimacy. He turned to her. "Ona. I am so sorry. There is no way I can buy it out. He told me that she couldn't sell you if she wanted 'cause of something about how she inherited you from her first husband. But, the lawyer said he could file papers to try and free you. Says Washington can't rotate you in and out of the state at his will."

"Me against the President?" She watched a gull dive into the water and laughed.

James sat back and paused before he spoke. "You're gonna run?"

She nodded. "What other choice I got? She can't even sell me for a million dollars if she wanted to. I can't go to live with Eliza."

"Stop and think. What would betray you if you ran? Your Southern manner of speech? Being noticed by one of the homes you had visited?"

"That's my fear. Missus Washington's like a butterfly, flitting from one house to another when people wasn't having tea or lemonade in her parlor. No. I gotta go to a place where nobody knows her so's they couldn't have seen me."

"Think they'll put out a notice on you?"

"Sure as the sun come up in the morning. I hear them talk once before like a runoff is taking gold coins outta their pocket. They paid a bounty to some blackbirders last year on a manservant."

"But you could let me try."

"Got to be real slow in thinking on this, James. No cloud picking or dreaming. Think on it. I got no baby to anchor me to a place. That's the reason I get moved with her. I'm easy to pack and unpack."

"But the lawyer—"

"He can say what he wants, but no judge is going to go up against the President. Fear the wrath of God if they do. Gotta do this on my own time."

"When are you planning?"

"When the weather breaks. Spring or summer be best so's I don't need to carry much in the way of food. I got a place to go, but I need to get there."

"Where?"

She turned to him and lowered her voice. "You don't want to know, that way you don't need to lie. Best you not see me no more after today or they'll go after you for aiding."

"You going to walk it?"

She laughed. "I can't read a map. I don't even know how to sound out letters. I gotta go with someone who knows the way. 'Sides, I gonna take some of my belongings too. Gotta. Ain't got no way to buy new things for a bit."

"I got money that I saved."

"No. They find cash money in my room, and they'll know what I'm thinking. I'll make my way." For a moment, he thought of Gabrielle and how he had promised her to make a way. But he failed and lost her. But Ona was different. He would do anything for her. Anything.

He glanced over his shoulder to be certain that no one was nearby before he pulled back the edge of his coat. The gold chain across his vest shined. He took his watch from his vest pocket and held it toward her without opening it or checking the time. "Ona. I want you to pay attention to what I am going to tell you. It is important."

She frowned.

The front of the heavy gold case had a circular crystal in its center, which exposed the protected hands on the watch face. When James opened the case, she saw that each of the blued steel hands had a small *fleur-de-lis* at the tip. "See that? It's a lily flower that kings had on their crests. Royal." He slid a button near the winding stem, and it played a small tune.

She smiled. "Why… it's a regular little music box. That supposed to cheer me into staying?"

"No," he said. "This is called a musical repeater pocket watch. You wind it by turning this stem and set a new time by pulling the stem up and turning it. Need to wind it every day to make it run."

"I know that much, about winding 'em."

"You heard the music part of it. Remember that it is a Bach lullaby. 'Repeater' means that it chimes out the time so's you don't need to look at it at all. Can tell the time even in the dark of night."

"Really?"

"Let me show you. There are two settings. They got French names. The big ring is the *grande sonnerie*. That setting rings a bell matching the hour, and then after a pause it rings the quarter hour. It's silent on the hour, one added bell at a quarter past, two on the half, three at forty-five minutes. In the *petite sonnerie* setting, it only rings the quarter hour. Now it is set on silent, but when I slide this button with my fingernail, it will ring the time. Next should be six fifteen."

"Why you showing off such a timepiece to me when we are talking on something so important?"

He placed it in her hand. "Look at it carefully. Hold it so you feel the ticking. It is like a living thing." She held it to her ear then to her breast. She jumped when it chimed six times, paused, and sounded an added bell.

She handed it back to him. As he slid the button to the right, he looked at her. "Can you remember how to make it sound if I leave it on silent?"

"Yes, it's that button, but why?"

"It sounds louder on a desk than in your hand. So when you want to tell someone about it, put it on a desk. Makes it louder. What are the two settings?"

She tried to mimic his words. "*Grand sunner* and *pet' sunner*. James, it's yours to brag on, not mine."

"Ona, I didn't buy it to be boastful. I bought this in France to have something of constant value, because their money was becoming worthless. I knew it was small enough to hide if I had to. Like you are going to have to. It is worth my passage back on a good ship, and then some. That's what I was going to do, go back, until I met you."

"James."

"You going free means more to me than my going back to France."

"Oh, James." Tears sparkled on her cheeks.

He unclipped the gold chain with the *fleur-de-lis* fob at its end and let it slip into his vest pocket. He brushed her tears away and held the watch for her to see. "Listen carefully! It's solid gold and the best French mechanism. If it's worth passage to France, it should get you to where you are going."

She pushed it back to him. "I can't take it. I won't tell you when or how I'll make my move. That'll keep you safe."

He silenced the watch, put it in her palm, and closed her fingers over it. "Don't wind it until you are ready to sell it. Let it run down so nobody will hear it tick or it won't sound by accident."

She stood. "Goodbye, James. I hope our paths cross again in better times."

He stood, facing her. Before he could say anything, she took his face in both hands and kissed him. Her soft lips parted slightly. Softer than he had imagined. He tasted chocolate. She pressed her body against his for an instant then turned, leaving him to watch the gulls that swirled behind incoming boats.

On Saturday, May 21, 1796, James woke to a hard rain against his window in the City Tavern. Rising slowly, he dressed for the day knowing he would need to be at the market by nine, whether the rain had stopped or not. As he dressed, he composed the menu for the celebration that eight bankers had scheduled in the tavern's private dining room. In his first week there, he had presented his credentials to the tavern's owner and offered to cater exclusive meals in exchange for his room and board. Quietly, the tavern owner had informed his most prestigious customers in the worlds of banking and politics that Jefferson's French chef could cater intimate dinners for those wishing privacy and luxury in which to conduct their business. During the several months that this had been offered, all but three days had been fully reserved. The increase in revenue was substantial for the owner, who then began paying James a salary.

At the market, the open-air stalls sparkled from the last of the rain. A brilliant sun broke through the thinning clouds. After selecting his vegetables and paying to have two crates of oysters delivered, James began the walk back to the tavern.

He saw her at the edge of the market, closest to the docks. He stopped to watch her move, measured like a dancer, her blue shawl swaying to her movements as she picked spring flowers from small buckets. She was the perfect lady's maid on an errand. She glanced up, as though knowing he was watching, and smiled at him before returning to her selections. He knew: It was only a matter of time and tide before she went.

As he walked along the harbor, he looked at the thirty-some ships at dock or at anchor, wondering which she had selected, or if she would go veiled in a stagecoach, and how far she would journey north for her freedom.

The sloop *Nancy* bobbed light at dock, having discharged its Northern cargo of barrels of rum, dried fish, carved clocks for mantels, and freestanding grandfather clocks. The lumber *Nancy* carried had been cut in Connecticut to the specifications of a builder who arrived dockside with two wagons to claim it. Captain John Bowles gave half of his crew liberty to take their noon meal at the tavern, hoping that the break in the rain would hold while they loaded their new cargo of grains and tobacco, kegs of brandy, barrels of potatoes, and molasses that afternoon.

During the appointed Saturday suppertime at the President's House late that afternoon, Ona offered to carry the vegetable trimmings to the stable for the horses. While there, two men met her. She knocked the straw away from the trunk she had hidden there earlier that day. Each of the men grabbed a handle and walked away with it. Ona followed them to a large stable near the dock.

At dusk Monday, crates of saddles, bridles, and boots were carried aboard the ship, followed by crates. baskets of food for the crew and Ona's trunk. Tuesday morning, she boarded at dawn and was shown to the rope locker in the bow of the ship where her trunk had replaced the coils of rope now stowed with cargo. The seven passengers came aboard by nine. The captain called for the sails to be set by ten.

Most of the passengers bound for Portsmouth, New Hampshire, remained on deck to watch the land slip away. Ona remained wedged into the small space under the bowsprit beside her trunk. Unlike the stability on deck, the bow exaggerated the ship's every dip and rise.

Holding her pillowcase of dried biscuits, dried beef strips, and apples on her lap, she wondered if she could really stay in the tight quarters alone for four days without losing her mind. The tight space had a keg of drinking water, a cup, a bucket for a chamber pot, and a candle on a spike driven into the hull near the small, covered porthole in the side of the ship. Warned not to open it in daylight or throw slops if her candle were lighted at night, she tried to sleep to pass the time. But there was no way the creaking of the hull and scratching of rats would let her find rest. Pulling the rough wool blanket over her head, she squirmed to create a solid resting place and then fell into a light sleep. Four nights of this and then land.

On Thursday, May 26, James ate breakfast at the City Tavern and glanced at a copy of Claypoole's *American Daily Advertiser*, which another diner had left on the long table. He searched it for notices as he had started doing the day after he saw Ona in the market with flowers.

Although he half-expected to find the notice of her escape from the Washingtons, he froze when he actually saw her name in print. He felt his vision narrow and grow spotty. He leaned on his elbows and sucked in air. After a moment, he steadied his hand and read the notice.

Ten Dollars Reward

Absconded from the household of the President of the United States, on Saturday afternoon, ONEY JUDGE, a light Mulatto girl, much freckled, with very black eyes, and bushy black hair - She is of middle stature, but slender and delicately made, about 20 years of age. She has many changes of good clothes of all sorts, but they are not sufficiently recollected to describe.

As there was no suspicion of her going off, and it happened without the least provocation, it is not easy to conjecture whether she is gone - or fully, what her design is; but as she may attempt to escape by water, all masters of vessels and others are cautioned against receiving her on board, altho' she may, and probably will endeavour to pass for a free woman, and it is said has, wherewithal to pay her passage.

Ten Dollars will be paid to any person, (white or black) who will bring her home, if taken in the city or on board any vessel in the harbor; and a further reasonable sum if apprehended and brought home, from a greater distance, and in proportion to the distance.

May 24, 1796   Fred. Kitt, Steward

His most ardent hopes for her and his gravest fears collided. Had she made passage and sailed? Was she holed up in the city waiting for interest to abate before she left? Had they never seen that her eyes were the color of almond husks and that her smile was like the sun? A hundred other questions without answers haunted him.

CHAPTER 24

It took James almost six months of asking around Philadelphia and watching to find where her trail started. While he worked at the tavern, he asked every arriving captain if he had seen her. He spent his days off quizzing sailors in the shabby waterfront bars, in the hope that one might have seen her and offer that information in exchange for a drink. He had no luck. He asked abolitionists and ministers. Months into his search, when he had never blackbirded anyone or sought a bounty, some people in Philadelphia listened more attentively to his questions. It took weeks at every step of her jagged path. He unraveled most of it through friends of friends and a network wider and deeper than he could have imagined.

Each step was discrete and removed from the one before and the one after. No one knew it all. He spliced information together and felt confident that she had sailed to a Northern port. He quit his job, travelled north, and asked after her of black tradesmen and at their small churches near Northern harbors. His contacts in Boston suggested Portsmouth as a safe destination.

He paid a call on each of the ministers of the churches near Portsmouth. Finally, in the fall of 1796, when one told him to watch and pray for a week, he took a room in a musty inn and remained either on its porch or in his room. Five days later, a young girl asked for him and said a minister wanted to see him. James sprinted to the church.

Entering the small building, James felt a chill of anticipation. He saw a portly man sweeping. Recognizing him, he called, "Reverend?"

Leaning on the broom, he smiled. "James, she said that you would be a welcome visitor. Thank you for your patience. Let me give you directions to her cabin." When James pulled a small notebook from his pocket, the minister put his hand out to stop him. "You can't write."

"Yes, I can."

"No. I mean it is not safe to have such a document on your person. Listen to my instructions and remember how to get there. Landmarks will be evident, if you know what to look for." Trusting the man's word, James pulled on a worn coat and left his new coat folded in his bag. He gathered his things from his room and started walking. From town, he took the post road, wide enough for two wagons to pass in most places but shaded by tall trees with leaves turning to yellows and reds. From the post road, he followed the third creek from town and walked a mile downstream. When he came to the first pathway up a hill, he paused and straightened his coat and buffed the dust from his boots by rubbing them against the back of his trousers. He saw the shake roof of the re-mote cabin peeking above the hilltop. He took a deep breath.

The cabin was off the creek by a hundred steep yards up a graveled pathway under an archway of crimson branches. A breeze carried the smell of hardwood smoke and sent a few of the dried leaves spinning down to the path. Just before he crested the hill, he heard a woman hum-ming a gentle tune, like a lullaby or perhaps a work song sung softly. He glanced past the hilltop and saw the late-afternoon sun full on the back of a lean woman in a dark blue dress.

She stirred a steaming cauldron over an open fire. His first thought was boiling off sheets but then the smell hit his nose. Rancid. Smoky. Harsh. He gagged at the stench of rendering fat. The huge black iron pot was suspended above a blazing fire. A forged loop on the pot held it above the flame on a long pole between tall sawhorses. Long logs were fanned out under the pot like a sunburst so she could push them for-ward as needed to hold the correct temperature. She put her weight into the long paddle that came almost to her shoulder. Stroke after stroke matched the tune he had heard. He stopped, traded coats, and ran his hand over his short-cropped hair. He wondered if his pulse was racing from the hike or his anxiety. Ona! A woman who treasured freedom as much as he did, who was braver than any man he had ever known, and who was her own beauty.

He looked around as he waited for a break in her song so as not to startle her. He hoped she was Ona. He'd seen soap-making from afar. He backed away a few steps and waited. When he heard only the rattle of the leaves and pulse of the paddle hitting the huge iron pot, he scuffed his boots deep into the pebbles to announce himself.

Caution stiffened her back. She turned. In a flash, a smile of recognition replaced the fear in her face. "James? That you?"

"Ona?"

"Get up here. Let me see you."

James trotted to her and stood, hands on his hips, for inspection. "Well. Don't you look fine! New coat. Tight haircut. And here I am, sweating over a soap pot?"

"You look good."

She relaxed into a welcoming smile. "You too. Coming up here for some fancy cooking job?"

"No. I came looking for you."

She hung her head. "And here I be, making soap. Gonna be another hour before I can take my leave now that the fat's melted and the potash's ready to add."

He paused, wondering why his coming did not merit a happier reply. He stared at the steaming cauldron. "You learn to make soap at Mount Vernon?"

She laughed the easy, deep laugh that he remembered. "No. I was in the house from when I was ten years on up tendin' Miss Martha or her grandchillen. The Jacks family took me in right when I got here. This is their place. I help them how I can. They showed me how. Helps pay the way."

James pulled off his coat and took the paddle from her. "Just stir it like you were doin'?"

She nodded. "Thank you."

"Pleased to help."

She walked toward a barrel resting on a small platform and took a five-gallon crock from under the drain plug in the barrel. Dragging it over to the heated pot of fat, she reached for a long dipper. "Stand away for a minute. This lye'll burn the skin off you if it splashes."

"That so?"

"So! They keep a bottle of vinegar at hand so's if you get any on you, it'll take away its sting."

After adding the lye, she ducked away from the acrid steam, put the crock back under the barrel, and returned to his side.

The clear fat and amber potash curdled into a milky substance when he stirred it.

"They taught me how to render the fat from the trimmings of the winter butchering. Got them from farms and the town butcher in exchange for some of the soap. Learned to boil down the trimmings, strain off the meat and gristle, that's cracklings, to get a clean run of fat. I make my own potash as well."

"What's in the barrel that makes it so dangerous?"

"That's called a leaching barrel. Got stones at the bottom, a layer of straw to hold in the ash."

"Ash?"

"Just hardwood ash. Collect it all year long from my hearth. Then I get some from other people. Trash to them but when you put boiling water over the ash and let it steep like a tea in a pot, then you can drain off the potash. Took me a while to get the right strength."

"How do you know when it is right?"

"Float an egg in it, careful to use a wood spoon and not touch it. If the egg floats with just this much out of the lye, it is the right strength." She gestured to the pad of her thumb. "Too weak and it sinks and you need to boil it down. Too strong and you need to water it down some." She laughed. "But don't eat that egg after."

He laughed. "Good idea."

"This batch is just washing soap. Last week I made some hard soap with lavender branches for ladies. We sell 'em to the mercantile in town."

"Enough to make your way?"

"Not really. But that's changing now. I got a housekeeping job of work starting in a few weeks. Just marched myself up to a door in town and told 'em that I'm a good maid. I do washing. I can tend to anything that's under a roof. And I'm looking for a God-fearing house to work in."

He laughed. "You said that. So bold?"

"Can't see as I had any other choice. Got a job caring for an old lady at the third house. This is my day off. But they want me to do simple cooking as well. I gotta learn enough cooking to pass. Missus Jack is teaching me."

"I could teach you."

She glanced away. "You cook too fancy for the old widow lady what wants a companion and housekeeper to make a simple plate. Woman's had a patch of illness, so needs help all day now."

"I could teach you foods for the infirm. Read about that in an old cookbook in France."

"Only food I'd ever want to learn is that good ol' stew like my mama used to make of okra and tomatoes and whatever meat we might have."

"Kingumbo?"

She grinned. "I miss that. Never even seen okra up here."

"Met a man in France. We got to talking food and I told him of king-umbo. Then to my surprise, he says it just a bit faster than I did. Said he heard it when he was a cook on a trading ship that brought goods from Angola. Said it means 'okra soup or stew' in Mbundu. That's what they talk in Angola."

He continued to paddle like he was stirring a cauldron of soup for fifty guests in Paris. But he realized that what he loved of Ona's spirit and independence suddenly felt like a threat. She had been alone for months. She had earned every bit of her confidence. He wondered if she would have been happier to see him if he could have found her sooner. His tone became more somber. "You been well?"

"Yes. Scared at first up here. But they's a free black family and kind to me. Once I leave, they can help another traveler. Everyone know they do it, and no one say boo."

She took the paddle and tested the strength of the mixture. "Got about another ten minutes before it gets a trace. That's when the paddle starts leaving a trail when you draw it through." She drew through the thickening mass with ease. She nodded to the pail on the porch of the cabin in the shade. "Want a drink of well water? Dipper's in the bucket just there."

"Thanks. Think I will."

He drank and looked at her focus and strength. Had he misinterpreted their time together? How was Gabrielle so open and Ona so shy? Had he expected more? The sweat on the back of his shirt cooled and chilled him in the light breeze in the shade. He shivered and wondered if it was just the shade or if he had missed the love of his lifetime. He returned to her side and took the paddle from her again. She asked, "Tell me. How was your travel here?"

"Too long. I stayed silent a while, like you said. Then I started asking. Churches mostly. Let them check on me, 'cause I didn't want to cause no harm or lead nobody to you."

"You really been looking for me?" He nodded. She tipped her head, puzzled. "Just to see if I am fine?"

He nodded again, watching her expression change. Her smile was not the smile he had hoped for. There was no embrace. It was only a friend's smile.

"Well, James. I am fine."

He forced a smile. "Good. I've got news from Virginia."

"Tell me!"

He smiled at her. "First, about your sister, Philadelphia."

"How is Delphi?"

"Fine, I hear. She was given to Eliza, Missus Washington's daughter." He stopped himself before he said, "in your place."

"That poor child. Eliza can be so ornery." She paused a moment. "But Delphi is a strong gal and can fend for herself."

"Sounds like they gettin' on just fine. But I see how Eliza's not your cup of tea, you so independent and all."

She cocked her head as if to wonder what his intention was. "How'd you hear about this?"

"I was down in the Federal City to make some arrangements."

"You see her?"

"No. Just heard she's doing well."

"And my family at Mount Vernon?"

"I don't have any other news on that. But my sister, Sally. Even though she's taken up with Mister Jefferson for years now, I try to get her to come north. She won't even let me ask to buy her freedom papers."

Ona shook her head and watched how he pulled the paddle slowly. After a long while, she said, "There, it's thicker now. Look at the trail it leaves." She started to take the paddle from him. "Go sit a spell. Let me. It's gonna be another hour yet."

He kept it. "Let me help a bit more."

She left and went into the cabin for a few minutes. Crows were arguing with each other in an oak tree. When she returned, her headscarf was freshly tied, and a clean apron was over her dress. "Stay for dinner? Missus Jack got a welcoming way about her."

"I don't want to impose."

"I want you to stay." For a moment he searched for the depth of this welcoming. He hesitated, wanting to ask her to leave with him right then. She cleared her throat and said, "Please. I want you to meet John."

"John?" He suddenly heard his pulse pounding in his ears.

"John Staines." She pointed to a tumble of boxes beside a small shed and took the paddle from him. "Can you get those molds for me?"

As James brought them over to her, he asked, "Who's he?"

"Good man. Met him at church. Might be coming by after dinner tonight."

"Sounds like he's courting you."

She smiled then looked away. "Might be. Hope so."

"Maybe I'll meet him next time I'm up in these parts."

"Wish you could stay."

James forced a smile. "So do I."

Returning to Philadelphia, James resumed his former position and worked until spring, when he took his leave and again travelled north. Ona was no longer at the small cabin in Portsmouth. Recalling that she was sweet on a man named John Staines, he ventured to the newspaper office in Portsmouth in search of either the news of her capture or of her marriage notice, fearing either.

He found her marriage notice, posted on January 14, 1797, contacted the officiating minister who then sent a boy to ask Ona if James would be welcomed. The following day, the boy led James to Ona's small cabin outside Greenland, some miles past Portsmouth.

Ona was arranging the last of the wet sheets over the long clothesline strung between two trees near her own cabin. This cabin was even smaller than the one she had in Portsmouth. It was far enough into the woods that it wouldn't be found by accident. James called to her. When she turned, he gave the boy a silver piece and sent him on his way.

Hands on her hips, she smiled and shook her head. "Bless me. I was wondering how long it would take for you to visit again. Come in."

The interior of the tiny cabin was neat. Dusk was falling. He asked, "Want me to light the fire?"

"Please."

He dropped his canvas bag by the hearth. She watched as he easily stacked wood chips and struck steel to flint. After it flamed, she watched as he added thin branches. "I'd offer you a drink, but we keep a temperate house."

"Water's fine. Or tea. I brought some provisions. Always like a cook to buy too much local food to try. Can I cook for you and John tonight?" He added a few small split timbers and then a decent-sized log.

"He's at sea. Back in a month or two."

James stood quickly. "Should I leave? I don't want to make trouble for you."

She chuckled. "No one to see or care about my callers. But thank you."

Ona took the kettle from the small table and shook it. Finding enough water in it, she hung it on the hook above the flame. "How'd you find me? James, you still need to heed the blackbirders. Now some of 'em are working for the law. Snatch you off the street."

"Why'd you leave Portsmouth?"

"I had a scare and had to disappear. So? How'd you find me?"

"The way you said his name when I was here last time, I figured you got married the proper way, so I went to the newspaper in Portsmouth. Asked to see the old papers, looking for your marriage notice. I saw a name that looked like yours. Married for months now! Good fortune I got to see the papers at all. A lady there questioned me a good bit about if I could read or not before pulling out the papers and showin' me. Good-hearted though when I said I was looking for my lost sister."

"Am I your lost sister?"

"You are more a sister to me than my own blood, I tell you that. We see the world in a like manner. Always did. That paper spelled it John Stanes and Oney Gudge. Almost missed you 'till I sounded it out. That how you spell your names?" He paused and looked away, remembering that she could not read.

She poked him. "No need feel shame for saying that. My man reads and is teaching me so's we can read Scripture together. No notion why the paper spelled our names such. His is Staines and mine was Judge, like the man sittin' in the courthouse. But how'd you connect me from that? We wasn't married in Portsmouth."

"I went to Portsmouth's South Church and found the preacher who married you both, even if he did it here in Greenland. Reverend Haven's a cautious man. Not easily parting with how to find you. Made me tell him something about myself so's you could say if you knew me. But he was not so bold as to say it outright. Sort of danced about like, how you know this woman, who do you know in common, things like that. Very protective, he was."

"When his runner come up on the house where I do day chores for the lady, he be so winded that I feared that John's ship had…"

"Sorry to give you a fright."

"Then he says, 'Do I know a man called James Hemings who knows Hercules.' Then he laugh. I was so scared, then so happy I laugh too, until we both were sitting on the stoop, tears coming. Me 'cause I know it's you what found me, again. Him because he thinks you fought off some myth monster."

"Took me two days of waiting at the tavern in Portsmouth before the Reverend summoned me. Sent a boy to lead me here. I felt like a hitching post, sitting outside the inn for two days. Waiting for your permission."

"Sorry I caused you that expense."

He smiled. "Paid for part of my room by playing my fiddle in the dining room of the boarding house while I waited. Some dance tunes and then some French music."

"I'm glad you still play. I thought in Philadelphia, you'd just look to cooking for making your way. Hercules said you got a gift there."

"Been lucky. Played a violin for some elegant dinner. Fiddle at some barn parties. Same instrument, it is just how you look at it and what you ask it to do."

"'Lot like folks, I guess."

He nodded. "Imagine. You're a married lady now. I'm glad for you. Your John, he's a good man?"

"Yes. God-fearing and good to me. We both are working hard to hold on to our time here. I work for two houses, doing hard chores, nothing like being a lady's maid." She looked at her broken fingernails and chapped hands. "No sewing on silk any longer."

"I remembered you as a woman of faith as well as grit, so I hoped for the best. You safe here now?"

She took a deep breath. "Hope so." She rubbed her belly. James then noticed how she had filled out.

"Why'd you quit Portsmouth. What spooked you?"

"One day I saw the daughter of Senator John Langdon on the street. Lady Washington had visited her father's home in Philadelphia more than once, with me attending her. About had my heart stop, but I just put my head down so's my bonnet shaded my face and kept on walking right past her. She made no mention or call to me. But I thought I might die right there."

"Must have been awful."

"Was. After a few weeks, I figured I was on the good side of mercy. Then what happens? The Senator comes to my very door and tries to sweet talk me into going south on my own. I tell him 'no, sir' and close the door, figuring he'd be back with some rope to tie me up, so's I go visiting for a few weeks. Nothing. Then the Customs Master comes calling and makes me a similar offer, but nicer I say 'no thank you' to him too."

"You just said go away and they left?"

"Pretty much. Think Missus Washington don't want no stink over me running. Now that Customs man sorta gave me some light in this darkness, saying he was not to do more than relay the President's 'entreaties' to me. That's his word, 'entreaties.' But it was just a bale of feathers, and I knew it. 'Come home. I free you right off,' he say. How stupid do I look? If he wanna to do it, he can just send me papers up here, but he can't. I's a dower slave. You know, she don't own me so she can't set me free. Besides, I never hear her say a word in favor of letting any slave go. So that's a laugh. So's I tell him 'no, sir.' And he goes away."

"You know there was a notice in the paper when you left."

"I expected so, but that was a long time past."

"Think it's over now?"

"No. He comes back a couple months later, and his heart ain't in it at all. He say 'so precious freedom is' and I figured out later that President Washington is about to go back to Mount Vernon and that man's gonna be outta his job soon as Mister Adams gets into that seat, so he don't care a fig no more."

"How'd you hold fast to your hope?"

"Just did. Some many weeks later, a man called Burwell Bassett came up asking around. He was a nephew of Missus Washington and also a Senator. But nobody did nothing, really."

"By now, there must be slave hunters who know about you."

She nodded. "I figured time was past for them to be on the quiet about trying to get me back. So, I move to outside this little town."

"Here?"

"At first we had a room in a home in Greenland. It may be just under ten miles from Portsmouth, but it may as well be a thousand. But it was in town and people can talk."

"True."

"Remember that family I lived with at first?"

"The Jacks?"

"Yes. He died and his wife and daughters moved to this cabin here with me. Since John is at sea so much, we all live here. I don't think they wanted too much dust kicked up over me when Washington was President, but now, I'm just a sack of corn that she owns and wants back. Slave hunters looking for a profit could find me there all too easy. But not out here."

"They coming back soon? The Jacks ladies. I'll make a larger pot."

She shook her head. "No need. They's off to a relative for a visit, be back tomorrow."

"You sure you are gettin' on here?"

"Yes. What with my work cleaning houses, doing laundry here, and my sewing for others, we make a nice home. He's a sailor and gone most of the time, but when he come home, he brings his wages all at once and turn them over to me. Good man. Then off to sea again."

"You women are here alone?"

"Got friends, so's we never really alone."

Rather than return to Philadelphia and its memories, James worked for passage on a merchant ship that was making deliveries along the coast. It was at dusk, two weeks later, when the ship arrived at the port of Baltimore. James remained on the wharf after the delivery and ate with two crew members at an inexpensive tavern in Fell's Point they had frequented on prior trips. After his meal, he asked the innkeeper if he had a room for the night, which he did, and if he was in need of a cook.

The innkeeper told James about a larger tavern that might have need of help—Bay House, he called it.

CHAPTER 25

The Bay House and Tavern was neither the largest nor the most elegant of the lodgings for travelers in Baltimore. But it had the advantage of facing the city's main piers requiring any disembarking sailor with a thirst or passenger in need of a room to pass by its door.

James found it from the description provided by the innkeeper at Fell's Point. It was the only three-story, red-brick building with glossy black-framed doors and windows at the foot of the pier. It was an easy place to find summer or winter, drunk or sober. Even those landing at Fell's Point often found their way to the Bay House and Tavern, having either stayed there before or heard of it from shipmates. More often spoken of than the lodging or the food were the ample pours by the innkeeper, Charlie Singer, who ran an honest house.

When James entered the tavern at mid-morning, he was impressed by its orderliness. The first floor was dominated by a long dining table, several smaller tables for four, and six rocking chairs around a welcoming and ample hearth. At the rear of the room was the stairway to the lodging rooms on the second and third floors and a long bar that cradled several kegs of ale and cider. Beside the kegs were crockery jugs of rum, brandy, whiskey, and a large pitcher of rainwater. He wondered if each of the thirty-some seats were occupied once or twice for the dinner service. Thirty dinners to cook at the least; sixty or more if the inn were busy. A lean man with lead-gray hair delivered a tankard to a fellow at the long table and then came directly to James. "Help you?"

"I hope so. I am in need of Mister Singer."

"That's me."

"I heard you might be looking for help."

"You a cook? Mine's leaving soon."

James smiled. "Actually, I am a chef."

"What's the difference?"

"A cook makes the food you ask for, but a chef makes something new of familiar ingredients, makes what you wanted without your ever knowing you had a longing for it."

Singer chuckled. "And where have you, uh, *chefed?*"

"In France. At the Monticello Plantation in Virginia. In Philadelphia and New York."

"That's a lot of travel for a young man."

"I was chef to Mister Thomas Jefferson."

"The Vice President?"

James snickered. "By just three votes in the Electoral College."

Singer shook his head. "Well, half the folks here will love you for that and the other half won't. You a free man?"

"I am, sir." James started to reach for his papers when Singer shook his head. James nodded and continued. "I answered your questions, but I would prefer that you judge my cooking on its own merit."

"When could you start?"

"As soon as we come to terms after I see the kitchen."

Singer turned and limped toward the rear of the dining area. James followed him and saw a small but serviceable area with reasonably new pans. "What does the cook make here?"

Singer reviewed the tavern's current menu that relied heavily on fresh fish, crab, and cornmeal in mush or cakes. When he stated a wage, James grimaced and cocked his head. "Board included?"

He smiled at the negotiation. "Could be. How about I throw it in for two weeks while you cook, then if I think you are *chefing*, I'll make it part of your pay? Fair?"

"How many plates you serve a night?"

"Thirty to forty."

"If I bring that up to sixty by the end of two weeks, I get the board thrown in and a raise in six months."

"Deal." Singer pushed out his hand.

James soon felt at home in the Bay House kitchen. Singer occupied the suite of two rooms on the top floor overlooking the piers. James was given the small room next to his. A bell for late-coming lodgers hung on the brick facing of the tavern between their two windows so any pull to the chain by the locked door would wake them both. While the climb was inconvenient some nights, James found the view from the top worth it —as well as the boost in his salary when he took over the nightly cleaning of the dining room and answering the bell for late arrivals. He also tended to serve many of his meals personally to make certain that his customers were completely satisfied.

After six months, the dinner customers increased to the point that the lodgers had to eat at four in the afternoon or pay an added fee to dine later. In the summer, sailors ate early, crossed the bridge over the Patapseo River, found cheaper drinks and loose entertainment on the water at Fell's Point, and somehow made it back by midnight when the door of the inn was locked.

During his first year there, Singer's profits rose after James convinced him to use only the finest products, increase the range of fresh vegetables, have a dessert, and try some French sauces. James sought out the local farmers, fishers, and stockmen for their best offerings. Soon he was known to all the purveyors who stopped at his back door on their way to market. His reputation drew diners even in the heaviest of rainstorms or icy winter days. His craft and resourcefulness were tested in the severe winter of 1799 when the harbor was blocked with ice, travelers took refuge in the tavern, and both fishers and farmers had difficulty getting their products to town.

As the summer of 1800 began, James found his patience tested by the early discussions of the presidential election and the outright falsehoods that he overheard. In addition, his legs had begun swelling and bothering him when he stood for more than a few hours each day on the stone floor. By trading his boots for his old clogs from France, his feet were no longer pinched when they swelled. By wrapping his calves and focusing on his tasks, James tried to ignore his pain. He also tried to restrict his movement to the kitchen and pay little heed to the political arguments about which of the several presidential contenders should be selected for the ballot.

Soon, the Federalists had nominated both President Adams and his party's second choice, Pinckney for President. They were opposed on the Republican platform by Jefferson, who was the current Vice President, and Burr. All four were active contenders for the presidency.

By late summer, conversations over plates or tankards were punctuated by repeated arguments: Adams was senile, a monarchist, and a man of ill temper. His running mate, Pinckney, was at best mediocre and wanted to reduce the states' powers. Jefferson was said to be a coward who lived in luxury, too taken with the French to be trusted, and suspiciously unmarried. Burr was consistently derided as a power-grabbing madman, even by some in his own party, but at least he was not an atheist like Jefferson.

Some thought Jefferson, as Vice President, should automatically assume the presidency as Adams had from Washington, ignoring the fact that there had been an election. Others wanted to retain the free-for-all open slate of contenders without regard to party by which the President-elect was whoever garnered the most votes and the Vice President was second in the count, regardless of their affiliation.

The debates that had simmered through the summer came to a full boil during the fall. Adams, it was argued, wanted to strengthen ties with King George III against the bloody revolutionaries in France and alter the trade relations between nations. Jefferson supported France because it had supported the new nation against its colonial monarch, and continued trade benefited both countries. Hamilton's efforts to foment anger against France and rabid support of Adams led some to name his faction the "Ultra cause."

When James found the debaters lingering longer, he presented an idea to Singer. "As the election nears, they will want news fresh from the capital, not just to keep squabbling with each other."

"Yes. I would too. Should I go the expense of a courier?"

"It may be easier than that."

"How so?"

"The *Baltimore American* has a courier, and its editor is recently widowed and loves my cooking. If we had him dine here every night, his courier would have to come here with the news for him. Our customers would know the happenings even before the type was set at the press."

"Every night?" Singer paused to calculate the cost.

"That free dinner would cost you much less than a courier and make your tavern distinctive. With more diners, think how many more men would stay late at your kegs awaiting news."

Singer nodded. "I'll propose it to the editor the next time he is in."

During the fall, debate was somewhat muffled by reminders that the Sedition Act made it a criminal offense to speak ill of the government or its officials. This threat was frequently made by those in support of Adams. Jefferson took this as a violation of the right of free speech and many of his followers said so, even at their own peril.

Each of the sixteen states of the Union elected their delegates to the Electoral College at various times in November. In eleven of the states, the legislature elected the delegate, so most people presumed that votes would follow the pathway of the party holding the state assembly. Other states limited their representatives to the Electoral College to property-owning or tax-paying white men. Some states had a winner-take-all system; others let electors split their votes. Only one thing was certain: each state had to send its elected delegate to its state capital for the vote on December 3. The sealed ballots cast by the delegates were then transported to the new national capital to be opened on February 11 of the following year. Once those 183 men cast their vote as delegates to the Electoral College, the mathematicians and speculators went to work.

The rumors thickened until December 12 when the *National Intelligencer* had ferreted out the numbers and reported that Jefferson and Burr were tied with seventy-three electoral votes each, Adams received sixty-five, and Pinckney sixty-four. This only elevated the tone and volume of the fireside debates. Threats that Virginia would secede from the Union if Jefferson was not elected President echoed in the tavern's dining room and were met with the opinion, by those of Federalist leanings, that Burr should be elected.

Rumors flowed through the travelers and couriers with conflicting news of offers and counteroffers and of threats to the Union if either Jefferson or Burr were elected. Singer had to intercede during more than one debate and cut off cider to two of his regular customers who made their opinions known with their fists.

James shook his head when he overheard a farmer repeating Hamilton's faint endorsement that he thought Jefferson less dangerous than Burr. Fearing that the rumor of a tie could be true, word was sent to members of the House of Representatives to convene on February 11 to be present when the electoral ballots were counted. When the tie was officially announced, it fell to the members of the House to elect the President. Given the winter weather and distances to travel by horse or carriage, some people doubted that even a majority of members would be able to be present when the House was gaveled to order. In spite of a fierce snowstorm that swept through Virginia and all but crippled the new Federal City on that day, all but one of the 105 members were present for the vote count. And then to cast their own ballots to break the tie. The absence did not impact the outcome of voting on February 11, 1801.

They debated and voted. No majority was found. They voted again. The same result emerged. Again and again. Vote. Debate. Recess briefly. Vote yet again. At three in the morning they recessed, having cast nineteen votes on roll calls, and all ending in deadlock.

With the tie, and the repeated failure to break it, the Union faced a new threat. If the President were not elected, there would be a nine-month void of leadership until Congress reconvened in December 1801. This was a crisis that the new nation might not withstand.

Tavern customers tended to linger late at the fireplace or at tables over their tankards as much for the news of the election as for the food and drink. Hearing of the deadlock, the debates stilled. An iced silence saturated the room. Late Saturday night a courier arrived with news that the House was still at deadlock after thirty-three ballots. The next chilled courier reported that after two more votes, the deadlock remained, and the House would recess briefly.

When the House of Representatives reconvened on Tuesday, February 17, Jefferson was elected President on the thirty-sixth vote of the House when Representative Bayard of Delaware abstained in the vote.

A runner for the *Baltimore American* arrived at the tavern with the news of Jefferson's election. James retreated to the kitchen and privately raised a glass of brandy to the new President. On the other side of the door, tempers flared for a moment as others cheered in the tavern and along the pier. To quell the groundless speculation as to why Bayard had abstained, Singer offered a toast to the Union and the transfer of power was without the revolution and bloodshed that was consuming France.

A week later the few men at the fireplace took little notice when a young courier walked through the door. He could as well have been just another traveler. The snow on his heavy coat steamed before it started to melt. His coat, muffler, and wide-brimmed hat were heavier than those of the customers. Stamping the snow from his boots and brushing it from his shoulders, he proceeded directly to the innkeeper, who was at the beer keg drawing a tankard.

Singer looked up. "Good evening. What can I get you? A pint, some supper, a room?"

"Is there a Mister James Hemings here?"

"The cook?"

He nodded. "Yes. He cooks."

"Come along." Singer limped toward the back of the tavern and shouted through an open door into the small kitchen. "Mister Hemings? You have a caller."

The kitchen was barely ten feet by eight. James had his sweat-soaked back to the doorway and was frying scallops on a brick stove with iron plates.

James looked at the pan, not his visitor. "Be with you in half a minute."

The courier frowned. "Mister James Hemings?"

His eyes still focused on the scallops, he answered, "That be me."

The courier removed his gloves and unbuttoned his heavy coat. "Sir, I have a personal letter for you from President Jefferson."

He slid the sizzling scallops onto a plate of cheesed cornmeal grits, scattered a dusting of his spice blend over the top, and handed it to the courier. "How 'bout you give these to the innkeeper while they're hot and then we can talk."

The courier took the plate, smelled it, delivered it, and returned quickly. He stamped his feet to get some feeling back. The snow on his hat started melting. "Never seen anything look that good."

James downed a glass of water. "Tastes even better than it looks. Have a plate?"

He shook his head and sighed. "Wish I could, but I have orders to give you a letter and return immediately with your reply."

"Orders?"

The courier stood taller as he said, "From the President himself."

James looked up. "Want a cup of coffee? A brandy?"

The young man rubbed his hands together. "I said the President."

"I heard you."

He looked at the steaming mug James poured for himself. "A cup would be welcome. There's a chill out, sure enough. Most of the storm's blown past, but it's gonna be a cold ride back."

James looked at the courier, whose face was flushed and eager. "Here's the coffee. Dose it as you wish."

"Thank you, Mister Hemings, just the coffee. Been riding six hours."

As he reached for the steaming cup, James put his hand over it. "Have a glass of water first. Just hold the coffee to warm your hands."

"Why should I?"

"Your choice. But as cold as I think your teeth must be, this hot coffee could snap them off in a heartbeat."

He reached for the tepid glass of water James offered and nodded before taking a sip. He then took an envelope from his inner pocket and gave it to James.

After wiping his hands on his apron, James opened it with his paring knife. He read it, smiled, leaned against the wall, and read it again. He folded the letter and shoved it into his pocket. Then he stirred the last of the grits. He dropped a knob of butter into the hot pan and gently slid in two goodly portions of fish. "Like rockfish?"

"Sure, but I ain't got no allowance for that expensive a meal."

"Go warm yourself by the fire while I make you a fine waterman's dinner."

"But, the President..."

James smiled at the young man. "He has waited for my dinners before."

"But he told me to return with your answer soon as I could."

When James turned the sizzling fish, he gently shook the pan. "Ride back to the capital tonight? You're mad. That's forty-some-odd miles. That's a full day of travel."

"Might be for a carriage at a stiff trot, but not for my bay mare. She can get me back by daybreak. Got a full moon tonight and soon, the sky should be clear. He said 'straightaway,' and that's what I aim to do."

James divided the remaining grits between two plates and laid portions of the lightly browned rockfish on each. "And so you shall, when I give you my answer in the morning."

The young man looked alarmed. "I can't pay for a room and stable."

"Nobody asked you to pay." He sprinkled his seasoning powder over each plate and handed both to the courier. "Go sit down and start. I'll be back in a minute, I'm gonna ask Mister Singer to stable your horse and give you a room."

"I can't stay."

"Gotta. The weather's turned against you. Riding at night'll get you killed—and most likely that bay mare you are so fond of to boot."

Later that evening, when the fire was just embers, and the chairs were upside down on the tables, James swept the floor slowly. The courier started for the stairs to his room. James stopped. "Warm enough?"

"Yes, thank you."

"I'm almost finished. Want to join me in a brandy?"

He shook his head. "Wish I could."

"Then do. As my guest."

"It would be my pleasure to join you, sir."

James poured a short glass for each of them and walked over to the last of the fire. After he handed the courier his, James fell back into the chair.

"You all right, sir?"

"Fine. Just stiff from the day."

"Sir. That was the finest fish I ever had in my whole life. Thank you."

"Didn't like the grits?"

He blushed. "Of course I did."

James chuckled. "Come back in summer for the crab. It's really something special. What's your name?"

"Simon. Simon Farnsworth."

"How'd you get yourself into running messages for the President in the middle of a snowstorm?"

"My father said I should work for the new government. It was the first job I could find."

"What'd you do before?"

"Worked in my father's hardware store in New Jersey."

"Best you learn to read the weather. It wasn't going to clear nearly as soon as you hoped. You'd be in the middle of an ice storm if you'd left when you said. Now what good is a frozen messenger to anyone?"

"But the President..."

"Isn't in charge of the weather. Talk to a farmer or sailor or get a book. Learn that science if you plan to live through this job."

"Yes, sir."

James was tired and leaned back. "The President sent someone else before you. A week past. Right after he was elected. You know that?"

"No, sir."

James took a long draw on his brandy. "To summon me to the capital to cook for him. Thinks we're in Paris again. To *summon* me. I declined."

"But he is the President."

"And I am a free man. Not to be summoned by a master, a king, or even my President." James finished his drink.

The courier sucked in his breath and stared at him "You really told him no?"

James was precise in his answer. "I told his messenger that I would not be summoned but could be *invited.*"

"Is that what I brought, Mister Hemings? Your invitation?"

"I'll see you here at first light with my answer over breakfast. Storm'll pass by then. *Dormez bien.*"

"What?"

James smiled at his slip into French. "Sleep well." As he made the slow climb to his room, he thought of France. Unwrapping the bandages that calmed the pain in his legs and held down the swelling, he hoped he would dream of those days again—and of Gabrielle.

James declined the President's invitation and continued to work at the Bay House and Tavern in Baltimore. In May when the crabapple trees bloomed and hinted at summer, James created new dishes at the tavern, and dismissed thoughts of working again for Jefferson. As became his habit on Sunday mornings, James rose early, filled a mug with fresh coffee, and went to the end of the dock well before he expected the boats to return with the overnight catch. From his seat on a piling, he watched gulls dive between the whitecaps on the surface of the gray ocean that was still angry from the passing storm.

James felt the heavy footfalls on the planks of the dock. Turning, he saw a well-dressed man walking toward him. A young boy tagged after him, hurrying to keep close. He pulled a long twig behind him and let it chatter across each plank.

"Good morning, Mister Hemings."

James stood and looked at the man. Familiar face but his name escaped him. The man extended his hand. "Broadhurst. From Philadelphia."

"The lawyer." His gut tightened, remembering his failure to protect Ona.

He nodded. "We are visiting family here. My wife wants to be closer to her parents. I'm meeting with the Abolition Society here tomorrow to see if they could use my assistance when I move my law practice."

When James stared at the prayer book in his hand, Broadhurst asked, "Do you attend services?"

"No. But I know my Bible stories from Missus Jefferson's talking to us and my mam telling us about the folks of the Bible and about Jesus's caring for sinners. You a Quaker?"

"Why? Because I am an abolitionist? Does that require me to be a Quaker, Unitarian, or Methodist now?"

"No, sir. I mean nothing by it."

"No offense taken. I was an Anglican. But after our breach with the Church of England, I am now an American Episcopal. I owe no allegiance to their King, but only to my God."

After a pause, James said, "You'll like Baltimore. I've cooked in a tavern here for some time and find it most hospitable."

Broadhurst smiled. "Awaiting the fresh catch?"

James smiled and nodded toward the incoming boats under full sail. "Hard life being a waterman. Hope they had luck in last night's storm." The first of the boats dropped sail and turned to gently slide alongside the pier.

"The birds look contented enough with their leavings."

The small boy glanced at James and tapped his stick on the dock.

Broadhurst put his hand on the boy's shoulder. "Eli? I would like to introduce you to my friend, Mister Hemings. You might recall that he visited us in Philadelphia."

James shifted his mug to his left hand and reached down. "I am pleased to meet you, Eli."

"Thank you, sir." Eli extended his hand, slowly. James shook it once and was surprised when the boy pumped his hand several more times before releasing it and looking up at his father.

"Would you like to go and watch them unload the fish?"

"Yes, sir."

"Just that one boat. And wait for me there."

Eli tossed the stick over the side and ran to watch the baskets of fish come off the boat, some headless and gutted, others still squirming in deep containers.

Once his son had left, the lawyer turned to James. "It was Ona Judge, wasn't it? Did you ever find her?"

He nodded. "She's made a life for herself." He looked out to sea then back at Broadhurst. "I appreciate all you did."

"Where are you cooking? I might bring my wife."

"Bay House. It is suitable for families. Come soon; I'm thinking of trying my hand as a ship's cook so I might not be there much longer. Cooking for a full house, almost a hundred some nights, is wearing on me. Cooking on a ship might be a good change." James surprised himself at how easily he said it, then smiled.

"Well, best to you Mister Hemings."

Several weeks later, James was drying the last of the dishes in the kitchen when he heard the tavern's heavy door open. Only one oil lamp on the desk remained lighted in the large dining area.

Standing before him was a man dressed casually for a horseback ride in the country. James squinted at him and looked for a travel case.

"You need a room for the night?"

"Uh. No."

"Just closed the kitchen, but if you're hungry, I can make you a cold plate."

"Mister Hemings, I came to see you. I regret the hour but needed to speak to you in private."

James took a closer look as the man removed his hat. "That you, Mister Broadstreet?"

"Broadhurst."

"Of course. Come in. We can talk while I finish cleaning up. Been a long day."

"Thank you." He followed James to the small kitchen and stood in the doorway.

James picked up a glass that was draining on the counter and dried it. He looked at the man, who was fidgeting with the brim of his felt hat. He was attired in a light coat over a spotless white shirt. His trouser cuffs were soiled. "Well?"

"I am trying to think how to start. First, I believe I owe you an apology."

James held the glass to the oil lamp and when satisfied that it was polished brightly, he put it down and picked up a wet glass from the sunken tub that fit into the countertop. "Why? You did what you could do."

"On that matter, we were stymied by the manner of her ownership. But it is more than that. I think I was out of line when I lectured you on the law being what it is, limiting our actions. I was wrong. The law is made by the strong. *Justice*, however, comes from a higher place." He paused to find his words again. "There are things beyond what the law considers that are simply right and imperative to do."

James put down the glass and leaned against the counter. "Owner's gone to bed. I'm on my own time now. Want to sit down with a cider?"

Sighing, Broadhurst seemed relieved. "That would be most welcome."

James grabbed two pewter tankards from the rack and motioned toward the chairs by the fireplace. He drew the ciders, handed a tankard to the lawyer, dropped into one of the chairs, took a drink, and waited. The last of the heat from the fire still radiated off the bricks and felt good on his swollen legs.

"Mister Hemings, I have often reflected on your selfless effort to help that young woman and how I was not able to help you on that matter."

James laughed and held up his hand. "I was being far from selfless. I loved her and wanted her to be free so she could love me too."

"Did you ever tell her that?"

He shrugged. "Things changed."

"I am sorry. Do you know if she is still in bondage?" James took a long, slow drink but did not answer. "Sorry. I guess that is none of my business."

James shook his head. "As you told me, the law's the law." He expected Broadhurst to leave then, but the man remained rooted to the chair, staring into his tankard. James wondered at his comment. "This isn't about that, is it?"

"No. You started me thinking that sometimes there's a greater good than what the law allows. What'd you say? 'Sometimes the law isn't what's right.' Do you still believe that?" James frowned as Broadhurst continued. "Because, if you do, there are many in need of assistance who are beyond the reach of what the law allows."

James studied Broadhurst's face for a hint of his purpose. "You joined the Abolition Society here like you planned?"

"Yes. But they are not why I am here. Several of us have chosen to put our efforts into additional measures, beyond writing writs and lobbying for a remedy to this most loathsome assemblage of laws regarding slavery."

James leaned forward and placed the tankard at his feet. "Such as."

Broadhurst lowered his voice to a whisper. James put his elbows on his knees and moved in even closer to hear. "We assist the occasional *traveler* on their journey northward."

"Who is 'we'?"

Broadhurst shook his head slowly. "I am here on my own, with their approval. But because what I am about to propose has some element of risk, I regret I cannot provide their names."

"What are you to propose?"

"In the Negro section of town, there has become available a small house for sale that would benefit our activities."

"For an office?"

"No. Not for an office. A station."

"'Station?'"

"Like a stagecoach station. A place of passage. It would look better if someone else bought it. Someone like you."

"Someone with a darker face?"

"Someone who would not attract attention in that section of town."

James sat back. "You want me to buy a house? You think I'm made of money, just 'cause I came to see you once in a nice suit and now have steady work?"

"No. I considered asking for your assistance because I believe we are of a like mind on some matters."

"Our opposition to slavery?"

"That and the need to act now and not just wait for some miracle. Or for the law to change."

James crossed his arms. "How much is this going to cost me?"

"I will provide the funds if you were to purchase it for our use."

"And what would that use be? Specifically."

Broadhurst chuckled. "Must you ask?"

Frowning, James said, "Yes, if I am to make an informed decision."

"It would serve as a temporary residence. An occasional place for one or two travelers to stay. We would maintain the house. Stock it with food and the like. You should never even go there after the purchase."

"But you want my name on the papers?"

He nodded. "Just to buy it. After the deed is recorded, we would transfer title from you immediately."

"How does that make it different from you just buying it straight out?"

"We would execute a quitclaim deed immediately, as though you sold the property. This removes you from ownership. But we would not record that transaction."

"How does that work?"

"We would ask that you not record your sale and the new owner would not record his quitclaim deed of purchase until or unless some issue of ownership arose."

"Meaning it's *my* name on the property if the law catches *you* harboring a runaway."

The lawyer drew hard on the cider and wiped his mouth on the sleeve of his coat. "Yes. That is exactly what it means. But, in your defense, you show that you deeded the property away before it was ever used. Because if it is not yours, the matter ends for you."

"And how are you protected?"

"There is a way, but I would ask your forbearance not to disclose that information to you."

"When would I need to decide?"

"Soon. The location is uniquely suited to serve its function. I would ask you to consider the matter right away, as we need to move promptly."

"It's not in Baltimore, is it?"

"No."

"Where's this house?"

"About ten miles from town."

"On the water?"

Broadhurst nodded. James frowned for a moment, then asked, "Elk Ridge Landing?"

"Why would you think that?"

"Can't dock big ships there anymore. Not since they dug all that iron ore outta the banks of the Patapseo River and let the tailings sluice into the harbor. Between the tailings and the incoming ships emptying their sand ballasts before taking on cargo, the harbor filled and became the sole province of smaller ships with shallow drafts. So, with access only by smaller craft, the exports and population thinned, homes were abandoned or sold on the cheap. There are not many eyes to see who comes and goes around there anymore. Those remaining work upstream where the waterwheels power the mills."

Broadhurst tilted his head. "I can't believe it. How did you ever…?"

"That's red clay on your trouser cuff. Red clay in Latin is *Bole Armoniach*, as Captain John Smith called it in his journal of discovery. That's why he called the river the Bolus River."

"Exceptional. How did you know about that?"

"Not exceptional at all. Anyone having access to those facts could do the same."

"I doubt that."

"Once, I overheard Mister Jefferson and President Washington talking about surveys they had performed. Washington said he laid out the Gun Road from Dorsey's Forge to Elk Ridge Landing so the soldiers could cart cannon parts from the forge to the landing. Then they'd go by water to Annapolis for final fitting into cannons. That was when it was a deep-water port, shipping out hogsheads of tobacco, iron ore, wheat, flour, and lumber. Not like today."

"And your grasp of Latin?"

"Read it in a book." James picked up his empty tankard, then leaned hard on the arm of the heavy chair to stand. "I got more dishes to wash."

"I am sorry to have troubled you, Mister Hemings." Broadhurst started to get up.

"You sit there and finish your cider and let me think on it. I'll be done in a few minutes." As James dried the last glass, he thought how different this was from finding Jefferson an apartment in Paris and how very important this could be.

Within the week, Broadhurst had drawn up the various deeds and drafted the will that James had requested. Once the deeds were signed and the first of them recorded, James became the owner of a house some ten miles from his lodging and work at the tavern. Broadhurst provided James with the quitclaim deed and retained a copy in his office.

CHAPTER 26

As spring shifted into summer, James found that he was drinking more and later into the night. He often thought of his time with Ona. Draining his glass, he closed his eyes and waited impatiently for sleep to release him from his memories and the pain in his legs. Saturday nights were, for some reason, harder than other nights. Maybe the laughter from the tavern was louder. Maybe he just was not looking forward to the extra time on Sunday morning after he made the simple tavern breakfasts when his mind drifted to Ona, who would never be his.

Summer thunder woke him. He fought his tangled nightshirt and reached for the dregs of his whiskey glass in the dark. It skidded off the crowded table and shattered. He slid to the floor on his hands and knees and pushed the broken glass into a pile under the table. He reached for the edge of the bed and started to pull himself up. He slipped and found himself kneeling, muttering her name like a prayer, and wanting his pounding heart to be matched by hers.

He curled into a ball in bed. In the morning, he dressed, made the breakfast platters, and cleaned up like he did every Sunday, but it felt different this time. He filled his heavy coffee mug and walked to the end of the pier. The first of the overnight fishing boats was coming in. The restaurants and taverns would take the best of the summer's catch of shad, drum, rockfish, and cobia while leaving the remainder for the home cooks.

He sat on the end piling of the dock, watching gulls swirl behind incoming boats, diving when the trimmings were tossed over the stern. One of the smaller fishing boats drifted easily against the dock. Its worn rope bumpers dangled over its side and groaned as the boat was tied up.

He remembered seeing Ona at the market in Philadelphia, nodding to him, smiling, before she turned toward the flowers. He thought of her holding a glass of water in the kitchen of the President's House. Such an everyday moment. Light shined on the rippling water. She sipped, like that's all she lived on. Light as a feather, she was. He blinked her away and took a pull of coffee. Married now. Making her own way. He sighed.

He watched clusters of well-dressed families walk along the promenade. *Early church must have just let out*, he thought. *The parade of the pious*, he scoffed and instead turned his attention to the last of the incoming fishing boats. Before they had unloaded the baskets of fish, a four-masted Spanish windjammer rounded the point and pulled toward the harbor. He waited to watch the larger ship dock and heard shouting on its deck. He had learned enough Spanish in his travels to understand that he was hearing an argument unrelated to the commands for docking.

James selected his fish and sent the fisherman to deliver the basket to the tavern. Soon the captain walked down the plank that extended from the ship's rail to the dock. He was lean and well attired. His onyx hair was captured in a fresh ribbon at his neck. In halting English, he asked James for directions to a hiring hall for sailors; his cook had disappeared at their last port of call.

James laughed and said, "I'm a cook. *Un cocinero!*"

"*Gracias a Dios por la buena fortuna!*"

James asked for a tour of the ship's galley. And although he liked the equipment and arrangement, he soon discovered that the crew spoke only Spanish. The smell of dried fish and mold suggested a larder too lean and ill kept for his liking. James thanked the captain and suggested a tavern in Fell's Point that usually had sailors seeking a new ship.

Several days later, a whaler came in for added supplies before setting out on an expedition of several months. The stench of rancid whale oil from the coal-fired vats drifted over the harbor like death and excluded that ship from any consideration. These experiences dampened his interest in cooking on a ship. He now thought that working in a smaller tavern might match his waning physical ability. The pain in his legs was now accompanied by a general weakness throughout his body.

That afternoon, James told Singer that he needed to reduce the strain of cooking for the inn's diners. James proposed turning over the main cooking duties to a helper while James coached him to ensure that the guests were properly fed and the reputation of the Tavern maintained. Singer found a catch in his throat as he started to agree, and so he just nodded.

On a cloudy Monday three weeks later, the *Marie-Claire* docked and began discharging her cargo. She was a three-masted barque. The fore and mid-mast carried square sails. Triangular fore and aft sails were rigged to her mizzenmast. Watching the activity from the pier, James could easily envision these sails billowing full above the helmsman holding the spokes of the wheel on the quarterdeck.

While the cargo was being offloaded by net and boom, the jib sails on the ship's bow were cut free. The older canvas fell in a heap on the deck. No sooner than they had been cleared, new sails were unloaded from a wagon, hauled into place, and tied off. Pacing her length along the dock, James guessed her at two hundred feet and her mast height at over a hundred. Newly painted but not new, she was well appointed and clearly well maintained.

Just before noon, a sailor James had seen on the *Marie-Claire* came into the tavern. He struck up a conversation in French and learned that she was a freighter running between Europe and America with few passengers. Her below-deck workings were reserved for cargo, with small carpentry and other shops tucked into the bow. When James asked if the galley and cook were good, the sailor hung his head. In rustic French, he reported the loss of the cook at sea to what James understood to be a rupture of his appendix or some other organ of the belly a week before landing.

"How did you manage?"

"Oh, everyone lent a hand and made it work. Good provisions and basic food, we did fine."

"And how is your captain?" On hearing that Captain La Salle was good and the crew amiable, James took his meeting the sailor as a positive omen and went to find the captain.

Managing the movement of freight on deck was a big barrel of a man who James asked to show him to the captain. He pointed to the door under the quarterdeck, which he said led to the captain's quarters at the stern of the ship. James went aboard, crossed a newly scrubbed deck, and opened the door.

Rather than entering the captain's quarters, James discovered a bright room with a stained-glass skylight and several hanging brass lanterns above a center table that easily seated ten, five to a side on benches bolted to the deck. Several velvet-covered side chairs were affixed to the deck in the room's corners, making it as welcoming a parlor as any on land. It resembled a smaller version of the salon area of the *Ceres*, but with a steep stairway leading to the quarterdeck.

On the port side, walnut doors were opened providing ventilation to the tightly fitted passenger cabins. Narrow stacked bunks were attached to the interior walls. The cabin closest to the captain's was the largest, with bunks on both walls and a wardrobe with slatted doors built against the hull.

Each of the rooms had a glassed porthole with a sturdy wooden hatch that could be closed when the weather demanded. All of the portholes were open. A good breeze flowed through the ship. Before he knocked at the captain's quarters, James glanced at the brass plates next to the open doors on the other side. All were marked by function: chart room, first mate, quartermaster, and doctor. None were marked for a cook or chef. Past the dining table, he saw the brass sign on the imposing door: *Jean-Paul La Salle*. No title accompanied the name.

James knocked twice on the captain's door and stepped back as it opened quickly. La Salle was a tall, wiry man with a thick head of silver hair pulled back and tied with a ribbon at his neck. He wore a simple black suit and held a rolled chart in his hand.

In the formal French manner, James bowed and introduced himself. He said that he understood that the position of ship's cook was available, and presented his credentials, all in French. When the captain looked skeptical, James offered to cook on board while they were in port for the number of diners and in the manner the captain selected. When Le Salle agreed, James asked for the list of stores and victuals the captain intended to put on board, the number of passengers and crew, and the duration of the ship's next voyage.

His weathered face broke into a grin. "Cook for me, tonight. If your dinner is half as good as your confidence, I shall dine like a king and we can come to terms tomorrow."

James nodded. The captain laughed and gestured toward his cabin. "So, come in and we shall discuss tonight's dinner."

The captain said that he was entertaining a banker from Philadelphia, had intended to go to one of Baltimore's better restaurants, and told James what he had been interested in eating that night was a soup, crab or duck, some vegetables, and a simple dessert. James said he could prepare it in the ship's galley if he had the proper equipment. Together, they walked across the deck to the freestanding galley and storeroom, which were wedged between the fore and mid-mast. The windows here were of thicker glass than James had ever seen, and which let in light but distorted the view. He thought the idea of cooking above deck would be welcome.

As the captain watched, James clattered the nested pans and baking sheets to test their strength. He tossed two skillets on the stovetop. "These won't last another week. Cheap tin." He opened the doors to the coal-fired oven and tugged the rail around the stovetop. It was not the rustic hearth cooking he knew as a boy or the complexity at Restaurant Combeaux, but functional. "Quite serviceable. Will your passengers use the dishes from the galley or finer settings?"

"There is a better set in the parlor."

James asked to see the settings. On returning to the parlor, La Salle opened the locked chest attached to the walnut bulkhead beside his cabin, and James scanned the variety of platters, plates, and bowls that were set into wells in the chest.

He grinned, "Limoges china and good silver. I assume your passengers have some sophistication."

"Most will."

"Tonight, will you have just one guest?"

"Actually, three men will join me."

James nodded. "How complex a dinner do you wish?"

The captain said, "Impressive."

"And the wines?"

"There are cases below of bottled French and a cask of Bordeaux."

"And how do you wish the dinner served? Individual plates, platters for you to serve, or a buffet?"

The captain seemed confused by the alternatives as he paused and then smiled. "You are who you say you are. Who have you served?"

"I was *chef de cuisine* for Mister Thomas Jefferson when he served as our ambassador in Paris. The Marquis de Lafayette was a frequent guest. Here, for Mister Jefferson as Secretary of State, where his guests were numerous."

"And the crew was how many?"

"On the passage to France, I was given to the cook simply to assist, not as a cook. But I do have some knowledge of shipboard cooking. Twenty, I would venture, were in that crew; they ate simply. Six passengers and the ship's officers had more elaborate menus."

"And what would you need to supply my galley to *your* needs as a chef, not a mere cook. Knives?"

James patted his side and opened his coat to show the dark leather sheath that held his ten-inch chef's knife, and a four-inch paring knife in a slot on the front. "I carry mine. That way I know they are sharp as a razor and not damaged by being knocked about in a drawer or misused."

"French?"

James shrugged one shoulder as he had seen Combeaux do in a manner both dismissive and at the same time acknowledging the innocence of the inquiry. "Sabatier."

The captain grinned. "As to the menu? Surprise me."

"Fine, but the wine needs to complement. If you have a white Bordeaux, a Côtes-du-Rhône, and a Sauternes, I will build a menu on those."

The captain nodded. "I do. We dine at six, four of us. Set the buffet service on the sideboard there."

James nodded. "And your budget?"

After they came to terms and the captain gave him money for the purchases, James quickly bought the freshest and finest of Baltimore's summer bounty and was cooking within the hour. At five o'clock, he inquired if the captain had opened the first two wines, assuming the Sauternes would be opened just before service. He agreed to open the wines promptly.

James inspected the dinner service once he had set the table. He polished two plates and three glasses with a white cloth, approved of the silver settings, and adjusted a knife that was askew. Once each setting met his approval, he returned to the galley. At five thirty, James saw the captain, wearing a dress uniform with a gold braid trim, greet well-dressed men on deck and escort them to his cabin.

At ten minutes before six, James slipped into the white jacket he had brought aboard, buttoned it to the throat, knotted a white napkin at the neck, and carried a tureen of corn soup with bacon and clams to the sideboard. He returned promptly with a platter of crabcakes with a side sauce of a caper mayonnaise that he had learned from Combeaux. Next, he brought two platters of duck, the breasts dressed with an orange sauce, and the legs with a cherry sauce. Bowls of small, butter-baked potatoes, fresh garden peas with mint, and carrots with dill followed. Finally, James delivered a platter with a large apple tart, enveloped in an amber glaze that sparkled. He noted that the wines had been opened and were all excellent vintages from reputable producers.

At the sound of the first bell from the watchman on the quarterdeck, James tapped on the captain's door. When he and his guests entered the salon, James bowed and said, "Bon appétit."

The captain gestured for his guests to proceed. He walked James to the door, shook his hand, and asked to see him the following morning at ten. James nodded and left. He went to the galley, changed back into his light jacket, and left his white coat folded beside the stove.

As James walked down the dock, he recalled a frequent Bay House customer by the name of Grimes. His wide stance was that of a man accustomed to a deck shifting under his feet. Now, he worked in a ship's chandlery only a few streets from the harbor. James went to the large warehouse just as Grimes was putting away a length of chain into a large bin and preparing to close. The door creaked when James pulled it open just enough to enter. The fresh sea air was replaced with the competing smells of mold and rust and grease.

James looked around the warehouse. Shelves were filled with all sorts of items needed to operate a ship. There were stacks of small anchors and oarlocks for tenders. Another area had larger items such as binnacles and standing compasses for the quarterdecks of bigger ships. Racked and labeled were row after row of items, including cased instruments for navigation and buckets of tar, caulking, and painting materials. New lines on spools taller than James and old rusted chains in bins lined the right wall. Past them, used sails were folded into bundles as tall as a man. It seemed to James that all manner of goods, replacements, and tools for the repair of ships were on shelves or in bins in the large warehouse.

Grimes called, without looking up, "We're closed for the day."

James said, "Here to see you, Mister Grimes. Want me to wait outside while you lock up?"

"Who is it? Can't see with the sun behind you."

"James. From Bay House."

"Oh! James. Be right out."

On the cobblestone street, James squinted in the glare of the late-afternoon light as he helped Grimes slide the heavy door shut. Grimes snapped a hefty padlock in place and turned to James. "What brings you down here?"

"Thinking about trying my hand at shipboard cookery. Can we talk over a cider or a beer?"

"Sure."

"I'm buying."

"Aye, that's better yet."

As they walked to a dingy waterfront bar, James asked, "I heard that you were a cook in the British Navy. Is that right?"

"Some time back. Before I fouled my shoulder."

"I need some help on deciding what should be in the larder and hold for a crew of twenty-some. I never had to figure a month of supplies and menus but thought you must have."

"I did. I had the last word, although the ship's quartermaster thought he did."

"Why'd you join up?"

"At sixteen, I left me da's farm in Ireland. My thinking was as simple as this: I was a farm boy who hated being on a farm in the middle of nowhere. I had skills none but went to the city anyway. Soon enough I figured that if you were a cook, you'd be near food, and I'd never be hungry again. And since there was more certainty of the work at sea, that was the course I set for myself. I'd never seen the ocean, and the job they found for me was as a cook's assistant. It was a good life."

"My thought too."

"Well, there you go, lad. Was head cook for several voyages and a couple battles royal. Nary a scrape. Then I had a fall during a storm that left this shoulder frozen in place. Broken so's I canna reach over me head.

Got drummed out of the navy on account of it."

They arrived at the dim bar. James ordered two ciders. Taking a seat at a scarred table, Grimes continued as though he had but taken a breath. "But I missed the sea and talked myself into a cook's assistant job on a cargo ship. Fed the officers and crew on cargos for a dozen years, even with just one good wing. Then I got landlocked by a wench. Me wife and I been here ever since. She passed a year ago."

"My condolences to you."

Grimes took a slow drink. "So, anyway, I'm looking to move south."

"South? Not for me." James shook his head.

"Hold on there. A few years back, this fella, Basil Hayden, left Maryland with a bunch of other like-minded folks. All Roman Catholics they was, like me. Went south to the new state of Kentucky, they made of a lower part of Virginia. Now down there, they offer a man 400 acres on what's called a 'crib and corn' agreement."

"A what?"

"Give you two years to grow a crop of corn and build a cabin. Get it done and the land is yours, free and clear."

"But you're not a farmer. You said you hated it."

"I do! But me da was a distiller when we had excess corn or wheat. I'm gonna grow corn and make whiskey. There be a plenty of lads willing to work my farm for wages."

James grinned. "Well, you'll never be at a loss for customers, good times or bad."

"My thinking too. You sure I can't interest you?"

James shook his head. "As I started to say, I got an offer to cook on a cargo ship, with a few passengers. Could I get your opinion on provisioning a ship's larder?"

He nodded. James explained he was considering signing on the *Marie-Claire* but wanted to be certain that the victuals were sufficient. Grimes took a long draw on his cider and leaned back in his chair. "Let me share a word of warning: Always be sure there's more than enough.

Good idea to steer clear of a ship that shorted provisions. Signed on one a them once, a fisher, and it was deliberately provisioned short. They had extra rations and rum aboard, but we had to use our wages to buy anything. A chit against our end pay. Some of the fishers do that, makes the sailors slaves to their debt. Debt servitude, it's called."

"I see how that could happen."

"Easy enough. Some of the long hauls and ships of the line that I sailed years before the Revolution had good victuals aboard, but they also used supply ships to restock in battle or on an extended voyage. Now most private ships couldn't do that. Some of the whaler expeditions pooled funds and had suppliers come out to them, but not often. What is the *Marie-Claire?*"

"Mostly cargo. Rooms for about ten passengers, in high style. Dining in a bay that looks like a fancy parlor. Sailor I met said the they were well provisioned."

"That's good. Any failing seems magnified if it relates to food or sleep." Grimes then looked at James. "How long is this sail your thinking of signing on to?"

"Here to Amsterdam then Le Havre and then who knows."

"Some of the shorter hauls, a month or so with a small crew and space available, carry livestock and butcher as needed. Takes some skill to use all the fresh parts in a timely manner, or you can brine off and salt your own beef."

"Any idea how? I've just worked with fresh products."

"Sure. Did it meself as a lad helping my da. We'd slaughter in the fall and winter, so's we have the cold to make the fresh meat last longer while it is salting up. Here's how we did it."

James took a pencil from his case and made notations as Grimes spoke.

"First, get your storage vessels in order. You'll need well-coopered barrels, so nothing leaks in the brining or in the dry storage later. Second, get enough salts. You need about four and a half gallons of white salt and one and a quarter gallons of bay salt for every hundredweight of boned beef. Now I say boned, and that means some minor bones might stay in for the curing, but my da was not one to pad the barrels with unwanted bones to squeeze another copper out of a ship's master. He himself had been to sail and saw what a short weight of rations did to a man and to a ship."

James nodded, trusting that Grimes felt the true dimension of his inquiry.

"Now pigs and cows can get salted off the same, just butcher them so the cuts of meat are of similar size, not larger than a hand's breadth at the thickest. Then dry-rub the beef with white salt. Let it dry a bit, an hour or so, then put it into a brine."

"White salt as well?"

He nodded. "Takes about four or five days in a brine to remove and replace the blood. And you want to do this because blood is what causes the meat to spoil. After the brine, pull the meat out, let it air-dry for a half day, then layer it into a dry barrel or smaller casks, layering in bay salt then meat. The final step is pouring in fresh brine to the top and capping it. The salted beef stays in the brine until you pull it, soak the salt off, and use it. Mind, it is still going to taste salty, but it'll be safe to eat."

"Do you have a brine formula?"

"A gallon of water will take three and a half or four pounds of salt, less if you start with seawater. Here's the test. Can it float a raw egg in its shell? If yes, it will preserve. If not, you need more salt. Test it before pouring into the barrel of salted meat."

"White salt for the brine?"

"No need to go to the added expense of the boiled-off salt. The sundried bay salt will do. Use that from France or Portugal if you can get it."

"Anything else?"

"Check for leaks every day. If the ship gets wind and the barrel gets knocked about or damaged and leaks as a result, you need to transfer or use up the meat right quick before it goes bad."

"How about for a month-long sail? I didn't really know what stock was on the passenger ship we took to cross the Atlantic, as I was just a helper in the galley then. I never got below to the stock pens."

"Cook I worked for had me measure out the provisions so's we'd never run short. I can tell you *exactly* how much per man per week. Two key things to remember feeding a crew: keep 'em fed all day and give 'em a tot at night. Keep an open supply of hard biscuits—just flour and water—and make 'em the size to fit in a man's pocket and take aloft. Figure a pound a day, seven in a week. Don't skimp here, as this is what keeps 'em happy on deck. Something to drink at night. Now if beer, a gallon a day; if wine, a quart a day; if rum, a half pint a night. Depends on the ship and its storage capacity. For cooking: four pounds each of salted beef, salted fish, and flour. Oatmeal, three pints a week; rice...four pounds a week; dried peas, a quart a week."

James glanced up from his paper. "All dried goods?"

"Yes."

"Of course, as much dairy as you can manage to hold fresh. Milk for a week, butter and cheese for a couple months, particularly in winter. Butter, a quarter-pound and hard cheese, a half-pound a week. Put the butter underwater. Holds cooler and longer."

"Under water?"

"Float it in a keg filled with water as a big lump. Water holds temperature and keeps varmints out, including the crew."

"Drink?"

"Some rainwater for the passengers, if snooty. Stream water for the crew. You can use seawater for most of your cooking if it is clear and boiled. But for drink, the Navy ran on beer."

"I thought it was rum."

"No. Beer when I sailed mostly the North Atlantic. Not the stronger ales like here, but a watery beer. You could down two pints and not feel a thing. Like I said, rationed a gallon a day. On a sail once, we got wine, had to mix it one-part wine to two-parts water to serve. They said it was to keep the water from stinking, but I think the real reason was to keep the men from working drunk. Same as why they water down the rum to grog."

James made notes as Grimes continued.

"Then anything fresh you can get along the way. Once, a flock of geese hit an ice storm. We sailed into a hundred of 'em in the water, most dead, but the captain lowered a boat and had the crew pick up a dozen still alive. Put some in crates below. Can't tell you the stink from them shitting down there. Wrung their necks as needed and had goose dinners for a couple nights. You aren't going south, to the Indies, are ye?"

"No."

"Pity. Got turtles at a couple hundred pounds, call 'em terrapins. Fat on 'em is like butter. Flesh is the sweetest and most tender I ever et. Steaks to soups. Generally speaking, if your captain allows it, keep a line overboard and use what the sea provides."

"What are the best vegetables?"

"Use anything fresh as long as you can. Then peas. Dried whole or split. Any color, but the green ones take a bit longer to boil. Navy issued peas on pork days. They go well together."

"Potatoes?"

"No longer than your first week out. Too damp below. They'll sprout or go to rot. If you keep them on deck, the sun'll turn 'em green and poison the crew. If your captain insists, just keep a close watch on 'em."

"What did you use instead?"

"Rice."

"Anything else?"

"Feed your crew oatmeal every day. Twice a week for the passengers for their morning meal, fancied up with some raisins. But if the sea is rough, plain oatmeal for the passengers. Calms the gut and gives a lot of strength. Navy put oatmeal in place of salt cod. Tried to cut back on the salt the lads had to suck in every day. Proved a boon to their lasting power on hard days."

James looked up from his notes. "Any ideas for the passengers?"

"Figure the same amounts, but of better quality of foods. Fresh if you can hold a pen of chickens for eggs and later stew 'em. A couple young hogs, if you know how to carve 'em. Now, you can fancy it up how you want but mind you, there's a pull between the captain's purse and what it takes to keep a man going. Look at them slaver ships. Kept them poor souls in the hold on two meals a day, mostly horse beans and lard. Sometimes boiled peas or yams."

James shook his head.

Grimes continued. "We be an exceptional type of being, not like horses or cows. We can eat just about anything and survive, but you need a strong and happy crew—that's where your skill comes in. Best you talk to the captain and get his take on how he wants the passengers and crew fed. Tell him you want to see his list. Come back tomorrow night with it. I'll take a gander at it for you."

James put his pencil down and took a drink. "Thanks. I will do just that."

Grimes finished off his cider and pushed the empty tankard a bit closer to James. "Got your sea bag or a chest provisioned for yourself?"

"Not yet. Got my bowl and spoon, clothes, shoes, boots, a book, and my violin." James reached for the tankard and stood to get it refilled. "What did I miss?"

Taking the new cider from James, Grimes started his inventory. "You got a bunk or need to take your own hammock and bedding?"

"Don't know," James said as he sat down again.

"Whatever you take for attire, figure it will last about a quarter as long at sea. Get some heavy trousers, wide enough legs to roll up to keep dry when doing water work on deck. Shoes. Take two pair extras. And bring something to amuse yourself and others. Some rock candy or tobacco besides your fiddle." James kept quiet about his book of blank pages to journal his travel or his writing instruments.

"You got a cannikin?"

"What's that?"

"Drinking cup of tin, everyone has his own. And a watch, if you want to know shifts or times without being told by the watchman or staying half-awake for the bells."

"Have any watches in the chandlery?"

Sliding a battered silver case across the table, he smiled. "No. Take mine. Time it went to sea again. She's good to five minutes a day, so set her by the noon bell."

"But you'll need it…"

He shook his head. "Might bring you luck. You play cards?"

"Not really. Should I?"

Grimes laughed so hard his belly shook. "Farthest thing from it. Every ship has a card player who'll gladly liberate you from your wages and then your belongings. Stay clear of those sharks."

James finished his cider. "Thanks. I've got to go. Care for another?"

"Wouldn't mind."

James got a fresh tankard of cider from the barman and put it in front of Grimes. "See you tomorrow about noon."

As promised, the following day, Grimes adjusted James's list, padding it for insurance if the wind failed or they hit bad weather. He added more dried goods for the crew and passengers. He also increased the feed allowance for the livestock.

CHAPTER 27

On the last day of June, James met with Captain La Salle in his cabin. The early light was strong through the window of leaded glass bound between two sheets of clear for strength. It was hinged at the top to open on fair days like this one. Beneath it was a long sofa that became a bunk at night. The large map table was fixed to the floor in front of it and a portable chair was pulled up to it. The captain motioned for James to sit in the chair as he slid onto the padded sofa. A ledger book, inkpot, and quill rested on the large table.

"The dinner you made last week for my friends was more than I could have expected. My business partners were quite impressed. Now, about terms: we are a merchant ship and paid when cargo is delivered. So, a share, not a fixed payment, is how we do it. I can offer you a dual share as cook and sailor if you agree. Payable at our first delivery in Amsterdam."

James held both hands up in surrender. "Cooking is enough. I won't be climbing the shroud to the crow's nest for a look-see. I managed to do it in a calm sea when I was younger, but not again." James stopped himself from saying that he was no longer that strong or foolhardy.

Opening the ledger book, the captain wrote *James Hemings* and entered his promised share as a percentage. James scanned the listing of crew names above his.

"More than fair, sir, but all I require is my passage to France. If I stay on after Le Havre, then we can settle on a share."

"You would work for free?"

"No. For passage. I need to go somewhere."

He held out the pen. "I need to have a manifest with all crew names for the authorities."

James took the quill and then paused for a moment.

"You hesitate?"

"I have not seen all the sailors. Are there any... like me?"

"*Gen de couleur?* I don't know the word in English. No. There are no *gen de couleur* on this crew."

"Are any of your men going to have a problem with me cooking?"

"No. I have had once before a carpenter who was like your color. But no. Not on my ship."

James signed on the line beside his name and share, then turned the book back to the captain. "I signed as requested, but I do not expect this share. Now, are there any special dinners for your passengers that I should include in the provisioning?"

"No. There were only two passengers, but they became ill at the last moment. Without passengers, I decided to refit the cabins during this trip. I'll start as soon as we are at sea with my carpenter, then complete the fine fitting in Le Havre. Plan to occupy the cabin nearest the door to the deck."

"I'd be fine below deck."

"I don't make requests, James. Also, I expect you to join us at the table for dinners. Eat where you wish for other meals but expect to dine with my three officers and myself, served buffet style. Your experiences interest me, and we all enjoy a good conversation."

James nodded and handed his list of provisions to the captain. After reading it, he nodded and gave it back to James.

"Oh, and although you speak French quite well, our quartermaster is an Englishman, Jacob Redding, so please conduct your business with him in English. I want no misunderstanding on your needs or stores. However, I expect French to be spoken at the dinners, with you assisting Jacob when he needs a word or two."

"Certainly."

"Your ration listing was excellent. I will fund Jacob to accompany you to buy the fresh goods tomorrow. Bring your kit aboard early. He can arrange for the dry goods and livestock today without your assistance. I'll have him get you tomorrow."

James finished his work in the kitchen quickly and went to the front of the inn in the mid-afternoon. Singer was drawing a tankard of beer for an elderly man. Waiting by the beer barrel until he was served, James watched how courteous Singer was with him and thought how much he had enjoyed his time working for him.

Singer smiled. "Anything wrong in the kitchen?"

"No. Cook's doing fine. All set for tonight." James motioned toward an empty table by the fireplace and followed Singer to it. "Mister Singer, I wanted to tell you how much I have appreciated working for you." James struggled for words.

"That's kind of you, but I fear there is more you have to say."

"There is. Today is my last day working here. I will be leaving for France. I have taken a position on a ship to get me there." Singer sighed. James continued, "My replacement is doing fine and is able to work alone. If you wish, I can leave now and take other lodging."

"That's not needed. You are most welcome to stay here until you sail. And welcome when you return, Mister Hemings."

That afternoon, James bought a large sea bag and assembled in it what he would need for the voyage. He also bought a sturdy cedar chest for his violin case, extra clothing, shoes, and books. He sold what he could and gave the remainder to the cooks and cleaners working at the Bay House and Tavern. That night, a messenger delivered a package for James. It was an Episcopal *Book of Common Prayer* with a note from Broadhurst wishing him well. Inside the front cover was written in the same careful hand, "To open the hardened heart and heal the broken heart." James put it into his wooden chest and wondered who would visit that cabin near the red clay.

At six in the morning on the first day of July, James carried his sea bag over his shoulder and amber cedar chest in both hands as he lumbered down the dock to the *Marie-Claire*. A sailor on deck took the chest from James and carried it to his cabin. James followed and had only unpacked half the clothing in his sea bag before he was interrupted. Jacob called his name, waited for him on deck, and marched ahead of James toward the marketplace.

As they worked their way through the market stalls, James thought that shopping with Jacob was nothing like the joy of being at Les Halles with Gabrielle. Jacob's transactions were swift, his manner curt, and he paid little notice to James or his remarks about the quality or pricing of items on the list. When Jacob complained about the lack of apples, James directed him to a vendor offering an early crop from the south. The outing had a sour overtone that James could not understand. The quartermaster seemed uncomfortable and hurried to complete their task. Over the next hours, all was delivered and put below decks. Later, when they passed each other on the ship, it was as though James had become invisible to Jacob.

James was on deck when the *Marie-Claire* left port late in the morning on the third day of July. As they cleared the harbor, two sailors went to the wood handles at each end of a long metal arm that pivoted above a bulky contraption. One man undid the binding and pulled up while the other reached overhead, grabbed the opposite handle, and pulled down. The function became clear to James as he heard the water splashing into the sea. His alarm was evident as he looked over the side. A passing sailor clapped him on the shoulder. "Not a worry. Just emptying the bilge."

"Are we leaking?"

He laughed and shook his head. "Just runoff from swabbing the lower decks and some rain. Best we lighten our load for speed and handling. Don't worry. She's a good ship or I wouldn't be on her."

James fired up the stove and oven. He cooked for the entire crew at once although the outgoing and incoming crews ate in two shifts, one right after the other. This reduced the use of fuel and insured that the hot food was eaten quickly. From his galley on the top deck, James simultaneously prepped the light, cold lunch for all and the dinner stew for the crew. He watched the sailors, who were in perpetual motion and whom he planned to make available an apple or biscuit for between meals. When something of interest occurred, a sailor would motion or call to him. Stepping to the rail, James would marvel at a pod of porpoises, or a line of pelicans passing low over the water.

When they lost sight of land, James grinned, thinking he was at last on his way to France and a new life. Jacob stopped by the galley to grab an apple from the barrel by the door. Looking at James, he asked. "What's the smile for?"

"Can't see any land."

He sighed. "If you miss it that much, you can scurry up the mainsail shrouds for a last look. You can see almost twelve miles from the top of the main mast."

James laughed. "Not I."

Jacob tossed the apple in the air and caught it with a downward swipe of his hand. Ripping a bite out of it, he turned and marched to the open forward hatch and checked on the livestock in pens and crates below.

Dinner that first night introduced both James and his cuisine to the other officers of the ship. Without instruction, James set the salon's long table with a white cloth and the best china and wineglasses while the crew's stew was still cooking. Although there was ample space for diners using both sides of the table, he set a place at its head for the captain, using a movable chair. The other four places faced each other, with the diners to be seated on the upholstered benches, which were bolted to the deck.

After sending the crew an excellent beef stew and a pot of potatoes mashed with cream, he laid out the buffet that had taken all afternoon to prepare. Making several trips from the galley to the salon, he arranged the metal bowls with hinged covers and platters of roasted lamb, carved and surrounded by small red potatoes that had been tossed with butter and parsley, bowls of blanched green beans with slivered, toasted almonds and another of minted fresh green peas. The captain had declined a dessert for the meal.

At the sound of the watch change at eight, three men emerged from their cabins in fresh jackets and stood chatting as James brought the soup tureen into the salon. The older man in a white jacket with silver hair, he guessed was Doctor Bretonneau. Jacob Redding, he knew was the quartermaster. The last man, tall with blondish hair, was regaling them with a story in French. "In Barbados, there is a beach with sand as white as a Dutchman's ass. Truthfully, the water is green. You can see the creatures crawling on the bottom. Warmest swim I ever had. Like being in your lover's arms."

The doctor turned to James and extended his hand. "André Bretonneau. Do you like swimming, James?"

He shrugged. "I don't know."

Poking him in the shoulder, the tall man said, "How could you not know? You do or don't."

"I don't know, because I never learned."

He howled with laughter. "What? A sailor who can't swim?"

Doctor Bretonneau asked, "Why ever not?"

"Once, I was enslaved," James said. He noticed Jacob shifting uncomfortably, but continued with his explanation. "Slaves were discouraged. Not being able to swim made escape more difficult."

The doctor broke the uneasy silence. "Captain says that you've cooked for the King of France. That was years ago, obviously."

James adjusted the platters so that all were perfectly aligned before turning to respond. "Once. I just made the dessert."

The tall man chuckled. "What was it? Eyes of pigeon soufflé?"

Before James could answer, La Salle entered and strode to the head of the table. All stood at silent attention until the captain sat. James waited until each found his seat before claiming his. Doctor Bretonneau was to the captain's right, the tall man was to his left. Beside him sat Jacob. James took the seat across from Jacob. The captain looked over the group. "Have you all introduced yourselves?"

The tall man extended his hand. "Jean Bouvier, First Mate."

The captain then asked, "James? What have you for us tonight?"

James motioned to the sideboard. "To start, I have prepared a crab and corn chowder. We have roasted lamb, baked red potatoes, and sides of fresh peas and green beans."

The captain stood and went to the tureen, ladled out a healthy portion, and returned to the table. Once all were seated again, James noticed that there was neither wine nor water on the table. He asked, "Should I have a water pitcher in the future, sir?"

"Yes, a decanter with short glasses. I neglected to bring the wine. Could you fetch the decanter from my side table? It's a claret from Bordeaux, just drawn from a large cask below deck." Conversation was minimal as all sampled the superb cuisine. After compliments were given, the diners found a balance between eating and light conversation about where they had sailed and how James learned to cook. To James's delight, each of the diners found a favorite food and returned for added servings until the platters were emptied.

James fell easily into the routine at sea, making oatmeal and scrambled eggs in large bowls to send below deck for the crew. Eggs were fried or poached with slices of ham for the officers. Lunches were simple cold meats and cheeses with apples, which could be eaten on deck or at the tables below. The tables hung from ropes, so that they moved with the ship and held the plates without sliding. Dinners were whatever James decided to make, to the delight of the officers. The second night, he presented a dessert of a moist chocolate cake with a hot chocolate sauce over it. Only after serving the dessert did James realize that it was Independence Day. He celebrated it alone in the galley by having a piece of cake and remembering the celebration in France years ago with ice cream in the heat of the city.

The third day out, James brought the captain's morning coffee to his quarters at precisely eight bells, as instructed. The captain was reading the scale on the stick barometer on gimbals near the door and frowned when James entered.

"Your coffee, sir."

"You know what this is, James?"

"A barometer. Mister Jefferson had one like it at Monticello and another in Paris. It had a round scale on the bottom. The mercury tube ran up a thin wood frame to protect it. Said it looked like a banjo to him."

"Know how to read it?"

"Not really. Just that when the pressure changes, it means a change in the weather."

He pointed. "See where I put the little brass marker yesterday morning? Look where the mercury is now."

"Much lower."

"Very much lower. Dropping fast. Just above the 'wet weather' mark, so I figure there'll be a storm by nightfall."

"Really? The sky right now is robin's egg blue and nary a cloud."

"Nothing to be alarmed about, but I thought you should adjust your menu. Expect some toss, so soup might not be the best idea tonight."

"I could serve it in mugs."

He chuckled. "A thought for another day. Plan to feed the crew early, hot food by three and have a cold buffet available after that. A bucket of apples and hard biscuits on deck and below for the men. I'll let you know if anything changes. Have you ever cooked in a storm?"

"Not really."

"Before it begins to pitch, I want your pans secured in cabinets and the fires doused. Not banked or scattered. Doused with water, both oven and stove. I'll take no chance on an ember hitting a sail or the deck."

"Absolutely, sir. I'll hurry the stew so I can douse my fires at any time."

As James left the cabin, he noticed the captain stacking the light side chairs and pushing them to a corner that had a hinged rod to contain them. He wondered how big a storm it might be, as the mercury in the tube now had fallen below the "wet weather" line.

By ten, white thunderheads filled the northern horizon. By eleven, the clouds were darker. Shortly thereafter the first mate arrived and asked if James could serve the officers dinner at two o'clock. James nodded. While selecting from the buffet of sautéed steaks and fried disks of potatoes with a side of green peas, the men did not engage in the light chatter that had characterized the first two dinners. Once they were seated, the captain was crisp and formal.

"James? Crew fed?"

"Yes, sir. Fires doused and pans secured. Just these dishes left to wash and get to their cases."

"Good. Jean, double tie the sails and break out the storm sail. We'll run with just the course and jib for now and set the storm sail in a bit." He held his hand to prevent a response. "I know. We'll sacrifice speed and distance for safety. We've had this discussion before, but as we are heavily laden, my decision stands."

Jean nodded. "Rig the lightning chain?"

"Yes, but don't launch the keg until my command.

"Doctor Bretonneau?"

"Ready. Surgery is prepared."

"Jacob? Cargo and stock?"

"Cargo is double lashed. I've secured the coops and pulled in the railings on the pens, so the pigs won't slide around. Put out extra feed to calm them. Should we keep the canvas or put on the heavier wood hatch cover?"

"Wood. Easier to get on and off."

The first mate sat taller. "Sir, my men are up to it. They know it's 'Save the ship, save your mate, and then save yourself.' They have big hearts and strong backs." The officers ate in silence and left when their plates were empty. James gathered the tableware on a tray and hurried to the galley to wash the plates and cutlery.

Sailors scrambled aloft and brought the sails on the fore and aft masts up into tight rolls along the yardarms and tied them even tighter with added coils of rope. Only the large course sail and jib billowing over the bowsprit remained. Their speed dropped and the ship rocked violently from side to side. James had to brace against the door jamb to dry the last of the dishes. For the first time, he felt the motion of the sea in his stomach and swallowed hard to fight it off.

The storm sail was brought from the forward hold by pulley. Once it was in place, the ship's speed increased again. The crew used the same pulley to haul up the solid wood hatch cover. The ten-by-ten foot cover had a foot-wide rim on it that snugged over the raised cowling of the hatch. Jacob then flipped the metal latches to secure it. The first mate sent a crew aloft to gather the course sail and tie it to the yardarm.

A sailor ran to the galley door. "First mate says you got biscuits for me to take below." As James filled a canvas sack from a barrel, he asked, "Why don't you just use the regular sail?"

"Storm's made of stronger canvas, double thick. Won't tear. See, we need forward motion, so she don't broach. If she goes sidewise, the waves'll hit her broadside. If they go over the rail, we could swamp, break up, or even tip her mast into the sea." James handed the canvas bag of hard biscuits and a second one of apples to the sailor, who then sprinted toward the rear hatchway.

The wind had picked up and now whistled across the hatch covers. Clouds had become a solid bank that looked like sooty snow.

Once the length of chain was on deck, a sailor strapped himself into the harness of the bosun's chair and took the ring end of the chain. Just as the rope tightened to hoist him aloft, Jean stopped him. "Back that line off, sailor. You ain't gonna be fried on my watch! We got a lightning charge in the offing. We'll walk the chain up by hand, so everyone stays grounded if we get a sudden strike."

The sea was rougher now. Trenches were as tall as a man. Foamy trails ran down the side of the breakers.

James finished drying the tableware and struggled to keep his footing as he crossed the deck to return it to the salon. Sailors scrambled up the shroud lines. The first mate gave a call and the large ring at one end of a chain was passed to the first sailor on the webbed shroud. The chain, with links as long as a forearm, was passed up on the call of "Hoist!" hand to hand to the crow's nest. With one unified last pull, the end ring was heaved once again and slid over the top of the main mast. The chain was released by the line of sailors and dropped straight along the mast. The remaining hundred feet of chain puddled on deck.

While the chain was being set, a stocky sailor carried a small keg to the railing and dropped it there. The keg had a twenty-foot line with what looked to James like a large canvas bucket tied to one end. The other end of the keg had a large metal ring on it. The sailor left his keg, took the end of the chain, and bolted it to the ring on the keg.

As James passed the sailor tying off the rope, he stared at the pile of lines and canvas. "Is this like a lightning rod?"

"Yeah. This here canvas is a sea anchor. Pulls the keg and chain away from the ship so's if we get a strike, it'll go into the sea, not the ship." James tried to smile but felt anxious as lightning arced between dark clouds and thunder rumbled in the distance. A second squall, heavier and longer than the first, wet down the deck and dropped the temperature. The wind increased over the next hour. By four that afternoon, whitecaps were blowing off the peaks of waves and the troughs ran eight to ten feet. The ship sailed steady, quartering the waves to avoid a headlong pitching or swamping in a trough.

Then the wind blew harder.

The low rumble within the thicker clouds in the distance grew to the sound of wagon wheels over stone. Within minutes, the sound increased to cannon booms. The bank of dark-gray clouds covered them, hastening the twilight.

"Away the sea anchor!" The first mate, Jean, shouted a second time. Only one sailor turned toward him. Jean ran along the railing, tapping sailors on their backs and pointing to get the crew he needed to hoist the keg and chain overboard. As the keg hit the water, the chain ran off the deck and scuffed paint from the railing. The keg drifted alongside and banged against the hull hard enough for James to feel the deck vibrating from the assault.

When the sea anchor caught, the keg pulled away like a kite on a string. The chain ran tight. The ship quivered and tipped slightly. James looked at the helmsman, who was now buckled into a harness. He put his full weight on the spokes of the wheel until the ship regained its balance.

Soon the roar of the thunder was as constant as a battlefield. The bolts slicing between the clouds lit the sea to a bright white. When the wind gusts came, they were strong enough to send the jib sideways and shove the bow to port.

"Jib! Line..." James turned to see the first mate gesturing for three other men to let out the jib line. They rushed and saved it from ripping off the ship. A moment later, the wind reversed. The sail and slack line snapped back.

"About! She's coming about!" As they were frantically hauling in the line, it snagged under a corner of the forward hatch cover and snapped it free of its four latches. The next gust pried off the wood cover and sent it spinning over the starboard rail and into the angry sea.

The sailors who saved the jib now dropped the top line and let the sail slide down enough for other sailors to grab a corner and gather it down on deck. While still attached to its lines, they pulled it over the open hatch and held it in place with their bodies.

They braced their feet against the cowling to avoid sliding into the hold when the ship pitched. In a moment, the carpenter arrived with lengths of batten. Working from the forward edge so the wind and water would run over the canvas, he nailed the wood strips securing the canvas to the cowling in just minutes. But by then the ship had taken on enough water to make her handling sloppy and unpredictable.

Jean skidded his way along the deck to the bilge pump. James saw him loosening the rope that secured the rear handle of the pump and ran to help him.

"We're taking on water! Jump!" He pointed to the high end of the rocker handle. James sprung up and barely grabbed the slippery handle. His weight pulled it down. Soon they were seesawing the rocker rapidly. Jean shouted then motioned for James to tie a line around his waist. James braced against the mast and tied on a line, leaving enough slack to return to the handle. As he resumed pumping, he saw the helmsman fighting to hold the ship's wheel.

CHAPTER 28

The rain squall passed. It was twilight when the first bolt struck the mast with a deafening crack. The lightning ran down the chain as planned. When it reached the keg, it exploded. The chain still ran from the mast, but now it draped over the port rail, glowing red, rainwater sizzling off it, and branding the outer rail and hull. The flash fell hardest on the helmsman, who was looking forward. He kept his grip on the wheel and held a steady course, although flash-blinded and unable to make out any but the largest of images for the next several minutes.

The ship heeled hard to her port side, her portholes nearing the waterline. Before the helmsman could right her, a second strike hit just under the chain's iron ring, severing the main mast below the crow's nest. The tip of the mast was over the water when the weight of the chain yanked the charred timber straight into the sea. The sudden loss of weight snapped the deck back past level, rolling hard to starboard for a moment. Sailors scrambled to keep their footing.

James felt like he was inside a ringing cathedral bell. His skin tingled and his hands throbbed like they were in an oven. He saw Jean's mouth moving. The ship righted. James worked the pump as hard as he could. Jean shouted something that James could not hear over the buzz in his ears. He motioned to pump faster.

The third lightning strike was to the foremast at the uppermost yardarm. The mast above it shivered, exploded, and sprayed burning wood across the foredeck.

"Fire!" Jean shouted as he dropped his tether and sprinted toward the bow. James turned to watch him. The shredded sail had sizzled, ignited, and was now a wall of flame. Looking back, he saw the helmsman's face covered in blood. He turned forward to call for help and saw all the sailors pushing the burning canvas and spars overboard with their bare hands. Once shoved over the railing, the tangle of canvas, rope, and timber formed a flaming island that was still connected to the ship by its thick shroud lines. Mast fragments the size of fireplace logs blazed on deck. Sailors kicked them to the rails, doused them with water, and threw them overboard.

James stayed working the pump. The burning island of shattered mast and tangled sail pulled at the foremast and heeled the ship to port. Sailors skidded down the steep deck and slammed into the heaving pile of broken rigging at the rail. Only James and the helmsman were still lashed in place.

The mass of floating debris pulled at the ship as if it were a harpooned whale. The carpenter grabbed the fire axe off the deck's mounting and hacked away at the shroud lines, which were the size of a man's arm. Chips of tarred hemp were sucked away in the shrieking wind. All but two of the lines had been severed when James saw it. A white shirt on the island. Someone struggling in the tangled ropes on the edge of the flaming raft of debris.

"Man overboard!" James screamed. Nobody heard him. With shaking hands, he struggled to untie the wet rope around his waist. When the last shroud line was severed, the raft spun in a whirlpool of the ship's side wash. The ship righted. The sudden pitch threw several sailors to the deck.

James shouted and pointed again. No one saw him. James watched as the man held on to a blackened spar with one hand and tried to climb onto the raft of ropes. He slipped and slid under water. The sea and rain quenched most of the flaming canvas. The little island was almost dark. James started to scream for help again as the man's head bobbed up. The sailor had pulled himself on top of the lines that were now twisted around his legs. He had collapsed, face down on the matted ropes, waves cresting over him.

James saw a loose rigging line attached to the debris sliding past him across the deck. He drew his knife, severed his tether with one stroke, and automatically slid the knife back into its sheath as he dove for the slithering line. The others were still in the bow, too far away to help. He grabbed the line, hoping impossibly that his weight would stop it. It dragged him on his belly toward the quarterdeck. He flipped to his back and bent his knees planning how he would brace into the railing, stand, and tie off the loose end of the line. He hit the rail. The force shot him to his feet. The line went tight. He saw the man slipping off the debris pile in the water.

James held fast and was launched overboard.

He felt the shock of the icy water but clung tight to the end of the rope. He sank into the silence of the sea. A moment later, he hauled himself, hand over hand, toward the debris. Saltwater stung his eyes. He could only see the small amber fire above him. He pulled on the rope to get beyond the surface and scrambled onto the floating island.

"Overboard! Man overboard!" James shouted into the wind's roar. As the ship passed him, he could see that the helmsman was looking forward and turning to starboard, away from the smoldering timber and canvas.

James pulled himself to the center of the mass on the tangled ropes just as the ship's wake tossed him high onto the debris pile. He grabbed the sailor's shoulder and rolled him over, pulling his face out of the water. His head fell to the side.

It was Jacob Redding.

"You can't die! Not now!" James slammed his fist against Jacob's breastbone again and again. The raft lurched. James's fist hit the man's soft belly. Jacob gagged and threw up seawater. When James hit his chest again, he started gasping for air.

Blood from a cut above his eyebrow smeared Jacob's cheek. He motioned to his limp arm by tilting his head. "My arm. I can't swim."

James laughed. "Me either."

James splashed seawater onto the smoldering canvas until all the embers were out. As dusk deepened, he cinched ropes around the charred timbers and sailcloth. Once he had mounded pieces high enough to hold their heads above water, he lashed Jacob to the top if the floating debris pile and hooked his own arm under the rope.

Then James passed out.

When he woke up, he saw Jacob tugging at the rope with his good hand.

The debris shifted. "The rope's gone slack. Tie me on again." Within an hour, the height of the storm passed. Somewhere after midnight, the sea calmed to a gentle slapping against their makeshift raft. James saw a half moon and stars. He heard Jacob talking to himself.

"What?"

"Nothing. Get some sleep now, if you can. I'll stand watch and wake you if I see anything or need you to spell me." After checking that Jacob's rope was still holding, James fell asleep.

At dawn, the clouds were high and light. James jerked awake and was relieved to see Jacob sitting as high as possible on the raft. James opened the pocket watch that Grimes had given him just weeks earlier for luck.

Jacob laughed. "You're late for starting breakfast."

"They'll notice us gone, soon enough." James held the watch as high as he could and randomly flashed it around. After a while, he asked, "They'd see my signal, wouldn't they?"

"Maybe. When they discover we're missing the captain will sail a series of triangles back to where he thought we might have gone over."

"How long?"

"He'll run the pattern a couple of days. Longer if I know him, and if others are missing too. We just need to make it easy for them to see us. Stay high on the raft. Keep signaling."

"Even if we can't see them?"

"Yes. Sort of like talking to God." Neither of them mentioned the real possibility that the ship might not be able to sail back and hunt for them until repairs were made.

James put away his dull watch and took out his knife. He held it high above his head and waggled it. An hour later he changed hands and continued to flash it at an uncaring horizon. The sea calmed to an easy roll. During the last of the rain, Jacob had tugged at the canvas to form several wells. They drank them dry by noon. The sun was bright. By three o'clock, both had blisters on their lips from the salt water and sun.

Just before the watch on the *Marie-Claire* changed at four, a sailor aloft in the bosun's chair saw a flash. He shouted to the helmsman and pointed off the stern. Jean, the first mate, ordered the course adjusted. Within a minute, the sailor saw it again and yelled a second time. Soon they were on a direct course. The flashes were continual and bright enough for the bosun and three men on the bowsprit to see. In moments, all were at the rail.

Captain La Salle ordered the signal cannon fired. Aboard the makeshift raft, the only thing James heard was the lapping of the waves and creaking of the timbers now barely lashed together. Jacob started laughing. James scowled. "What?"

"Didn't you hear it?"

"What?"

"Our salvation." On the second sharp report from the cannon, James fell back on the raft, laughing.

A half hour later, the *Marie-Claire* was within sight and the men at the davits were ready to lower the tender. James thought he heard the captain shouting, "Away! Away the tender." The wake of the ship passing them spun the mass of debris so that it followed the vessel. Now the distance between the ship and their floating island increased. James watched the sailors pulling hard on their oars.

As the tender approached, they saw the captain in the bow of the tender. La Salle gave the order, "Starboard ship oars." Sailors on one side lifted their oars and the tender slid sideways next to the charred debris. The sailors who hauled them into the tender were bruised and several had bandages on their arms. James asked, "The helmsman?"

La Salle smiled. "Lucky man. Just a nasty cut on his forehead. The glass didn't get to his eyes when the compass exploded. Everyone is accounted for, now."

When the sailors helped Jacob into the doctor's cabin, he was applying a salve to a sailor with a burn and then wrapping his arm in gauze. Two others sat at the table with their hands in gauze mittens.

The medical examination cabin still had blood-stained clothes piled in the far corner. The room smelled of sweat and rust like the butcher barn in Les Halles. James could see brownish smears and smudges on the doctor's light coat. His stubble was gray and his eyes bloodshot. Jacob sat on an elevated examination bunk while Doctor Bretonneau wrapped a length of sheeting around his ribcage and shoulder to hold Jacob's arm across his chest. "Bruises. Cracked ribs. Only a dislocated shoulder. I'd figured it for broken when they hauled you aboard. Keep it in the wrap for a few days, then in a sling. In a couple weeks you'll be right as rain. At least it's your left arm." He turned to James. "It is beyond me how you both didn't drown out there. The water's cold enough to have you lose grip."

James nodded toward Jacob. "He had us stay on the very top of the sailcloth."

Jacob turned with great effort to James and smiled. "The stock? How'd they fair?"

The doctor muttered, "Chickens and ducks fine. Pigs took a beating, one died."

Jacob asked, "Think you can dress it out?"

James shook his head. "It's not safe. Guts have tainted it by now. But we have plenty for the voyage, even with this delay."

Doctor Bretonneau did not look up from his bandaging. "Captain's turning about."

Jacob held the bandage in place. "I thought the carpenter could make a new top mast."

"He could cobble it together," Bretonneau said. "But the ship's rigging is in tatters. Crew has more heart than sense at the moment. And our compass is useless."

"Doesn't the captain have a spare? I heard him…"

The doctor withdrew a scalpel from a basin of bloody water and shook it. He pointed to a large iron bolt on the porthole and laid the scalpel against it. It held. "Magnetized. Once this happens you can't trust any compass, even his spare."

James asked, "Is the ship ruined?"

"No. A new compass can be set right, calibrated. That's what those large iron balls on the binnacle do, adjust the magnetic field to balance out the iron on the ship."

"How do we get home?"

"Captain's going to navigate by the stars." Tying off the ends of the bandage, the doctor then patted Jacob lightly on his back. He turned to James. "Could you help him to his bunk?"

Without answering, James took Jacob by his good arm and helped him to his cabin. James started to leave but hesitated in the doorway. "Can I ask you something?"

Jacob winced as he squirmed to get comfortable. "Yes."

"During the night, you kept talking low. I couldn't make out what you were saying. Were you praying?"

"I don't know a lot of prayers, but I do know my hymns."

"But you weren't singing."

"Just the words. I memorized the words to one that's most important to me. Maybe it was my prayer."

James nodded and went to check the condition of the galley.

It took the *Marie-Claire* ten days to limp back to Baltimore. During that time, the most severely injured sailors were bunked in the passenger cabins. Those with burned hands were fed by the able. Dinners for the officers and crew were served in three shifts in the salon. All were treated to wine and cuisine fit for a king.

James was at the rail as the harbor came into view. The captain announced his intention to anchor, take a tender to shore, and make arrangements to go directly into the repair dock. James reported that the kitchen was in order and asked to be relieved of duty and go ashore. Jacob came on deck from the salon and walked to the rail beside him. He looked at the sea bag and chest beside James. "Are you sure you won't change your mind and finish out the sail? It will be a good wage at the end."

"No. I think I am better on land."

He winced as he adjusted his left arm in the sling. "I don't think there is a man aboard who would agree with that."

Jean called to James from the quarterdeck. "Harbormaster's tender is coming off the dock now. Five minutes."

Captain La Salle came on deck with his tricorn hat in hand. He joined James and Jacob at the rail, watching the tender pulling toward the anchored ship. He turned to James. "I am not certain how to say this."

James smiled. "Sir?"

"You signed on for shares, but..." Jacob took a step away to allow them privacy.

James shook his head. "I expect no payment. I know that comes after the goods are sold."

"James! The men respect you and join me in hoping you will sail with us after the repairs are made. I will gladly pay your board ashore and a fee for the past two weeks of your service. But that is in no way the repayment you deserve. You saved the ship by manning the pump, and you saved someone's life." He nodded toward Jacob.

"You give me too much credit."

"I don't think I know another man who would have done what you did. But you risked your life for a man who showed you not the simplest of courtesy that I saw during any of our meals. Why?"

"We all need another chance."

"You showed him a mercy that was exceptional."

"Exceptional? I think not but thank you for saying so."

"We'll be in port at least another two weeks to fit a new mast and rig lines. You'd be welcome if you change your mind."

"I think my sailing days are over."

"But you said you needed to go somewhere."

"I do."

Jean then motioned to the captain, who went to the quarterdeck and waited there for the harbormaster's tender to pull alongside.

Jacob returned to his spot beside James and glanced over the deck. He spoke softly. "James? You asked what I was saying during that night. I was not very forthcoming with you."

James turned and looked at him.

He swallowed hard and started speaking as if reciting something he had practiced. "I'm from a little town north of London, a small village called Olney. Poor place of farmers and old women making lace. One of our own was a slaver, then he became a minister in my church. That's where I heard Reverend Newton preach. Most of 'em there can't read, so his sermons were cut of simple cloth of words and rhymes. There's a friend of his, Mister Cowper, what helped on that. He's a poet, so his ability with getting the words right is a blessing to Reverend Newton."

James sensed Jacob's discomfort and looked out to the water again.

"I hear him say his sermons when I'm home. He writes some of 'em as hymns in a book. I found that book in a store in Philadelphia. Published in ninety-one, some coffee or tea stains on it, but of no accord. It was like going home to read them. Keep it in my sea chest and read one or more every night."

James nodded. "And is that what you were saying? The words of a hymn?"

He nodded.

James frowned. "But I thought church hymns had music to 'em."

"Like I said, he wrote words. Let people put whatever music fits 'em, just so they sing 'em."

"I didn't know you were devout."

He laughed. "I'm a sorry sinner. Trying to mend my ways."

"You mentioned the pastor."

Sighing, he continued. "John was once a libertine. But he found himself. He left his ways as a profligate and slave trader to become our minister in Olney."

"You call him by his first name. Is that common in your church?"

"No. I knew John. We sailed together."

A shiver ran through James. "You worked a slaver?"

Jacob shook his head back and forth as though waking from a bad dream. "God forgive me, I did."

He took a folded page from the sling cradling his left arm and handed the paper to James. "Here is what I said that night. This is what gave me hope. I think I copied it right. Someday I hope you read it and think kindly of me."

James took the page and slipped it into his pocket. He shook Jacob's hand and picked up his canvas sack. A sailor carried his chest to the rail and tied a light line to the rope handle. The captain hurried past them and down the rope ladder. Once he boarded, James followed with his sea bag over his shoulder. When he got his balance in the tender, he took his chest from the sailor, who lowered it down to him.

That night he had dinner at the Bay House and Tavern. Mister Singer was not in the tavern. James took a room for the night from an innkeeper he did not know. The next morning, he pulled the page from his jacket and read it.

Mister James Hemings:
You asked what I was saying through our long night.

This is what brought me comfort.
I wish the same for you in your travels.

This is Hymn 41 of the Olney Hymnal.
Written by my friend and pastor, John Newton
with help from the poet Mister Cowper.
Please put it to what music you find pleasing.
He titled it as Faith's Review and Expectation:

> *Amazing grace! (how sweet the sound)*
> *That sav'd a wretch like me!*
> *I once was lost, but now am found,*
> *Was blind, but now I see.*

> *'Twas grace that taught my heart to fear,*
> *And grace my fears reliev'd;*
> *How precious did that grace appear*
> *The hour I first believ'd!*

> *Thro' many dangers, toils, and snares,*
> *I have already come;*
> *'Tis grace hath brought me safe thus far,*
> *And grace will lead me home.*

> *The Lord has promis'd good to me,*
> *His word my hope secures;*
> *He will my shield and portion be*
> *As long as life endures.*

Yes, when this flesh and heart shall fail,
And mortal life shall cease;
I shall possess, within the veil,
A life of joy and peace.

The earth shall soon dissolve like snow,
The sun forbear to shine;
But God, who call'd me here below,
Will be forever mine.

Ever your humble servant and brother in Christ,
Jacob Redding
This sixteenth day of July, 1801.

James blinked away his tears, folded Redding's paper, and placed it carefully on a small side table. After some minutes, he went downstairs for breakfast. James was enjoying his eggs and sausage when Singer came into the room and greeted him warmly. "James! I hope this means that you've come back to cook."

James laughed and put down his fork, genuinely happy to see his former employer. "No. Just to stay a while as a boarder. I did not recognize your night man."

"Just hired him to sweep up after closing. Did he give you the envelope?"

"What envelope?" James asked.

"The one the courier left for you just after you sailed. It has your name on it."

"No. I don't think your night man paid much attention to my name."

In a few moments, Singer placed an envelope bearing a wax seal on the table beside James. "I told the courier you'd gone to sea, but he insisted on leaving it."

"Thank you."

"Aren't you going to open it?"

"In a bit."

James finished eating and took the envelope with him as he walked to the end of the dock. Sitting on a piling, he slipped the tip of his smaller knife under the seal and opened it carefully. James read it slowly and looked over the harbor. It was a second invitation from Jefferson. This time it was to cook at Monticello during the President's summer retreat there in August and September. James let the page dangle from his hand as he looked at the horizon. Just for two months. A chance to see Mam again. Sally. Visit Bob and Dolly and finally meet their children. *This just might work*, he thought. The idea of cooking in the French style after so many years made him smile.

James sent word that he accepted the position and would be at Monticello by the first day of August. He left his sea chest and sea bag with Singer for safekeeping and traveled with just a small valise and a change of attire.

He stopped at Richmond to see his brother before going to Monticello. Bob and Dolly had a comfortable ease about them in their small attic room. Their children took to James, and soon he had both of them in fits of laughter with tales of when he and Bob misbehaved as boys. When the two fell asleep—Elizabeth on his lap, Martin beside him sitting on the floor—Dolly picked them up and got them into bed. Bob and James went outside and sat in the garden, shared news of their lives, and watched fireflies in silence. Bob did not mention that his brother looked and moved as though he was far older than his thirty-some years.

At Monticello, Jefferson greeted James with affection and asked about his adventures. Short who had again joined Jefferson, made a brief appearance to acknowledge his arrival. Petit stopped by the kitchen regularly to laugh with James and discretely encourage Peter to do more of the heavy work and task Lizzie with more of the preparation.

Soon, James limited himself to making the sauces and finishing the plates with decorative flourishes like delicately carved carrots or sprigs of dill. After the kitchen work was finished, James enjoyed his evenings and seeing his mother and other siblings again. The family told stories and laughed at the exploits James dramatically recounted. Sally remained in the big house and dined with Jefferson. Still dressed in the finery she had worn for dinner, smelling like lily of the valley eau de toilette, Sally visited her mother's cabin once a week for an hour or so to see James.

Before the summer's end, even assisting Peter in cooking the complex meals for scores of important guests every day was straining James's constitution. He reluctantly admitted to himself that even wrapping his legs no longer contained the swelling or reduced the pain.

In early September, James dressed in his old homespun shirt, vest, and long trousers after he had packed his valise. In spite of the summer heat, he buttoned his vest and tied the string at the neck of the shirt. He stopped just before the doorway to Jefferson's study and set down his bag. When the heard the scratching of the quill stop, he tapped on the doorjamb. Looking up with a frown at the interruption, the President snapped, "What? Can it wait?"

"I am afraid not."

Jefferson took a second look and then noticed the valise. "Where do you think you are going?"

"Away. Peter can manage well without me."

"Now? The summer recess is not yet over. I need you here until I depart at the end of September."

"Respectfully, you don't."

Jefferson shoved his chair back forcefully and stalked to the door to confront James. "What? You want to leave now? You are so ungrateful."

"Grateful I am, sir. Grateful for what my life has become. Grateful that you taught me to read so that my world opened, first, here in your library, and then you gave me a real world. I read your French lessons, but learned to pronounce words from Marie, just as you had planned. Grateful that your Latin primer was here too."

"I'll never understand you, James. Never. Latin? What could you have learned from that?"

"From your Latin book. There are two phrases that come to me almost daily now."

"And those are?"

"*Memento mori*—remember that you will die."

"Wherever did you hear that?"

"I overheard you telling Mister Short, lecturing to him before you left the first time for France. In your absence, I read and discovered it to be a Latin phrase suggesting he needed to attend to longer goals and perhaps his legacy."

"You got that from just my tone?"

"At first. Later I figured that you wanted to inform him that he needed to attend to his conduct lest he be ill remembered."

"You astound me."

"I applied it to my life. It altered how I saw my choices. I know my time is not infinite; that someday I will not be here."

"James?"

"Sir, I am dying. I have not told my family, lest they fret. But, I cannot return to this place. But you deserve to know why I quit you before the summer is gone. The work has become too much."

"*Memento mori.*" Tears welled in Jefferson's eyes. His face went pale.

"But even as modest as my life is, it is *my* life. To live. And that is what I intend to do. To my fullest capacity."

Jefferson hid behind his intellect. "And the other? You mentioned another phrase."

"*Ubi sunt.*"

Jefferson nodded and smiled. "*Ubi sunt qui ante nos fuerunt?* 'Where are those who were before us?' Why did you think of that?"

"Perhaps because you had underscored it in your schoolbook when you were a student. I tried to understand it. Even then, you were thinking of your legacy."

"Legacy?"

"How in centuries to come you will be remembered, as I will not. Not after Mam and Peter and Bob and Sally pass."

Jefferson nodded slowly. "And how do you wish to be remembered, James?"

"How? I hope as a good man. One who is honest and possibly a master of my craft."

"James. I do not know what to say."

James picked up his belongings. "I hired a wagon to take me to the stage stop. I shouldn't keep it waiting."

"Godspeed, James."

James turned back to Jefferson. "I beg you to consider your legacy. How do you want to be remembered? As the slaveholder who had a moment of enlightenment and freed his cook? Or as the man who severed the roots of slavery's poisoned tree for his country by stopping the importation of men and women and children in bondage. You know that act of kidnapping or rape begins every slave's life. You can stop it. You alone."

Jefferson blinked back tears. "I could have my doctor..."

"It would not change what I know to be true. My heart is failing."

Jefferson stood and grasped James's hand in both of his. "Then, so too, is a part of Monticello's."

"Au revoir, President Jefferson."

"Goodbye, Mister Hemings."

CHAPTER 29

Over the next week, James travelled to Norfolk to find a ship that was sailing to Portsmouth. Having booked passage, he went to the open-air market. By nine he had finished picking over the offerings for the best of its late-summer vegetables to add to his heavy canvas sack. He found carrots, celery, okra, onions, a small bag of flour, a larger one of rice, and a big knob of butter, and finally sassafras root, and ginger. At one of the last stalls at the far end of the market, a vendor sold a dried spiced sausage. He bought a link that was a foot long.

He boarded the *Pilgrim* at ten. The tide turned at eleven. The ship set sail eight minutes after the noon bell. James stood at the rail and watched the land disappear, then went to his small cabin below deck and put his legs up to stop the swelling.

He thought back on where his journey had taken him. From a plantation where slaves ate from their weekly allotment of a peck of cornmeal and a half a pound of dried beef, pork, or flour-salted fish from Jefferson. Anything beyond that came from their own gardening, trapping, or fishing. Jefferson even let some of them raise chickens and rabbits.

A new world had bloomed for him in Paris. Gabrielle. Eating truffles with what they called a capon, a rooster without its balls. James chuckled as he wondered who'd ever thought to cut the balls off a live rooster? Hold it down, make a knife cut at the base of the backbone by the second rib, put a long horsehair loop down a straw or hollow bone, catch them little balls, and pull the loop tight. Bam. All gone. Easy as that. Those French, going to such trouble just to create something different. A lot like Jefferson: never satisfied with things as they were. And Sally taking up with Jefferson, conjuring her idea of a future with him at Monticello.

He relaxed and let the ship's easy sway drift him into a light sleep. He dreamed of when he and Sally were little and the summer that they had grown too many watermelons. They sold them off to the big house and Missus Jefferson paid them a copper each and gave them a sweet. Long before Mam's hair was all white, when he was just a small lad and ran all day in the sun, when Sundays were big meals with the other children, when Missus Jefferson told Bible stories, and all his brothers slept in a pile like pups.

When the *Pilgrim* put in at Portsmouth three days later, James bought crab, shrimp, and fish from different boats. The deckhand on the last boat gave him wet seaweed and a small canvas bag to protect his purchases.

At the stable near the stagecoach station, he hired a horse for a week with the understanding that if he returned it sooner, he would receive a refund. An older bay mare was saddled. A feed bag and grain for a week filled her saddlebags. He lashed his valise and purchases to the horn, where they bounced against the bay's shoulders. In less than two hours, he was at Ona's cabin in Greenland.

James tied the mare to a tree near the cabin and rapped on the door. He stepped back three paces when a burly man yanked the door open. His oatmeal-colored shirt strained over his chest. "Yes?"

"Pardon me, sir. I was looking for Missus Staines."

The man stood taller and filled the doorway, leaning one elbow into the frame. "And who might you be?"

Before he could reply, Ona came to the door. A little girl toddled after her. "James? Is that really you?"

He pulled his hat off and bowed slightly to the shadowed figure in the doorway.

"Oh, James. It's been so long a time." She stepped into the light of the afternoon, took the man's arm from the doorjamb, and put it on her shoulder as she smiled at James. "This is my husband, John."

Extending a callused hand, John nodded. "Pleasure. Heard 'bout you."

"Pleasure to meet you, sir." He turned to Ona. "Had some time off, so I came to offer a down-home meal, like I promised you. Brought enough if the Jacks ladies are here."

"They go visiting when John is home. Courteous that way."

James nodded and pointed toward the bags dangling from the horn of his saddle. "That be the end of the good tomatoes and okra for the season, straight from Virginia. Thought I'd bring the last taste of summer up with me. There's a bag of Carolina rice in there too. Found good things at the dock in Portsmouth as well."

John clapped him on the shoulder and helped him untie the bags. "You ride up with all this on your horse?"

He laughed. "No. I sailed up from Norfolk and hired the horse in Portsmouth. Best I start to cooking if you want your kingumbo tonight. It needs to stew off a while. I thought to fix it up then be on my way."

Ona held the hand of the squirming toddler. "You stay and eat. Be a treat for us to have company and news." John nodded and took the reins of the horse from James.

The child hid behind her mother's long skirt. James smiled at her. "She's beautiful. What name did you give her?"

"Pearl." James started teasing her by whispering her name. Soon she was peeking around her mother. In a moment she was toddling toward James, who picked her up. Her short hair was like a frizzy halo that smelled of rosemary soap. But there was something else about her, like puppy breath or a meadow on a hot day.

John asked, "Got any of your own?" Pearl squirmed and John put her back on the ground.

"No. Never found the right person. Glad Ona did."

Ona glanced at her husband. John smiled at her and turned to James. "Hope you'll spend the night here, James. I'll put a blanket out for you by the hearth."

She touched John's arm. "Remember, I told you that when James visited before Pearl was born, all we could do was laugh on how the only thing we missed from the plantation was the food. Now look at us. He's cooked for kings and me up here where okra won't grow." She turned to her husband. "Ever had it?"

"Can't say I have."

She nudged her husband as they entered the small cabin. "At Mount Vernon, there was three kinds of kingumbo made in three different slave cabins." She laughed. "Each said theirs was the finest. What's yours like, James?"

James smiled when he smelled the freshness of the soap she had made. "Mam used tomato, okra in equal parts with onion and whatever meat we had. Rabbit or chicken, mostly. Marie, who worked in the kitchen at Monticello when I was a boy, said in New Orleans they add shrimps and sausages. Mine's a bit of all theirs. Then there be the last of the seasonings, salt and pepper, while it cooks. Hold off adding the sassafras leaves or powder until it's off the flame, lest it go bitter."

Ona said, "Never hear that."

John asked, "What can I do to help?"

"Get your biggest pot hot over the fire." James glanced around and discovered a smaller pot. "Can you start some rice? Got a bag of it just there."

John added wood to the fire to get a strong flame under the large blackened pot.

"While the big pot heats, I'm gonna get everything ready. They call that *mise en place* in France. Gonna shell the crabs and shrimps and *filet* the fish. Then cut up them vegetables."

John asked, "*Filet?*"

"They say *découper en filets*. Cut it so it got no bones in the pieces. Want me to do that outside or on the table here?"

John picked up the sack of seafood and a flat pan. "Let's go outside." As they left, he called to Ona, "We be out a while so wanna feed the baby?"

Ona nodded from the doorway and scooped up the toddler.

About twenty minutes later, the men returned to the porch. John stopped and rapped on the doorjamb. "You decent?"

"Come on in."

James carried the pan of prepared fish, crab, and shrimp. "All I gotta do now is chop my vegetables and sausage. I like to start with okra."

Ona threw her head back and moaned. "Oh, my. Haven't thought of okra in forever."

James asked, "John? Can you put a pitcher full of water in the pot to heat up while I make the *roux*?"

John frowned. "Make what?"

"*Roux*. Nothing but butter and flour. Take equal parts and stir it around in the skillet until it's brown as coffee. Gonna smell cooked but not burnt." He leaned over the skillet and let the butter come to a bubble before adding the flour. All the while he stirred and mashed the browning paste. John watched as he bent over from the waist.

John used his foot to nudge a stool closer to James. "Want to sit?"

"Thanks." James sat down hard. When he was stirring the flour into the bubbling butter, as he had done a thousand times before, he thought of how he had once longed for Ona, and now he wanted only her happiness. He found himself smiling and his shoulders relaxing. If she was happy, then so was he.

Once the *roux* was made, he scraped it into a side dish, and put more butter in the pan. He cut the okra into rounds while the butter heated in the skillet, then he added the slices. "Gotta cook it slow and easy 'till it gives up that ropey look. If you don't, it just goes to slime in the pot."

Ona watched as the okra changed under the gentle heat. "Can I cook with you? I'd like that."

"Sure, chop them carrots into rounds and quarter the tomatoes. Chop the celery and green peppers to whatever size you like. Then put it all in the pot."

John playfully tossed the toddler in the air. She giggled. James glanced at the child and laughed, hoping that sometime in her childhood

Ona had known this joy.

Ona held up an onion. "This too?"

"No. I'll cut them like the French do and fry them before they go in or else they push all the other flavors aside."

After he added the okra to the pot, he took his chef's knife from the sheath on his belt, sliced the onions into perfectly uniform pieces, and tossed them into the hot skillet and shook it.

John peered at the well-honed knife blade and whistled. "That's some fine toad sticker you got there."

"French. Served me well." James shook the skillet again and sniffed. After the onions lost their initial acrid smell and were translucent, he added them to the pot. "Good, now all we gotta do is toss in the sausage and let it start stewing." James washed and dried his knife and left it on the mantel out of Pearl's reach.

John pointed to the pan of seafood. "What about that?"

"We add 'em at the end with the last of the spices and the thickener, otherwise they'll just fall to shreds. Got about an hour to wait. Then we add enough water to keep it soupy."

Ona called out from the other room. "John? You want some ashcake to go with dinner?"

He smiled at his wife. "If it isn't too much trouble for you."

"Happy to do it. Why don't you men take the baby out for a while and let me get my cooking done in peace?"

James teased Pearl. "Ready for a walk? Really? Think you want to come with your daddy and me?"

She giggled as she toddled to her father. Walking past his small stable a minute later, John picked up a large bucket and motioned for James to do the same. John led down a path to the stream where he dropped the bucket and picked up Pearl. James placed his bucket on the bank and followed John as he walked along downstream. "Where're you from, John.?"

"Here. My father and grandfather were enslaved to a farmer in

Maine. In the war of Revolution, they fought for the British. I was just seven or eight, but they freed the whole family. We worked a couple more years on the farm for the man who had owned us. Then my father opened a cobbler shop in Portsmouth. Did saddle work too."

"But you went to sea?"

"So my brother could keep the shop with my father. There was not enough work to feed all of us." Several minutes into the walk, John saw James limp and slowed his pace. "How'd you come by cooking?"

"When I was no bigger than Pearl, just barely walking, I learned that the best food came from the kitchen in the big house, not the mush pot in a slave cabin. That was about the time I started working in the big house with my mother when she still had her health. Sweeping out the ash in the fireplaces and other simple chores. I watched the cook every time I could. Got to taste scraps too. Then I got a chance to go to France and really learn new ways. But sometimes the old ways still suit."

"I can't believe he just gave you your papers."

"He didn't. I had to bargain hard with Mister Jefferson for years."

"After Philadelphia, where'd you go?"

"Baltimore. I liked being my own man cooking in a tavern there." He neglected to mention his plan to return to France. Nor did he relate to John, a sailor, his experience on the *Marie-Claire*.

On the way back, John filled both buckets and carried them up the hill to his cabin. James and Pearl struggled to keep up with him. By the time they had returned to the cabin, James was out of breath. John poured the buckets into a large barrel by the door. He spoke to James in a quiet voice, saying, "If I fill it every time I go out, she don't need to run down to the creek anymore. Can't see her toting it by herself. You know, she takes in washing from townsfolk. Needs 'most a hundred gallons on those days. I tell her she needs to stop when I go back to sea, but she'll stop when she wants."

James chuckled. "Never one to bend to the will of others when I knew her, either." They went into the kitchen.

Ona had made the ashcake, sliced, and arranged it on a wooden trencher. James noticed that the rice pot was off its hook and at the side of the hearth keeping warm. "That rice all done?" he asked.

"Sure is."

James stirred the larger pot, tasted the broth, added the seafood, and the last of the spices. After five minutes, he declared it ready to eat.

Once they had filled their bowls with a layer of rice topped with the kingumbo and taken a few bites, John moaned in appreciation. "James, this is mighty fine. Thank you." He passed the ashcake trencher to James, who nodded appreciation.

Ona held Pearl on her lap and said, "It's better than any I ever had at Mount Vernon." He nodded. She dipped her finger into the broth and gave Pearl a taste, then looked directly at him. "You gonna cook for him again?"

"Told him that I wouldn't be his cook as President. Too many fussy people to feed, but I did go back to Monticello this summer and cooked for him there for a time. Got news on your sister while I was there. Should have told you right off."

"Delphi?"

He nodded. "She's doing fine for herself. Mister Law is quite the wealthy man in the Federal City after buying up parcels. Now that the capital has moved, there is a lot of building going on. Folks from all the states gonna need places to live when they meet in Congress. He got a nice big house and she says she's treated well."

"You see your mam much when you're there?"

John finished and refilled his bowl. He motioned to Ona, who handed her empty bowl to him with a nod.

"Yes. Lived with her back in our cabin." He laughed. "Seemed so small, even though just two of us were in it. Bob's still indentured out, paying off his debt to the doctor who loaned him buy-out money. He and Dolly are doing fine. Have children now: Elizabeth and Martin. Now they all are under one roof. Sally's still at Monticello living in the big house."

"She want her freedom? I know you worried on it."

James handed his bowl to John to refill and shook his head. "Sally? No. Never. She thinks all is perfect for her. I hope she's right. Still says her children gonna be free at twenty-one years of age."

"Your mam? She's old now. He gonna free her too?"

"No. If he frees her, she's gotta leave Virginia. That's the law. Then what? Sally thinks he just gonna give her 'her time' and maybe a cabin away from the slave row. But I don't know."

Pearl squirmed to stay awake, so Ona spoke softly. "You hear anything about folks at Mount Vernon?"

"Hercules ran."

"Figured he'd give it a try."

"They said it was a little before President Washington's birthday. I hear it both on the day or during the workup for the celebration. Either way, he left his family and went. Gone. Children are old enough to care for themselves. No word of where he got to."

Ona put the toddler to bed and returned to the men. "Going to go back see if he'll let you live at Monticello, even if you don't work in his kitchen? Be close to your family?"

James shook his head. "They're all where they want to be. Jefferson wanted me to cook for him again, but my brother, Peter, turned into a fine cook."

John gathered the empty bowls, washed them, and returned them to their rack on the mantel. He asked, "Where to next? Back to France?"

"Maybe. I sorta like Baltimore, so I might be there a while." He paused and reached into his bag. "You know, there is something I want to leave with you both. A man I met gave it to me. He was a slaver and repented his ways, if you can believe that. It's a hymn that his pastor in England wrote. It might interest your church here. He says just put it to any tune that matches the words."

Ona said, "I don't want to take your only paper, it's important to you. Can you copy it for me?"

James tapped his head. "I have it up here."

John grinned. "I'll pass it on. Best get our rest now." He stood and went to their bed. From under it, he pulled a blanket and brought it back to James. "Ought to make a good pallet on the floor. Call out if you need something."

Ona said, "Thank you for coming up and making such a fine feast for us, James." John took Ona's hand and led her to the bed. He pulled the thin curtain that separated the sleeping area.

James folded the blanket, undid his belt, removed his knife sheath, returned the big blade to it, and pushed it to the back of the mantel. About midnight he found himself chilled and pulled the blanket over him. He thought of the meal they had shared, of how Ona looked at him, of how Pearl smelled like promise and love. He drifted into an uneasy sleep.

He woke early, before the others, went to the outhouse, and returned to get his coat. He reached for his knife sheath, then stopped. He ran his finger over his initials on the handle of the large knife, then left it on the mantel. He limped to the small barn, where his horse was stabled. He looked for where John had put the saddle, then stopped, sat on a hay bale, and rewrapped his right leg. Once done, he started on the left, just as John filled the doorway. "Bother you much?"

"Some days more than others." By the time James had tied off the ends of his wraps, John had bridled the mare and put on the saddle blanket. He took the saddle up in one hand and easily centered it. "Want me to put your valise on the saddlebag with the feed sack?"

"Just the valise. Keep the feed here where you can use it."

When he had tightened the cinch, he turned to James. "I know she had feelings for you, and you musta too." James started to reply but John held up his hand. "Don't say anything. I know you gave her that expensive watch that got her passage to freedom."

"It was just a watch."

"A gold watch from France, she said. We owe you her liberty and our happiness."

James smiled as he struggled to bend his swollen leg to get his foot into the stirrup.

John laid a hand on his arm. "Hold on, brother. Let me help you." He tugged a large crate over for James to step on.

"Not too used to getting help. Been on my own for so long."

John took his arm for balance. Once in the saddle, James looked down. "She's lucky to have you. I see how you treat her."

He handed James the reins. "Can I ask you somethin' before you leave?"

"Certainly."

"Ona say that our baby is a slave to Missus Washington, 'cause Ona is still bound. Is that true? I know she pines to see her sister. I thought we could travel down if it was safe."

James grimaced as he nodded. "She tells you true. You go south for a visit, they'll get picked up by patrollers fast as you can whistle."

"Washington hasn't sent anyone after her for almost two years now."

"That don't mean he won't. She's a dower slave to his Missus. He's not President anymore, so what people think of him matters less to him now. Take caution still."

"We will. Thank you." John guided the horse from the stable.

Ona suddenly opened the cabin door and said, "Wait up, James. Pearl has something for you."

The sleepy child toddled out of the house. Her hair was pushed into a tangle on one side. She held her small closed fist in front of her. Her father hoisted her up. She looked at James, then reached toward him, and silently put a white pebble into his outstretched hand. He looked at it and carefully closed his hand around the gift. "Thank you, pretty girl."

Ona waved. James nodded and pulled the reins to the side. The mare turned and started off at a crisp walk. Now unencumbered by the bags that had rubbed against her shoulders the day before, the mare found an easy trot heading home.

CHAPTER 30

When James came back to Baltimore at the end of September, he declined Mister Singer's offer to return to his former position. He took a small room on the ground floor of the tavern and worked for board only, assisting the cook and sweeping up at night. But even these reduced demands exhausted him. The visit to Ona and the brief sea voyage had drained him physically but refreshed his spirits. He was himself again.

After a week back in Baltimore, James visited Broadhurst's office. The lawyer answered the door himself. Seeing James, he opened the door and with a wide grin, motioned him to enter. "Mister Hemings! How very nice to see you."

"You as well. I have some business to discuss."

"We should go to my office."

Broadhurst led him down a long hallway to his office and closed the door. Not until the latch clicked did he motion James to a chair. "I feared I would never see you again. I thought you were leaving our fair city."

"I did. Now I am returned."

"Although we hold the transfer papers to the house outside of town, it is not safe for you here. If you get arrested, it still might take some time for a judge to honor the deed of transfer as your defense and release you on motions or after trial. Do you really want that exposure to possible jail time?" Broadhurst watched for his reaction. When James shrugged, he continued. "Are you cooking again?"

"Only helping these days. My legs are giving me fits."

"Sorry to hear that."

"No need. I wanted to see how our *enterprise* is performing."

Broadhurst leaned forward and lowered his voice. "The *station* is operating well. We have a talented *conductor*, and frequent *parcels* and *cargo* are passing through the station." Even with the door closed, they used the coded language of the stagecoach system as a shield.

"As I had hoped. But now I find myself in a position to assist in more ways than merely as a face you once needed. I want to become a stockholder in the enterprise. I have funds to spare and want to know what I can do."

"What have you in mind? Buying another station?"

"Wish I could. But what I can do is assist in provisioning the one you have. I can make food that's just right for folks who are travelin'. I was a ship's cook. I know how to make hand biscuits that fit in a pocket and won't spoil for weeks. I know how to dry and preserve goods that can be left at the house for months without tending. This is what I know. What I can offer."

"A provisioning plan? Interesting! Let me discuss this with other shareholders and see if it is acceptable to them."

James rose, shook hands with Broadhurst, and left.

Within days, James was given the name of a local minister who would accept such donations of durable foods at his church, which was just past Fell's Point. If somehow those items made their way to the station and nourished those who were traveling all the better. Information about the manner of the transit of such cargo, their numbers or destinations, was never divulged. All James knew was that if he carried provisions in sturdy canvas bags with handles just out of town to the church, some good would come of it. Best not to know all the details.

Sundays became his day of provisioning the house that he owned but never visited. During the week, James collected foods unobtrusively. Air-dried strips of beef from a farmer who sold his products at the market every week. Hard-crusted breads unsold by a baker, waxed hard cheeses, and apples. Hand-sized hard biscuits that he made after the tavern closed using the last of the oven's heat. From his shipboard experiences, he knew that certain types of food would last until needed. Food that could be carried in a pocket. Food that would nourish without need of preparation. Food for travel.

On the first Sunday in October, James took two large bags to the church past Fell's Point, while the tavern's new cook made a simple breakfast for the lodgers. One day a week was all he asked for. This time was his alone, to do as he willed. A walk. A long coffee at an inn or on the pier. Talking to fishermen. Watching children frolic on the green. Somehow, during the following week, his sturdy bags reappeared in the kitchen of the Bay House and joined the stack that James used when he helped shop for the tavern's foods.

In the crisp air of the following Sunday, James adopted a steady pace from the piers down Pratt Street. When the bridge came into sight, he slowed down and listened to the water rumbling below. It reminded him of the summer, years before, when he first saw boys fishing this rapid river and laughing. He left the cobbled city streets for the dirt road that led past Fell's Point and into the country.

Less than a mile beyond the bridge was an abandoned tobacco warehouse. A white cross on its front door marked it as a church. When he left the bags just inside the rear door of the church, he took a deep breath. The air was still spiced with richness from the hogsheads of tobacco that were long gone. He knew that things changed, crops shifted, harbors silted up, and time itself sped away.

On the way home, he noticed how the overarching trees had shifted from the deep greens of late summer to the ambers and warm golds of October. He was alone with his thoughts until he crossed the bridge back into the city. He walked slowly along the waterfront promenade while others were at church, while shops were closed, shopkeepers still warm in their beds, and sailors who drank late in the taverns were still in their shipboard hammocks.

The bridge became his marker between his two worlds of old and new, of white and black, of city and country, and of freedom and longing. The bridge was barely wide enough for two wagons to pass, so if a driver held to the center, there was still space for James to continue walking. The low stone railings came just to a wheel's hub. The heavy planks were set side to side to prevent the narrow carriage wheels from binding but left enough space for a light snow to drop between them during winter.

He lingered empty-handed on the bridge, watching two old men fish on the banks below. The river's rumble hid their words but not the spike of their laughter or shouts when one would pull a fish from the fast-running water.

He thought that his life was like that river, tumbling onto itself, making a noise without meaning. As he walked back to the tavern that day, however, he began to understand its meaning—what had given him the strength and endurance to find his freedom and challenge Jefferson to act and honor his conscience. It was then that James decided to write the story of his life. He would write it for Jefferson, so the President of the United States would understand that James was born to a liberty that the law had stolen from him. Jefferson had only restored the natural order.

It was thus that James committed his evenings to writing his history.

Within the week, his pages were written, recopied into a clear hand, and numbered. Now he faced the daunting task of writing his transmittal letter. Late at night the following Saturday, James dipped his quill into a small glass inkpot. As the nib scratched across rough paper, he carefully formed letters in the ornate style of the Declaration of Independence. With the precision of an engraver, he bent over the desk and gave his full attention to each stroke of his neatly cut quill. Once the ink was exhausted, he paused, sat up straight with his shoulders back in the spindle-back chair, and sighed deeply. He chuckled to himself. His teacher had taught him well, as their letters were nearly identical. He leaned back to let the ink dry without blotting it or using a shaker of sand. He wanted the lines to be as crisp and perfect as he could make them.

> *To: The President of these United States of America, Thomas Jefferson*
> *In the care of Franklin J. Broadhurst, Esq. of Baltimore*

A rattling cough seized him. He turned away from the desk in his small room above the tavern and ran his ink-stained fingers through his wiry hair. Years working in kitchens had added heft to his frame and a web of pale scars to the backs of his hands. Larger scars swept up his forearms like swirls of cream not yet stirred into a coffee. He suddenly noticed the chill in the room and turned down his sleeves. An October rain blew across the harbor and hammered against his window. Lightning flashed briefly.

James stumbled three steps to his fireplace, leaned on a battered sea chest, and tossed a split log on the embers. The dry wood crackled and sent sparks swirling up the chimney. Pushing aside a scuffed violin case, he sat on the edge of his bed. His hands shook as he poured cider into a cup. Then he picked up a small square bottle of laudanum with a ground-glass stopper. "No! Not tonight." He slammed it down on the bedside table, unopened, and drank his cider.

Returning to his desk, he leaned down and rubbed his legs, which had swollen by this point into tree trunks and strained the seams of his trousers. Sitting up again, he took a moment to catch his breath and wipe the sweat from his forehead. He glanced at the pebble beside the inkwell and took a deep breath before dipping his pen again and continuing.

> *My Most Esteemed and Dear Sir:*
>
> *With all gratitude, and a full heart, I declined your most kind and generous offer in February to serve as your chef de cuisine in The President's House. I sent your messenger away with my refusal so that you could install the staff you desire and deserve for your*

great new venture. However, honor binds me to explain my decision, as painful as it may be. You did me more honor in asking than I could return. I feared that I could not serve you for the term or manner that you required.

When your quill wrote of our right to life, liberty, and the pursuit of happiness, you fired my imagination. Your assertion that all men are created equal is what sparked a flame in my breast. With this letter, I transmit to you the account of my life for your archives. It is the only gift which is mine alone to give in return for your many kindnesses to myself and my family at Monticello, where my life truly began, when you inherited me and my family, enslaved, from Mister John Wayles, who was my father and the father of your beloved wife, Martha and of my sister Sally.

James straightened the fifty-two pages before he reread his account of his life. He nodded. It was as he wanted it. Drunks leaving the tavern late that night in the rain laughed as they passed his window. The sharp smell after lightning lingered. Another thunderclap shook the window as the rain turned into hail, then a light snowfall that muffled shouts of sailors as they staggered toward their docked ships. The lamp on the edge of the pier was blurred by the snow. He stretched, rubbed his eyes, returned to his desk, and cut a sharp point on a new quill.

This summer past, I worked for you for wages at Monticello. Twenty American dollars a month you paid me as a free man. More than a fair wage. But within weeks, I knew that I could no longer cook at the level we both had known, and you rightly expected. As my doctor predicted, my heart is no longer strong, and my legs fail me after a few hours. After several weeks, I drew my wages from your new overseer and left your kitchen in Peter's good hands. I said my farewells to my family and friends and worked as a tavern cook here in Baltimore. I began writing my odyssey from slavery to freedom for your archives, the price of paper and my laudanum consuming a fair amount of my savings.

You achieved your dream of bringing the best of science and nature, of vine and vale, to our new nation. You held true to your belief in the equality of man and have made faltering steps toward the realization of that dream. You defied man's law when you taught this slave to write and read. You defied my fears when you took this enslaved man to Paris to discover a world previously unimagined. You freed me from the bondage of both slavery and ignorance.

Today I write to my President as a free man to thank you and to commend to your loving care my family and the enclosed account of my life.

As I bid you farewell and adieu, I pray that you will bestow on others the blessing of freedom and do everything in your power to rid this great nation of the curse of slavery.

May God bless you, Mister President, and the nation you have crafted.

Your most obedient servant,

James Hemings
Baltimore, Maryland

He placed the letter on the stack of pages that he had written and blew out the lamp. While the ink dried, he sat motionless, and spent. The embers had gone to ash in his small fireplace. The room was chilled and smoky. He lumbered to the window and saw that the morning light was filtering through a gentle snow. He laughed at himself for losing track of time and working through the night.

It is done, he thought. Perhaps later that day or the next, he would read the letter again, add a date when convinced that it was just as he wanted it, and entrust it to a messenger. As he packed the last of the provisions in the cloth bags to take to the church, his breath came harder. *I must remember to pen a note to release my belongings and remaining savings to Mister Broadhurst*, he thought. He then decided to leave that letter in his room for the day his heart failed, and he did not wake up.

He smiled as he pulled on the heavy overcoat with the high collar Jefferson had given him. He remembered wearing a thinner coat on winter mornings in France when he had struggled in gusty, early-morning weather to reach his job at Restaurant Combeaux. James picked up the small white pebble from the desk where it glowed in the dawn and then put it in his pocket.

As he walked away from town, the faint breeze blurred the few tracks in the light snowfall. Some other early risers, perhaps a hunter, had braved the cold before him. He shortened his stride after almost falling where the cobblestones were uneven and hidden under the snow. He tightened his grip on the heavy bags.

The wet snow on the bay trees spiced the air. He thought of Gabrielle naming spices for him to learn. "*La feuille de laurier*. Bay laurel leaf." The morning was so quiet that he heard the rush of the river well before he reached the bridge. After another minute, he saw a few smudged footprints on the wooden planks.

And then noticed the man partially hidden by the trees near the far end of the bridge.

James stepped onto the slick bridge and slowed. The man's face was in the shadow of his hat, his jaw obscured by his upturned collar. Pausing, James turned and saw a second man step onto the bridge behind him, a small truncheon in his right hand.

James hurried his pace. The man in the hat strode quickly toward the bridge, blocking his path. James stopped. Both men began a steady march toward him. He felt his vision tunnel and his heart begin to gallop.

Trapped, James dropped the bags. He reached for the knife that was no longer there and then quickly opened his hands and extended his arms out to his sides.

"Where ya goin' with them bags, boy?"

"Boy?"

"You're that Hemings cook? Right?"

"I am *Mister* James Hemings." The man with the truncheon advanced. His partner was just five feet away. "I asked, where you going? I want to know the place. And who runs it." He opened his coat. A short sword hung in a scabbard on his hip. Beside it, wrist shackles. "Tell me!"

"No."

Moving closer, the man pulled the shackles off his belt. His voice went higher. "Tell me now or I'll drag you to jail and beat it out of you."

"No, sir. I will not!" James slowly heeled back, turned, and stepped over the rail. He lowered his arms and slid his hands into his pockets. His right hand closed around the pebble.

"Stop!" shouted the man with the truncheon as he sprinted toward James, but his words were lost. James looked at him flatly, then stepped off the bridge.

And into the air.

EPILOGUE

When President Thomas Jefferson heard the rumor that James Hemings had died, he sent a special investigator, William Evans, to Baltimore. Witnesses were interviewed. Some said Hemings was drunk and slipped off the icy bridge alone; others thought he jumped. It was thus reported that James had died by his own hand, not of foul play, at the age of thirty-six.

Of the several hundred slaves owned by Jefferson, James Hemings was the only one whom he freed unconditionally during his lifetime.

Robert Hemings bought his freedom through an indenture and worked off that bondage to eventually become a free man.

Sally Hemings lived with Thomas Jefferson until his death. In his will, he freed each of Sally's children that he fathered on their twenty-first birthdays. Sally was given "her time" as an elderly woman—freed only of her duties, but not of her enslavement.

Ona Judge Staines died at the age of seventy-five, in Greenland, New Hampshire, still enslaved yet living free, as were her children.

Six years after James Hemings died, President Jefferson signed the Act of Congress that ended the importation of slaves to the United States of America.

ACKNOWLEDGMENTS

My sister and I were lucky. Our parents were readers and explorers of American life and its regional cuisine as a window to a culture. We were a military family. Any new posting required field trips to historical monuments, local libraries, museums, and the exploration of cultures and foods that were new to us. We made cornbread from cornmeal ground at George Washington's gristmill. Visits to the colonial kitchens at Mount Vernon and Monticello sparked my interest in both culinary history and the hidden history of the enslaved men and women whose skill and forced labor built and operated those plantations but whose lives were missing from my schoolbooks. We are just starting to fill those gaps.

Our first visits to Monticello showed only the old colonial kitchen with iron pots suspended over an open hearth. After restoration in 2004, the kitchen now reflects the safer methods of cooking brought from France by James Hemings, who was America's first French chef and Jefferson's industrial spy. Archeological work in 2017 confirmed the existence of the safer French kitchen implemented by James.

I lived with the idea of James for decades. Unable to find a definitive history of the man, I began my formal research and drafting in 2005. Friends and family encouraged the exploration, as obscure as it was.

I found inspiration in the works of historian Annette Gordon-Reed, author of *The Hemings: An American Family* and the books and blog of Michael W. Twitty, culinary historian and James Beard award winning author. Toni Morrison's admonition to writers to "write the book you would want to read" empowered me to continue with this project when it seemed impossible to weave the few fragments known about James

Hemings or his culinary contributions into a whole.

First and always in her support of my writing is my sister, Maureen Shanahan. Her encouragement and wise observations are unfailing and invaluable. My brother-in-law, Dennis F. Shanahan M.D., M.P.H., generously shared observations and guidance as well.

My valued friend, Dan Smith, encouraged my research and supported the idea for this project for a decade. His comments on the last draft enriched it.

As only a French woman could, Sarah Pourquier translated, improved my French with humor, and offered insight into the French perspective of their history. Thank you for helping me discover Jefferson's Paris on paper and on foot.

On the technical side, my editor, Laurie Gibson, brought her clear vision of this project and her technical prowess to it with her usual depth and timeliness. I am profoundly grateful for her devotion to detail and awed at how she improved and clarified my work.

Any errors of fact, infelicities, or fictional excess to spackle over historical gaps or in pursuit of the story are my responsibility.

Principal References
and Resources

On Language

A comment on three culinary terms of French derivation:

Restaurant: Frequently used in this book. While Jefferson was in Paris, the French government authorized a guild of "traiteur-restaurateurs" to receive customers at what we today would recognize as a restaurant after development during the prior decade. English usage began in 1804 per Merriam-Webster.

Café: Limited use in this book. Used only as the name of a particular establishment, but not generally used in the modern sense during Jefferson's time in France. The more common term "coffeehouse" is used in this book. English usage began in 1802 per Merriam-Webster.

Baguette: Not used in this book. Today's ubiquitous French bread, noted for its staff-like shape and fast cooking time, was developed in steam ovens after Jefferson left Paris. It was variously referred to as "the wand" or "stick" in the 1800s and officially named in 1920 when its size and cost was codified. English usage began in 1926 per Merriam-Webster.

Institutions

Bibliothèque nationale de France; Paris, France
Founders Online
Library of Congress (U.S.A.)
Massachusetts Historical Society
Mount Vernon Association
National Archives (U.S.A.)

National Park Service (U.S.A.)
The James Hemings Foundation
Thomas Jefferson Foundation (with particular thanks to Gardiner Hallock, the Robert H. Smith Director of Restoration and Collections, and Interim Director of Facilities and Anna Berkes, Research Librarian, Jefferson Library.)
University of Virginia, Special Collections Library

Bibliography

BY JAMES HEMINGS

Hemings, James. *Inventory of Kitchen Utinsils (sic)*, handwritten, Titled *Kitchen Furnishings February 20, 1796* (presumably by Thomas Jefferson), Library of Congress. Washington, DC. http://www.loc.gov/exhibits/jefferson/jefflife.html#070

CULINARY, COLONIAL LIFE, AND PARIS

Bon Appétit Magazine Supplement. *A Taste of Colonial Cooking, Recipes of the American Revolution.* Mount Morris, Minnesota: Hamond Inc., 1974.

Breig, James. *Speaking of the Past: the Words of Colonial Williamsburg.* https://www.history.org/foundation/journal/Summer01/words.cfm 2001.

Craughwell, Thomas J. *Thomas Jefferson's Crème Brûlée.* Philadelphia: Quirk Books, 2012.

Dosier, Susan. *Colonial Cooking (Exploring History through Simple Recipes).* Mankato, Minnesota: Blue Earth Books, 2000.

Garnier-Audiger, Athanase. *La Maison Réglée Et L'art De Diriger La Maison D'un Grand Seigneur & Autres... Avec La Véritable Méthode De Faire Toutes Sortes D'essences, D'eaux Et De Liqueurs.* (Facsimile reproduction) Charleston, South Carolina: Nabu Press, 2011.

Guy, Christian. Translated by Elizabeth Abbot. *An Illustrated History of French Cuisine.* Paris: Les Productions de Paris, 1962 and New York: Orion Press, 1962.

Harris, Jessica B. *High on the Hog: A Culinary Journey from Africa to America.* New York: Bloomsbury, 2011.

Harris, Jessica B. *Iron Pots and Wooden Spoons: Africa's Gifts to New World Cooking.* New York: Ballantine Books, 1991.

Harris, Jessica B. *The Welcome Table: African-American Heritage Cooking,* drawings by Patricia Eck. New York: Simon & Schuster, 1995.

Hess, Amanda, ed. *Martha Washington's Booke of Cookery.* New York: Columbia University Press, 1981.

Kaminski, John P., ed. *Jefferson in Love, The Love Letters Between Thomas Jefferson and Maria Cosway.* Lanhan, Maryland: A Madison House Book, Rowman & Littlefield Publishers, 1999.

Lynch, Jack. *A Guide to Eighteenth Century English Vocabulary,* 2006. www.andromeda.rutgers.edu/jlunch/C18Guide.pfd. (Note: "lunch," not "lynch," is used in the web address.)

Mendes, Helen. *The African Heritage Cookbook.* New York: Macmillan, 1971.

Mercier, Louis-Sébastien. *Paris Delineated, From the French of Mercier Including a Description of the Principal Edifices and Curiosities of that Metropolis, Vol II*, translated to English (no translator given). First published: London: H.D. Symonds, 1802; (facsimile reproduction). Miami, Florida: HardPress, 2017.

Mercier, Louis-Sébastien. *Tableau de Paris et Le Nouveau Paris*. Paris: Mercure de France, 1994.

Metzner, Paul. *Crescendo of the Virtuoso: Spectacle, Skill, and Self-Promotion in Paris during the Age of Revolution*. Berkeley: University of California Press, 1998. http://ark.cdlib.org/ark:/13030/ft438nb2b6/.

Oliver, Sandra. *Food in Colonial and Federal America (Food in American History)*. Westport, Connecticut: Greenwood Press, 2005.

Randolph, Mary. *The Virginia Housewife OR, Methodical Cook, A Facsimile of an Early American Cookbook*. New York: Dover Publications, 1993.

Simmons, Amelia. *The First American Cookbook, A Facsimile of "American Cookery" 1796*. New York: Oxford University Press, 1958. Reprint, New York: Dover Publications, 1984.

The American Heritage Cookbook and Illustrated History of American Eating and Drinking. American History Publishing Company, distributed by New York: Simon & Schuster, 1964.

The University of Virginia Hospital Circle. *The Monticello Cook Book, Containing Recipes of great Worth and of the widest Variety. Secrets of the delectable Dishes from Ancient & Modern Times by the good Ladies of the City of Charlottesville and the County of Albemarle*. Richmond, Virginia: The Dietz Press, 1950.

Tipton-Martin, Toni. *The Jemima Code: Two Centuries of African American Cookbooks.* Austin: University of Texas Press, 2015.

Twitty, Michael W. *The Cooking Gene.* New York: Harper Collins Publishers, Inc., 2017.

Wheaton, Barbara Ketcham. *Savoring the Past, The French Kitchen and Table from 1300 to 1789.* New York: Simon & Schuster, 1983.

Zola, Emile. Translated and notes by Brian Nelson. *The Belly of Paris (Le Ventre de Paris).* New York: Oxford University Press, 2007.

AMERICAN HISTORY:
THE FOUNDERS AND THE ENSLAVED

_____. *An Introduction to the WPA Slave Narratives, Born in Slavery: Slave Narratives from the Federal Writer's Project. 1936–1938.* Library of Congress. Washington, DC.

Baptist, Edward E. *The Half Has Never Been Told: Slavery and the Making of American Capitalism.* New York: Basic Books, 2014.

Brodie, Fawn M. *Thomas Jefferson, An Intimate History.* New York: W. W. Norton, 1974.

Chernow, Ron. *Washington: A Life.* New York: The Penguin Press, 2010.

Crafts, Hannah, Henry Louis Gates Jr., ed. *The Bondwoman's Narrative, A Novel.* Ann Arbor, Michigan: XanEdu, a Division of Pro Quest Information and Learning, 2002.

Dargan, William T. *Lining Out the Word: Dr. Watts Hymn Singing in the Music of Black Americans.* Berkeley: University of California Press, 2006.

DeCatur, Stephan, Jr. *The Private Affairs of George Washington, from the Records and Accounts of Tobias Lear, Esquire, His Secretary.* Boston: Houghton Miffin/Riverside Press, 1933.

Douglass, Frederick. *Narrative of the Life of Frederick Douglass, an American Slave, Published by the Anti-Slavery Office of Boston, 1845.* Reprint, New York: Dover Publications, 1995.

Du Bois, W.E.B., Introduction by Arnold Rampersad, Henry Louis Gates Jr., ed. *Souls of Black Folks.* New York: Oxford University Press, 2014.

Dunbar, Erica Armstrong. *Never Caught, The Washingtons' Relentless Pursuit of Their Runaway Slave, Ona Judge.* New York: Atria, 2018.

Franklin, Benjamin, Charles W. Eliot, ed., *The Autobiography of Benjamin Franklin.* New York: Collier & Sons Company, 1909.

Gates, Henry Louis Jr., and Hollis Robbins, eds. *In Search of Hannah Crafts, Critical Essays on The Bondwoman's Narrative.* New York: Basic Civitas Books, 2004.

Gates, Henry Louis Jr., ed. *The Classic Slave Narratives.* New York: Signet Reissue edition, 2012.

Gordon-Reed, Annette. *The Hemings of Monticello: An American Family.* New York: W.W. Norton, 2009.

Hamilton, Alexander, James Madison, John Jay. Written under the name of Publius. *The Federalist Papers, 1787/1788.* Reprint, New York: Dover Publications, 2014.

Jefferson, Thomas. *Deed of Manumission to James Hemings. February 5, 1796.* Albert and Shirley Small Special Collections, University of Virginia Library.

Jefferson, Thomas. *Notes on the State of Virginia 1787.* Reprint, Digireads. com Publishing, 2017.

Jefferson, Thomas. *Promise to Free James Hemings, September 15, 1793,* Handwritten, Library of Congress. Washington, DC. http://www.loc. gov/exhibits/jefferson/jefflife.html#108.

Jefferson, Thomas. *The Autobiography of Thomas Jefferson.* 1821. Reprint, Mount Pleasant, South Carolina: Arcadia Press, 2017.

Jennings, Paul. *A Colored Man's Reminiscences of James Madison.* New York: Palgrave Macmillan, 2012.

Keckley, Elizabeth. *Behind the Scenes, or Thirty Years a Slave and Four Years in the White House.* 1868. Reprint, Hillsborough, North Carolina: Eno Publishers, 2016.

Kilmeade, Brian, and Don Yaeger. *Thomas Jefferson and the Tripoli Pirates: The Forgotten War that Changed American History.* New York: Sentinel, Penguin Random House, 2015.

McCullough, David. *John Adams.* New York: Simon & Schuster, 2001.

Meacham, Jon. *Thomas Jefferson: The Art of Power*. New York: Random House, 2012.

Middlekauff, Robert. *The Glorious Cause: The American Revolution 1763–1789*. New York: Oxford University Press, 1982. Revised and expanded, 2007.

Minges, Patrick, ed. *Far More Terrible for Women: Personal Accounts of Women in Slavery*. Durham, North Carolina: John F. Blair, 2006.

Nichols, Frederick D., and James A. Bear Jr. *Monticello, A Guidebook*. Monticello, Virginia: Thomas Jefferson Memorial Foundation, 1967.

Northup, Solomon. *Twelve Years a Slave*. Published in 1853. Reprint, New York: Open Road Media, 2014.

Roberts, Robert. *The House Servant's Directory, An African American Butler's 1827 Guide*. Reprint, New York: Dover Publications, 2006.

Taylor, Elizabeth Dowling, Foreword by Annette Gordon-Reed. *A Slave in the White House, Paul Jennings and the Madisons*. New York: Palgrave Macmillan, 2012.

Truth, Sojourner. *The Narrative of Sojourner Truth, a Northern Slave, Emancipated from Bodily Servitude by the State of New York, in 1828*. Reprint, Digireads.com Publishing, 2014.

Watts, Isaac. *Hymns & Spiritual Songs*. Circa 1758. Reprint, Louisville, Kentucky: GLH Publishing, 2013.

Wilentz, Sean. *No Property in Man: Slavery and Antislavery at the Nation's Founding*. Cambridge: Harvard University Press, 2018.

Yetman, Norman R., ed. *When I Was a Slave: Memoirs from the Slave Narrative Collection.* New York: Dover Publications, 2002.

MARITIME AND CLIMATE

Boston Public Library, Leventhal Map Collection, *Maps of the South Part of the Island of Madagascar and Africa, specifically Angola.* 1732–1736.

David Rumsey Historical Map Collection, *Congo et Angola, Afrique No. 41, 1827.*

Fagan, Brian. *The Little Ice Age: How Climate Made History,* 1300-1850. New York: Basic Books, 2007.

Grays Harbor Historical Seaport, Washington. Interviews and shipboard (the brig *Lady Washington*).

Maritime Museum of San Diego, CA. Interviews and aboard multiple sailing ships.

Ocean Institute, Dana Point, CA, Interviews and aboard the *Pilgrim.*

Smith, Hervey Garrett. *The Marlinspike Sailor.* Camden, Maine: International Marine/Ragged Mountain Press, 1993.